The
Lost Season
of
Love and Snow

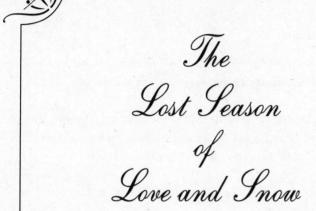

The
Lost Season
of
Love and Snow

JENNIFER LAAM

ST. MARTIN'S GRIFFIN
NEW YORK

THE LOST SEASON OF LOVE AND SNOW. Copyright © 2017 by Jennifer Laam. All rights reserved. Printed in the United States of America. For information, address St. Martin's Press, 175 Fifth Avenue, New York, N.Y. 10010.

www.stmartins.com

The Library of Congress Cataloging-in-Publication Data is available upon request.

ISBN 978-1-250-12188-2 (trade paperback)
ISBN 978-1-250-12189-9 (ebook)

Our books may be purchased in bulk for promotional, educational, or business use. Please contact your local bookseller or the Macmillan Corporate and Premium Sales Department at 1-800-221-7945, extension 5442, or by email at MacmillanSpecialMarkets@macmillan.com.

First Edition: January 2018

10 9 8 7 6 5 4 3 2 1

For Liz and Brett

The
Lost Season
of
Love and Snow

Prologue

A man says he will die for you. A woman is taught to lower her gaze and blush before hiding once more behind a silken fan. Men are given to self-aggrandizement, while women flatter egos and keep men tied to this earth. Such is the way of the world, or so I was taught in the days before I gained a reputation as the villain of St. Petersburg.

I know better now.

When a man declares he will die for you, sometimes a woman must take him at his word. For to allow one's husband to perish on the field of honor is a shameful affair, worse even than murdering him by your own hand.

The solemn men who gather at our flat fall silent as my husband draws his final breath. A prickly chill, like the first wave of a fever, washes over me as I realize my husband is gone. The sorrow tightens my chest and clamps down, squeezing until I think my body will snap in two. I sway on my feet and believe I will faint. Only the invisible force of my will keeps me upright. Dark blood still seeps from his abdomen and a sharp metallic scent clings to the air.

For two days my husband had been one of the waking dead, suffering a cruel and lingering death. Though I was not present at the duel where he fought to defend my honor, the image of Alexander collapsing, his blood staining the snow crimson, haunts my every thought. I have slid into despair, veering between hysteria and hopelessness, while Alexander's wound festered and his once vibrant face distorted with agony.

His friends stand in a semicircle around his body, backs erect, mouths set in stern lines, and expressions stoic even as their eyes dampen with tears.

"What a waste," I hear one of them mutter. "A genius lost over a woman."

The words echo in my head. I was the wife of a distinguished man of letters, the greatest in our land, and I let his life slip through my fingers. These men suppose I care only for material comforts and romantic diversions and don't believe I possess the wits about me to appreciate my husband's talent. Rumormongers have convinced them I love the empty-headed Georges d'Anthès or have fallen prey to the advances of our iron-jawed tsar. They consider my behavior traitorous, as terrible in its own way as if I had joined the ranks of the Napoleonic soldiers who once threatened our very heartland.

I will confess to basking too long in the attention of Georges and even the tsar himself, yet I am no Jezebel, merely human, as vulnerable to flattery as any other creature. Much as I may wish to do so, I cannot change the past. The damage is done. A fresh wave of tears threatens and subsides, as though nothing remains inside me to expel. I wonder how long I will live with the torment of my guilt and the censure of those who claim to love my husband.

At the moment I feel lowest, I hear faint voices below our flat call Alexander's name, and I tear myself away from the death mask that was once my husband's face. When I cross the room to stand at the window, the world outside blurs, the ice-encrusted buildings blending with the storm-clouded sky. My spectacles are in a beaded reticule hanging at my side. I place them on the bridge of my nose.

People have congregated outside in overcoats and fur hats and cloaks dusted with snow, holding candles with fragile flames that twist in the wind. I quickly lose count of the number of admirers, a hundred perhaps. They wave copies of Alexander's works; I spot *Evgeny Onegin* and an edition of his Russian fairy tales in verse. One of the women has affixed a jeweled pendant to the scarf around her throat, a portrait of Alexander placed in the center. A few mourners catch sight of me at the window, and I wonder if I should withdraw and return to my private grief, but my feet will not budge. Women call my name in high, sweet voices. To my surprise, they aren't angry. They don't consider me a villain, but a gatekeeper: the guardian of my husband's works and memory.

As I watch the women shield their flickering tapers with small, mitten-clad hands, I wonder if there might yet be time to recast my role in this drama, to make a sacrifice and prove my worth. I must ensure Alexander's words remain freely available to the people who gather below our flat in the snow. I may have failed my husband in life, but in death, I will ensure he is never forgotten.

My vision mists with tears and my shoulders tremble, but I now cling to a bittersweet hope. I make a silent vow that the world shall know the truth of our story, the power Alexander and I held over one another. It may not have the happy ending of a fairy tale, but deep in my heart I know it is a tale of true love.

One

I didn't want to attend the dance master's ball that night. If my sisters hadn't insisted, I never would have met the greatest poet in Russia, and my life might have taken a different course altogether.

Admission to the ball cost five rubles each, and Mother had made a grand show of dispensing the needed coin. While my sisters spritzed one another with the lavender-scented perfume our aunt procured on a recent trip to France, I cast a longing look at the mahogany writing table, blemished with age, in the opposite corner of our sitting room. There I kept my leather-bound notebook, feather quill, and embossed inkwell atop red linen embroidered with curving black arabesques. Though always in need of a sturdy book to prop a broken leg in place, this table was my favorite spot in the house and certainly preferable to the bedroom I shared with my sisters. Over the winter holidays, I had reviewed my French translations and an essay on the history of Russian poetry. I wished to spend the evening engrossed in that work.

Instead, I was expected to make myself pretty and amicable for the benefit of strangers, gentlemen I would not even truly see. My vision compromised by shortsightedness, I could hope to gain no more than fuzzy impressions of their faces from a distance, and would need to wait until they drew near in order to determine whether or not they were handsome. Tonight, my spectacles remained safely encased in their fabric cover on the writing table. Mother might allow for a fashionably discreet lorgnette at the ballet, but the last time I tried to wear spectacles outside the house, she told me I looked like a man and threatened to grind the lenses under the heel of her boot.

Ekaterina and Azya pushed in front of me, leaned in closer to our looking glass, and pinched their cheeks to make them glow. Mother sat before the dying fire in the hearth, perched in her favorite armchair—generously proportioned rosewood with worn floral cushions frayed at the edges. The quivering shadows made her high cheekbones appear even more severe than usual. Though busy mending a pair of stockings, she caught me gazing at my writing table. I turned away quickly, as though I'd been caught staring at a clandestine lover like some swooning girl in a gothic romance.

Slowly, Mother set her yarn back in her wicker sewing basket and rose to her full height. Dressed in gloomy black from head to foot, with her hair pulled under an old bonnet, she towered over us. When she wasn't speaking, she appeared more a statue than a living being. She approached the looking glass where my sisters and I had gathered.

"I trust you will be on your best behavior." Mother reached out to adjust my cream-colored cambric gown, revealing more of my décolletage. I was sixteen, hardly a spinster, but the need for a husband had been made clear since I had my first monthly cycle three years earlier. "And I trust you will display every courtesy to the gentlemen present."

I caught Mother's judgmental eye in the mirror before I realized I'd been biting my lower lip, a habit I had tried and failed to break. I forced a smile.

"Natalya still looks grim as a constipated granny." Ekaterina's rectangular face had an honest, salt-of-the-earth quality that might have been appealing had she a more pleasant manner.

"This will cheer Natalya . . . and attract an eligible gentleman!" Giggling, Azya waved a tiara crafted of faux gold in the air. Her merry pink face flushed with pride, she placed it over my hair, centering it on my forehead. Her wide-spaced, light brown eyes were tender as she worked. "Like Venus herself."

I moved closer to the looking glass, squinting to better see my reflection, the pale contours of my face and the glint of gold against my dark auburn hair, which had been pulled back into a loose bun with curls framing my face.

"Quite suitable," Mother said in her husky voice. "You should thank your sister for her generosity. She could have kept the bauble for herself."

"Or given it to me." I couldn't quite see Ekaterina's expression, but her tone sounded surly enough.

"Jealousy is hardly becoming," Mother warned my sister. "Now off with you."

We headed in a line to the foyer, where our pelisses hung neatly on hooks by the door. Outside, it was snowing, and I would have much preferred an overcoat, as men wore. We would freeze, but I supposed this small sacrifice well worth the charming picture we would create in our snug, fur-lined garments.

Our three brothers, ranging in age from thirteen to twenty, lined up by the door, pretending to be footmen. As we approached the gabled entranceway, their ruddy features took on garishly pompous expressions. The eldest, Dmitry, played the charade best, but then God had granted him a handsome face and blond hair, an anomaly in our family, and he did most everything best. Our middle brother, Ivan, was also well formed, though his pale forehead loomed too prominently even in the dull lamp light. Little Sergey, long since deemed the runt of the litter, had already gone plump, though sweet-faced enough if you could tolerate his habit of holding one hand to his mouth and blowing hard into it to imitate the sound of an old man passing wind. As I stepped around him, Sergey's eyes crossed and I stuck out my tongue. Unfortunately, while my sisters had remembered to lift their gowns above their ankles, I neglected to do so and stumbled over my own feet.

"You must be more careful, Natalya," Mother intoned. "And stop squinting or you'll be wrinkled before your time. All of you, take care you are home by midnight. You wouldn't want to upset your father."

Ekaterina and I exchanged looks. For all our disagreements, we united in our poor opinion of our father. How I wished Mother would stop talking about him as though he were still an active presence in our home. One of Ekaterina's supposed friends had made a catty remark about seeing my father stumble home from a tavern in the Arbat, vomiting on the street as the girl's family passed by on a sled. To Ekaterina's credit, she had lunged at the girl and I held her back. When one of our brothers got into a scuffle, Mother's anger was the raw material of legend and I could only imagine how she might react if one of her girls came home with a blackened eye.

Azya gave a nervous glance in our direction, her face clouded with worry. "We will, Mother."

"Your behavior in public is a reflection on our family, and your success in society an important step toward securing your futures. Be kind to the gentlemen. After all, one of them might wish to make you his wife."

Sergey sputtered at that. I tried to kick him, but he was out of reach.

Mother returned to her armchair. Her lazy brown tabby had sprawled on the faded Persian rug before the hearth, hind feet twitching in a dream. She bent down to stroke the cat's fat stomach and I considered the once proud animal's willingness to submit to such degradation. As terrified as I felt about going to this ball—and how much I dreaded being evaluated like fresh fruit at a market—staying here forever under Mother's thumb, soul slowly crushed, would be far worse.

"I shall expect a full report in the morning," Mother said. "Take advantage of this moment and your beauty. Make your family proud."

I've heard it said the Christmas season is a magical time in the countryside, with all manner of opportunity for fortune-telling and mischief with comely boys. Living in Moscow, I had not yet experienced such pleasures. Despite my reservations, I hoped the dance master's ball might mark a change in direction of what often felt like a dull and hopelessly domesticated life.

When my sisters and I entered the ballroom of the mansion, I remembered to hitch my dress to make it easier to walk across the smoothly polished floor. I tried to picture myself as a ballerina gracefully taking the stage, though I knew I'd never have made it as such without my spectacles. "Your face is your fortune, Natalya," Mother often told me. "That and your figure. Perhaps you have not been blessed with the ability to determine this for yourself, so trust me on the matter."

I focused on the exquisite surroundings nearest my line of sight, drawing in the woodland scent of pine boughs and holly mingled with the heavy aromas of melting wax, French perfume, and hair pomade. Gilt candelabras lined long side tables heaped with iced sherbets, jewel-toned sugar plums, and delicate Viennese pastries dolloped with frothy cream. A tingling sensation teased the back of my shoulders, and I felt alive with the possibilities of the night. I tapped the modest heels of my satin slippers to the lively tune of a mazurka. On the dance floor, underneath a banner emblazoned with the imperial double-headed eagle, gentlemen lifted their ladies from the floor and turned them with brisk and powerful steps.

All schoolgirls practiced this popular dance with one another, though I had once thought such lessons a waste of time. Now, I nervously eyed the row of men to the side of the floor, turning their heads this way and that, trying to look blasé as they evaluated potential partners, and felt grateful for the instruction. As we made our way farther inside, several heads swiveled. My face grew warm and yet I confess I enjoyed the attention.

Azya looped her arm around mine and stood taller so she could whisper in my ear. "The men are all dressed in elegant brocade evening coats and have the shapeliest legs in their breeches.

The women's dresses are wonderful confections as well, so colorful they make us seem like simple country maids." She covered her mouth as she emitted a nervous snicker. "We must convince Mother to spend more on our gowns. Oh, but the mansion is decorated so beautifully for Christmas, Natalya! Can you see the tree on the other end of the ballroom?"

I squinted and made out a green pine. Glowing candles in copper holders were fastened to its branches, along with dangling silver trinkets, beaded garlands, and fragile glass balls.

"A tree like the Protestants have in the Prussian lands?" Ekaterina's head bobbed in distress. "Inappropriate for an Orthodox celebration, if you ask me."

"Oh hush," I told her, irritated. "Since when do you care what Protestants do in their lands? I think the tree looks pretty."

Ekaterina's cheeks flushed pink. Too pink. I wondered if she hadn't snuck some rouge from an apothecary.

"And you need to stop acting like her crutch." Ekaterina turned to Azya. "What would Mother say if she heard you whispering to Natalya like some foreign trickster begging for kopeks? Do you want everyone to know our sister is blind as a mole?"

"I only want her to enjoy the night," Azya whispered fiercely.

"She'll enjoy it." Ekaterina jutted her prominent chin at the tiara. "With that bauble on her head, the gentlemen will mistake her for some sort of countess. And what does that make us? Her daft ladies-in-waiting?"

"Still preoccupied with the tiara?" I hissed, touching the gold circlet on my forehead. Even I had seen in the looking glass that it flattered my hair, whereas it would have been lost in Ekaterina's mousy mess of curls. "How would you like it if I threw it at you?"

"You couldn't hit me if you tried, you blind bat."

"I can see well enough to hit your giant jaw."

"You try throwing that thing at me and I'll pop you in the nose."

"Ladies, I trust you are all behaving? Your mother asked me to serve as your chaperone and I do want to be able to tell her how admirably you conducted yourselves this evening."

At the sound of the refined female voice, we pivoted in unison and curtsied. Mother's half-sister and Ekaterina's namesake, Aunt Katya, was nearing fifty years of age, but her features retained a softness our mother's lacked. Her hair was still jet black and her lips so full and rosy that a gentleman young enough to be her son stopped to give her a bold wink. Over the years, Aunt Katya's looks had served her well; she had a seemingly endless supply of dramatic gowns and expensive jewels to show for her success at court and wore a peacock-blue ball gown with puffed sleeves and richly embroidered gold floral designs at the hem of her full skirt.

"Now, enough of that. Mind your manners." Aunt Katya tapped the base of her lace-and-gauze fan gently against Azya's bare shoulder, thin and vulnerable in her slim gown. My sister winced. "I'm sure the gentlemen want the favor of seeing your lovely faces. No kitten fights."

Azya and Ekaterina quickly righted themselves and searched the room for potential dance partners. I wished I could convince Azya to walk with me to the tree. I wanted to see the decorations up close and gave not one whit if the tradition came from the Protestants. Even without my spectacles, I could tell the tree was divine.

Aunt Katya must have caught my wistful gaze, because she inclined her head toward mine, so close I could smell the fresh powder on her face and the rosewater she dabbed behind her ears.

"I don't wish to alarm you, niece, but I spot a gentleman making an advance. I expect you will attend to him with both the dignity and generosity your mother might expect."

I opened my mouth and then shut it abruptly, unsure how to respond to my aunt. With as much grace as I could manage, I turned.

A heavyset man with a mop of thick hair and side whiskers approached. His movements had a clumsy charm about them, like a trained circus bear. He would likely make an enjoyable dance partner, though he was a grown man in his early forties, at least, and I doubted my conversation sufficiently sophisticated to hold his attention. Besides, when I looked at him my heart did not skip a beat, flutter, jump in my chest, nor come to a standstill . . . all of which were reactions I had read in novels when the heroine met the man she was meant to marry. If this gentleman was somehow destined to be my first romantic suitor, I felt disappointed at my heart's lack of response.

"Mademoiselle," he said with a gallant if inelegantly executed bow. "We haven't formally met. My name is Fyodor Tolstoy. I have the honor of friendship with your older brothers, Ivan and Dmitry. They said their sisters might attend. Based on your brothers' description, I am guessing you are 'little' Natalya."

"Not quite so little anymore, I suppose." I was nearly as tall as this Tolstoy fellow.

"May I have the pleasure of this dance?" he asked, offering his hand.

My heart beat furiously. We would now take our place among the couples already on the dance floor and my aunt would watch our every step for impropriety. I already felt Ekaterina's contemptuous glare: the audacity of her younger sister, attracting a partner before she did, and an attractive one at that. I anticipated she would spend the rest of the evening complaining.

No matter what happened next, vexing Ekaterina made the entire night worthwhile.

I placed my hand on Tolstoy's shoulder and waited for him to lead.

Deftly, he steered me around the circle of waltzing dancers. Despite his size, he was light on his feet, easy to follow, and spoke freely as the orchestra played. "I don't believe I have seen you at a public ball before." He had switched to French, like any ambitious Russian.

"This is my first ball, monsieur." I replied in Russian, not yet comfortable enough with my spoken French to attempt anything beyond the simple *monsieur*. My mouth felt as though Ekaterina had stuffed it with cotton to make me hush.

He returned to our native tongue. "I thought not. I would have remembered you." At that, he gave a wolfish grin, but his words seemed practiced and I sensed it was the sort of compliment he might pay to any young woman. I wasn't flattered, but remained intrigued. His clear voice had a flat cadence to it, as though he had traveled abroad and picked up some remnant of a foreign tongue.

Desperate for something to say, I ventured: "I detect a hint of an accent."

"Oh you noticed? I spent some time abroad in Russian America."

"America!" I knew nothing of America except snippets in poorly written textbooks, which focused on the unruliness of government by the people and vague insinuations another revolution would occur, and that the cocky republicans who had overthrown their king would soon endure their own set of trials. "Is America as wild as one would expect?"

Tolstoy let out a boisterous laugh, but no one turned to look. Men could laugh as loudly as they pleased, while Mother would flay me alive for such a display. "Oh, I daresay more so. I spent my time there on the Aleutian Islands. Dumped by my fellow sailors after traveling with them all along the western coast, the heartless bastards." At that, he seemed to remember he was talking to a lady. His back stiffened and the tone of his voice formalized. "Do you know where these islands are located, mademoiselle? The Alaskan Peninsula? Have you heard of this place?"

"I have," I informed him, grateful it was the truth. Why did men assume women had nothing better to occupy their thoughts than gowns and balls and future husbands? Of course we considered such matters closely, but only because our futures depended on them. Our interests often extended beyond such practical affairs. "Do you intend to return one day?"

"I've seen enough of the place for one lifetime, thank you very much. I had to find my own way across the sea and then all through Siberia to get home in the end. But make it back, I did. Ever since then my chums have referred to me as the American."

"I would like to hear more of your travels, Monsieur Tolstoy. Or perhaps I should say Mr. Tolstoy, since you are the American." I smiled, pleased with my sudden burst of wit.

"I would like to share more of my adventures, but that wouldn't be fair to my friend."

I slanted my head, confused. "Friend?"

"I confess, I had an ulterior motive for asking you to dance. You see, I am here with a fine fellow quite taken with you at first sight. Truth be told, I have never seen him in such a state. He wanted to approach you himself, but his nerves got the better of him. He called you Venus and Madonna wrapped in one enchanting package."

The reality of my presence could not possibly compare favorably to such a majestic fantasy. Still, after such a compliment, I already deemed Tolstoy's shy friend a clever fellow. "Why will he not speak to me then?"

"He asked that I seek your acquaintance first and then ask your opinion of him. He fears you will not feel as taken with him as he with you, and that would only break his heart. You see, he has a most tender heart. The soul of a poet, one might say. As his friend, it is my duty to protect his ego."

Now this was the sort of romantic game playing that occurred in novels and I intended to make the most of it. "So who is this mysterious and tenderhearted chap?" I cast a furtive glance around the room. "Might I have the pleasure of at least knowing his name? Or is the strategy that you will show him to me first?"

As the music came to a halt, Tolstoy the American slowed his steps and steered me toward the beautiful tree. Closer now, I saw fruit-shaped marzipans and robins spun from sugar affixed to the branches. I caught a glimpse of black curls, and then spotted the tips of polished boots behind the tree and beneath the lowest bough. This must be Tolstoy's friend, then. I felt as though I might burst from the agony of anticipation, but had no wish to ruin this moment of revelation. "Your friend is shy. I feel I must slow my steps so I don't startle him and cause him to take to the sky like a skittish bird."

"Oh, ordinarily he's not shy at all. He adores being the center of attention, but I have never seen him take to a woman as he did when he saw you this evening. He clasped my shoulder, asked me to speak to you immediately, and then ran to hide." Tolstoy raised his voice. "Why, he's hidden himself so well he can't possibly expect you to get a good look at him. I have never seen a fellow behave so foolishly over a woman."

I managed a laugh and decided not to mention that in order to see his friend without the aid of my spectacles, I would need to get very close indeed. "He adores attention? In what sense? Does he tell humorous tales at parties?"

"He enjoys it when someone asks him to read one of his works aloud."

"Works?" Intrigued, I thought of my writing table at home and my notebooks. One of them was devoted to Russian poets, a small but talented group. I had felt keenly patriotic when I started this modest history of our poetry. "Is your friend a poet, then?"

"Actually, yes. It is even possible you have heard of him."

At that moment, Tolstoy's friend stepped out from behind the tree, and I drew in a swift breath. The black curls and side whiskers. The dark face and intense, searching look in his eyes. Thinking of what Azya had said about the men's legs earlier—how shapely they looked in breeches—I glanced down. His muscular calves were swathed in tight black boots. In my mind, I saw him as he appeared in his author's portrait: a loose blouse unbuttoned at the neck and his chin thoughtfully posed in one hand with a quill raised high in the other, as though he were about to be endowed with divine inspiration.

And then, the world shifted beneath my feet and my heart skipped a beat, just as the novelists promised.

Tolstoy leaned in close to me. "Perhaps you have heard of Alexander Pushkin?"

Two

Everyone had heard of Alexander Pushkin: the author of *Evgeny Onegin*, the tale of a St. Petersburg dandy, as well as adored poems in our own Russian tongue and many other works. Tolstoy the American gently smirked while I regained my composure, a task complicated by my heart's brisk pace.

"May I present my new friend, Natalya Nikolaevna," Tolstoy continued, addressing the poet. "I know her brothers and she was kind enough to accept an invitation to dance."

Alexander Pushkin stared at me and shifted his weight from one foot to the other while his fists tapped his sides in a rhythmic motion. His face appeared much as it did in portraiture. It was not especially handsome, the nose a little too big, and the eyes a shade too pale for his olive complexion. Yet for all he might have lacked in conventional looks, Alexander Pushkin was lavishly gifted with intensity. His gaze focused so attentively on mine that I did not dare turn away.

Tolstoy raised his voice a notch once more. "I say this is my new friend, Natalya."

"Mademoiselle!" Pushkin snapped to attention, lowered into a graceful bow, and then righted himself and extended a hand. My heart thundered as I realized what I was supposed to do next. Pretending to play the role of cultured princess, I offered my own hand for a kiss. His lips pressed a moment longer than proper and I should have considered it a liberty, except all I could think was that the greatest poet in Russia had asked a friend for an introduction because he was too nervous to approach *me*.

Since this was my first opportunity to make a good impression, I was determined to comment intelligently on his work. I had read *Evgeny Onegin* to myself aloud so that I might bask in the musicality of the words, the flow of the rhyme that made my heart so happy. In the latest chapter recently published in a journal, the useless but pretty coxcomb Onegin killed his friend, Lensky, in a duel. I had thrown the pages against a wall, frustrated I would have to wait to learn what happened afterward. When the next chapter was delayed, rumors spread that Pushkin had no idea what was to occur, the entire project had been a lark, and any reader expecting a satisfying resolution would be sorely disappointed.

"Is it true you don't know what is to become of your character, Evgeny Onegin?" The words flew out before I could stop them.

His broad brow furrowed. I panicked, thinking I had unwittingly insulted him. "I meant, is it true that you don't yet know? I am sure you will think of something . . . or have thought of something . . ."

Tolstoy had moved behind his friend but remained in the vicinity, perhaps to rescue the poet if needed. He started to titter. Perhaps I simply needed to hush.

The orchestra struck up the tinkling notes of another waltz and I wondered if the poet would ask me to dance. Perhaps not.

Perhaps I had forever ruined the chance of forming a friendship—or more—with Pushkin. Were Mother here, she would claim I had been rude, but then I didn't think a poet the sort of gentleman she wanted me to spend time with tonight anyway, even a poet as well-known as Alexander Pushkin. Though famous, his income couldn't have been overly lavish, for his dark blue evening coat and bright red cravat, though rich in color, were shabby. Nevertheless, when he turned his soulful gaze to mine, his attention was like a spark of lightning and I felt as though he could read my every thought.

"I enjoyed the latest installment," I added, "and long to read the next."

The poet bent closer to my ear, so I could hear him over the music. "I require inspiration to continue Onegin's saga."

His voice was low and like a gentle caress. I held back a little gasp of delight, instinctively understanding that to hold the attention of such a man I couldn't submit to his charms so easily. I kept my tone steady and formal, with only a hint of playfulness. "Is Tatiana not inspiration enough?" Like many girls, I was quite taken with *Onegin*'s romantic heroine, who had been brave enough to declare her love plainly.

"Tatiana is an angel, and yet the best muses are flesh and bone, those you can see and touch, who whisper in your ear and allow you to press your lips against theirs."

My first ball and already the creator of Tatiana was trying to claim me as his muse. It began to seem less like a flight of fancy and more natural that this man before me in his frayed coat and loose cravat, with the beguiling olive-toned skin and the wild black curls, should say something so bold.

Still, I knew well enough what happened to women who allowed such attention to go to their heads. I lowered my face and tried to will a blush to appear on my cheeks, though I was likely already flushed from dancing. In truth, I didn't feel embarrassed in the slightest. I only wanted Alexander Pushkin to talk more.

"Natalya is a skilled dance partner," Tolstoy interjected. "If I'm not mistaken, that is the sound of another waltz."

Pushkin offered his hand. "I would be honored."

"The honor is mine." His fingers pressed against my bare wrist and I felt a jolt, as though I had been sleeping for all my sixteen years and only now sensed the full scope of the world.

As he led me to the floor, I took in his scent: sandalwood and citrus cologne, sweet tobacco, oil and horses, and a tantalizing saltiness. Coming from a home with three boys, I knew masculine aromas well enough, but there was something newly seductive about this particular combination. Pushkin placed his hand on my back and pulled me closer, the velvety fabric of his coat against my naked arms. I glanced over his shoulder and caught a glimpse of Aunt Katya, flanked by my sisters on either side, staring at me as I danced. When we glided past them, I saw Azya's expression—placid but for a dreamy, faraway look in her pale brown eyes—and I knew she was happy for me. Meanwhile, Ekaterina glowered and Aunt Katya raised her fine black eyebrows. I had heard Mother mutter often enough about the licentiousness of the waltz, the inappropriate close position between the partners, but I believed my aunt sophisticated enough to understand the honor of waltzing with Alexander Pushkin.

I tried not to make too much of this moment, but then his whiskers skimmed my cheek, and a thrilling wave of panic descended. I wondered what might happen should we find ourselves isolated. Would he move his lips to mine? Or would he tease me first, tucking curls behind my ear as the tips of his fingers brushed the sensitive skin of my neck?

"Do you not care for attention?"

I realized I hadn't been looking at the poet, but straight past him, that the thought of being alone with him had simultaneously made my insides melt and my shoulders tense. "I am not accustomed to it."

"You must learn to adore the spotlight! How will you avoid it? Every man in this room noticed you. I'm sure they are all madly in love."

"You flatter me, Monsieur Pushkin."

"Please, call me Alexander, at the very least. Sasha if you are so inclined."

"Perhaps Alexander for now."

"Will your chaperone be scandalized if we disappear?"

Scandalized. He let the word linger on his tongue, imparting it with delicious drama, like the hiss of a snake. My cheeks burned and I looked down for a moment to keep time with his nimble steps. "I believe my Aunt Katya would be concerned, monsieur . . . Alexander. She serves in the court of the tsar and her sense of propriety is impeccable."

"A shame." He skillfully guided me around the circle of dancers once more. "I have my own connections to our good tsar. He claims to enjoy my work, though he keeps a close eye on it for words of sedition." Alexander clicked his tongue as though scolding himself. "Nevertheless, Mademoiselle Natalie, I believe young women are allowed some freedom of movement . . . might I call you Natalie? I feel it suits you."

"You make me sound as though I belong in Paris or some other city of the west."

"Perhaps you do. Who knows where life might take you. An enchanting face can motivate great adventures. You've heard of Helen of Troy, have you not?"

"I doubt my face will launch a thousand ships."

Alexander beamed with pleasure, and I wondered if he'd posed the reference to Helen as a way of testing my knowledge of antiquity. That struck me as not quite fair, and yet if this were a test, I wished to pass with high marks.

"Please know I would do nothing to tarnish your reputation. It would be a crime to do anything to prevent you from attending future balls. You were born to be admired."

I glanced again at Aunt Katya, whose eyebrow now seemed perpetually cocked, and then at the poet before me, who curled the fingers of his right hand and pressed them lightly against his mouth, trying to contain the grin now brightening his face. As though allowing himself the unadulterated happiness of a smile would only lead to disappointment.

It was a habit I would grow to know well, and worry over more and more in the years to come. At that time, however, that happy Christmas when I first came to know him, it only seemed one of Alexander Pushkin's many charms.

"Perhaps a few moments outside in the courtyard for fresh air," I told him. "What's the harm in that?"

I remember everything about that night, about my first moments alone with Alexander. The glow of the crescent moon scarcely penetrated the clouds and birch branches drooped under the silvery weight of new snowfall. In the center of the mansion's courtyard, a marble fountain, dry for the winter, housed a statue of a voluptuous nymph in a toga with outstretched hands. Two gentlemen stood near the fountain, bundled deep into overcoats and leering at the nymph.

"Your patience with my dancing is much appreciated, mademoiselle." Alexander tightened his own coat against the sharp wind and tapped his fashionable walking stick against the ice-flecked cobblestones of the mansion's square courtyard, keeping time to the quick tempo of a mazurka playing inside the mansion's ballroom. Upon closer inspection, I saw his stick was topped by a charming figurine of a bear cub ascending a tree stump. "I never did develop a talent for it. I fear dancing lessons were a trial in my youth."

"I thought you were marvelous," I said.

"Your skills far surpass mine. How old are you . . . if it's not too presumptuous."

I had not the experience to determine if the question was presumptuous or not and so simply answered: "Sixteen."

"Sixteen years old and already wearing a charming tiara, as though crowned the most beautiful woman in Moscow." His breath misted in the air. The men in bulky overcoats pitched curious looks in our direction, for one of them had poked the other and pointed at Alexander. "When I was but sixteen, I was no beauty. Not as I am now . . ."

He stopped tapping his walking stick and rubbed his hands together as he said this, and I knew he was trying to be funny, but I didn't think it kind to laugh. Though Alexander's features were not traditionally handsome, even I knew of his popularity with the ladies in St. Petersburg, Moscow, and all other points of the empire if rumors were to be believed. Lacking that which made some men fetching had not hindered Alexander's power to attract. Surely he knew this.

Still, I did not laugh.

Despite its thick lining, my pelisse was no match for the stubborn chill of the night. I shivered and drew it tighter around my chest, but tried to appear sophisticated and nonchalant, as though accustomed to spending evenings out in the cold wind with the most famous poet in Russia. Alexander stole a glimpse at my feet, the tips of my satin slippers peeping out from beneath my gown, and then his focus moved once more to my face.

"Though I suppose I had my moments," he said. "At sixteen, I was in the junior class at the Impérial Lycée, a year away from being graduated. I had my own room. My own writing table on which to place a sheet of paper and scribble my thoughts. Can you imagine the thrill of such a space?" He flashed a roguish smile that made my heart pump faster and I longed to keep him out here to myself as long as possible. "My imagination soared."

When I attempted creative work at home, I was always interrupted by one of Mother's endless needlework projects or Ekaterina's complaints about a rude shopkeeper. I longed for the luxury of privacy. "I've heard it said you read for Derzhavin as a schoolboy."

Derzhavin was the most celebrated poet of Catherine the Great's time. As a child, before misfortune diminished our family's finances, I lived for a short time with my grandfather on his estate near Kaluga. In the basement of the main house, he kept an enormous bronze statue of Catherine that I always found an excuse to visit, trying to imagine a world where a woman might rule men. Ever since, I had taken a particular interest in Catherine's reign and knew Derzhavin's epic "The Waterfall" practically by heart.

"I did!" Alexander declared, clearly pleased. "My chum Delvig was keen to meet Derzhavin and declared he would 'shake the hand that had written "The Waterfall."' He made me wait with him in the school's foyer. When at last the front door creaked open, we heard the tap of his cane against the marble floor."

To illustrate the point, Alexander pounded his walking stick on the cobblestone once more, startling the men in the courtyard who slowly backed closer to the mansion's thick, lemon-yellow walls. My teeth chattered, but I endeavored to extend my time alone with Alexander. "Were you two humble students allowed to meet the great man?"

"He had more pressing matters. A footman asked if he needed anything. Derzhavin responded with equal gravity." Alexander's voice rumbled as he impersonated the poet. "'My good man,' said he, 'where is the privy in this place? I need to piss like a work-horse.'"

Alexander stifled a laugh, punching his fist to his mouth. A few sputters escaped and then he doubled over and his laughter was so infectious I started to giggle as well. "I suppose you were all quite disappointed your hero was given to such base human needs," I said.

"Never, my dear lady! I found him all the more appealing for it. However, I can't say the footman felt the same. The fellow's cheeks reddened until he looked like an apple. Once they had shuffled away, Delvig turned to me, said, 'Great man, my arse!' and stormed off."

My corset stays tore into my stomach as I laughed. I still felt amazed I was even speaking to a man such as Alexander Pushkin, let alone that he was comfortable enough to say "arse" in my presence. Without thinking, I grasped Alexander's wrist.

Alexander stared at the patch of exposed skin above his gloves, where my flesh pressed his. Suddenly shy, I withdrew my hand

and took a deep breath. The cold air roughened my nostrils and throat. I averted my gaze, poking the cobblestone under my satin slipper. "Was this the last you saw of the famed Derzhavin?"

"Certainly not." Alexander still stared at the spot where I had touched him. A few droplets of snow speckled his black whiskers and he withdrew a handkerchief from his front pocket to pat his face. "We were all scheduled to recite poems for him as part of our final exams. I confess, I was nervous waiting for the other poor devils to deliver their lines. Watching the old man's head slip to his shoulder as he nodded in and out of sleep."

"He fell asleep during the exams! The boys must have been mortified."

"Indeed, they were. I was mortified as well. What if the great Derzhavin should snore in the middle of my recitation? And then I decided to view his somnolence not as a problem, but a challenge. Someone needed to rouse the poor man from his torpor and it might as well be me. I strode to the center of the room, surrounded by my instructors and their pretty wives all dressed to the nines, stepped onto one of the diamond-shaped tiles, and gave the best reading of my life. At least I thought it so. Then I saw it happen: the old man awoke and cupped his hand to his ear so that he might better hear my words."

I could picture the scene: Alexander as a brash young man, his olive skin and mass of wild black curls, hand flung high in the air as he read a particularly dramatic line. "Did you ever shake the hand that wrote 'The Waterfall'?"

"After my recitation, I fled the room. Truth be told, the pressure grew too immense and the fact that he adored my poem felt devastating." Alexander fingered the little cub atop his walking stick, and then shook his head and screwed his eyelids shut. Faint creases appeared at the corners of his eyes. "Success alarmed me. I feel a fool saying that aloud."

"It's not foolish at all! You dreamed of success. Once attained . . . well, what then?"

Alexander opened his eyes and his gaze fell squarely on my mouth. I understood him. Perhaps he was unaccustomed to feeling understood. I felt certain then that he would try to steal a kiss. Without thinking, I closed my eyes, wanting to feel his lips on mine, choosing not to worry who might see. I was ready.

I waited, but felt nothing. I opened my eyes once more to find Alexander grinning. My lips were still foolishly pursed, but he had not taken advantage. He tossed his walking stick into the air and caught it deftly in one hand, as though celebrating this small victory.

Out of the corner of my eye, I watched the gentlemen by the fountain re-enter the mansion. The cold now felt like painful pinpricks of ice, reality sinking in once more.

"We should return before we are missed," Alexander said. "I trust Tolstoy to keep your aunt occupied, but the poor chap can ramble and I don't want her to suffer too long."

I nodded, trying not to betray my disappointment. We needed to return to the ball, but the night was not yet over and already it seemed an eternity until I might again see Alexander.

"Aren't we fancy?" Ekaterina declared as we alighted from our carriage and navigated the slippery walkway to our house just before midnight.

"What do you mean?" I spoke against my better judgment, for

I knew Ekaterina was trying to provoke me and I should refrain from snapping at the bait.

"You were on the dance floor all night! With the same partner for the most part. That dark fellow?"

After our initial waltz, Alexander had asked me to dance again, but by no stretch of the imagination had he monopolized me. "I danced with Alexander a few times, no more than was appropriate. And that 'dark fellow' is the author of *Evgeny Onegin* and other works."

"Oh, everyone knows Alexander Pushkin," Ekaterina said slyly. "He has been involved with a number of elegant ladies, from what I understand."

"How would you know?"

Ekaterina shrugged. "I'm only repeating what Aunt Katya said."

As we crossed the threshold into our dim and silent home, I tried to compose myself. Ekaterina wanted to embarrass me. I would not allow guilt to sully my complexion when we spoke to Mother.

The fire in the hearth had already been put out and the front room was chilly. I thought Sergey would have remained near the door to harass us the instant we arrived home, but Mother must have shooed the boys off to bed. She sat alone in her armchair with the lazy tabby prostrate on her lap. I did not understand how either of them could tolerate the cold, nor the dank scent of mildew. I wanted nothing more than to sink under the blankets of my bed.

"I trust you had a fine time," Mother said. "Your father would be here to ask himself, only he worked himself to the point of exhaustion today and has taken to bed."

I tried not to flinch at Mother's blatant lie. Father likely lingered still at one of the taverns along the Arbat. For all I knew, he was sleeping on the street these days. He had chosen alcohol and misery and despair over his family, and I could no longer find room in my heart for him.

"Natalya had a grand time," Ekaterina announced.

The harsh lines of Mother's face shadowed in the dull light from the dying fire. "Oh?"

The tiara felt tight on my forehead. "There was a Christmas tree and I found it lovely."

"She spent the night dancing with Alexander Pushkin," Ekaterina said. "The writer? You have heard of him, haven't you? Didn't he get in trouble over some rebel nonsense in a poem?"

"That was years ago and besides, Natalya only danced with him a few times." Azya could always be counted on to defend me. "No more than was proper."

Mother rose to her feet, dislodging the tabby who emitted a screech of complaint and glared at Ekaterina before darting out of the room. "Girls, you get straight to your beds and tell me the rest in the morning. You need your beauty sleep, after all."

We nodded and curtsied, and I prepared to follow my sisters upstairs.

"Natalya, why don't you wait a moment while your sisters go first? I think we should have a few words."

As I watched my sisters scurry off, the stairs creaking under their heeled slippers, my heart dropped to my stomach.

"Alexander Pushkin. I believe I have heard this name before." Mother stroked a tarnished silver crucifix strung around her neck on a beaded chain. "The poet?"

"The one." I was tired and did not know what Mother expected of me.

"He lived in exile for some time under our previous tsar, this poet of yours. It seems such a man will always find himself under the crown's scrutiny, along with his family and associates."

Mother drew closer to the table where I kept my notes and inkwell and oval-shaped spectacles. I chewed my lower lip as she removed the spectacles from their fabric case and turned the thin, fragile frames over in her hands.

"Your great-great-grandfather was a practical man. A man of this world. He lived in the time of Tsar Peter and thought to himself: what might this powerful man need? Then he looked to the grand ships being built in the harbor and knew the answer. Such ships would sail through the wind with what? Cloth . . ."

I bowed my head, bracing for the all too familiar family history lesson that was to follow.

". . . and so he set to manufacture cotton and linens and expanded to paper products and made a fortune that brought honor to this family and helped make this empire what it is today. The Goncharovs remained great, retained their fortune . . . until your grandfather brought the French laundress home with him after the war."

I had been born in 1812, so I knew of the war with Napoleon only from hearsay, but Mother had told this family story so many times I felt I had borne witness to it. My grandfather, Afansy Goncharov, spent the war abroad. After Napoleon's armies had been driven from Moscow, and Grandfather finally returned home, we learned he had left his wife and replaced her with a clever Frenchwoman named Babette. As far as Mother was concerned,

Babette was to blame for all the family's financial problems since. How exactly this was so had never been made clear. It seemed more a coincidence of timing to me and yet the legend endured.

Mother would never admit the truth: that it was not some random Frenchwoman, but my father's drinking—his bouts of crying, his sudden screaming fits on those rare occasions when he did come home—that accounted for our troubles. Ever since he was thrown from a horse and made the decision to soothe the pain of his injuries with drink, my father had been useless. I had been a small girl at the time of his accident, and could only now comprehend the extent of the damage he'd done.

"I appreciate the appeal of poetry, but it is nothing more than fantasy," Mother said. "In reality, a husband must support his wife and her family as best he can manage. In this world, poets are not capable of such generosity. Better to turn your favor to a more practical man who sees a need in this world, fills it, and is compensated handsomely for his trouble. One who steers clear of politics and the petty intrigues of the tsar's court. Do you understand?"

I could barely look at her, but nodded.

Mother handed me my spectacles. I took them with one hand, removed my tiara with the other, and then positioned them on my face. As though a spell had been cast, the world came into sharp focus around me: the pointed corners of the writing table, the needlework unicorns and maidens on the fading, old-fashioned tapestries hanging from the walls, products of my family's once lucrative mills, and the last glowing embers of the fire in the hearth.

"You are young and gifted with great beauty. You can attract a practical man. You're a good girl, Natalya. You understand our family's precarious situation. Now, off to bed with you. I know at your next ball you will make a wise choice and do that which is right for us all."

My mother spoke of wise choices as though such matters were clear as day and night, and life provides only one true path to security and satisfaction. I have since learned that the choices we make in this life are a complex, nuanced array leading to both joy and despair. A comfortable partnership with a practical man might have granted me contentment, but I believe I would have spent that life forever looking over my shoulder, wondering what might have been had I chosen the poet instead.

Three

Over breakfast the following morning, Azya spoke of nothing but the ball. As we waited for the chilly room to warm, Ivan and Sergey scarfed down hot buttered buns and slurped cinnamon-flavored cocoa while my sister told them of the dancing and decorations. "They had a pine tree with candles on every branch!"

Mother took a silent sip of her plain black tea. "As in the Protestant lands? I didn't realize society was so taken with Prussian custom."

Ekaterina gave a triumphant snort.

"Yes, but it was beautiful!" Azya insisted. "And one of the girls told me at this time of year there are all sorts of spells you can cast to learn the identity of your husband. They say if you look in a mirror at midnight on Christmas Eve, you will see his face."

"Sounds like a foreign trick," Ekaterina huffed.

I looked steadily at a pat of butter on my chipped Sèvres plate, a bun warming my mouth. At the word "husband," Alexander's face appeared in my mind. That was no trick.

"Not foreign at all," Ivan cut in authoritatively, his wide forehead creasing. "It's an ancient Slavic tradition."

"Either way, it seems like nonsense to me," Ekaterina said.

"They played mazurkas until the dancers were exhausted, and the waltz at least five times by my count," Azya continued. "Natalya danced every one of them."

"Yes," Ekaterina said slyly. "First with some man you all know. Tolstoy or some such?"

"The American!" Ivan declared. "Nice fellow. Arrogant, but Natalya could do worse. He said he might visit soon. I wonder if we should expect him."

I thought Mother would frown again. So, apparently, did Ekaterina, who took a moment away from primly tasting her cocoa to give me a knowing smirk.

"It is a credit to us all that your sister is so popular," Mother said.

Under the table, Sergey kicked my shin. It smarted and I scowled at him, but he kept his plump features maddeningly neutral. So I kicked him right back and he cried out in pain.

"Her partner for the next few dances was a dark-skinned fellow with the most unusual hair," Ekaterina droned on, oblivious to Sergey's yowling. "If you know this Tolstoy the American, perhaps you have met his friend too. Alexander Pushkin?"

"The poet? With our Natalya . . ." Ivan eyed me suspiciously, as though it was beyond his ability to ascertain why I might be of interest to someone like Alexander Pushkin.

Mother pressed her lips into a thin line and I was sure she was about to say something to Ivan or perhaps even to Sergey for kicking me, but at that moment the one footman who remained in our household entered the dining area. Over the past few months, he had assumed a variety of duties, despite an unavoidable decline in his pay. Now, he hovered patiently at the threshold, waiting to be summoned. Mother nodded and he approached bearing a small visiting card printed in elaborate lettering I did not recognize.

"A visitor this early?" Mother dabbed her mouth with a linen napkin and carefully took the card, dipping her nose closer to it.

Though I couldn't make out the name of the visitor, I caught the rich scent of sandalwood and citrus emanating from the card stock, the same cologne Alexander had worn the previous night. I recalled the jolt of excitement when his hand touched mine and my heart fluttered, the descriptions in French novels proven correct once more.

My eldest brother, Dmitry, bounded down the stairs, late to breakfast as usual. He gave Mother a peck on the cheek and prepared to take his customary seat. Before lowering himself onto the chair, he leaned over her shoulder to view the calling card.

"Alexander Pushkin!" Dmitry had always been hard of hearing and spoke as though everyone else suffered from the affliction as well. "Who in this house knows a poet?" He gave a hearty laugh and stabbed one of the sausages on a platter in the center of the table. "Sergey can hardly write his own name." He looked over at Ivan, who was fussing with his hair, trying to push it forward to better cover his high forehead. "Was it you? Are you trying your hand at poetry? Trying to get a damsel to roll in the hay with a choice word or two."

Ekaterina gasped loudly while I felt vexed Dmitry would not even consider a man so famous might be here to visit me. "That's enough," Mother said, but handsome Dmitry had always been her favorite and could say whatever he liked in her presence. She was still frowning at the card, apparently saving her disapproval for someone more deserving.

"Natalya, breakfast is nearly over. I believe you will be more comfortable upstairs. You are far too young to receive a gentleman so early in the morning."

My gaze shifted to the calling card. Last night before falling asleep, I had thought of more questions I wanted to ask Alexander about *Onegin*, questions I hadn't the presence of mind to ask during our private conversation at the ball and I had hoped, somehow, the fates would conspire to bring him to me again.

I remembered what Mother had said about the importance of finding a practical man—someone like our Goncharov ancestor who provided the sails that set Peter the Great's Russian naval forces to sea. And then I thought of my grandfather, Afansy, still responsible for our family factories in the countryside south of Moscow. I wondered what he might make of Russia's greatest poet calling on his granddaughter.

These thoughts occurred to me in quick succession, but I did not yet possess the strength to oppose Mother.

She gave our footman a stiff smile, rose to her feet, and returned the card to his gloved hand. "After waiting up for the girls last night, I feel fatigued. I believe I made a mistake in rising so early. Please tell Alexander Pushkin that if he wishes to call, he needs to make his way to my home at a more appropriate hour." Mother followed the footman out of the dining room. I listened to the heavy trod of her footfall on the squeaky stairs, and then the meow and tapping paws of her tabby as he followed her up to her room.

She was trusting me to leave of my own accord, testing my loyalty.

Ekaterina gave me a sideways glance. "Aren't you supposed to go upstairs as well?"

I stared at the sausages and took another sip of the sweet cocoa.

Perhaps I should have, but I was not about to do so at my sister's behest.

If I had been quicker to heed my sister's nagging or follow Mother's lead, everything might have been easier in the end, for myself and for my family. The memory of Alexander Pushkin would have been condensed to one magical night, a charming encounter but with no more impact on my future than the decorative tree the dance master had procured for his ball.

Instead, I remained firmly fixed to my chair. Then I heard his voice, the silky tone I recalled from the previous night sending a delicious shiver dancing lightly across my shoulders. "Surely if they are enjoying breakfast, I might keep them company."

"The lady of the house is in bed. I'm not sure it's appropriate for you—"

Alexander bounded past the footman and into the doorway, scanning the faces around the table and quickly finding mine. In an instant, the room lost its chill. He wore a dark frock coat with long tails that flared out at his hips, a matching waistcoat, and a loose green cravat about his neck. Snow had flecked his unkempt black curls. In one hand he held his silver-topped walking stick with the little bear cub and in the other, his floppy top hat. I remembered how badly I wished to kiss him last night. As though he could read my mind, he gifted me with a lavish smile and wink.

Every sensible thought fled my brain. I couldn't even find it in me to say hello, but only stared at his face, which now seemed to me the most blissful sight in this world.

Thankfully, Ivan spoke first. "Alexander Pushkin! My mother isn't here to greet you in person, but you're considered a friend of this family, dear fellow. I believe we are both acquainted with Tolstoy the American, that rascal."

I had not realized Ivan fashioned himself a dandy. His tone had the rakish offhandedness favored by that set and Alexander responded to it well enough. "Indeed! Why the American can be long-winded, but a good sort all around, wouldn't you say?"

"A daredevil!" Ivan declared. "But it seems you have a bit of the revolutionary in your soul as well. Are you a supporter of Simón Bolívar?" Ivan indicated the hat in Alexander's hand, which I remembered now had been dubbed *chapeau Bolívar* and was said to be all the rage in Paris. Evgeny Onegin himself had worn one. I thought it bold of Ivan to ask Alexander about politics, but I was curious to hear Alexander's answer.

Alexander tossed his top hat in the air and snatched it back in his hand. His relaxed air put me at ease and I giggled at this show of dexterity, but our footman pressed his lips together and straightened his back. Perhaps in Mother's absence he felt someone needed to play the role of disapproving adult.

"I believe in the sovereignty of independent states in the Spanish empire. Why shouldn't these republics follow the lead of their neighbor? Surely North Americans have no monopoly on personal liberty."

"A poet and a politician. This is an honor." Dmitry stood and introduced us all, except when my turn came, he said, "I believe you had the pleasure of meeting our little Natalya."

Alexander clicked his heels together in a raffish manner. "Mademoiselle Natalie." His gaze intensified when his eyes met mine and a pleasant giddiness stirred in my chest.

Of course Ekaterina could not let any moment pass without

commentary. "You shared many dances with my sister last night. I wish you had found time to chat with Azya and myself." She gestured toward Azya, who appeared embarrassed to be included in the complaint.

"An oversight I hope to remedy this morning," Alexander said.

Ekaterina tilted her chin in Alexander's direction. Really, if my chin was large as a melon I would take care to tuck it in close to my throat, but Ekaterina had no shame. "You said you were in favor of sovereignty for the nations of the New World. I understand you take an interest in such matters in our land as well. For example, the Decembrist traitors who attempted to overthrow our tsar? Such men were your friends, were they not?"

Sergey chose that moment to loudly slurp the last of his cocoa, but the rest of us remained silent. Ekaterina had been unspeakably rude. I would have kicked her shin except she sat out of foot's reach. No one could think of anything further to say.

Three years earlier, a group of elite officers had attempted to defy the presumed heir to the throne, then Grand Duke Nicholas. Tsar Alexander was on his deathbed and had no sons. The Decembrists, as they were called, supported Constantine, the brother of the dying tsar, who was said to hold liberal ideas regarding governance. Ultimately, however, Constantine refused the throne and Nicholas stood next in the royal line.

Nicholas held far different political views than Constantine and favored strong autocratic rule. This did not sit well with Constantine's supporters, and in December, the officers gathered three thousand men to oppose Nicholas's accession to the throne. Safe in Moscow, I heard of the confusion in St. Petersburg only through whispered conversations between adults in the parlor. From what I gathered, the rebellion had been immediately suppressed, the leaders publicly hanged, and countless others exiled to Siberia. Even now, every so often, another officer was found guilty of complicity in the revolt, and people gathered on the street to watch him, pretty wife at his side, taken by the police and escorted out of the city to the frozen hinterlands.

I knew Alexander had been a friend of the Decembrists. It was even rumored his poetry inspired the rebellion. The old tsar had found Alexander's poetry subversive and prior to the revolt, Alexander had been forced from both Moscow and St. Petersburg for a few years, though exiled to the south rather than a work camp in the harsh north.

I expected Mother might dredge up this ancient history, but how dare Ekaterina be so boorish as to raise the subject now, while Alexander was a visitor in our home. My cheeks burned with resentment. I resolved to get her back by tying all her hair ribbons in knots while she slept.

Alexander managed to hold his smile. "Tsar Nicholas spoke with me personally to ask if I supported the revolt and I gave him an honest answer. I was not in the capital at the time."

"If you had been?" my sister asked.

Alexander punched the hat in his hand. "I would have supported the Decembrists. He asked me to speak plainly and I told him as much."

At the sound of those words, my stomach soured. The sausages that had smelled so appealing when first set before us were now revolting. I admired Alexander's passion, but to speak so frankly in our presence, considering he had already been exiled once for seditious language, seemed rash at best.

"I find it hard to believe the tsar let such impudence slip through his fingers."

"What impudence?" Alexander tilted his head playfully, but Ekaterina remained immune to his charms.

"A poet inspiring his friends to rebellion," my sister said.

Dark purple splotches blossomed on Alexander's cheeks and around his whiskers.

"The tsar accepted your answer?" Dmitry cut into the conversation, his voice so loud I was certain Mother could hear from upstairs.

"He asked me to reconsider my politics and I told him I would do so," Alexander said. "Since then, I have shown him nothing but allegiance. Though I understand their way of thinking, I now believe the Decembrists were merely a misguided lot, poor devils. Hearts in the right place but heads in the muck and mire."

"Surely the tsar keeps you under close watch," Ekaterina said.

"He has assured me he does not. He only asks to read my work before it is published."

"Perhaps he is looking for something to serve as an excuse to send you away."

I bit my lip so hard it grew numb, wishing my sister would shut her rude mouth but understanding the sense of her words. I had not thought it fair of Mother to deny Alexander based on his financial prospects, nor past clashes with a long dead tsar, but neither had I realized he had been so bold with our new tsar, the man who held power over our very lives. I could end up like one of the pretty Decembrist wives, following my husband to exile in Siberia. My family, already on the precipice of financial devastation, would be ruined.

My hands trembled, but I dabbed my napkin to my lips before I rose from my chair. "Excuse me. It's quite early and I don't believe it appropriate for me to receive a caller."

The stiff sound of my own words made my heart plummet, and

yet I didn't know what else to do except remove myself from Alexander's presence as artfully as possible. To leave the room, I needed to pass him. I drew a deep breath and kept my gaze fixed on the floor. I caught the warm scent of Alexander's sandalwood cologne and sweet tobacco and saw his boots, damp with wet snow. The footman moved aside, but Alexander stood his ground. I was forced to look up, to face the misery in his eyes. The heaviness of his gaze entranced me and for a moment I forgot my siblings and only wanted to melt into his arms and beg him to take me from here.

"I hope I have not offended you, mademoiselle." His words were innocent enough but his voice felt like silk on bare skin. "I only thought you had taken such an interest in the fate of Onegin that you might be compelled to further our conversation."

Nothing would have pleased me more. I met his gaze and opened my mouth to pose a question about how Tatiana's feelings for Onegin might shift after the duel. But I felt the burning stares of my siblings. At this distance, their expressions were fuzzy, but I saw Ekaterina's disapproval and an anxious twitch in Dmitry's handsome face. Life had been difficult enough since Father had taken to drink, and I could not further jeopardize our family's already precarious circumstances.

"Good day, sir," I said, snatching my spectacles from the writing table before I ascended the creaking staircase.

Once I made my way to the bedroom I shared with my sisters, I sat down hard on the divan near the window and ran my fingers over the threadbare patch where the tabby had clawed the cushions. Stinging tears threatened, but I forced them back. I was behaving like a fool. I barely knew Alexander. How could I imagine we shared a magical connection?

I placed my spectacles on the bridge of my nose, adjusting them under the tips of my ears. They fit poorly and since Mother refused to "waste" money on a new pair, I centered them as best I could. Suddenly, the world came into focus. Outside, snow fell gently, clinging to the birch trees that edged the small park across from our house. I tried to take pleasure in the sharp contrast between the white snow and the jewel-toned buildings on either side of the park, but the day had been ruined.

Alexander's carriage was parked just below my window, a closed coach with the wheels converted to sleigh runners to better navigate the winter streets. His horses pawed the snowy ground, breaths fogging over their halters. My heart caught as I spotted Alexander approaching the carriage, his *chapeau Bolívar* pulled so low over his forehead it covered his eyes. He strode deliberately, pounding his walking stick against the icy cobblestones. He seemed angry and I was deeply sorry, but his bruised ego could not be helped.

He turned and seemed to know exactly where he might find my window. Mother would have insisted I remove my spectacles in the presence of a potential suitor, not that she considered Alexander as such. But hadn't Catherine the Great herself suffered from myopia? It was nothing of which to be ashamed.

Alexander quickly located my face. If the spectacles were off-putting, nothing about his features betrayed this fact. When he spotted me watching him, he smiled broadly, removed the hat, and gave a low bow. Then he made his way inside, and the coachman snapped a whip, calling his team of horses to attention. They trotted off, the sound of jingle bells on their harnesses slowly fading to nothing.

I remained at the window for the rest of the morning. No

matter how prudent my behavior with Alexander might have been, I couldn't shake the sense that I'd held something wonderfully precious in my hands and then allowed it to slip away. I felt like a foolish maiden or prince in a fairy tale who captures the elusive firebird but cannot manage to keep it and is left with only a sparkling feather in hand.

As it turned out, Alexander was less willing to abandon his pursuit of me than I supposed. Each morning that week, he attempted to call. Each morning, Mother sent me up to my room and allowed for no more than a passing word with him. As the evenings progressed—and my sisters went about their usual bedtime routine of cleaning and scrubbing and lathering their faces with rose-scented cold cream—I could scarcely summon the will to change into my nightclothes. Even the strong smell of their cream offended my senses.

I opened one of the rattling drawers of our bureau and withdrew the latest installment of *Evgeny Onegin*. If I re-read the last passage, I might conjure Alexander.

As I settled into our canopied bed and opened the thin pages of the journal, Ekaterina scowled. "Don't tell me you're still moping over the rebel poet? He's not even handsome!"

"That's most unkind," Azya said. "I think he has a certain charm about him."

"He's little as a dormouse." Ekaterina finished braiding her hair and slapped a gigantic white blob of cream on her jawline. I thought to say something catty about how she might save some of the cream for me, but my mind was too dulled to summon a jibe. Alexander might not have been tall, and he might not have had the classic good looks we were taught to admire, but anyone with half a brain could sense the passion in him, the depth of emotion in his eyes.

I remembered the sensation of his hand on the small of my back, the spark at his slightest touch. Yet surely it did not mean more than the welfare of my mother and siblings.

Surely not.

"Are we even certain he's in so much trouble with Tsar Nicholas?" I mused.

Azya turned to me, eyes wide as those of a peasant waif in a staged tableau. Ekaterina had turned her attention from her face to her large hands and smoothed lotion over her palms.

"His work is put through the censor. He said as much. I'd wager he's being followed by the tsar's secret police. Reasonable, given his history with the traitors."

"Not that you were obliged to raise the topic at all." I loathed the petulance in my voice, but if Ekaterina hadn't brought up this issue, it might never have occurred to me to do so. "Certainly not on his first visit to our home."

"Mother wasn't present, so I simply acted as she would expect me to act."

"You have no idea how Mother would have acted."

"She wanted you to leave the room before the poet even made it through the door. Should I have carried you out over my shoulder like the insolent child you are?"

"You're just mad because you didn't dance as much as I did at the ball."

"And you're just lucky Azya guides you around so you don't bump into every table and pillar. I'd like to see how many partners you'd attract if you wore those ridiculous spectacles."

"I'll likely never see you attract even one aging fool." My voice sounded high and disturbingly shrill. Azya motioned for us to quiet down. Mother probably could hear our row, but I was quickly ceasing to care what Mother or anyone else might think.

"And I wanted to wear the tiara," Ekaterina hissed at me. "You had no right."

I tried to slam the journal shut, but the paper was thin and the sound not particularly satisfying. I glowered at Ekaterina, but she had tossed her long braid behind her shoulders and returned her attention to the looking glass, satisfied she had upset me enough for one night.

"You could ask Aunt Katya for help," Azya said in a small voice. "I heard Mother say she is visiting tomorrow afternoon to speak with the boys."

I turned to her sweet face, squinting out of habit.

"If Alexander Pushkin is under government surveillance or in danger of future exile . . . well, Aunt Katya is acquainted with everyone who is anyone. She would know. Or at least she could find out."

I tossed the blankets aside and the journal to the side of our bed. "Azya, you are a marvel." I rushed to give her a hug.

"She'll only verify what we suspect." Ekaterina shrugged. "Either way, Alexander is still a man of letters. How much income can a poet hope to earn?"

"Now you do sound like Mother," I said, exasperated.

"I'm only speaking common sense. His fortune will always rely on the whim of the public's taste and the tsar's censors. And what kind of life would you make for yourself at court with such a man? Under scrutiny and worried about whether or not you're in favor. Why the tsar could decide to send you to Siberia if it so pleased him. No, thank you." Ekaterina gave a firm shake of her head. "When I marry, it will be to a man in the army or civil service at the least, with a stable family income and a reliable pension."

I hadn't the energy to taunt Ekaterina further, so I settled for a frustrated sigh. Let my sister dream of a bland military man to buy her baubles; I wished for more. If there was a chance I could allow Alexander to pursue my heart, I would give him the opportunity to do so.

Four

The next few weeks were a torment, or at least what one considers a torment when but sixteen years old. I spent mornings over glum breakfasts, listening to Ekaterina and Mother attempt to outdo one another with their endless complaints about life, and afternoons in our musty parlor, bent over yet another embroidery project. I had no talent for handiwork, and maintained my sanity only by clinging to hope of the future, recalling the sensation of Alexander's hand on mine and the velvety sound of his voice. While in the sitting room with my sisters, darning socks on a cold but cloudless winter afternoon, I indulged in schoolgirl fantasies of balls, concerts, even a lavish wedding. I dreamed of evenings spent in salons, listening to Alexander present his latest work to a rapt audience.

"Get your head out of the sky," Ekaterina snapped. "I can't carry on a conversation with you at all these days—not that you were ever so keen on talk that requires common sense."

I tried and failed to remember what my sister had been saying when my thoughts wandered. I stuck my tongue out at Ekaterina, just as I would if Sergey were heckling me. She tilted her square chin up in disdain and unleashed a frustrated sigh of disapproval.

When Aunt Katya finally arrived at our door, I endeavored to find a moment to approach her alone and learn what she knew of Alexander's standing with the tsar. I was constantly foiled. My brothers launched a torrent of queries about various military or civil appointments. My romantic fantasies seemed shallow in comparison to their future careers, and so I allowed my brothers' needs to take precedence over mine. Besides, I understood the pressure on my brothers to leave our household and earn incomes of their own. Even Sergey, always such a practical joker, approached Aunt Katya to see if she knew of anyone in the Ministry of Navy who might have need of a seaman. I tried to picture little Sergey making his way across Alaska and Siberia on his own, as Tolstoy the American had, but could only summon an image of him irritating his senior officers when he made noises.

Of course the boys were not the only ones compelled to make their own ways in this world. Once Aunt Katya had finished with them, she had a cedar trunk brought in from her carriage. The trunk had been filled to the brim with extra silk and lace and even entire hand-me-down dresses. She helped us gather stiches around the waist, so as to better fit into gowns that once belonged to grander and stouter ladies.

"It is still becoming," Aunt Katya told me after apologizing that the dress she offered was five years out of fashion. "Of course it is too short, for you are wonderfully tall, but we can add length with more silk gauze to the hem."

In truth, I would never have known the difference, though the gown did retain the sweet woodsy scent of my aunt's cedar trunk mingled with feminine perspiration. Intricately patterned crimson lace and metallic needlework lined the deep round neckline and the dark green shade brightened my dark eyes. As we peered together at my image in the looking glass, I discerned the pride in my aunt's smile and knew I would find no better opportunity to speak to her. I caught her eye as she fussed with a smudge on the fabric. "May I have a private word?"

Aunt Katya must have sensed the solemnity in my tone, for she glanced over her shoulder at my sisters riffling through the remaining hand-me-downs in the trunk. Mother always made sure I had first choice, making it no secret she thought me prettiest and thus most likely to make a lucrative match. I knew I should have felt guilty over this—and more generous to Ekaterina and Azya—but the gowns were so beautiful it was hard to refuse the privilege.

"As though we don't know what Natalya will ask." Ekaterina smirked, picking at some thick brown dog hair stuck to a velvet frock. "It was Azya's idea."

"Never mind," I said quickly. "They can stay."

Azya appraised me now with her wide eyes. "Natalya wishes to ask about her suitor? The poet? I knew it!"

"Alexander Pushkin." Aunt Katya swung back to look at me, one delicate eyebrow arched. "He has been here since the dance master's ball?"

"Alexander . . . Monsieur Pushkin came to call on us the next day," I explained.

"You enjoy his company?"

"He is darling, but you see I have a concern . . ." Out of the corner of my eye, I watched Ekaterina raise an eyebrow, parroting my aunt. "I mean we all had concerns, really."

"Regarding his intentions? You are concerned he is not the marrying sort."

This caught me by surprise. Though I had only a vague notion of what Aunt Katya meant, I suspected it had something to do with the tales I'd heard whispered behind gauze fans, of men who cared naught but for their own pleasure. With all the wisdom and experience of a sixteen-year-old, I told my aunt: "Well, I certainly do not desire to find myself alone and with child!"

My sisters tittered, but Aunt Katya remained poised. After twenty-five years at court, no comment ruffled her composure. "My dear, I trust all of you to behave well enough that it will never become an issue. Now, what is it you wish to ask?"

I straightened my shoulders, hoping good posture might add gravity to my words. "I know Alexander had trouble with the tsar due to his former association with the Decembrists. I couldn't in good faith allow a courtship if I thought his attention endangered our family. Do you know anything more? Is Alexander still under the tsar's watch?"

Aunt Katya held my gaze but I could ascertain nothing from the blank expression on her pretty face. I imagine this look served her well at the court's gaming tables. "I have no idea."

Azya sidled next to me and took my hand. "I suggested Natalya ask you."

"I can ask some subtle questions here and there, I suppose, but the only person who knows the reality of this matter is Pushkin himself."

"That's not true," Ekaterina said.

"I'm lying?" Even though Aunt Katya and my mother were only half-sisters, I heard the same imperious tone in her voice that Mother used with us.

Ekaterina had sense enough to soften her approach. "I only meant that perhaps he is under watch and doesn't know it. You know the creative types: daydreamers lacking in common sense. Pushkin might not be aware of his true standing. In that case, Tsar Nicholas himself is the only person who knows the truth."

At that, my heart fell, for how would I ever find myself in a position to ask the tsar about Alexander? I might as well ask for the moon to fall from the sky.

Aunt Katya gave a sly smile and I saw her dimples. "You find the poet attractive?"

Azya stifled another giggle and Ekaterina emitted a loud snort, but I had grown weary of their foolishness. We were old enough to marry, after all, so why must I pretend to feel embarrassed that I found a man handsome? "I do and I believe Alexander has taken an interest in me as well." My confidence lasted only a moment before I remembered my conversation with Mother that first night, after the ball. "Though I'm not sure Mother thinks a poet's income sufficient to provide for a proper household."

Aunt Katya thumbed through the dresses and found a mauve gown with fabric rosettes sewn into the sleeves. She held it up before Azya and stroked my sister's chestnut braids. "This one will need a cleaning, but it flatters your complexion, dear."

"So I don't know why I am even giving the matter further thought." I allowed a note of hopefulness to counter my words.

Her gaze still focused on Azya's gown. "If you feel strongly for this man, I see no reason to reject him, at least not unless we have evidence he is in danger of exile."

"I agree," I said, heart soaring. "Only Mother . . ."

"I don't believe she fully understands the honor of being courted by Alexander Pushkin. Your mother may act the sovereign in this house, but she cannot rule her daughters forever. Leave her to me."

Aunt Katya played the angel, as she had so many times before and would so many times in the future. Early the following Sunday morning when we were all gathered for breakfast—Sergey once again kicking my shin—the footman entered the dining area with a calling card formally propped on a silver platter. The scent of Alexander's cologne wafted past me as the footman passed the card to Mother. Sergey stopped kicking and twisted his chubby little lips, pretending to be engrossed in a prayer book. Though I wished to jump out of my chair, I needed to remain patient and let Mother take the lead. As she scrutinized the card with a frown, and the antique copper timepiece on the mantel ticked away every precious second, my heart felt as though it might leap free of my chest.

"It seems this Pushkin is a man of God," Mother paused. "He may accompany us to the service this morning."

Inside, I let out a cry of delight. Not wanting Mother to change her mind, I remained the picture of modest propriety on the outside, giving only a small smile. Mother pressed her lips together and I understood what had to happen next. I removed my spectacles and placed them in the beaded reticule I carried with me to church every Sunday. Even Mother couldn't argue with the notion that I might be allowed to see well enough to enjoy the beauty of the gilt iconostasis under the candlelight, and besides, services were hardly the place for vanity. However, the tone of the morning had changed. Today I was to perform a role

Mother thought even more important than devout Christian: the beautiful young woman of marriageable age.

We devoured the last bites of our meal and then gathered our cloaks while the boys buttoned their overcoats. Once we finally burst out the front door, my heart danced when I caught sight of Alexander outside. I drew close enough to see the flush of color in his dark cheeks, the curve of his lips when he saw me, and a playful glint in his pale eyes. Now, I understood the joy and fascination of staring at a beloved gentleman's face, bewitched. I wanted to make my mother and Ekaterina and all the rest of my siblings disappear, and for Alexander to lead me away from this place, to a home of our own where he would read to me in his silky voice and wrap his arms around me at night, kissing me until I felt faint.

Of course the real world moved at a much slower pace than my conjured fantasies. Alexander tapped his heels together, but extended his arm to Mother. The best I could manage was to follow them down twisting cobblestones still damp with melting snow, trying to catch a snippet or two of their conversation while we walked to church.

As we passed the park across from our house, I caught the scent of fried dough and smoke from a festival. I squinted to see better and cast a longing look at tables heaped with dumplings fried in butter, colorful bonbons, and toy bears situated between two wooden sticks; the bear danced when the sticks were squeezed together. From inside an enormous cage designed to emulate the elegant lines of a palace, doves cooed at one another. Farther afield, a headless doll had been stuffed with hay, tied to a long pole, and set afire. Flames danced, bright orange against the stark white sky, to represent the passing of winter to spring. We approached a red-and-blue-striped tent, where a handsome young man with a rosy countenance placed a wriggling bunny inside a compartment and then carefully positioned a stiff top hat on the table. When he caught me looking in his direction, he winked. I returned his smile before turning quickly away, cheeks burning.

A hard shove from behind made me trip over my feet. I turned to find Ekaterina's gray eyes glaring at me as she readjusted her fur muff. "Watch yourself," she whispered. "Isn't it enough to have the little poet's attention? You have to flirt with the sideshow acts as well?"

I hadn't thought an innocent smile disrespectful to anyone, but before I could snipe back, we were distracted by a silver-haired woman in a flowing red gown. She sat before a clear globe perched on a black pedestal in her booth. I wanted desperately to hear my fortune. I caught Ekaterina gazing wistfully into the distance—a few random snowflakes drifting past her ears in the chilly air—and figured she wanted a few moments with the fortune-teller as well. Of course we would learn who we were to marry, for no fortune-teller would believe a young woman wished to hear anything but the identity of a future husband. But I had so many other questions regarding my future: would I journey to foreign lands, be received at court, receive credit for my translations, or perhaps even write the type of poetry that had made Alexander famous? Nevertheless, when the question of my future husband arose, I assumed she would see Alexander in her magical ball. How could she not?

It would not do to leave Alexander to Mother's camaraderie now though, even if that was the conventional course of action. I quickened my steps so that I might better overhear their conversation.

Mother spoke slowly, voice husky in the cold air. "Of course, I avoid setting foot in shops, for you never know what rabble you will encounter on the streets these days. I send my most trusted men out with a complete list of our family's needs for the week . . ."

"Mmm," Alexander said and I rolled my eyes. Mother had the most prestigious writer in Russia at her side and she could find nothing more fascinating than her errands to discuss? And "the most trusted" man in our household was also the "only" man in our household, our poor footman, the last of our male servants. She just didn't want Alexander to know of our financial troubles.

"Every week the price of bread rises, and I wonder if we'll soon have to make do with half the amount we purchase now. The tsar in his wisdom might grant an order of some sort to fix the price and ease the burden on good Russian families."

I pitied Alexander for remaining trapped in such banalities; likely he was accustomed to far wittier conversations at salons and readings, but I adored him for putting up with Mother for my sake. As she prattled on, I dared extend my arm and patted Alexander on his back, where the light snowfall had dusted his overcoat. He flashed a quick grin over his shoulder that made me giddy.

"Now that we're outside, I can better appreciate the red in your hair. You look beautiful this morning, my auburn-haired Madonna."

I didn't think this comment wholly appropriate, particularly considering we were on our way to church, but Mother let it pass and I simply basked in the compliment. And then Alexander winked, just as the magician had a few minutes before. This time, however, I didn't look down and blush, but winked right back.

Alexander's eyes widened in surprise, and I bowed my head,

shocked at my own boldness. I needed to appear serene and proper. I didn't want Mother revoking her permission for Alexander to walk with us. My sister Azya, however, had no such restrictions placed on her behavior for she wasn't the object of a man's pursuit. She saw the looks we exchanged and then immediately piped up: "Alexander, would you care to stop and have your fortune told? They've set up a booth and it looks wonderfully intriguing."

Mother's eyes were hard in her stern face. "We're on our way to worship. There is no place for such frivolous pursuits on a Sunday morning."

Azya just rolled her eyes. Despite her modesty, I believe of us all, she was least afraid of Mother. "Perhaps after the service, then."

Alexander turned his attention away from Mother to the tents. "Fortune-telling is not for everyone. Those women abide by an impenetrable code of ethics and must remain honest at all times. You may not care for what you hear."

"You see? Don't be a boor, Azya." Mother allowed Alexander to take her arm once more and we proceeded on. His mysterious air made me wonder what destiny had been predicted for him, but Mother had trapped him into another conversation about the price of bread, so I cast one last longing look at the festival before hurrying on.

I had hoped Alexander might ask me to join him on one of the sleigh rides scheduled to tour the city at the end of Shrovetide, with a succulent pancake breakfast to follow. Unfortunately, Alexander seemed to time his arrivals to coincide solely with our weekly walks to church. I grew accustomed to watching the back of his head, the mass of unruly black hair curling in Moscow's early spring drizzle. I came to know his gait by heart, the restrained spring in his step as he kept pace with Mother's trod, and the tapping of his cane against the cobblestones. ·

He and Mother must have reached some understanding, but I couldn't imagine such limited contact would hold his interest for long. His visits remained regular, but their frequency didn't increase and I couldn't shake the feeling that grander ladies competed for his attention.

I endeavored to find a way to keep his focus on me. I still wanted to win a kiss from him, but had not yet conspired to find a place for us to be alone together.

After several weeks, Mother finally allowed Alexander to walk beside me on the way home from church. Perhaps she felt the services had been sufficient to put God in our souls and foremost in our minds, and so nothing untoward could possibly happen.

One Sunday, while the city was enjoying an unusually warm early spring sun, Alexander seemed strangely quiet. I did not think I could ask a man if he needed to stop and rest without insulting his ego, but I needed to say something. "Do you not feel well?"

"Fit as a fiddle," he said, huffing in the warm air.

"You seem . . . distracted."

He pounded his walking stick against the cobblestone, the tiny bear cub atop the cane bobbing up and down. In those days, I still had a rather naïve view of the inner workings of the male mind. I supposed Alexander was attempting to contain his anger, to remain strong, and that were I only clever enough to get him to talk about whatever plagued him, it was a sure sign we were meant to be together. "I hope you feel you can talk to me of any trouble you might face. I would never judge you, nor fear what you might say."

Alexander stopped to withdraw a linen handkerchief and wipe his brow, but I saw the corners of his lips pulling into a smile and I knew I had said what he wished to hear.

He shoved the handkerchief back into a pocket and withdrew a thin sheet of paper. "From one of my fellow men of letters. Look at this, my Natalie . . ."

My heart soared. I was *his* Natalie. In those days, I was still foolish enough to find a man's presumption of possession flattering. With difficulty, I found it in me to concentrate on the letter he had thrust in my hands. After dismissing one of Alexander's recent poems, the author referred to Alexander as the descendant of a "blackamoor slave" with insinuation that little could be expected of him due to this fact. Alexander claimed an African ancestor in his family's lineage, a princeling of that land, and had even started a novel about how this gentleman came to find himself in Russia.

"The impudence! He threatens to publish this dreck. Should I not call this scoundrel to task for his disrespect?"

I envied Alexander the passion so evident in his voice and wished I might speak in such a heated tone whenever Ekaterina said something vexing. "This is certainly not well put."

Azya, who had been keeping pace close to our side—and apparently eavesdropping—suddenly exclaimed: "How dare they! Who did this to you?"

"Bulgarin, the bast—" My brother Sergey caught up with us and, overhearing Alexander, started to guffaw. Mother and Ekaterina had been walking in front of us and turned to frown.

Alexander caught Mother's eye and concluded: ". . . bastion of bad taste."

"This Bulgarin fellow is likely only envious of your talent," I told him.

The comment calmed Alexander, and he lowered his voice. "I take it he refers to my mother's grandfather, Abram Gannibal, the close confidante of Peter the Great and a distinguished engineer in his own right. And is the swine not aware my father's family traces its noble routes for centuries past, back to the days of the boyars in Ancient Muscovy? We're older than the House of Romanov. Do I not then deserve some measure of respect?"

I wanted to respond, but felt hampered in the presence of Mother. The Goncharovs were still considered relatively new to the aristocratic orders and I knew only too well how easily family fortunes change. The thought left me glum, and between the heat of the morning sun, Ekaterina's disdainful stare, and Sergey's attempts to make me giggle by crossing his eyes, I could not summon one intelligent comment. I simply smiled.

I felt empty relying on my beauty alone.

"What of you, my Natalie?" Alexander pressed. "I have made a show of my troubles. Forgive me." He drew his hand dramatically to his chest. "We speak so little of you on these walks."

I bit my lip. "I wish there were more to tell of my days."

"If your days are not to your liking, then you must change their form." As we turned the corner, he veered to the right to avoid a brood of ducklings splashing in a large puddle. "What do you want most from this life?"

"Marriage. Children. A secure home . . ." Giving this answer, I felt like an automaton cuckoo in a clock, saying only what was expected.

As though reading my very thoughts, Alexander said, "This sounds more like what you have been taught to answer than the true feelings of your heart."

His voice was tender and he had slowed his steps enough that we fell behind the rest of my family. He placed a gentle hand on my arm to indicate he wished me to stop for a moment. I paused and he looked deep into my eyes, as though trying to determine the nature of my soul and what might be hidden beneath my polite exterior.

No one in my life had ever bothered to look at me this way, nor thought to ask what I might desire. When I met Alexander's gaze I felt a deep, piercing longing, for I had found not only a man who made me feel I would yield to anything, but at the same time made me stronger, as though I was finally living as my own true self.

"I do not yet know what I want from life," I whispered, no longer feeling empty. "For now I only want to discover it for myself and control my own destiny."

Though I felt confident with my answer to Alexander's intense question, I still feared I was too uneducated for the greatest poet of our land. These fears seemed founded when Alexander announced the tsar had granted him an opportunity to tour the south and the Caucasus to research new writing projects. He would be away from Moscow for several months, likely not returning until late autumn. Tipping his hat, he declared he would see us all when he returned. And though his gaze fixed on mine for several moments before he left, he gave no indication as to what might happen between us then.

I fixed a smile to my face when he shared this "good" news, and tried not to think about the women he might stay with along the way, well-educated and sophisticated ladies, nor brood over whether Alexander would even wish to return to Moscow. I could not even blame this turn of events on Mother and her dull talk of bread. I hadn't found a way to get Alexander alone and steal a kiss, and I felt certain my own failure to speak intelligently had destroyed my chance to find happiness with him. After such a long trip away, I felt assured he would forget me.

Without Alexander's Sunday visits, my life once again fell into a dull routine, and even as the weather grew warmer and flowers blossomed, I felt as though I were receding into a flat and barren existence.

And then his first letter arrived by post: a short stanza dedicated to me, with a note on the side stating he hoped I enjoyed the verse and had not overstepped his bounds. I brought my hand to my mouth and let out a little cry of delight. On the back of the poem, he'd sketched a picture of my face in profile with charcoal pencils. It was the view he would have had of me when we were attending services, my eyes squinting. In the portrait, I wore my hair in an elaborate bun with curled braids to each side of my ears and the same tiara and cream-colored gown I had worn to the ball where we first met.

I allowed myself to hope I had not been such a fool after all, that Alexander's absence truly had been motivated by his need to write. I tacked the picture near the looking glass, to Ekaterina's consternation. "It's not like you can't see yourself in the mirror."

"I don't have anywhere else to display it and I think it's a nice likeness, don't you?"

Ekaterina snorted, which I took as grudging agreement, and

then commenced brushing her thick hair. "You can let the little poet moon after you as you wish, but I suppose you remember he was friends with Decembrists. I hear they couldn't hang them all on the first try. They had to redo the whole affair with three of them, and even then their bodies were twitching for twenty minutes. Can you imagine?"

My hands clenched into fists. Of course I could imagine, just as I could understand the horror gripping their families' hearts as they watched, and all of the large and small ways the tsar could punish those left behind: devastating finances, sending his secret police to keep watch for any sign of sedition, not-so-veiled threats of torture.

"You know how the court of the tsar works. One insult to a powerful man, rumors spread, and you're ruined." Ekaterina leaned forward, jutting her chin at me, a smudge of face cream still clinging to her cheeks. "Why would you desire such a life? Mother will never consent."

I stared blankly at my own hairbrush on the vanity. Ekaterina didn't understand what it felt like to want more from life than a snug home and pretty trinkets. She thought only of comfort, not adventure. Besides, Mother had been looking at her account ledgers more frequently of late, no doubt calculating how much lower her monthly expense would be with one less daughter at home. "Mother will be glad enough to have me off her hands."

"Then why did she not entertain your poet's proposal?"

My head shot up. Ekaterina set her brush down next to mine, leaned back, and crossed her arms triumphantly.

"Alexander has proposed?" How could Ekaterina know and I didn't? I couldn't believe even Mother would be cruel enough to keep such information from me.

"Within a week of meeting you, he sent that fellow Tolstoy to Mother on his behalf."

"Why didn't anyone tell me?" I cried.

"Mother saw no need. For God's sake, he hardly knew you. Foolishness of the highest order."

That proposal may have been impulsive, but if another were offered, I would make sure Mother had no grounds to refuse. My destiny might already have been decided—perhaps was even visible in some carnival fortune-teller's magical ball—but I intended to take every opportunity to ensure my life unfolded the way I desired.

Five

While Alexander was away, Sergey and Azya attempted to lift my spirits by performing impromptu musical numbers in our parlor. Azya sang a folk tune while Sergey crouched and kicked his feet out from under him, eyes crossed the entire time. This show distracted me well enough in the evening, but when I lay abed at night, shivering and waiting for the blankets to lose their chill, I couldn't help but imagine Alexander's adventures with elegant women. I tried to pour my heart into poems and lyrics, attempted to express the pain and beauty of how deeply I missed Alexander, but all my words seemed feeble. In the end, I tore the thick paper from my notebooks and shredded it into tiny pieces, frustrated at my lack of talent.

On the few occasions when other men approached me, I laughed at their jokes and blushed at their compliments. In the case of one attractive prince, I even allowed my hand to rest on his arm. Except that only reminded me of the time I had spent in the courtyard with Alexander at the dance master's ball, and my attempts at flirtation ran dry. Needless to say, men did not flock to the Goncharov household, and I resigned myself to the idea of spending the rest of my life in our cold parlor knitting with Ekaterina and Mother until I finally withered away from boredom.

At the end of November, Aunt Katya paid us a visit and deftly sidestepped my brothers to inform me she had secured a spot for me in a *tableau vivant* at a reception to honor the tsar's visit to Moscow for the start of Advent. I might even have an opportunity to be presented to the tsar. I was to appear in a tale from the *Aeneid*, looking on in horror as my sister Dido, the Queen of Carthage, prepared to run a sword through her chest and throw herself into a funeral pyre over her failed love affair with the Trojan warrior Aeneas. The thought of performing before the most powerful man in Russia, the most powerful man in the world as far as I was concerned, left me struggling to catch my breath.

Ekaterina wormed her way into hearing distance and quickly cut in: "Before the tsar! But Natalya has no acting experience."

This wasn't strictly true. I had appeared as Pyramus in a production of *Pyramus and Thisbe* orchestrated by one of our governesses, though I only secured the part because the governess determined that the tallest girl in our group should play the male lead. Even so, I thought I had done a fine job of it. When the time came for me to pretend to kiss her, the girl who played Thisbe had leaned in close and whispered, "Do it."

Aunt Katya immediately dashed my dreams of becoming a great actress: "It's a tableau, not the London stage. She is only required to stand there and look decorative."

My governess had told me to imagine the story of Pyramus and attempt to relate it to my own life. I tried to do the same for Dido's sister, but couldn't envision either Ekaterina or Azya throwing themselves into a fire nor claiming their own life with a sword. Ekaterina would find it gauche and Azya would cry too much to manage the logistics. Nevertheless, my role in the tableau was a great honor and I endeavored to make the most of it, practicing my expression of horror for hours on end in front of our looking glass until Ekaterina scowled and said, "Think you can manage this grand drama without your spectacles? It would be a fine thing for you to trip over your own feet and fall offstage before the tsar and his court."

I stuck my tongue out at her, but that never provoked my older sister as it did Sergey, and Ekaterina walked away as though she hadn't a care in the world.

Ekaterina's comments undermined my confidence. No one wanted to see Dido's sister in spectacles. ("Why does a girl need to see anyway?" Sergey had said once, before I stomped on his toes until he howled.) On the other hand, I didn't wish to make a fool of myself. The evening of the tableau, Mother caught me trying to stash the spectacles away in my reticule and promptly snapped them out of my hands. "In front of Tsar Nicholas? Are you mad?"

By the time I made it to the backstage area, and a maid had applied carmine rouge to my cheeks and a hint of black color around my eyes, I was convinced I would trip over the unfamiliar folds of the toga and make a fool of myself. Dido was being made up in the chair next to mine, elegant from a distance, but smelling of claret up close. I caught a glance of my brightly made-up face and costumed form in the looking glass, draped in a toga with a crown of golden laurel leaves tucked into my braided hair. I needed to focus, to transcend my petty concerns and make the audience believe I was a Carthaginian maid.

The other girls and I took our places behind the red velvet curtain. The embossed golden double-headed eagles were a clear reminder of who was in our midst. I took a deep breath as the sonorous voice of the master of ceremonies described the scene: Dido had just instructed her sister (me) to construct a pyre and burn her worldly belongings. Now, she would throw herself in the fire and declare eternal war between Carthage and Troy. Slowly, the curtain rose and I stood under a warm spotlight, intense dread gathering force inside of me like a tempest. I fixed my features into a look of horror at the artificial flames constructed onstage and maintained this expression, even when it hurt my face to remain still and the spotlight made a droplet of perspiration slide down my brow. It tickled, but I dared not move. The tsar was watching and held all our fates like crippled birds in his hands. With the favor of the tsar, I could leave my family's house to seek out my own life. No one could control me, not even Mother.

When the curtain dropped to the thunderous applause of the audience, I felt a surge of satisfaction. I made my way off the stage and into Azya's waiting arms.

"You looked magnificent! The audience was enthralled. I've already heard people whispering about how gorgeous you looked."

She meant well but the remark irritated me. For once it would have been nice to be complimented for something other than beauty, a trait I had not earned and over which I had little to no control. "It only required the ability to stand still."

Azya squeezed my hand. "After the curtain fell, I positioned myself near a group who had been sitting with the tsar. He wants to meet you."

My stomach turned, the image of young officers hanging from gibbets in Palace Square fresh in my imagination. Men killed by order of the tsar. Men who had been Alexander's friends and read his poems for inspiration. And yet, this was my one chance to wrestle control of my own destiny. "It would be an honor to meet Tsar Nicholas."

By the time we made our way down to the main floor, the velveteen cushioned chairs set out for the audience had been moved to one side to make room for dancing. The great hall of the palace was ornamented with pine boughs and holly and even a tree with candles in golden holders. The scent of the greenery mingled with that of Turkish pipes in the smoking room. It reminded me of Alexander, his feet peeping out from the bottom of the tree at the dance master's ball nearly one year ago. The intense focus in his pale eyes. The flutter in my heart when I realized the greatest poet in Russia wanted to dance with *me*.

My train of thought was disrupted when I caught sight of Tsar Nicholas. Tall and broad across the shoulders, he wore a uniform with medals that gleamed in the candlelight, setting him apart from his fawning courtiers. At the time, all I considered was my good fortune at the opportunity to speak to him directly; I would not learn of the tsar's reputation with women until later. Personally, I did not find Tsar Nicholas a particularly attractive man, but I knew myself to be in the minority among the ladies of Moscow. As a young grand duke, he had been handsome: a strong jaw, soft mouth, and full head of reddish hair. Though now only a few years past thirty, the demands of office had aged him prematurely. His hairline had thinned, his paunchy midsection pressed tight against his uniform coat, and his eyes began to droop in the same trajectory as his trim mustache. Without the signifiers of rank, he would have looked like a middle-aged shopkeeper who kept overly long hours.

I had not intended to catch the tsar's eye, but he saw me and flashed a sudden smile, greatly improving his looks. He bent to whisper something to one of his courtiers and then the entire assemblage moved in my direction, perhaps eight or nine men, along with three maids of honor hovering on the perimeter. The tsar's wife, the former Charlotte of Prussia, walked at his side, in a slim crimson gown with embroidered sprigs of mistletoe along the hems and a traditional *kokoshnik* headdress heavy with jewels, her pretty but sharp Germanic features fixed in neutral affability. They progressed forward as deliberately and gracefully as a corps de ballet, all parts of one single-minded creature.

I dropped into a low curtsy, as did Azya. Thankfully Ekaterina was nowhere to be found. Perhaps she had finally found some dull soldier to squire her about and would leave me in peace.

"Enchanted!" the tsar declared once we had risen back to our feet. "Delightful tableau. I believe you captured the passion of the moment most vividly."

My stomach raged with fear, but I could not lose myself to agitation and miss my chance to speak with the tsar. I only needed to find a means to summon intelligible words.

"Thank you, Your Majesty. You are most kind." I spoke in French, as the tsar had, while the orchestra played the opening bars of a waltz.

At the sound of the lilting music, the tsar's ears perked up and he turned to me. "What grand timing. Might you do me the honor of a dance?" He extended his hand.

Azya drew in a quick breath and the empress's eyes pinched as my pulse quickened. I could not pass on an opportunity to command the tsar's full attention, but I had hoped for a less intimate dance. I had been raised to fear his power, to put this man's needs and desires, no matter how slight, above all. A demigod had asked me to dance. How does one say no to that?

Tsar Nicholas led me to the dance floor, resting his hand low on my back and pulling me tighter than necessary, which made it difficult to gather my thoughts.

"I know you, by reputation at least." The tsar led me around the floor for the first time and I caught the scent of mint sprigs on his breath. "My wife informs me you're the same young lady who captured the heart of our Alexander Pushkin at a ball last winter."

I tried not to pay mind to the other dancers, even though I was certain the finely dressed men and their ladies were staring at me, wondering who I was that I should be so presumptuous as to dance with the tsar. Perhaps they had even heard Alexander's name in connection with mine, like the empress, and were laughing behind their fans and snuff pouches at the silly little girl who thought she could win the heart of a poet. Shoulders tensing, I missed a step.

"Watch yourself," he said playfully.

At least now I wouldn't need to conjure a clever way to broach the subject. I dared not waste this opportunity, so I cast my gaze straight ahead, eye level with a star-shaped medallion attached to his formal uniform coat. "I found his attentions flattering of course, but my first thought now is to ask of his standing with you."

"His works are not always to the taste of my censor and yet I find most of them charming. His fairy tales tell of strong-willed Russian men and the ladies who love them. What is not to like in that?"

I believe the tsar was being lighthearted, so I managed a soft laugh as we made another turn about the floor. "I would never entertain the attentions of a gentleman who was anything other than patriotic."

"My Pushkin? Are you implying he isn't a patriot? I admit some of our poet's bolder language has troubled me in the past. Of course the fellow's rhetoric vexed my brother entirely. He would have sent Pushkin to Siberia if he had his way, but some officer or another convinced him a prolonged stay in the south would drive the point home well enough. After all, it's one thing to travel and have a jolly time and quite another to know you can never return home."

I realized I had been holding my breath. My heart pounded so hard I thought it must have been visible under the thin chiffon costume. "You believe the point was driven home then?"

"Are you questioning my judgment? Do you believe I should sentence our good man to another exile abroad? Perhaps there is validity to that course of action. The man as much as admitted he sympathized with the Decembrist traitors."

"No," I said, louder than I intended, and the corners of the tsar's mouth twitched while I thought I might collapse, wondering if I should go down on my knees to apologize. I hadn't yet spent five minutes in the tsar's company and I'd already sentenced Alexander to banishment. I pictured the moment when the hangman released the ropes and the bodies of the condemned young officers convulsed and shuddered. "I mean . . . I would never question your judgement."

"Once the whole sordid plot was uncovered, I called our poet to my chambers and asked him what would have occurred had he been in the capital at the time his rebel friends took action. He looked me in the eye, as best the fellow could manage being rather slight, and told me: 'I would have joined the ranks of the rebels.'"

My feet still moved in time to the music, but otherwise I was frozen. I had hoped Alexander had been exaggerating when he related that story to my family, bragging for the sake of my brothers' entertainment. All my dreams of the future, of dimly lit salons and stolen kisses, collapsed in on themselves. "I see. I couldn't commit to such a gentleman then."

Tsar Nicholas still held me too close, but his voice reverted back to the smooth, honeyed tone he used earlier. "Forgive me, but perhaps you do not see." Again, his lip twitched and I realized he had been toying with me. My fear was meant for his amusement. "I only wanted to see your reaction. I see by the look on your face that you are concerned for our great poet. I admired his honesty, but had to press the matter. I asked if he might be persuaded to think differently. He thought on it and assured me his attachments to the traitors had been severed, and I believed him when he said he had no foreknowledge of their actions. We may not have started off on the best footing, but I now consider him my Pushkin. Russia's Pushkin."

Despite my irritation at being manipulated, relief surged through me. "That is a great honor."

"Indeed. I believe you should soon call him your Pushkin as well." Tsar Nicholas smiled, his face slightly more appealing now. "Why shouldn't our great poet pursue the most beautiful woman in Moscow?"

He squeezed me tighter and I fought the impulse to pull away. I was so close to what I truly wanted. "So you approve of my suitor?"

"Most decidedly, dear lady . . . I rather like the ring of that. My dear Lady Pushkina. Might I address you in the English manner? And your Pushkin comes from an ancient family. God knows we've all heard him speak of it often enough. Such a title of respect is surely warranted. As far as I'm concerned, you and our dear poet are free to wed."

Even as he delivered this good news, a trace of coldness returned to the tsar's voice. I should have recognized it. At the time, however, I could only count my blessings that the one person in the world who could overrule my mother approved of Alexander.

Word reached me that Alexander had returned to St. Petersburg from his travels in the south, but he did not visit us in Moscow. When two weeks passed and still I did not receive a letter, I began to lose hope. And then one gloomy afternoon in late January, Tolstoy the American paid us a surprise visit.

He was jovial as ever, his boisterous personality breathing life into the dull spaces of our chilly house, cheering my brothers out of the stupor they had fallen into ever since Mother insisted they hound Aunt Katya for appointments. When it came time for Tolstoy to leave, I endeavored to pass a moment alone with him. Mother's keen eye appraised my every move while I was in the parlor, but allowed me to escort him out without a chaperone, while my brothers remained behind, hooting and hollering.

Tolstoy extended his arm in a gentlemanly fashion and I accepted, walking with him past our neglected shrubbery to a team of black horses prancing before his carriage as though they couldn't wait to get home. Tolstoy's dark green coat and trousers were embellished with fine gold braiding and epaulettes. I thought to compliment how fine he looked as a means of opening a conversation, but then he might think me a coquette. Instead, I got straight to the point. "I am surprised not to have heard from your chum, Alexander."

"Why, that's not fair. He has friends to visit in St. Petersburg and the post is notoriously slow. I'm sure you will hear from him once—"

I had lost all patience for half-truths. "I meant that given the amount of time we spent together last spring, I would have expected him to have returned to me and . . . well . . . introduced more pressing issues into our conversation by now."

Tolstoy drew in his breath as if scandalized, though I sensed he was mocking me. "Are you trying to tell me he has taken liberties with you?"

"Only in my own mind."

Tolstoy gave me the same wolfish smirk he had flashed the night of the dance master's ball. I straightened my shoulders, trying to regain my dignity.

Tolstoy took in the indignant tilt of my chin. "Are you trying to ask why you have not yet received a proposal?"

Something about his tone made me fear I was about to hear the exact opposite of what I hoped. I looked down at my shoes, the impression they left on the snowy ground, before pressing forward: "I have since learned he already proposed once, but hardly at the most appropriate time. Is he so easily discouraged?"

"You must understand, Alexander feels he has received no encouragement and the fellow has no shortage of pride."

I suppose some of Alexander's passion had rubbed off on me by then and I took care to pause and modulate my voice so as not to upset poor Tolstoy. "I have been most hospitable."

"Hospitable is hardly the same as encouraging, mademoiselle."

I couldn't help but sigh in frustration. What did men expect of us? If we were too forward, it was considered unfeminine. If we held back, we were cold and discouraging and no doubt also unfeminine. It was all so exhausting.

"He has extended his time away from Moscow because he heard rumors you are interested in Prince Meshchersky," Tolstoy told me. "He has heard you might even marry this chap. His heart is breaking at the thought."

"What could have given him such an idea?" I thought back to the prince's attentions, our vapid conversations. He was handsome enough, but had taken up archiving his family records as a hobby, and I quickly tired of hearing him boast of his family's marriages into the royal families of Europe. Still, I had touched his arm. Apparently such a liberty was grand enough to agitate the rumormongers. I remembered Ekaterina grinning at me while the prince rambled on about his cousin's latest match and wondered if she had been responsible. "I thought Alexander understood his visits were most welcome and enjoyable."

Tolstoy gave a loud laugh. "Enjoyable, is he? The fellow will be happy to hear that."

"You know what I mean. I initiated this conversation with the intention that you should communicate my feelings clearly to Alexander."

"Since you're so forthright with me, I must return the favor. There is one other person who stands in Alexander's path: your mother."

I should have known. Mother had never been convinced of Alexander's financial solvency, even if she did want me out of the house. Perhaps she still aspired to find a wealthier match. I imagined myself as a fragile vase she held gently in her hands, eyeing the crowd at the auction house for a higher bid. The idea that Mother might stand in the way of my happiness made me resent her even more than I resented my absent father, and over the years I had come to loathe that man completely for the pain he had caused our family.

"His friends call her 'Mamma Kars.'" Tolstoy withdrew a linen handkerchief from the pocket of his overcoat and used it to wipe his nose, which had grown red from the cold. "You are familiar with this phrase?"

Kars was a Turkish fortress, rumored to be all but impossible to penetrate. "I suppose it could be worse. He could have made that his nickname for me."

Tolstoy coughed abruptly. I then realized that if "Mamma Kars" was my mother then I was "Kars." My cheeks burned.

"I don't know why I should be expected to have control over my mother's personality. I hope Alexander will judge me on my own merits and that his actions are guided by the strength of his feeling for me."

"Can I take this as a sign of encouragement then? Alexander would have good reason to approach your mother should the spirit move him?"

"I would hope the spirit does move him," I said, feeling bold. "Why I even spoke to the tsar of Alexander and he approved. Mother can't possibly object!"

"Alexander will be happy to hear it. Perhaps I can find a way to get the two of you alone together once he returns to Moscow."

The very idea of being alone with Alexander thrilled me, but Aunt Katya had taught me to maintain my composure. "It is kind of you to help. You're a good friend."

Tolstoy gave his nose one last wipe before stuffing the handkerchief back in his pocket. "We are best of chums. Now. Who would have thought it?"

I tilted my head. "What do you mean? Were you not friends before?"

"Not in the slightest," Tolstoy declared, too merrily considering the subject. "Why we almost came to blows in the past. Apparently, Alexander got word I'd said some drunken nonsense about him when he wasn't present. Buffoonery, I assure you. And yet he challenged me to a duel over it! Threatened to put a bullet in my brain. One of us might have ended up like Lensky and the other Onegin. Can you imagine?"

I could imagine it only too well, but I tried to put the thought out of my mind.

When Tolstoy next appeared at our door, Azya was ill with a head cold, but he asked Ekaterina and me to accompany him to a charity concert to raise funds for Moscow's Eye Hospital. I did not believe Tolstoy's sudden appearance a coincidence, but rather destiny. This was exactly the sort of event that would attract Alexander if he had returned to Moscow.

As soon as we arrived, Tolstoy spirited Ekaterina straight inside the auditorium while I lingered in the gilt-encrusted foyer, feigning a dizzy spell. The lobby was crowded with people. Whenever a finely dressed lady walked past, jealousy flickered as I imagined her commanding Alexander's attention. A group of women in loose gowns with low necklines set up a little entertainment near one of the tall picture windows looking out to the snow-covered square. The women wore long lengths of chains and necklaces, and bold gold hoops glittered in their ears. While they rattled tambourines and sang, I kept a desperate eye on the Corinthian columns at the theater's entrance, hoping to see Alexander coming in from the cold, tossing his walking stick from one hand to another, his eyes sparking when he saw me.

As though a spell had been cast, he appeared, tired around the eyes but still Alexander. At once, he spotted me, his intense gaze fixing on my face alone. My heart soared, dreams at last reality. Tolstoy must have known Alexander planned to attend this evening. It was meant to be a surprise and I felt marvelously emboldened.

He tipped his top hat and then removed it as he stepped inside. Doubt crept into my soul. What if he passed me by? While Alexander greeted friends, I could not still my fidgeting feet, nor keep from working the lace on my handkerchief through my fingers. I wanted to leap forward and claim him before another woman could steal his heart. I wanted to throw all sense of propriety to the wind and make him take me away from the theater, away from Moscow, far away from Mother, so that we might start a life of our own.

Alexander marched past the other women, toward me. "Mademoiselle Natalie! I hoped I might find you here . . ." He gestured toward a woman with long black hair and tiny bells strung along gold chains on her ankles, who was strumming a three-stringed balalaika in a high-pitched melody. "I always wished to take you to hear such music!"

My lips trembled as I smiled. "Now is as good a time as any."

He took my hand in his, leading me to a space in an alcove, near enough to enjoy the music but with some measure of privacy. My skin felt delightfully aflame.

"I wish for more of Onegin's saga. Were you able to write while away?"

"Not as much as I'd hoped. I did hear a most intriguing tale from an Austrian soldier of fortune. He claims a rumor has taken hold in Europe that the genius composer Mozart died not of natural causes but by murder at the hand of a jealous rival named Salieri. I should like to turn this into a tale of my own."

"I suppose you identify with Mozart?" I teased.

Alexander sulked, though I could tell he was playacting. "Why should I not want to take on the role of genius in my own life's story?"

"Who is your Salieri then? Which rival is so jealous that God gifted talents to you rather than themselves? Who might be driven to murder you?"

"No shortage of fellows at court could play that role well." He waved his hand dismissively. "Not enough talent between them to fill a schoolgirl's notebook."

I blushed. I hadn't yet been brave enough to let Alexander know I kept my own schoolgirl notebooks at home, and though I was no Mozart, I hoped he would never view me as a talentless Salieri either. "And what of your other escapades?"

"My Natalie, do you wish to travel someday?" He gathered my hand in his once more and I envisioned a life of travel and reading and writing for us. *My Natalie.* "You make me think such adventures are within my grasp."

"Anything you wish for in this life may be yours."

Before I could think of anything further to say, he leaned in close, and my thoughts grew disordered. His soft lips pressed against mine and though I knew I should pull away, I relaxed into the kiss and let my lips linger on his. At first, I was too nervous to focus, and then he put his hand on the small of my back, and I forgot my worries and lost myself, limbs softening as he held me in his arms.

"I'm sorry." He drew back, but it didn't sound as though he truly regretted the kiss. "I was taken with your beauty. I won't let it happen again."

I wouldn't have minded if it happened again. I didn't even care if Ekaterina saw and chastised me afterward. She would say Alexander should marry me and that was exactly what I wanted. I was so tired of caring what other people thought, and wished now to follow my own desires. "I did not mind. I did not mind at all. Kiss me again if you wish."

"I need to know then." He gathered my hands once more in his and kissed my palms, sending a thrill of anticipation down my spine. "Do I have a chance?"

"A chance in what regard?" I asked coyly.

"A chance with you." His eyes widened, as though his very being depended on my next words. "I love you."

The audience inside the theater started to clap along to the opening music—a rousing orchestral piece. In that moment—despite all the worries in my head clamoring to be heard—I knew beyond a doubt that I loved Alexander.

"You have always had my heart," I told him. "It was only a matter of claiming it."

Six

Perhaps I had read one too many novels of romance, but after we kissed I assumed Alexander would propose straightaway. As days of embroidery and prayers passed without word, I began to worry I had misconstrued his intentions and the "chance" he spoke of was not meant to imply marriage but a more lurid proposition. Strangely, I did not feel offended, only intrigued.

Lively carnivals and sleigh rides soon gave way once more to the ominous quiet of the holy season. Mother insisted on strict adherence to the rules of our Lenten fast, and so I spent the next few weeks in misery, not only from heartbreak but the constant pangs of hunger in my stomach. I grew sick of thin mushroom soup and mushy apples and the vile bread the Church approved for Lent, made with a false butter that only made you long all the more for the real affair. As Moscow prepared for the greatest holiday on our Orthodox calendar, I spent my afternoons quietly plotting escape from what felt to be a dungeon.

A week before Easter, the city began to rouse once more from slumber like a restless bear. Predictably, Mother disapproved of the raucous markets, but we were able to slip out. My sisters gawked and giggled at the forbidden pastries and sweetbreads as Dmitry herded us past handsome boys singing and hawking hand puppets and giant red balloons to mark the arrival of the holiday and the coming spring. I tried to enjoy the excitement, but couldn't lose the stinging sensation of disappointment at not yet hearing from Alexander. I was seventeen and already my world had come to an end.

The night before Easter, as we ate vegetable stew and coarse black bread, my siblings remained uncharacteristically silent. We had spent the day dyeing and polishing eggs and Mother had prepared *kulich* cakes, filling the house with a divine sweet scent. Later, we would walk to church for services to celebrate the resurrection.

As Azya began to clear the dishes from our meager supper, Ekaterina passed around one of the eggs she had designed and intended to hang outside our door. Affixed with an intricate pattern of red and black diamonds, it glistened, tantalizing under the candlelight. The bell at the front door rang just as my brother Sergey handed the egg to me. Startled, I dropped the delicate prize and the egg fell to the floor, shell cracked and the design splintered. I waited for Ekaterina to rail against my clumsiness, my lack of care with *her* things.

But to my surprise, Ekaterina only said, "It's a good thing I made extras."

Our footman appeared with a letter for Mother. I saw Alexander's name, the flamboyant handwriting, and caught the scent of his cologne. My heart rate escalated. Was it possible Alexander had come after all? Would he accompany us to services this evening? At midnight, we formed a procession to declare Christ had risen; how much more gratifying the transcendence of that moment would feel at Alexander's side.

"Thank you." Mother glanced solemnly at the clock. "I suppose I have time to indulge this gentleman before we leave for services."

I looked at Mother.

"Close your mouth, Natalya," she told me. "You appear a simpleton."

Ekaterina smirked, and my cheeks grew hot. It was unfair to keep me waiting. Mother might still be playing games, waiting for a proposal from someone with more money than Alexander. It was all I could do to force my anger down as I rose to help Azya clear the dishes. As though nothing at all had happened. As though my very future were not hanging in the balance on the most sacred night of the year.

After the dishes were cleared, Mother retired to the parlor to read the letter. When the minutes stretched on and still she did not approach me, I began to wonder if she kept the contents to herself to spare my feelings. Perhaps I had been fooling myself and could not truly see matters as they were. Perhaps the letter did not include a proposal at all, but instead Alexander had cut things off and apologized to Mother. I bit my bottom lip. During his travels, he must have met another woman. Perhaps many women. Perhaps he'd decided the bachelor's life was more suitable for a poet and I had no place in his future.

As I brushed my hair in front of the looking glass trying to get in my one hundred strokes to give it sheen—for even on the holiest night of the year we were expected to look our best—I resolved to see the letter for myself. Once Mother finally shuffled off to her room to get ready, I put on my spectacles.

The room was excessively cold. Knowing we would be out for the evening, Mother had all the fires in the hearths extinguished early. I pressed forward and found the letter alongside knitting notions in her sewing basket. Mother's tabby had been busy stalking some unseen phantom in the kitchen. When I started to bustle about, he poked his nose through the door and emitted a loud meow at the prospect of playing with yarn. I hushed him and he sat back on his haunches, surprisingly receptive to my command. I heard the bed from Mother's room creak and glanced upstairs. I held my breath and waited, but no one came down.

Mother's full name was emblazoned on the front of the envelope in Alexander's now familiar bold hand. Shivering with cold and nerves and excitement, I carefully withdrew the letter and began to read.

It was a proposal of marriage.

The oddest proposal.

Alexander spoke at length of me, praising my beauty, wit, charm. He gave a full account of his finances and spoke of how well he would treat me as his honored wife. I clasped my hand over my mouth and rocked back and forth on the balls of my feet as I crouched over the basket. The room no longer seemed so cold, nor life so bleak.

However, in the next section of the letter, Alexander put forth his concerns. He claimed that though he loved me, he would make a most unconventional husband, for a creative spirit must have room to breathe. He trusted we would always be in good spirits, even if our lifestyle might not be as grand as our neighbors, for we would always depend on the whim of publishers. I sighed and then frowned. It seemed odd to express all of these reservations in a letter to my mother, and besides, he said nothing I didn't already know. I wanted an unconventional life.

I settled in on Mother's old rosewood chair and continued to read.

He spoke of another woman he had spent time visiting while in St. Petersburg: a Polish lady named Karolina. Envy clouded my vision and the words began to run together as I imagined this woman, a beauty no doubt, full of wit and gossip and fascinating tales of time spent abroad. Naïve as I was in those days, I still knew Alexander should not mention another woman in a letter meant to focus on me. He explained to Mother that while he had been seen often with Karolina, his heart had been claimed and he wanted to spend the rest of his life with me.

Then why feel compelled to mention another woman at all? Unless, an angry voice inside my head insisted, there had actually been an affair with this Karolina. Perhaps Alexander feared the news of this affair would reach us via other channels and he hoped to diminish the impact by telling us himself.

Footsteps creaked on the stairs behind me. "So you see what he has written."

I broke from my demure façade, and for the first time in my short life, I braced for a fight with my mother. Alexander had proposed. My time of playing the meek and obedient daughter was coming to an end. "I had a right to know."

"You have no rights. You are still under my protection."

My hands bunched into fists, a gesture I had borrowed from Alexander. If only I could explain how much I resented her protection and wished to break free of it. "I have been dying of curiosity."

"Oh do not be dramatic, Natalya." Slowly, Mother made her way down the stairs, past the faded unicorn tapestries and toward the kitchen. She scooped the tabby into her arms and began to stroke behind his ears until he purred. "The poet is a charming enough fellow, anyone can see that, but to maintain his success, he will forever be subject to the dubious fortunes of court life. Before I shared this letter, I wanted time to consider what your poet had to say. Have you not thought how this possible engagement might affect me?"

Always her. Never a thought that I might be a human in my own right, with my own desires and ability to make decisions. Still, Mother's tone held a note of acceptance and so I decided to focus on hope. "Did you find what he said to your liking?"

"I had not expected him to be quite so candid regarding his faults."

I didn't expect this either, but still it irritated me more that Mother saw fit to hide the letter from me. "I would expect nothing less than complete candor from Alexander. He is an honest and honorable man to tell me about . . ."

I found I couldn't utter Karolina's name aloud, but Mother finished for me: "Yes, but why mention another woman now?"

"Oh." I had felt so sure of myself a few minutes earlier, but the mention of this Karolina put my thoughts once again into disarray.

"Does it make you hesitate?" Mother released the tabby who scurried back to the kitchen.

"I wish he hadn't talked about her."

"I'm not sure I agree. As you say he is an honest man. Every man thinks of other women, considers them before making a proposal of marriage. I believe he must think well of you to be so forthright."

I felt momentarily confused, for I had expected Mother to use this part of the letter to persuade me *not* to marry Alexander. "It shouldn't concern me that he was courting someone else?"

"He is a popular gentleman. Did you really expect otherwise?"

I suppose I had not, but I hoped he would never speak of it to me.

"Despite my prior reservations, I must admit his proposal does great honor to this family and to you. You have a chance at a better life now, with a famous husband and a substantive income. Perhaps your experiences at court will be positive." A faraway, dreamy look entered Mother's eyes then, something I hadn't seen before. "I should like to see you married in the Church of the Ascension."

Mother still did not mention love. "I don't care where I get married. I care who I marry."

Mother cast a glance upstairs. "As long as your father approves. That's all that matters."

I knew my mother had once served at court, as Aunt Katya did, but then left that world to marry my father. He should have been here now, interviewing Alexander to ensure he was good enough for me. Father hadn't been home in weeks, and yet his absence still had the capacity to wound me. I recalled how he had been once upon a time, when I was a small girl living in Kaluga with my grandfather. When my father came to visit, he swung me high in his arms. He still played his violin then, still used the elegant paper from my grandfather's mills to transcribe sheet music. I liked to think I had been the center of his world—at least for a short time—his adored youngest daughter. I hoped somewhere deep inside he knew I was on the verge of marrying a man I loved.

No matter. I would rely on my own counsel and my heart was quite clear. I may have been jealous of this other woman, but that only proved the strength of my feelings for Alexander. All that mattered was we loved each another. And at midnight, the church bells would ring to declare Christ had risen, and we would spend our first Easter Sunday together as an engaged couple.

A month later, we sat in the great hall of Afansy's estate in Kaluga where I had come for a spring visit; Alexander had joined me for a week so as to become better acquainted with my grandfather. I stared, enchanted with the way Alexander's elegant fingers turned a thick sheet of newly pressed paper in his hands and the movement of his lips when he munched on a fresh cucumber. I remembered his mouth pressed against mine and silently vowed to find time for us to be alone in a quiet space, away from prying eyes, hands intertwined while his lips ran across my shoulders, my neck, the tender spot behind my ears . . .

"So what do you think of it?" my grandfather asked, putting a sudden end to my reveries.

Alexander shifted his weight in one of the pine barrel chairs around the massive dining room table and gently slapped the paper with the back of one hand. "It is a fine quality to be sure. Your family has performed a great service to my industry."

"I told you as much!" Afansy sat across from us and his kindly features, more lined now than when last I saw him, beamed. His frail voice echoed in the nearly empty room. "A man could get much writing done on such fine paper. I like to think the Goncharov family might contribute to your success in this way."

"You have already gifted me with an angelic muse." The chairs were spaced so far apart around the formal table that Alexander could not pat my hand, but I saw the reflection of his smile in the giant looking glass on the opposite wall.

"Listen here, chap." Afansy straightened his shoulders as his common-law wife—the so-called French laundress named Babette—entered the room with a steaming tray of fried cutlets, the aroma of which made the room a little more inviting. "It was good of you not to make too great a fuss over Natalya's dowry. My granddaughter has asked me to love you as much as she does and I cannot refuse the darling. So I'll tell you what . . . Take as much of the paper as can fit in your spare valise. Set to work right away with it."

"That is most kind. Why, I have a proposition to start a new journal and almanac modeled after the English style, which I intend to propose to a few fellows of my acquaintance. I shall use the first sheets for that endeavor." Alexander nodded at Babette as she offered him a cutlet. Her gray curls were tucked modestly under her kerchief, and while even my weak eyes could see how much my grandfather had aged, her youthful features seemed as impervious to the passing of time as Aunt Katya's.

I tried to smile and thank Babette for my cutlet, but I was distracted by the man who had followed her into the great hall. He staggered about, unsteady on his feet.

My father.

It had been Mother's idea to have him join us, insisting he had a right to know his youngest daughter's fiancé better and claiming the country air might do wonders for his condition. I suspected Mother simply wanted him out of her way. The country air had done nothing for him. His hair was askance, his eyes drooping and vacant, and his words slurred when he deigned to speak at all.

I could no longer determine where his sad dependence on drink ended and an ailment of the mind began, for they had become one and the same. I had begun to wonder if we should consider a sanitarium, with professionals, but Dmitry always dismissed the idea as rubbish. Of course, Dmitry had never been charged with our father's care.

Afansy sliced into a cutlet with relish and then took a long sip of iced lemonade. He had long since learned to ignore Father. "Once you have gone through the paper in the valise, we can agree to a reasonable sum on your future supplies."

Father was at the table now, reaching for a cutlet with his bare hand until Babette slapped his hand away. "Now, now," she said, a nervous laugh in her voice. "We spoke of this before, dearest. We shall take our supper in the kitchen."

My father pouted like a small boy, a bead of drool forming at the corner of his mouth, while Alexander concentrated on the barnyard rooster pattern edging his chipped china plate. I caught him sneaking a peek at Father, clearly trying not to let his disgust show. Though he was buttoned tightly into a brown coat, he shivered.

My heart sank. Embarrassment of my own father flooding me. I knew it was wrong, but I wished Alexander had never seen him.

"I have one more matter to discuss," Afansy said, "regarding a grand lady."

"Oh?" Alexander gave a last glance at Babette as she ushered my father out of the great hall.

"I believe you might know of the old girl. Empress Catherine herself! Now, the family tale is the empress was meant to visit our humble estate during one of her tours of our great land." Afansy swept his arm to indicate that this room itself might have been so honored. "It is said my grandfather commissioned a likeness in bronze from a factory owned by Prince Potemkin."

When I lived with my grandfather, I often visited the bronze statue of Catherine the Great, cobwebbed and forgotten in one of the storage houses on his estate. I knew he must be conniving to rid himself of the thing. He had done naught but complain of it for years, but the thought of losing Catherine saddened me. "What of it?"

"I was hoping your fiancé might use his connections to fetch a good price for the statue. It's time to let the old girl go."

"No!" I cried. "You won't get rid of her?"

"She might best serve this family now as part of your dowry. Surely your fine poet knows people in the capital who would be honored to care for such a statue."

"I'll see what I can do," Alexander muttered, returning his attention to the cutlets.

"That is all I hoped to hear," Afansy said.

Alexander may have accepted that my family could not provide a significant dowry, but I don't think he anticipated my own grandfather might want to use him for his own ends, as a purchaser of paper products and disposer of unwanted heirlooms.

A loud snorting sound and maniacal laughter rang out from the kitchen. Clearly my father had broken free of whatever charm Babette used to keep him quiet over dinner. It was the last straw. I could not abide the thought he might return to the dining area and try to snatch food from our plates. I scooted my chair back and it screeched along the wooden floor, startling Afansy and my father in the other room, for he suddenly quieted. "I'm sorry, but I feel faint."

Alexander left his chair at once and came to my side, gathering my hands into his. "What is it, my love? Are you not well?"

"It is just a bit hot today . . ." Though the summer was indeed warm, the great hall remained chilly, and yet how easily men were distracted by female illness.

"Do you need to lie down a bit?"

"I think rather that a walk in the garden would do me some good. Will you join me?" I raised my eyebrows.

Alexander gave a sly smile. "I see. Well, much as I'm enjoying this meal, I certainly cannot deny my wife-to-be." He turned to my grandfather. "May we be excused, my good man?"

Afansy waved his hands diplomatically in the air. I supposed he had gotten as much from Alexander as he could over one meal. "Go, go."

I made a show of struggling to rise from my chair as Alexander gathered his walking stick, before taking his offered hand. We strolled out of the great room, toward the front entranceway, past a freestanding grandfather clock that never kept good time and the low divans lining the walls, awaiting guests who no longer visited. As we passed the kitchen, my father made another cackling attempt at laughter and I cringed.

"I take it this need for fresh air is due more to mental rather than physical complaints?" Alexander asked.

I turned my head to ensure we were out of Afansy's earshot and then blurted: "I'm sorry. I'm sorry my grandfather is behaving like a horse's arse. I'm sorry you have to see my father as he is now. If only you had known our family when I was small. My father played the violin so beautifully. It would make your heart weep. And my grandfather was a sophisticated man of business. I looked up to him so." I bit my lip.

Alexander pulled me close. "Think nothing of it. Why, wait until you meet *my* family. My little brother Lev is a charming devil but of no practical use to any woman, state, or organization. My father never met a kopek he could not somehow slip in his pocket and save into perpetuity. And my mother . . . well, you shall meet them all at our wedding so I suppose I shall save you that particular pleasure. My sister Olga will likely be to your taste, but I don't know that she'll stick around the rest of them for long."

I gave a small laugh. "The wedding is still on then? We haven't completely frightened you away?"

"Never," Alexander declared. "Why, I am made of stronger mettle, my dear lady. You would need to turn into an eight-eyed monster before I might consider a change of plan, and even then I should find myself under your spell."

"Perhaps if I threatened to take a bite out of you? Then you might reconsider?"

"A bite taken by the right person can be most delightful."

I longed to know exactly what he meant. If only we weren't confined to this empty old house. We were just in sight of the entrance, with its large windows that opened up to the gardens. "I think once we reach the end of the path we should keep walking. It is springtime, after all. We will be forgiven for taking advantage of the lovely weather, and I hear there is a carnival nearby."

"A carnival! Have you a hankering to see a puppet show?"

"I wish to have my fortune told," I said. "I wish to know how much longer I must suffer my family before the two of us might be married."

Alexander tapped his walking stick lightly, but his voice was strained. "Don't you remember, my Natalie? I can't abide fortune-tellers."

"I remember! You told us when we passed the fair last year. Did you receive a bad fortune from a roadside seer, my love?"

"I had my palm read by a vicious old woman. She said I would die."

"That's hardly a fortune. We shall all die."

"She said I was fated to die at the hands of a tall, fair man. It was too specific for comfort. Never again."

"Oh . . ." I could not summon a better response. But despite my lack of true faith in the practice of clairvoyance, I promised myself that in the future I would steer clear of tall, fair men.

Seven

"You know what they say about marriage, don't you?"

I sighed, wondering if somehow my sister might grow distracted and I wouldn't have to acknowledge her questions. They weren't really questions anyway, merely her opinions in question form. I set down my needlework, gazing out at the gray snow blanketing the park across the street. Despite the howling wind and gloomy winter weather, I wished a handsome man might pass by on a white stallion to distract Ekaterina from her tiresome commentary.

"A man's heaven and a woman's hell," Ekaterina said triumphantly.

Mother had been bent over an old set of linens she hoped to repurpose for my kitchen with the addition of embroidered violets and lilies. She raised her head grimly. "Language!"

"I have never heard this maxim." I allowed a note of pomposity in my tone, even as my shoulders shivered from the chill in the room.

"There is much you haven't heard of, little Natalya." Ekaterina poked her needle through the hem of an everyday shift for my modest trousseau. "This is a wonderful occasion, of course. The wedding supper will be absolutely splendid. Just don't expect much . . . afterward. I hear it said men take all manner of pleasure for themselves with not a thought for the bride."

I turned to Mother with imploring eyes, but she only pressed her lips tighter, focusing on her sewing. Her hands were encased in the old mittens she wore about the house on especially cold days. She had encouraged the same of us to save money on fuel for the fires.

"Two of my friends are already married and so know something of the amorous relations between a man and a woman," Ekaterina prattled on. I think she took glee in shocking Mother. "They tell me it's a trial, at least for the woman."

After sharing kisses with Alexander, I took a different view, and chose to believe the physical aspects of marriage could be enjoyed by wives. "Maybe they're just bad at it."

"It isn't a matter of good or bad, but rather how matters stand. My friends both say they're done with marital 'bliss.' They hope to make babies quickly, so they might be excused from their duties for a few months at least."

I refused to wind up like Ekaterina's friends. I wished for babies, but did not want to be defined solely by my relationship to them. "I don't believe their experiences will mirror mine."

"I suppose every woman thinks that before their wedding night when they have not yet had the experience of a man's touch and—"

"That's enough," Mother cut in. "Mind your conversation or retire upstairs."

Ekaterina smugly returned to her stitching. I had not been in a good mood before my sister regaled me with her friends' opinions on marital relations, and now that she had been silenced I felt naught but emptiness. Alexander and I had hoped to be married as quickly as possible, but an outbreak of cholera meant strictly enforced quarantines kept Alexander confined to his family estate in the countryside, where he had been busy writing. The quarantines closed much of Moscow's social life as well, sentencing me to remain in the sitting room with Mother and Ekaterina, re-reading Alexander's letters, and yearning for a stolen kiss.

Meanwhile, our father still left every night for parts unknown—likely a tavern. On those rare occasions I saw him, he wandered our house, glassy-eyed, violently shaking his head, and mumbling to an invisible companion. My brothers were kept busy with their pursuits of professions; Dmitry in particular was so anxious over his new position at the Foreign Office that he snapped at anyone who so much as looked at him. Even Azya had lost her lively spirit and took to moping around the house, reading Alexander's verse and sighing mysteriously.

During this forced extension of our engagement, Aunt Katya had presented me with a delicate silk nightgown as a wedding gift. She claimed the pale green shading would make my brown eyes appear hazel in the right lamplight. When I tried it on, I gasped. The green may have brought out the highlights in my eyes, but who would notice? The neckline was so low my cleavage poured out of the gown and made my nipples visible through the thin material.

When Mother walked past my room and peeked inside, I

expected a firm admonishment of some kind. She merely lifted her brows. "That suits. I believe you will please your husband."

I wish she had ordered me to return the gown to the shop or made some confession that it hurt to lose her little girl. Instead, she continued past my room without further comment, as though her work with me was finally done. I had completed the transition from daughter to most valuable possession.

I vowed to put this life behind me. I did not have the sensibility at that time to understand precisely what I wanted from life or marriage, but I knew I was meant for something better. I could not shake the feeling that I needed to abandon my family to save myself. I could not wait to start my life anew.

You have no doubt heard tales of bad omens plaguing the wedding of Russia's esteemed poet and his youthful bride. The ceremony took place at the Church of the Ascension, a grand, domed affair of oversized gilt icons and scarlet floor runners. A bride could not ask for a more beautiful setting, nor for a groom who looked happier than Alexander in his finest fawn-colored frock coat with Dutch ruffles. And yet . . . I cannot call the day a success. During the ceremony, in his nervous haste, Alexander dropped the rings, and the candle meant to represent our united lives flickered out before we even left the cathedral. I placed little stock in pagan superstitions, but Alexander turned ghostly white.

"It's all right," I whispered to him later, as we made our way inside the hall where our wedding supper and reception was held. "It means nothing."

He shook his head and walked away. My heart dropped. Marriage meant facing adversity together and already my new husband had created distance between us.

But my soul soothed as he turned to beckon me to his side once more, and we headed toward an older couple hovering near the long oak table weighed down with appetizers and treats. A stout, older man smeared black caviar on bread while his raven-haired wife, hair streaked with gray, picked at fruited jelly candies in a crystal dish.

"My parents," he murmured in my ear. "This will not go well."

I had heard him speak of them enough times to appreciate how apt his descriptions had been. My new father-in-law did indeed look like a man who had given up on all but the pleasures of food and drink, and his mother, though clearly once a great beauty, had her pretty lips twisted into a scowl even as she popped candy in her mouth. "I want to meet them," I said, to make him feel better.

Alexander stiffened. "I suppose we'll need to get it over with. It's not as though we can avoid them our entire lives."

After a perfunctory introduction, I watched Alexander interact with his parents, the formal handshakes and awkward hugs. Alexander's mother glared at her son and then gave me a tilted, bemused smile. "You're lucky to have her," she said, seemingly under her breath but loud enough that I could hear. "You always were a funny-looking little thing. Take care with this beauty or you'll lose her."

I drew in a quick breath, dreading the look of horror I would see on Alexander's face. It seemed we had both suffered under the hands of a domineering mother.

"It is nothing more than how she has regarded me all my life," he said, not bothering to lower his voice. "Pay no mind."

His mother looked away.

I squeezed Alexander's hand, but he only patted my arm unconvincingly. He had been wounded. It was my job to protect him and already I had failed.

Alexander may have pretended not to care what his mother said, but the next day, he woke with the sun and spent the morning and afternoon out with friends, drinking or gambling or what else I did not know. I had hoped to prove Ekaterina's friends wrong about a woman's capacity for passion in a marriage, yet we had been so exhausted after our wedding supper that our carnal union had been vigorous and quick. I had to bite my lip to keep silent during the first moments of pain. Once again, I felt I had failed him.

Now I was left to wander our new home alone.

Prior to our wedding, Alexander had rented a brick house in the Arbat District and through the windows I could hear street vendors and horses and hurried shoppers. The place still smelled freshly cleaned, like lemon polish, and I admired the feminine pattern of the flowered lilac wallpaper. Alexander had made an effort to please me. Even so, the emptiness of the rooms, the bareness of the walls and hardwood floors, and echoing *tap, tap, tap* from the heels of my slippers made me feel a stranger in this place and quite alone, despite the bustle outside. I missed the faded unicorn tapestries hanging in my family's home and the mildew scent clinging to the worn upholstery of our furniture. God help me, I even missed Ekaterina.

I collapsed onto the floor in the middle of one of the unfamiliar rooms, empty save for a billiards table covered with a green canopy, overwhelmed and trying not to cry. I wanted to please

Alexander, not only because this was my sacred duty, but because I wanted physical pleasure as well. I had always loved the way he looked at me and wondered what thoughts ran through his head, how he wanted to touch me. My imagination was not fully sufficient to fill the gaps. I wanted lingering caresses and kisses tracing their way down my body.

By the time Alexander came home that night, I had gathered myself once more. After a light supper, I changed at once into the revealing green nightgown.

"My angel." When he joined me in bed, Alexander gently held my wrists over my head with one hand and explored the curves of my body under my delicate silk nightdress with the other. His whiskers tickled and I giggled.

Surprise flashed over his face. I had been stoic during his previous advances, but only because of nerves. Alexander buried his face in my stomach and then between my breasts, thinly covered underneath the gossamer gown. This tickled even more and I squealed in delight. He still had my wrists bound above my head with one hand and though he didn't hurt me, the light of passion in his eyes excited me. I held his gaze, daring him to continue.

At last he released my wrists. I liked how it had felt, to have them stretched high over my head, and so I left them in that position, thrusting my hips up, offering myself to him. He moved down, his whiskers still tickling me but in such a pleasant way that a soft moan escaped me. He licked me gently as well, lapping between my thighs, tasting me. Waves of desire coursed through me, and all thoughts left me and I considered only the pleasures of the moment and a blissful passage to sleep.

A few hours later, in the silence of the night, I stirred. In the study of the adjoining room, a pen scratched thick paper. Disoriented, I thought it morning. I reached for my spectacles on the nightstand so that I might check the time, and accidentally knocked over a vase of flowers the maid had placed there the night before. I heard Alexander set his pen down and his bare feet trod back to our bedroom.

He stood at the doorway for a moment, gripping a candle holder aloft. In the flickering light, I made out the broad vertical stripes of a silk dressing gown he had acquired during his travels in the south. I tried to imagine him in the somber garments of a shopkeeper, but it was impossible to do. Such bland men would remain the purview of Ekaterina and her dull friends.

I started to remove my spectacles, but Alexander strode to our bed. "No, please. Leave them on." My gown had fallen over one shoulder and I was conscious of the heaviness of my breasts so near to his chest. He made no move to straighten my gown, but reached for my hair, smoothed it back, and then gathered it into a severe bun, nothing like the current style with loose curls to frame the face.

I pulled him nearer, an echo of quivering pleasure from what had passed between us earlier still stirring.

"Wait." He pressed gently on my arms to stop me.

My heart fell. "I thought you might wish . . . to find pleasure . . ."

He gathered one of my hands in both of his and kissed me softly on the palm. "Oh, I do wish it, angel, only I must work harder to earn the right."

"You have earned the right. You are my husband."

"That is not what I meant. I wish that you treat me as your servant made only for your pleasure."

A thrill pitched my shoulders. "You wish to dress as a footman?"

Alexander laughed and kissed my hand again. "I like how you think. That is a fine notion, my Madonna. Consider this another time. For now, I wish you to remain frigid."

"I have no desire to remain frigid. I wish to give you pleasure."

"You will," he said. "I want you to resist until you can no longer control yourself."

The word "resist" made me frown. It called to mind a drunken prince in pursuit of serf girls. "If I wished to resist you, I would never have married you."

He planted a kiss on my forehead, but it was not yet the kiss of a lover. "You are a dream. Let me explain one more time. I only ask that you not falsify your reactions. When I begin to make love to you, sit still as marble. Return the embrace only when you feel compelled, when you feel you cannot stand it any longer. I think you will find the sensual rewards grand."

"I shall try," I said uncertainly.

"Then I shall start. Remember, only once you cannot stand it any longer, only then abandon yourself to me."

I tried to do as he commanded. I remained still when his lips moved over my neck and my shoulders. Though my body already responded to his caresses, I focused on a spot on the wall, trying to inhabit another persona as I had when performing in the tableau. I was a Madonna. A goddess. If this mere mortal wished to possess me, he would need to earn his prize. He moved down, cupping my breast with his hand and running his lips over its fullness. I wanted to throw my head back, drinking in the sensation. I wanted him to devour me, but I fought. I remained still. I let out a little sigh as though bored by the entire affair.

I knew he would not be deceived. My whole body had gone limp; my nipples were small and hard. My feigned indifference spurred him on and I felt his firmness against my thigh. His fingers moved to the softness between my legs, massaging me while I grew wetter and wetter. He concentrated on a small patch of skin, exquisitely sensitive to his touch, and I could not continue the charade any longer. I screamed and arched my back, moving my body to pull him into me. He removed my spectacles and tossed them aside while I shook my hair free and dove deeper into his embrace.

I awoke sore and happy, Alexander snoring at my side. Tendrils of weak winter sun streamed through the thin drapes, illuminating the floral design on the wallpaper. I found my spectacles on the floor and wondered if I would ever wear them again without a powerful surge of arousal.

The ormolu clock on our mantel confirmed it was not yet six a.m., but I was too excited to sleep further. I pounded playfully on Alexander's bare shoulders. "Wake up, lazy boy."

"Not yet, wifekin." Without opening his eyes, he pulled me in for a slow, deep kiss, but when I continued to pound on his shoulders he batted my hands away like a kitten.

I would come to learn my husband required strong Turkish coffee, the morning papers, and a cold bath before becoming sensible. I was not so patient. I was flying. I snatched a thin robe from the bureau, barely wrapped it around my shoulders, and proceeded to the dining room—spectacles on, hair unbound, and feet bare. I would never have dared such an appearance before Mother, but I was the lady of this house.

I had never felt so free.

The house may have been sparsely furnished, but it no longer seemed so intimidating. I located a servant's bell hanging from a cord and pulled until the pealing sound filled the room.

A thin, meek-looking maid peeked out from the kitchen. She could not have been more than fifteen. Alexander had introduced me to her, along with his elderly valet and some other servants, but I had been so flustered by our wedding I could scarcely keep their names straight. "Madame Pushkina?"

It took me a moment to realize she meant me. I nodded, now slightly embarrassed. I knew the flush of my conjugal night clung to me yet. "What is your name?"

She gave a quick curtsy. "Elizaveta, but I prefer Liza. Would you care for something to break your fast? I'll inform cook."

"Hot cocoa?" I said. "And perhaps some scones with extra butter?"

She scurried back to the kitchen. While I waited, I decided to poke around. I felt too shy to explore Alexander's personal study, but he kept an additional writing table in the parlor and a shelf crammed with books. I found myself drawn to a silver framed portrait and leaned in for a better look. Alexander's African ancestor, Abram Gannibal, returned my gaze. His hair was tied back into a short ponytail with a bow and he wore the formal naval uniform of the seventeenth century. His gold buttons gleamed. There was something of Alexander in his expression; he stared out at the world with a teasing glance. I might have thought it strange Alexander kept a picture of Abram Gannibal but not his parents, except now I had met them and their hearts of stone. Little wonder he related better to his long-dead ancestor.

Next to the portrait, a bound journal smelling of fresh leather rested. I thought of my own writings, safely tucked away in one of my valises. I had dabbled with some verse before our wedding, trying to capture in words the glorious anticipation that stirred inside me when I gazed on Alexander's face. And yet, now that I could compare my own weak attempts so closely to the magnificent words of my husband, I felt it my fate in life to be a reader, rather than a writer, and kept my own creative expressions to myself.

The notebook had a hook across the front, but had not been locked. I cracked it open, lightly running my hand over Alexander's random scribblings and drawings: notes on Mozart, rants over Onegin, and a drawing of petite feet in ballerina's slippers. These gave me pause. I had never worn such slippers and wondered whose feet he meant to represent. I did not dwell long, however, but turned the page quickly and then recoiled as though bit by a snake.

Alexander had drawn the figure of a slim young man in a military uniform and heavy boots; feet tied together, hands tied behind his back. The gallows stood shaded in the background. The young man's neck fit tightly in a noose and his head drooped at an awkward angle. My heart began to palpitate. When I turned to the next page, I saw a similar picture, but this time with five men hanging in a row on the scaffolds.

I slammed it shut. Clearly Alexander's lost friends remained on his mind. What if he intended to write about the Decembrists and word of it reached the tsar? I had heard whispered stories of late-night knocks on the door, the secret police forcing men from their beds at night while their wives and children cried and pleaded for mercy. They might take Alexander from me and throw him into the dungeon at the bottom of Peter and Paul Fortress in St. Petersburg. Men had died there, alone and forgotten, starved or drowned when the Neva's waters rose too high. An image of Alexander's face as a mask of death, sallow and drawn, flashed in my mind and I shook my head to rid it of the horror.

"What have we here, then? Investigating my work?"

I let out a cry and spun around, the sound of his voice startling me, as he came up behind and hugged me. When he saw the pictures, he released me, backing away.

"I was snooping about . . . I'm sorry about your friends." The tsar's dungeon masters could not have extracted a confession more efficiently than the mournful look in Alexander's eyes. I nodded toward the sketch of a soldier swinging from the gallows. "You still think of them?"

"I was not there to witness their deaths myself, but I have heard the day described often enough." His voice was so soft I ducked my head to hear him. "Sometimes I dream of it at night. With the slightest turn of fate, my neck might have snapped under the weight of the ropes."

"But it did not. You were meant to be of this earth."

"Perhaps. But a mere trifle saved me from that fate. I was on my way to St. Petersburg that December. I would have arrived in time to join the officers in their revolt. By God, I would have, for I believed in their cause. A constitution! Can you imagine it, my Natalie?"

The passion in his voice alarmed me and I wondered if he risked speaking this way around others. "I have not dared to imagine it."

"It was a hare who stopped me. A small beast! The fluffy scoundrel scurried across the road in front of our sleigh. Missed the horses' hooves by a fraction and hopped along his way without a care, while I was in a frenzy. You have heard this is a bad omen, have you not? A hare crossing your path?"

I bit my lip listening to Alexander's story, leaving it plump and sore. "I thought black cats were bad luck."

"Black cats? Why on earth would one consider such magnificent creatures bad luck? You sound like an Englishwoman. No, I ordered the driver to turn around and delayed my trip to St. Petersburg rather than risk bad fortune. A hare kept me from meeting with the Decembrists. A hare kept me from being strung up on the gallows along with them. Now tell me how much thinner the line between life and death could possibly be but by a *hare*. Tell me that is naught but folk superstition."

"I will tell you no such thing. I only wish we could find that darling animal and make a pet of it to show our gratitude."

"Yes, well . . . I don't much care for the beasts, but perhaps we might keep a cat or two. Black cats, I think."

The maid, Liza, entered the room with my hot cocoa, and Alexander asked for his usual strong coffee before sinking onto a divan. Soon the aroma of java mingled with chocolate filled the room and I felt better. A fire blazed in the hearth, flames twisting and snapping. Through the window, I watched snow falling onto cobblestones and heard the distant jingling of sleigh bells. Perhaps we might arrange things so we never left this flat, remaining forever in our little cocoon, safe from the rest of the world. Then Alexander could never share his rebellious thoughts on a constitution with anyone who might report such words to the tsar's spies.

Once Alexander finished his coffee, I found my way onto his lap. He refused to kiss me, claiming the coffee soiled his breath, but his hand slid beneath my gown. I worried for a moment that one of the servants might see. Yet this was our place, and we were married, so I could do anything that gave me pleasure and the world could not stop me.

"First, I've something delightful to show you." His face flushed as he withdrew his hand.

I followed Alexander as he sprang up from the divan and approached his writing table. He lifted one of the ink blotters and retrieved a small silver key from underneath. "I want you to see what keeps me occupied when I am feeling low or restless or any of the many moods that plague a man from time to time."

At last, I was to become his true muse, entrusted with his work, offering valued opinions and suggestions. I nodded, expecting to soon read his new verse.

Alexander crouched to reach a lower drawer and turned the key in a lock. He opened the drawer and I peered over his shoulder.

"Oh!" I said as he lifted a rectangular wooden box and opened the lid. Inside, a pistol with a pearl-colored handle and a long barrel nestled in a velveteen lining, the way a piece of jewelry might. Or a corpse in a coffin.

"Beautiful, isn't it?" Alexander stroked the pearl handle with the same loving attention Mother lavished on her brown tabby. "A fellow never knows when he might need it."

I stared, dumbfounded, at the weapon. "I did not know there were guns in this house."

"I have it safely locked away." Alexander centered himself and pointed the pistol at a random spot on the wall. "I find it most calming when I need to think. Stand back for a moment. And you may want to cover your ears."

While Alexander straightened his shoulders, I stuck my fingers in my ears as instructed. His form was perfect, one arm extended and one arm carefully behind his back, while his bare feet stood shoulder width apart. His eyes focused intently on the target before him.

Alexander liked to play the role of Evgeny Onegin: the perfect Russian dandy. He had drawn sketches of himself wandering the bridges of St. Petersburg with his fictional creation; apart from the wild black curls under the top hat of the figure meant to represent Alexander, you could scarcely tell the two apart. Nevertheless, despite his perfect stance, I could not picture him as Onegin right now, but Lensky, crumpling to the ground under the fatal bullet.

"No, Alexander . . . Sasha . . ." I used the term of endearment to see if it might have a soothing effect. "Perhaps you could take target practice outside."

"I assure you I know what I'm doing." Alexander fired and the pistol erupted. A wax bullet struck the wall, making a pocked mark sizzling with heat.

"Perfect!" he declared, striding forward. "I tell you this is great fun. At my old bachelor's flat, I spelled out my name. If you like, I can assist with your form and you can start your name."

My heart pumped so quickly I thought I might expire. "I believe I can find other occupations to keep my hands busy."

"I am certain of that." He gave me a sly wink.

I looked down demurely though a chill spiked in my chest. If Alexander grew restless enough to write his name by firing wax bullets into a wall, I would need to keep him busy. I had thought we would be safe if we kept ourselves apart from the rest of the world, but now I saw how wrong I had been. Certainly our private pleasures would command his attention, but I thought it best we partake of the pleasures of social life as well. Anything to keep him away from his prized weapon.

Eight

My desire for distraction was soon granted when we were invited to a public costume ball and concert to raise funds for victims of the recent cholera epidemic. It was to be held at the Bolshoi Petrovsky Theater, and I thought it would be great fun to dress in costume for the occasion. I still had fond memories of the evening I portrayed Dido's sister and thought I could repurpose the gown into a reasonable likeness of the love goddess, Venus. Inhabiting such a sensual persona would surely make for a pleasurable night afterward. In this spirit, I approached Alexander one morning while he was on his way to his study and began to rub his shoulders.

"So affectionate, my angel." When I caught his gaze, I saw light in his eyes, the subtle spark when a man is completely yours. There is an intoxicating power to it.

"I should like to assume the persona of Venus for the ball next week," I told him.

"I can think of nothing more appropriate."

"Will you consider joining me as Mars?"

Alexander grinned, but his shoulders tensed in my hands. "You see me as a god of war?"

"I see you as the lover of Venus." In my mind's eye, I had a quick vision of Mother gasping, but I banished it. She had no further hold on me in real life and I should not allow her to haunt my imagination.

"It is a charming idea, of course." Alexander spoke quickly, the tenderness in his voice replaced with casual flirtation. "Unfortunately, I don't think we can handle such an expense at the moment."

"I thought we keep our expenses to a minimum."

"Yes, but you see, I had a bit of bad luck when last I visited the English gentlemen's club for faro . . ."

I had not known Alexander continued to visit the card tables. My smile struggled to hold. I had hoped that as a married man he would find more genteel pursuits. Silently, I resolved to pay closer attention to our financial ledgers in the future.

"I hope it doesn't disappoint my angel, but I think we should conserve our limited funds."

"This isn't a problem," I said. "I intend to use the toga I wore when I performed for the tsar as Dido's sister. You remember when I mentioned this, my love?"

Alexander flinched. "Of course. Of course."

"I do not think it would be such an expense to dress you as Mars and we would make a striking pair, don't you agree?"

"You will." He gave a tight smile.

"We will together," I insisted.

"I shall think about it." Gently, he lifted my hands from his shoulders. "Now I must face my stupid fit for the day."

I tilted my head. "Stupid fit?"

"Only what I call my writing." He shrugged and looked away with a twist of his lips that suddenly reminded me of his mother, the way she had looked at our wedding. "Sometimes all the happiness in the world comes from this endeavor, but I swear writing mostly drives me mad."

He disappeared into his study and shut the door. Though the news of his gambling losses vexed me, I accepted his reasoning. I had spent far too many years watching Mother slowly lose her soul over her household budget, and I wished to cause my new husband no pain in this regard.

I kept my purchases to recreate the goddess of love to a bare minimum.

The following week, we arrived at the theater: Alexander in a black evening coat and myself in the same toga and frayed crown of artificial laurel leaves I wore when I portrayed Dido's sister. I had added a touch of gold braiding to my waist, but knew that without Mars at my side, the meaning of my costume was unclear. Still, I thought it suited me well enough.

Unable to shake Mother's admonitions from my mind, I chose not to wear my spectacles, and squinted to admire the chandeliers ablaze with candles, and the thick red carpet runners placed along the parquet flooring. Tsar Nicholas's imperial insignia had been writ in an elaborate tapestry above the threshold. The lobby was humid and rife with exotic flowers imported from the south. I wondered if the money spent on the flowers might not have been better spent on victims of cholera, but kept this thought to myself.

Alexander was immediately flanked by admirers. Many of them had not met me yet. My hand was kissed so often that a thin sheen of moisture formed and I wondered how soon I might find a washroom and scrub it clean.

"My dear." An older man with graying whiskers added his own spittle to the mess on my hand. "As beautiful as they say and yet I had not known you were so tall."

I was accustomed to people commenting on my height, particularly men, but had yet to find an appropriate response to such a vapid observation. I simply nodded and lowered my gaze, staring at my slippers, the low heels scuffed from overuse.

"Indeed!" Alexander said, accepting a flute of champagne from a passing footman. "I find standing beside her a rather lowering experience."

The men chuckled at that, but I could not join in their merriment. I hadn't realized Alexander minded our difference in height. If anything, I thought he rather liked it.

They carried him off in a wave of questions and entreaties about the new literary journal Alexander had proposed to start based on an English model, with short pieces on literature, economics, and politics. The men's voices competed with one another, asking if he might read and comment on their work, while I was left to sip a sweet cordial and pretend to admire a silver candlestick on a table near where I stood. Without my spectacles, I could see little else. I tried not to mind, but wished Alexander had thought to take my hand and lead me off with him, for I wished to stand next to my husband as proud wife and presumed muse. It seemed I now had the freedom of which I always dreamed while still trapped in Mother's house, and yet somehow that wasn't enough. I tried to concentrate on the strumming of the orchestra from inside the theater as they warmed their instruments for the concert, but the high sweet notes of the violin made me think of my father before his accident, when he still played his own violin on cold winter nights.

Fortunately, I could not linger too long in the past. A pair of young women in togas stood next to one of the picture windows, under a garland of fresh orchids. A blonde rested her hand on a brunette's shoulder, cupping her other hand to whisper something in her friend's ear and then nodded at me. As they drew near, I squinted, trying to make out their features. They both had coiffed curls, glowing cheeks, and smiles filled with white teeth.

"Mind if you're joined by two of the Muses?" the blonde called out.

I managed to fix a smile on my face. What else could I do? At least the cordial was going to my head and the room around me grew fuzzier.

"You are the poet's wife?" The blonde held a grinning mask in one hand so I assumed she was Thalia, the Muse of Comedy. "We've heard so much about you, Madame Pushkina. I'm Idaliya. Call me Ida." She nodded at her dark-haired friend. "And Alexandra here wishes to be called Alix. Like a foreigner." They giggled a bit at that.

"Nice to meet you. Thank you," I said awkwardly, and then realized she hadn't paid me a compliment. Already, I felt a fool.

"You are as beautiful as they say!" Alix declared, perhaps reading my thoughts and wishing to spare me further embarrassment. She had beaded stars affixed to her toga, so she was likely Urania, the Muse of Astronomy. "I would expect no less from our Pushkin."

"I am disappointed you didn't dress up though!" Ida said. "I heard you charmed Tsar Nicholas when you appeared as Dido's sister over the Christmas holidays."

They exchanged meaningful glances. They knew full well I had attempted to appear in costume this evening, as it was not the custom to trot about Moscow in laurel leaves and togas. At that moment, I missed Ekaterina. She would have had something sharp to say to the Muses.

I tapped the gold braiding about my waist. "I meant to portray the goddess of love, but had not the time I wished. Alexander and I have been occupied as of late."

"Of course!" Ida said. "Newly married and all."

They giggled more and I caught a whiff of alcohol on their breath. A memory of my father staggering around our house came to my mind and I wanted nothing more than to retreat.

Alix had been examining my dress. Her gaze lingered for a moment on my cleavage and I detected a sneer of disapproval as she pointed to something on my dress. "Oh dear. I'm afraid you've had an accident."

I paled. What could she possibly mean? I glanced down. A faint smudge, like facial powder, marred the gown. It was not my own powder as I was still too shy to make such a purchase from the apothecary and too vain to think I had need of it. The smudge must have been left over from when I had been made up to appear as Dido's sister under harsh stage lights.

"There is a washroom downstairs," Alix told me. "You can tend to that stain."

This was nothing more than sound advice, but I had a feeling she wanted to find fault with me and I didn't care to give either of them such pleasure. "Oh, it is but a trifle." I kept my voice falsely merry. "I'm sure no one else will notice." Out of the corner of my eye, I made out Alexander approaching us, not a moment too soon.

Alix retained her smile. "I only meant to help."

"I'm sure," I said lightly, "but you see I would rather spend time with my husband than fuss over a smudge."

"Even so, you wouldn't want anyone else to notice, poor girl."

I straightened my back, emphasizing my height so I might look down on them both. "I have not heard my husband offer any complaint about the way I have dressed tonight."

"Ladies." Alexander took my arm. "I do hope the Muses have made a show of delighting my wife with the secret hope of inspiring me."

"As though you would need our help," Alix declared.

Alexander smiled and a spark of jealousy flared in me, but then he tapped his heels together. "If you'll excuse me, I would like to show my wife to the dance floor. Madame Pushkina?" He offered his hand.

As we left, I heard Ida say, "I believe they came in costume after all. I heard it said they're Venus and Vulcan. A mismatch."

"You mustn't!" Alix declared. "A mismatch indeed, but only because he is a great man while she has an empty head."

I drew in a sharp breath and glanced at Alexander, praying he hadn't heard either comment. Mars was the handsome lover, while Vulcan was the homely husband the god Jupiter had chosen for beautiful Venus to keep her out of trouble. A husband she had never loved. A husband she had cuckolded on more than one occasion. If I was thought to have an *empty head*, I was surely also thought capable of such cruelty.

Alexander's hands worked in and out of fists. I remembered the wicked comment his mother had made after our wedding and squeezed his upper arm.

"They hate me," he said in a low voice. "I'm sorry, but you will need to get used to it."

"Who hates you?" I asked, horrified. "Those two?"

"Not Alix, but the blond one, I think. And any of those here who see fit to praise my writing while treating me like I'm beneath their contempt when I dare arrive at a ball. It is no more than how my mother made me feel when I was forced into dancing lessons and she called my clumsy appearance a shaming mark on our family, but never mind."

He rubbed his hands together and I took them in my own to still his trembling. His mother. I wanted to slap the woman. "You should never be made to feel such."

"To the devil with them anyway. Someday I should like to get away from all of this. I would like to take you to the country where I might have you to myself." My touch had calmed him and the good humor began to return to his expression. He kissed my hands, glanced over his shoulder, and then pinched my thigh playfully. The small gesture of our intimacy, the reminder of what would pass between us that night, was all the more exciting for having been in public. "I can only imagine what I might do with an entire country house at my disposal and no worries in my head. None of the shallow distractions of cosmopolitan life. You as muse."

I inclined my head to speak directly in his ear. "Don't give another thought to the false Muses. Urania's stars covered a flat bosom. And Thalia might pretend to be the Muse of Comedy, but her face was a tragedy."

Alexander laughed heartily at that. "There's the girl I love. My Venus with a squint."

. . .

After our night at the Bolshoi Petrovsky, Alexander decided we should host a small party in our own home. He may have spoken fondly of the country, but he seemed determined to show Moscow that small-minded gossip about our supposed mismatch was nothing more than the jealous rumbling of fools.

I felt far more nervous playing hostess than appearing at a ball and needed help. Fortunately, Aunt Katya was in town visiting Mother. I called on her one afternoon when I knew Mother and Ekaterina to be out running an errand.

"All eyes are on you now," Aunt Katya informed me after we had taken seats opposite one another in Mother's parlor and between sips of the hot cocoa we both loved. "You are married to one of the most famous men in the land. Of course you must host an affair."

I set down the mug of cocoa, feeling awkward in the old rosewood armchair; the frayed cushion made me itch and I had to cross my arms and rub them up and down, for Mother still kept the parlor excessively cold and the hot drink was only starting to warm my insides. I appraised the peeling wallpaper and took in the dull, musty scent that still clung to our family's home. I had not visited since my wedding day three weeks earlier. It all seemed even shabbier now than when I had lived here, and it had seemed shabby enough then. "Alexander's income is rather . . ." I tried to think of a way I might phrase it without alarming my aunt. "Unpredictable."

"Surely that's not your problem."

"I do not wish to be a burden to him."

"His duty is to support you. He's no fool. He knew this before he married you and social life in Moscow comes at a price."

"This is not why I married *him*," I insisted. "I knew his income was modest. I knew that when I accepted his proposal."

Aunt Katya leaned back in her chair. It made an ominous creak, as though struggling to support even my aunt's modest weight. She picked up her fan and slanted the base in my direction. "You say these harpies noticed a smudge on your dress. Is this the same gown?"

"Of course not." I wore a simple lilac shift from the hand-me-down box Aunt Katya had brought from court. It was a bit worn, but Alexander had been pleased enough with its effect on my figure when I modeled it for him earlier that morning.

"This one has a rip in it." Aunt Katya pointed her fan accusingly at my sleeve. "Did you not notice?"

I tried to smile, but my aunt was not treating this lightly, as I'd hoped she would. "I suppose I had not."

"You might use a lorgnette . . ."

"What does it matter?" I said, exasperated.

"You came here for help. Do you want my advice or not? Stop trying to make sense of it. Success is predicated on appearances. You must take greater care with the way you present yourself. Take care with your clothes. Treat them as a knight would a coat of armor and then you can face any insult these shrews might care to throw your way."

I bit my lip. Mother preferred simplicity in all things, including dress, and spent little time attending to our wardrobes. And Alexander lived so fully in his own head, I don't think he noticed much about my clothes save for the way they flattered my figure. "We have not the money to spend on clothes," I protested weakly.

"You will need to persuade Alexander to find the money. A beautiful wife who rules over society will be a tremendous credit to him. You must spend a substantial portion of your budget in order to have greater wealth in the future."

"You sound like that man who goes on and on about the wealth of nations." Though I would choose a novel over an economic treatise any day, even I had heard of Adam Smith's ideas.

"The English are wise with their money . . . if an uncultured lot in many respects." Aunt Katya flicked her wrist. "They have mastered a concept called 'investment.'"

"I have no clue what this means."

"Think of it this way: your mother hoarded money and guarded every kopek like a hawk. Did this make her happy?"

I said nothing. No one needed to confirm Mother's unhappiness. It was established fact.

"The English see money differently. They would advise your mother to spend some of her money wisely now in order to make more money in the future."

"One can make money last, though. We could save money by moving away from the city. Alexander mentioned he was productive when he was away at his family's estate. Perhaps he will be productive in the country. We can live on less income there."

"He is spending time in the country?"

"He has spoken of moving us away from the small worries of society."

"Oh no." Aunt Katya shook her head. "Oh no. That won't do."

"Why not?" It seemed a reasonable enough solution. I wouldn't feel terribly upset if we had to cancel our little party or if I wasn't forced to deal with women like the Muses again.

"Perhaps some time in the country might be good for Alexander's writing, but he would tire of that quiet life soon enough. And where would that leave you?"

"Happy? Free to read all day and wear my spectacles whenever I wish?" Free to enjoy certain pleasures all night, I wanted to add, but knew this would be tactless. For all her sophistication, even Aunt Katya might take offense.

"During the first few weeks, perhaps." My aunt raised her eyebrow slyly, making me suspect she knew what I was thinking even though I hadn't uttered it aloud. "Perhaps even for a year. Then what? Trust me, child, you will get bored as easily as your husband will. You'll long for the excitement of Moscow and St. Petersburg. You're a beautiful girl! I should say a beautiful woman now. All eyes are on you."

"What if I don't want that?"

"Every woman wants that, but let's say you truly have no desire to be admired. You have others to consider."

"Alexander's words speak for themselves."

Aunt Katya set her fan down and stirred her cocoa with a tiny pewter teaspoon. "I was not thinking of Alexander."

My stomach twisted as I sensed the direction this conversation was to take. "Who then?"

"You have two sisters of marriageable age, yet they have no husbands, nor many prospects from what I understand. They now have an advantage they had not before: a sister with the potential to occupy the highest position in society."

I looked down at my hands. "I suppose I could make introductions—"

"Precisely. So what is a little debt here and there? Think of the benefits. Your sisters are lovely enough, even if they pale in comparison to you. Ekaterina is sharp with her tongue, but we can rein that in, and Azya is a sweet little thing. With the proper introductions, they will have no trouble marrying noblemen or soldiers or whomever else they desire. Any expenses you spend now will seem a trifle in comparison. An investment in your entire family's future. Your husband can't possibly object."

Perhaps not if I put it to him that way. Still, I didn't feel entirely comfortable with the scheme. "How will we fund this *investment*?"

"Alexander is a popular man and from a noble family on his father's side, if I remember correctly. Surely he has no problem securing credit."

"I suppose not . . ."

Aunt Katya patted my arm. "When you are next in St. Petersburg, I shall be happy to accompany you to the finest French shops. Once you see how you look in the latest fashion, I am confident you will not only see the wisdom of what I say, but the fun. After all, what is life without a bit of fun?"

That sounded like something Alexander would say and I smiled.

"You are in an enviable position," Aunt Katya said. "We shall make the most of it."

I did not have time to shop for anything new to wear prior to our party, but I did take particular care with the menu and listened carefully to the opinion of our new cook on popular items to serve. Together, we decided on a French spread consisting of onion soup, crusty baguettes with butter, and a duck with orange sauce. When Alexander saw the proposed menu, he shook the paper as though he thought he might somehow make it less dear. "It's lovely, wifekin, only I dread bringing these expenses to our steward."

At first, I was tempted to relent. The only experience I had with household management was listening to Mother battle with our family's steward over every kopek spent. Yet the chat with Aunt Katya had convinced me there was a better way to manage money. "You have mentioned you wish to start a new journal. Such a venture will require funds, I assume."

He narrowed his eyes, but his lips curved into the start of a smile.

"You know as well as I that appearances are important. If we wish people to"—I stumbled on Aunt Katya's word—"invest in your journal, we must convince them our finances are in good order."

"Invest? Are you an Englishwoman now?"

"The tsar himself referred to me as Lady Pushkina in the English manner."

"The tsar himself. I see." Alexander tightened his smile. "Well, then order champagne in copious amounts as well. We want to ensure everyone leaves happy at the very least."

It was a charming event. At least I thought so. Alexander invited an elderly nobleman named Prince Yusupov who graciously told stories of his time as a young man in the court of Catherine the Great, a topic that still intrigued me. His stories were not as coherent as they might once have been; I appreciated the effort nonetheless. The food was delicious and the champagne plentiful, but I felt more conscious than ever of the unfashionable design of my gown. Even worse, our housekeeper set out the repurposed table linens Mother had embroidered for my trousseau. The stains never truly washed out and the fine dishes beside them only served to highlight their dinginess. Finally, there was some confusion as to where pots and platters should be placed on the overcrowded side table. One of the guests—one of Alexander's poet friends who had traveled all the way from Odessa—sneered at the muddled dinner service.

I resolved to speak with Alexander the next morning.

By the time he rose at midday, I was already dressed and waiting for him in our parlor. I had fixed my hair, taken extra care in choosing my gown, and made sure I had time enough to swallow down some hot cocoa and a bit of breakfast before we spoke.

Alexander crept into the parlor as though every movement hurt. He wore his red-checkered silk robe and had drawn a green scarf around his neck to ward off the chill of the morning. He placed a lavender sachet on his forehead as he sank onto our new chaise longue with a moan.

"Damn success last night," he told me. He never held his tongue when he spoke to me, a quality I still appreciated. "Yet I should have stopped after the port."

"You were a delight!" I ran to him, took a seat on his lap, and kissed his hands. They were large, especially considering his stature, and I felt safe when they were enfolded over mine.

"You think so?"

"The wit and charm our guests might expect from a night at the theater." At some point, I supposed, he might tire of my flattery but then again men never seem to tire of women telling them how wonderful they are. He kissed my hands, before drawing them to his chest to feel his heart beat. The movement aroused me, but I would not allow myself to be distracted from my goal.

"They came for you," he said. "I was merely homely Vulcan to be tolerated so they might catch a glimpse of Venus in all her glory."

My poor poet was still wounded it seemed. "I am only your wifekin."

"You are far more than that." I fancied he might ask then about my own notebooks full of poems and translations, but I still had yet to share my literary aspirations.

"I hope you might approve of *investing* money in our table linens and service ware for future events. It might even make sense to hire additional men for the evening so that our guests might be served properly."

Alexander opened his eyes, sat straight up, and flung the sachet aside. "Served properly? Why, I would not have been ashamed to serve such a meal to the tsar."

"I didn't mean it like that."

"What *did* you mean? Speak plainly, woman."

I knew eventually we would have our first quarrel, only I had not thought it would be over linens. "It makes sense for a man of your position to spend more on such accouterments."

Alexander's features relaxed. "Rubbish."

"It's my fault. As the hostess, I should have attended to such matters, except . . ." I blushed. "The nights we spend together are such a joy all other thoughts leave my head."

Alexander pulled me up so that I straddled his legs. He kissed me gently while placing his hand underneath my skirt, kneading my thighs and powerfully distracting me, though I remained determined to get one more question out before giving in to raw pleasure.

"So it is all right if I spend some of our income on new

furnishings?" I whispered in his ear. "Perhaps a new gown or two as well."

"Whatever you wish." His cheeks had darkened and his hand moved up my thigh. He might not have heard what I said, but that was not my concern.

Later, when Alexander had retired to his study, I lingered at his writing table in the parlor. He had taken his portrait of Abram Gannibal and leather-bound ledger with him, insisting he would at last get to work. Several unbound pages were strewn about, the ink still glistening on the thick Goncharov paper. We had not really discussed whether or not I might read Alexander's drafts, but I managed to convince myself that as his wife, it was both my right and duty to evaluate his work-in-progress. I hoped he might come to value my opinion. Carefully, I gathered the stray pages. They contained random turns of phrase that made no sense and Alexander's usual jumble of sketches: a sad-eyed horse with no rider, that dandy Onegin under a streetlamp, and furry balls with perky ears, meant to be sleeping cats.

At last, I spotted my own face, hair done up and neck long, my cleavage prominent. On the page opposite my picture, he had composed a new poem. I read eagerly and quickly realized this was no work to be published for profit. The first stanza talked of a passionate lover, a wild woman, while the next stanza spoke of a more subdued, gentle, and even cold woman only doing her duty. By the end, however, the poet had pleased the reluctant woman.

My cheeks burned. He was the one who had instructed me to act coldly during our lovemaking. He was the one who had wished me to hold out until I could not help but give in to passion. He had asked me to play that role for the benefit of *his* fantasy.

I heard some movement from Alexander's study and placed the papers back on his writing table before laying back on our chaise longue. I grabbed a bit of embroidery I kept out in the parlor in case I needed something dainty with which to occupy my hands.

Alexander entered the parlor. He looked at the writing table and then at me. In my distress, I had stacked his papers neatly, rather than leaving them in their previous disarray.

"Did you like my latest?"

I threw the embroidery aside. "I lack passion in it!"

"You do not." He came to me and took my hand in his once more. "Why, your fire burns through in the words."

"Your passion is the only catalyst for mine."

"Why should that matter? I am your husband. Of course I'm the one who should open you to passion. You were a virgin. You were innocent."

"I was, but . . ." Words failed me. I couldn't explain, only knew the poem made me feel as though my sensuality, and by some extension my very being, depended on Alexander. This was appropriate for a wife and yet I did not like it and did not know how to explain this without injuring his pride. "It is well done." To change the subject, I added: "I should like to help you with your transcriptions. I have a fine hand. I might help copy your rough drafts into a readable form. I would like to comment on them as well if I might."

"Of course." Alexander made an elegant wave with his wrist and leaned in to kiss me. "That sounds delightful."

"And the poem . . . I assume it will remain a private matter between us."

"It is a private poem. A love note." He smiled, but he had not truly answered the question. Alexander was not the sort to keep his work to himself. I suspected some of his friends would read the poem. Already my reputation was being fashioned and it seemed I had but limited control over its final shape.

sisters needed to meet eligible bachelors and so I thought it best to stay near a city.

We agreed to try our luck in the small village of Tsarskoye Selo, near St. Petersburg where Alexander had fond memories of his student years. The village was the summer home of the tsars and dominated by great palaces. Even so, we were able to secure a rented wooden dacha for a reasonable sum, which made me feel slightly less guilty about the money invested in new clothes, linens, and furniture.

In our country house, Alexander's study was above the parlor and the wooden floorboards creaked when he set to work. He re-arranged his routine, deciding now that he was a "married fellow past the age of thirty," it was no longer seemly to lie abed all day and write at night. He committed to his so-called "stupid fits" of writing by rising early, taking a bath in a tub chilled with cubes of ice, and then locking himself in his study by nine every morning. He did not leave until he had ten pages of new material, at which time he changed into his red peasant's shirt and put on a straw hat so he might enjoy a horse ride with me along the trails that ran the length of the gardens and around the lake of the imperial park. I rode a beautiful black mare named Matilda on an English saddle and wore a jaunty English top hat.

It was a wonderful time in our lives.

While Alexander worked upstairs in the morning—and after I had transcribed his pages from the previous day—I returned to my schoolgirl's history of Russian poetry. How odd to find myself a part of that history now, the wife of the greatest Russian poet to date. During those quiet mornings, I wrote of Alexander's *Little Tragedies,* including his tale of Mozart and Salieri, and dabbled once more with a bit of my own verse to celebrate life as a newly-

Nine

The moments of greatest happiness in life are so small you can't properly appreciate them until later. When I think back on such times, I return to relaxed mornings in the countryside during the first year of our marriage, birds singing from birch trees, and one of the stray cats Alexander had taken to feeding, yowling for milk. I recall the sweet taste of lemonade on my tongue and the fresh scent of newly cut paper from my grandfather's factory, the ink still wet from Alexander's scribbled verses and the satisfaction I felt when I dipped my own feathered quill into the inkwell to transcribe the drafts of his work into a legible hand.

We had all one could desire: a loving nest for ourselves, and greater purpose in the world. I wish I'd had the foresight to savor every moment.

Alexander wanted to live as inexpensively as possible, which was impossible in Moscow. Rents were high and carriages a necessity to navigate the sprawling streets. At the same time, my wed. Alexander had dedicated a love poem to me; I should return the favor.

I relished the time away from the watchful eyes of my family in Moscow. While Alexander finished his poems in the afternoon, I took long walks in the garden, pleased to have so much time alone with my own mind, although I confess a part of me missed the excitement of the costume balls, just as my aunt had predicted, and I had started to think about the fall social season in St. Petersburg.

On one such afternoon, I grabbed an expensive red shawl Alexander had bought for me and flung it over my shoulders before pausing at a looking glass near the door. Aunt Katya had said I must always inspect myself before I left the house, so that I was well in practice and would never appear again in public with smudges or rips in my gowns. Instead of reaching for my spectacles, I chose a more fashionable lorgnette. I could hardly walk with a lorgnette before my eyes the entire time, but I knew the path well and would content myself with the heat of sunshine on my skin and the colorful blur of flowers. I adjusted my shawl before inspecting my white dress, making a full turn to view it from all angles. I then located one of my new wide-brimmed hats from the rack and perched it on top of my head, tilting it at a stylish angle.

Stretching my arms out wide as I strolled through the gardens, I stroked the silky leaves as I passed, tipping my head back to watch the dappling effects of the sunlight through spindly branches and fluttering green and yellow leaves. When I needed a break from the sun, I dipped into a blue-and-white pavilion along the shores of the lake.

As I continued down the pathway, past a marble statue of a

half-nude Apollo in a plumed helmet, I made out the figures of a couple promenading in the opposite direction. I did not particularly wish to talk to anyone, but at least I had taken care with my appearance today. I didn't think I would need my lorgnette, so smiled and walked confidently forward until their faces became clear to me.

I held my smile, but my chest constricted and my jaw tensed as I realized I was heading toward Tsar Nicholas and Empress Alexandra. Silently, I chided myself. I had been raised to revere the tsar and yet I could not deny the bristling ripple of fear, an echoing memory of the tsar's broad, flat hand too near the base of my spine. Alexander would have known how to handle this situation. He would stop and bow low to the tsar and compliment the empress. I was not Alexander, though, and wanted to avoid talking to Tsar Nicholas altogether. I wondered if I might suddenly veer to the right unseen.

While I mentally fussed, the tsar bellowed: "My dear Lady Pushkina!"

The empress, her voice surprisingly low in pitch for a woman, spoke up as well: "If it isn't Madame Pushkina!"

"Indeed it is."

It seemed I would not avoid company today. I lowered myself into a curtsy and kept my gaze fixed on the ground, on the tsar's polished black boots and the tips of the empress's slippers peeping out from her gown.

"Come, come girl. We're not in court. It is a pleasure to see the beautiful wife of our Pushkin taking fresh air."

I rose to appraise them properly. When I saw her last, the empress had worn formal court attire with a high *kokoshnik* ornamented with jewels. For her afternoon stroll, she dressed simply. The tsar's forehead looked enormous and his unruly mustache drooped, but he still cut a dashing figure in his gleaming scarlet-and-gold frock coat "Dido's sister!" He seemed proud to have made the connection. "I remember you as such."

"You are most kind. I was a mere trifle in that affair. My main purpose was to hold a look of horror while fighting a tickle in my throat. How horrifying a cough would have been!"

"It would have extended the length of time to admire you."

I smiled politely at the empress, and wishing to shift focus away from me, said the first words that came to my mind. "I believe you know one of my aunts. Ekaterina Zagryazhskaya?"

"Oh yes!" Her features relaxed. "I didn't know she was your aunt."

"My mother's half-sister."

"She must present you formally at court."

"We would like that very much," the tsar added. "Perhaps our Pushkin might be persuaded to come to court more often now that he has a beautiful wife at his side."

Alexander did not come to court because he had no formal title by which he might appear. I thought it best not to mention this fact. "Aunt Katya has been most kind to me over the years." I remembered our recent conversation and added, "Myself and my two sisters."

"Are they as charming as you?"

"More so for they are older, but I'm sure I shall soon catch up with them." That comment came out more coquettish than intended, so I shut my mouth. The tsar's gaze held mine longer than appropriate, but then who was to say what was appropriate when it came to our holy tsar. After all, I had not thought he would stroll through public gardens like a provincial landowner. Later, thinking back on that afternoon, I'd find it arrogant of this man to believe his people had nothing but love for him and that he was forever safe from harm, that we were all willing serfs, happy with our lots. We were all the tsar's to command.

"Perhaps I might send another one of my ladies, a girl named Alix Rosset, to visit you," the empress said, freeing me from the downward spiral of my thoughts. "She is a great admirer of your husband's work."

My shoulders stiffened at Alix's name—she who considered Alexander a great poet and me a woman with an empty head. Still, I could not refuse. "How lovely. Of course." I resolved to post a letter to Aunt Katya this very afternoon to see what she knew of this Alix Rosset.

"We should be off then." The empress took the tsar's arm in her hand. "I am sure we will see each other often now that we are neighbors."

"We are . . . neighbors?" I had assumed the tsar was merely visiting for a few days.

"Surely you've heard! The cholera epidemic reached St. Petersburg. The entire court is moving to Tsarskoye Selo for the summer." He still held his wife possessively with one hand, but his eyes had never left mine and I found myself drawing my shawl closer to my chest, covering every bit of flesh. "Surely you would not deny us the pleasure of your company whenever we should so desire it?"

Alexander and I were not fated for a quiet life after all. "We would be honored."

"We?" The tsar gave an abrupt laugh, but I sensed an undercurrent of annoyance. "Surely you would allow us the honor of a visit even if your husband were indisposed?"

I could not tell if that was a question or a demand. Ultimately, it didn't matter. "Of course." I worked myself into one last curtsy.

As they left, the tsar turned back briefly. I couldn't see his face for they were too far out by then, but I had the distinct impression he had pursed his lips as though to send me a kiss.

Even in the warm sun, with my shawl wrapped tightly around me, I felt frozen to the core. The next time I took a stroll in the gardens, I would keep to a more isolated path. Our days of tranquility had come to an end and I began to long for the bustle of a city once more, where I would be but one of many prizes upon which the tsar set his sights.

Alix presented herself at our doorstep before I had a chance to contact Aunt Katya. When I read her name and caught the heavy scent of vanilla and cinnamon on the calling card—beguiling and vexing at once—I pressed my lips together and managed a nod to our footman.

"Oh, you are as charming as I remember!" Alix exclaimed when she saw me. Her dark hair was parted straight in the center and she wore a day gown with billowing sleeves. I gathered we were supposed to kiss on both cheeks then, in the French manner. I detested the idea but could not avoid it. When I leaned in close, I once more took in the scent of vanilla and knew she had not added it to her décolletage for my benefit.

Alexander's boots clomped down our wooden stairs. It was not yet noon, but apparently he was willing to make an exception to his strict writing regimen for this visitor. "Alix! How good to see you!" They kissed on both cheeks with no hesitation and I caught the flutter of lashes over her wide-spaced brown eyes.

It was nearing time for our luncheon, so I invited Alix to dine with us and tried to make chitchat over borscht and egg salad. She seemed less interested in conversation than in casting a keen eye over our furnishings, which were still modest as we had not been long in Tsarskoye Selo. "This is delightful." Alix popped a pickled herring into her pert, pink mouth. "Still, surely you need greater sustenance to keep your creative juices flowing."

Alexander laughed. "I manage."

A tempest of jealousy stirred in my chest. This woman addressed my husband freely without bothering to string more than five words together for me. And not that it was any of her concern, but our meal was light as we had plans to attend a charitable musical event in the evening. By the time dessert was served—gooseberry jam with imported Devonshire cream—I thought it appropriate for Alix to make her way back to the empress.

Alix slathered a bit of jam onto a bread roll twisted into a little bow. "I would love to hear some of your new verse."

Alexander's lips lengthened into a broad smile. My husband couldn't resist the sound of his voice reading his own words, and Alix would no doubt provide an enraptured audience. "Nothing would give me greater pleasure."

I wiped my lips with one of our new linen napkins, ready to keep a watchful eye on Alix, but as she and Alexander rose to their feet, I realized I had not been asked to join them. In fact, they were already heading up the stairs. Alix's little fingers trailed along the oak banister of our staircase and she glanced over her creamy shoulder with a look of supreme satisfaction. Alix might not have cared to steal my husband, but she wanted me to know she could if she so chose.

I would not become an object of pity in my own home and

bypassed the stairs as though this had been my intention all along. "Enjoy yourselves," I called gaily, taking a seat in my favorite armchair where I could pretend to sew while listening in on them.

"I'm sure we will," Alix said.

"Alexander! I shall be ready at seven in a new gown. I chose it to beguile you."

He stopped and turned his head, tilting it curiously, while Alix sneered. I gave a playful shrug and commenced to rummage through a wicker basket I kept filled with embroidery thread.

Soon enough, Alexander's voice was raised in a dramatic baritone as he read a few lines. I was confident nothing more would happen between them upstairs.

After a few minutes, something else began to bother me, something worse even than the presence of a girl who fancied my husband alone in a room with him, though that was vexing enough. Alix had specifically requested to hear new verse, yet Alexander was reading from his historical play *Boris Godunov*, which he had finished long ago. Perhaps Alexander had nothing new to read and did not ask me to accompany them upstairs for this reason. Perhaps he did not realize how easily his voice carried in this little house, through the thin walls and floorboards, nor think I would recognize the lines.

I thought of the gowns and furnishings I had purchased over the past few months, confident we'd soon enjoy a fresh infusion of income. I still transcribed verses for Alexander in the morning, but how long had it been since I'd seen more than a stanza or two? Why had he not yet spoken of when these verses might be sold?

It took only moments for vague suspicion to evolve into

full-blown panic. If Alexander had nothing new to offer for sale, what had he been doing up there all day? Drawing pictures? More erotic verses about me, or worse yet, other women? It was only a matter of time until a baby was on the way and we had no money to spare. Rather, we owed creditors. I tossed the embroidery thread back in the basket. I had always been hopeless with stitching anyway and the design on the pillowcase had taken the shape of a malformed bird. It had only been meant to serve as linen for guests, but I didn't want to scare anyone, especially not if we would soon depend on the charity of our friends for income. *No, don't think that way.*

I grabbed a pen from Alexander's writing table and dipped it into ink to compose a letter to my eldest brother, Dmitry, who was officially charged with our family's finances even if Mother still held the purse strings tight. If worse came to worst, I would get Ekaterina and Azya on the next train to St. Petersburg, meet them there, and make proper introductions. If one of them found a wealthy suitor, our troubles would end.

And then I stopped cold. I was thinking as Mother had before my marriage. Her only concern had been Alexander's financial situation and she hadn't given a second thought to my happiness. I would not turn into Mother. I wanted my sisters to find love— even Ekaterina. Perhaps love would change her personality for the better; she could pursue that soldier she so desired. I hoped Azya would have better sense than to marry into the military, instead finding a gentle nobleman whose interests lie in breeding sports dogs or collecting French art.

I began to write, scratching the nib of the quill onto my grandfather's elegant paper. If it did so happen that one or both of my sisters made brilliant matches, money would no longer press so heavily on our minds. With such pressure relieved, Alexander might start to write again.

"Desperation has a sour scent, like spoiled milk." Aunt Katya straightened the lace ruffles at the back of my gown. "This is true in both romantic and professional matters. If one gets the sense of it about a person, one moves on."

I had hired a carriage to take me to St. Petersburg to go shopping with my aunt. It felt good to be out on an adventure. We stood now in her small formal parlor, a quaint and distinctly feminine space filled with knickknacks and handmade lace doilies. Aunt Katya and her adolescent maid, a nervous girl whose face was still spotted with pink pimples, helped me try on a gown before a full-length mirror. The gown had fashionably puffy "leg-of-mutton" sleeves and an equally fashionable low neckline, along with elegant bows on each shoulder. I thought the name for the sleeves ridiculous and their shape impractical, but it would keep me apace with the stylish Alix Rossets of the world.

"I understand," I told my aunt. "I want to make sure we are prepared for the season."

"The balls in Moscow are intimidating, and yet imagine a thousand times that in St. Petersburg. You will be evaluated not as a young maiden, but the wife of a prominent man. That is a different matter entirely."

Something sharp poked my thigh and I yowled. My aunt's maid had accidently jabbed me with a pin while adjusting a seam. I wished I had brought Liza with me. Aunt Katya slapped the poor girl on her wrist and then said, "I've heard Alix Rosset has been to visit."

"She is one of Alexander's readers." It was not purely a coincidence that I had timed my trip to take place exactly when Alix had declared she would be back in St. Petersburg. If she wished to visit my husband alone, she would have to be clever about it; I would not open the door for her. "She says she is an admirer of his work."

"The empress sent her?"

"She suggested we might become friends."

"Are you friends?"

"I confess we are not." And then I blurted: "She takes far too much interest in Alexander and too little in me, but I am attending to that and assure you she has been put in her place."

"Perhaps."

I caught my aunt's eye in the looking glass. "You do not think I am capable of defending myself from women who take too much pleasure in my husband's company?"

Aunt Katya turned to the still pouting maid. "Find some drapes to clean. If you prick them, they will not bleed."

The girl scuttled away. Even so, Aunt Katya spoke in my ear. "Be careful. The tsar takes an interest in women and sometimes has them scoped out prior to his advances. His wife . . . she learned long ago to turn the other way."

You would allow us the honor of a visit even if your husband were indisposed. I remembered the sensation of ice in my chest when the tsar looked at me. If Aunt Katya was right, and the empress had no compunctions about the tsar's affairs, Alix might have been sent to see whether or not I might be a willing mistress to the tsar. And that would mean she could spend all the time with Alexander she pleased. If our marriage dissolved, she might even step into the role of scandalous yet revered poet's mistress, all with the approval of Tsar Nicholas.

I should not let my imagination run away, yet the theory remained lodged in my mind. "I will avoid the tsar as best I can, and take care not to signal interest, no matter how slight."

My aunt managed a tight smile, her lips rosy and powder impeccable, though tiny creases at the corners of her mouth were starting to betray her age. I knew what she was thinking. After all, she was a lady of the court and had no doubt spent a great deal of her time avoiding the advances of powerful men. If the tsar wished to have something, neither of us could stop him.

Ten

"I miss Paris in the autumn," Alix was saying one afternoon in early September. She continued to make weekly visits to our rented home in Tsarskoye Selo. As was her practice, she sat between Alexander and me while the luncheon china was cleared and Alexander's favorite dessert of gooseberry jam took its place. "It is the only way to learn French properly and to absorb the culture as one should."

My husband had never seen the great cities of the west, so I'm not sure what this comment meant to accomplish other than to intimidate me. Alix cast a pitying glance in my direction, though she had not mentioned whether or not I should see Paris. As I sipped tea, I checked the rage seething inside of me.

"Alexander, you must travel there someday," the tiresome woman continued. "You would be the darling of the salons."

"Sounds grand." Alexander beamed at the compliment and dug into the gooseberries. Unlike me, he relished the hint of bitterness in the fruit and his mouth puckered with positive delight; whether this was from the dessert or the praise, I couldn't say. I smashed the tart berries deeper into the sugared preserves while Alix's eyes shifted about, taking note of the housekeeping, as though this might somehow bring to her mind the exact state of our marital affairs. Any neglect she spotted in our home was due to the fact that I still spent every night with Alexander in bed and woke too tired and happy to oversee the housework properly.

"Of course the foliage is quite lovely in Moscow this time of year," I prattled, smoothing my white day gown, needing them to remember I existed. "The park across from Mother's house appears on fire for a while in autumn. Do you remember, my love?" I gave Alexander a coy smile and then addressed Alix politely. "You speak of the French capital with such love, but how much time have you spent in Moscow? The very heart of Ancient Muscovy? I was born and raised in the ancient city, shepherded about its winding streets."

Alix looked at me as though I were an intruder who had appeared at the door with a pistol in each hand. I tried to swallow my contempt, but observed that somehow her chair had maneuvered closer to Alexander's. A stranger would assume she was the wife and I a mere visitor in my own house.

"I've seen Moscow many times," she said coldly. "With the tsar's family. When they are in town, I stay in the Kremlin."

"Oh, of course." I imagined how much fun I might have gossiping about Alix with Ekaterina. I could see my sister's stout jaw jutting with disdain and a queer pain struck me then. How I wish Ekaterina were there to subtly comment that the shade of Alix's dress did not flatter her skin tone or that she had been particularly sloppy with the rouge so obviously applied to her cheeks. "By the way, do you think it might be a particularly mild winter? Why, I stroll in the gardens late into the afternoon and not even a hint of snow touches the air."

"Really?" Alix said. "I had heard those from the country had a peculiar ability to remain in touch with the weather and such."

"From the country?" I raised my eyebrows innocently, trying to capture the polite disdain my aunt was so practiced at conveying with this expression. Alix had just made a fatal misstep and I wondered if she would be clever enough to see it.

"Muscovites are countrymen to you?" Alexander said lightly.

"Of course not, only having been born and raised near St. Petersburg, I don't have such talents." Alix's voice stammered a bit, but she soldiered on. "I was raised to spend my days discussing paintings and my evenings at the opera and ballet. I'm sure you understand, Sasha. You were raised the same."

Sasha. I took a sip of raspberry tea to hide my smirk.

"I even heard you've made a joke of it," she continued, oblivious to Alexander's—or should I say *Sasha's*—souring mood. "The Gates of Moscow? You said the city should adopt a slogan: abandon all intelligence ye who enter here." She laughed for effect.

"And yet I was born in Moscow." Alexander's voice shook with hurt feelings. "I hope this doesn't mean you think my talents are better suited for weather divination than the arts to which I have devoted my time."

Alix opened her mouth into a simple oval and I smothered a triumphant smile.

"I guess that is all we are," I told her, wondering if now Alexander might be persuaded to lie to Alix, saying we had an engagement this afternoon so she would have to amuse herself elsewhere. "Two country mice from Moscow trying to make our way as best we can."

• • •

Country mice. Despite Alexander's efforts and initial bursts of creativity, nothing could be further from the truth. As Aunt Katya predicted, life in the country did not suit Alexander long. For all he might praise the clean air or the crisp pine trees, he found excuses not to write. He rose later and later in the morning and summoned numerous reasons to stroll in the palace gardens or take his horse for a ride before his ten daily pages had been completed. He stopped asking me to transcribe drafts and I feared this was because he had no new words to offer. While I sat downstairs after yet another late breakfast—bent over a needlework pattern of birds and flowers meant to edge table linens or pillowcases—I kept my ears perked for the scratch of Alexander's nib from his quill on fresh paper.

All I heard was the click of metal against metal as Alexander cleaned his pistol. He had not yet shot holes in the wall as he had in our house in Moscow, but I knew we could not stay in our dacha much longer. Alexander was growing too restless. Truth be told, I was restless as well. I had escaped Mother's house knowing a better life awaited me, and much as I adored Alexander's company, I wished to venture out in the world more often.

And so, together, we took up residence in St. Petersburg, and I made my first appearance as a woman of the capital's society at the palace of Count de Ficquelmont, the ambassador from Austria. The night we arrived, it was ablaze with light from dozens of candelabras and chandeliers. The scent of wax and cologne and the savory late-night buffet of wild mushroom soup and beef croquettes filled the heated air inside as a haunting and lovely tune by Mozart played in the background. *Eine kleine Nachtmusik.* The composer had hailed from Salzburg and I assumed this a nod to our Austrian hosts, though I fancied it had been timed for Alexander's appearance, in honor of his story *Mozart and Salieri.*

We stood in the entranceway, under a vivid fresco of Persephone abducted by Pluto, flowers spilling from her arms as she was dragged down to the underworld. While we awaited our formal introduction, I smoothed the folds of the pale pink gown Aunt Katya had helped me choose. It had been delivered earlier in the week so that I would have plenty of time to let out the stays. I had gained a little weight in my stomach and harbored a secret suspicion as to why my waist widened and I felt woozy in the mornings. I wished this was a costume ball, for I would have preferred to slip into another persona for the evening rather than be stuck with mine. I felt insignificant and uncomfortable at once, as my corset pinched so tightly I was forced practically to stand on my tiptoes while I struggled to breathe.

"I am more nervous than I anticipated," I whispered to my husband. "Perhaps I should have pleaded a stomachache and stayed at home."

Alexander kissed my hand. "How can I keep such a ravishing creature all to myself at home? It wouldn't be just."

I smiled, but it sounded more like something the tsar would say than Alexander. "You wouldn't be content with a simple wifekin then? I suppose the poet of our time needs an elegant lady of society at his side."

Alexander stared at my hair, which I had dressed atop my head with curls near my ears. I did not think the tiara I had worn when I first met Alexander was appropriate for a married woman, but I wanted to give some reminder to my husband of that magi-

cal first night when we met, so a tiny diamond circlet rounded my
forehead, with one tiny diamond dangling in the center. No one
who saw us this evening would think for a moment we needed to
concern ourselves over money. Aunt Katya would be proud.

Alexander extended his hand—sheathed in a silver-colored
silk glove—and pressed the jewel until I felt its smooth, cold sur-
face against my forehead. "I love you as you are, my angel. If only
I could take you home right now and show you what I mean."

His low voice called to mind all the pleasures I took in his
company when we were alone, yet something was wrong. As Alexander took my elbow to guide me up the steps, I sensed the
fidgeting and shifty glances. "I overstated my case of nerves," I
whispered, pausing to catch my breath once more as we ascended.
"You needn't worry."

He gave a high laugh, as though he had been caught in an
illicit act and needed to talk his way out of it. His next words
struck me as false. "I'm not worried."

"Then why are you fidgeting?"

"I only hope you are happy with the company you find here
tonight. There is not as much talk of fashion at these affairs. The
chat takes a more political bent, as at a salon."

"Do you feel I cannot keep pace with such talk?"

"I only wish you not to feel bored."

I hesitated. It occurred to me that Alexander never would have
imagined Alix Rosset bored by politics. He had been trained at
the Impérial Lycée and no doubt Alix, Karolina, and other women
he attracted had the female equivalent: poor in quality compared
to the education given to men, but far superior to my sporadic lessons at the hands of governesses who taught me French and dancing, along with the proper way to hold a cup and saucer in polite

company and a bit about the dramatic arts, but beyond that left me responsible for my own endeavors at learning. I wondered now if this bothered my husband.

"Are you embarrassed by me?"

He opened his mouth in mock shock. "Madame Pushkina! You wound me!"

I lowered my voice. "Do you think I lack the sophistication needed in St. Petersburg? I haven't seen Paris, after all. Unlike . . ." I could not bring myself to say Alix's name, afraid I might unwittingly summon her presence.

"I have not seen Paris either." Alexander pulled his hand to his chest with dramatic flair. "I said as much."

"You are well educated. Your French puts mine to shame."

"You have a charming wit," he said.

"That is not the same as a formal education."

For a moment, his features reminded me of Ekaterina, for Alexander was pouting. His voice took on an injured tone. "You are well-read. Familiar with the classics."

"You're still evading my question," I said. "Are you embarrassed by me?"

"How could Vulcan ever be embarrassed by Venus?" He kissed my hand again. That was as direct an answer as I would receive, but must he still bring up that tired comment? I supposed his self-doubt might account for his anxiety and the concern I had regarding my own lack of education was a mere reflection of my own insecurity. It was our duty now to learn to live with these foibles and support one another. By the time our names were called, we entered the white-and-gold ballroom hand in hand.

I knew all eyes were on me. The faces were fuzzy but their

stares weighed heavily on my exposed shoulders and back. I was prepared for this, however. Aunt Katya had warned me of what to expect.

"The goddess of love herself," a voice in the crowd muttered. Near the back of the room, I spotted a tall man with a drooping mustache speaking to other men in uniform. With a sudden flush, I recognized Tsar Nicholas. I didn't see the empress.

The tsar caught my eye and his face lit like the dawn. I could not avoid his gaze, nor pretend I had not seen him, but I didn't want to approach him. Alexander was determined to say hello, so we proceeded forward, his hand still firmly in mine.

"Here's the beauty we've all waited for," Nicholas said. "I thought I would see more of you in the gardens at Tsarskoye Selo but I haven't caught sight of you since."

"Most unfortunate," I murmured.

"I hope you have not chosen to avoid me."

"I would never." In truth, I *had* been avoiding a second run-in with him.

Alexander squeezed my fingers. "We were quite busy during our final months there, and then, of course, we came here, and with all the moving and what have you . . ."

Fortunately, the tsar changed the subject, focusing his majestic attention on Alexander. "How goes your writing?"

Now it was Alexander's turn to look embarrassed, his face growing splotchy. I thought of the verse he had read for that strumpet Alix Rosset and how I had neither seen nor heard anything new. Perhaps a gentle nudge from the tsar would be just the thing to set him in motion. Something positive might yet be gained from this awkward encounter.

"You have such a delicious distraction at your side now," the tsar added amicably. "I'm quite sure I would be helpless as an infant were such a grace in my home."

Alexander clenched my hand tighter, nails pinching my skin, but smiled and modulated his voice so he sounded genial as the tsar. "I take that as compliment and know my wife takes it as a great credit as well."

"I do." I gritted my teeth. Nothing could have been further from the truth. I wondered how many other lies I would tell to negotiate my position in society. It seemed lying was a survival skill like any other, easier with practice.

"And yet it wouldn't do to have the voice of our great Russian poet silenced completely." The tsar raised his hand in the air and casually snapped two fingers together to draw the attention of a boy in ill-fitting livery passing by with a tray of champagne flutes. The tray wobbled in the poor boy's hands as he approached our group. "Surely you have some love ditty or another I might read to my wife when I wish to sweeten her mood in our private boudoir."

I drew in a deep breath, offended both on behalf of the absent empress and Alexander—whose poems were far more than "ditties" to be shared and forgotten on a whim.

Alexander's smile was placid as he straightened his shoulders and kept his voice even.

"As you have no doubt heard, I'm starting a new journal . . ."

"I *have* heard." The tsar took a flute of champagne, but his gaze never left Alexander's. "I understand political discourse is to be a planned part of this endeavor."

"Simply the conversation of a few literary sorts."

"Nothing of our history even? Our modern history?"

My stomach went cold, but Alexander kept his tone cordial. "Trifles to address the more meaningful events."

"As your friends the Decembrists were a trifle?"

Now I did not dare look up. I imagined Alexander's hand like ice in mine as we made our way to a poorly insulated cabin in the farthest reaches of Siberia.

"You no doubt realize some recent events must be excised from our history, for the good of all." The tsar's upper lip twitched underneath his mustache. "Certain aspects of our history are harmful to the welfare of our land. I can't have poets gathering under cloak of night to reinforce their feelings on the injustices of life lived under a tsar and then publish it for the world to see."

I had thought this matter behind us, but clearly the tsar had misled me when he said he held no ill will toward Alexander. Dark purple splotches mottled my husband's face and I knew his composure was breaking. I needed to help him.

"Injustices?" I said, as quickly as the words came to me. "I can't even imagine my husband listening to such words without issuing a challenge. Why I have heard nothing but praise for your generosity. Were I a jealous woman I should call the tsar my rival!"

At that, the tsar let out a booming laugh and slapped Alexander on the back while my husband maintained his stiff posture. "I would not dare consider myself a rival to such a beauty! But I trust I will see you both at my home, the Anichkov Palace, for the winter holidays as well. I suppose that will be the next time I have the pleasure of seeing Madame Pushkina." He nodded at me. "My dear Lady Pushkina."

"I will be out of town attending to business in Moscow." Alexander was meeting with my brother Dmitry, hoping to put our financial affairs in order before the turn of the year. "I'm sure my wife will be pleased to attend."

"Very good," the tsar said, taking a sip of champagne. "I shall count the days."

He bent to kiss my hand. There was nothing particularly inappropriate about his behavior. From Aunt Katya's tales, I knew people in court and society engaged in romantic games all the time, amounting to nothing. Some husbands encouraged their wives to flirt with the tsar, thinking the attention flattered them as much as their spouses.

I turned to my husband. His powerful arms were tight at his side, his hands squeezing in and out of fists. Alexander was no such man. He wanted me all to himself.

Later that night, after I had sunk into bed, exhausted, Alexander did not join me. He had never left me to sleep alone before and my eyes remained open, despite my fatigue. I listened to the minutes tick by on our clock on the mantelpiece. I knew Alexander was angry, but couldn't articulate his emotions. I wondered if this abandonment was meant as punishment. Once the hands of the clock had reached four a.m., I could no longer tolerate the uncertainty. I covered my thin nightdress with a silk robe and crept to Alexander's study. I hesitated at the door, which had been left ajar. Normally, I would never enter his study without permission, but I was determined to catch him unaware and thus measure his true state of mind.

When I entered the study, I found him crouched over the dark red covering on his round writing table, paper and quills strewn about, still in his striped dressing gown. I hoped a sudden burst of inspiration had prompted him to jot down a few words before retiring for the evening. "Are you working?"

My voice startled him and he turned quickly. I saw his pistol on the writing table, its pearly handle gleaming in the moonlight.

"What are you doing with that?"

He picked it up and assumed the same pose he had at our flat in Moscow, aiming at the opposite wall. "I thought I might leave a memento of myself behind in this place. My initials on the wall for all to admire. I still regret that I had not the presence of mind to do so at our dacha in Tsarskoye Selo."

"I ask that you do not." I liked our flat here in St. Petersburg and didn't want to see it ruined. Besides, we could not afford any damage accrued added to our list of debts.

"You do not think the think the tsar would approve?"

"I only wish to keep our home in a good state."

"Why?" he pressed. "You will attend the ball at Anichkov Palace, I suppose. As the tsar's personal guest. Do you plan to show him the flat afterward? Sit provocatively for him on our mahogany sofa so that he might admire your beauty undisturbed?"

"Why would I do such a thing? You're allowing unwarranted jealousy to cloud your judgment." If Alexander intended to be petty and snipe at me, I had no intention of playing the submissive wife. "You were the one who accepted that invitation on my behalf. It's not my fault you will be in Moscow at the time."

"In a way, it is your fault. How much did the gown you wore this evening cost?"

"I have purchased nothing more than that which we need to pursue the social season. Are you suggesting my gowns cost more than your gambling debts?"

I shut my mouth abruptly. Though I had never actually

witnessed Alexander in action at the faro or whist tables, his taste for high stakes were well known and his debts to fellow members of his gentlemen's club easy enough to spot in our household ledger. I would not accept the entire blame for our financial situation.

Alexander dropped the pistol onto his desk and sank to his chair, head in his hands, black curls splaying out around his fingers. "I'm sorry. I should not have spoken in such a manner to you. I shall attend to the debts as soon as I am able. I need to write more. I have failed you."

The harm I had so clearly caused with this accusation was etched on his face. I could hardly bear it. I approached him and placed my hands on his shoulders. "We will see our way through it. I only worry about you. Before our marriage, you were so productive and now that you and I are one . . . I fear the words are slower and I am to blame."

"You are an angel. I am to blame." He rubbed his hands furiously. "Every time I put pen to paper, I remember our debts and my heart pounds so furiously that I can think of nothing else."

I massaged his shoulders the way he liked, wanting to distract him, make him remember why our marriage was worth the expense. But I also felt I needed to introduce two subjects weighing on my mind. "I know it was not easy for you to marry a woman with no dowry. I know my mother is a trial and my father . . ." I could bring myself to say no more. I still could not shake the feeling the Goncharovs were a disaster and that Alexander lowered himself by marrying into our mess of a family.

Alexander's expression softened as he gazed up at me, blinking rapidly, like a child seeking approval. "I would have married no other."

"I shall try not to forget that, my love." I held his shoulders softly in my hands, immobilizing him. Now that my family had been called to my mind, I could not let go of the thoughts plaguing me regarding my sisters' predicament. "Perhaps our happiness means we should show generosity to others. Ekaterina and Azya are still in need of husbands. They should marry well. We could help them in this respect and then . . ." When I brought up my sisters, Alexander's gaze hardened once more. "There will be more money available for the entire family."

"You would have me live off the charity of a brother-in-law?"

"Of course not." I hadn't the heart to tell him I had already written to Dmitry and asked for help. Or that my brother was already sending me money and grumbling over Alexander's lack of responsibility with our finances. "An advantageous marriage for one or both of them would relieve so many financial pressures that might ultimately fall to us."

"Such as?"

I pressed my lips together. "Care for my father . . . Mother can't do much anymore, and we can't always rely on Babette and my grandfather to see to him." Alexander snorted. "If we can host my sisters for a season, and they make successful matches, afterward they will be off our hands for good."

That came out more brutally than I intended, but Alexander had stopped listening after the first sentence anyway. "Host them?"

I withdrew my hands from his shoulders and shifted uncomfortably. "We have room. It would make it so much easier for them. Their prospects in Moscow—"

"—are not good because they do not have you there to make introductions." He groaned. "But all of us? Under one roof? You and Ekaterina never seemed to take to one another. Will I forever listen to the two of you sniping?"

"Not forever," I said, raising a finger. "Only until she marries."

"What is the guarantee of that? It's possible no one will want her and then we're stuck."

I had considered the same possibility, likely with even more apprehension than Alexander, but had already thought of an answer. "Ekaterina is far too prideful to stay here indefinitely. She may return for a second season, but after that I am confident she would return to Mother." If not, I would order her to leave.

"A house belongs to a husband and wife." Alexander's shoulders sagged, and despite his words, I sensed he was starting to relent. "Having others running about is bound to cause trouble." He reached up and tickled my side until I squealed. "I want to enjoy you whenever I want. How will having your sisters here affect that?"

I climbed onto his lap and threw my arms around his neck. "I shall make sure you are constantly pleased."

"I will do the same for you." He leaned in and kissed me. I let out a soft moan, desperately wanting to lead him back to our bedroom, but there was still one last matter.

"Besides . . ." I tried to sound casual as his lips moved down the sides of my neck. "I don't believe we will live alone much longer. It might be nice to have my sisters here to help."

He pulled back slowly, flush with excitement. "You mean . . ."

"Yes," I told him. "I believe you are soon to be a father."

Eleven

I was fortunate to gain most of the weight in my stomach, which assuredly meant a son. Or a daughter. Or a child that would have great fortune in life. Every person I spoke to offered a different theory as to what the baby's future might hold, even when the creature was a mere speck inside me. In May of 1832, I gave birth to a beautiful, raven-haired little girl we christened Maria and called Masha.

During the first few days, Alexander carried Masha around the nursery in a circle, arms and shoulders stiff as boards. Now, nearly a month since she'd made her entrance into the world, he understood how to best cradle the back of her little head in his hands. I was grateful my husband felt comfortable doting on our daughter, and even managed to hide his disappointment our first-born was not a son. While he toted Masha about, I had a chance to brush out my hair properly and catch a moment to read.

I was enjoying just such a respite, lounging on our bed and making notes on a bit of verse I had experimented with prior to Masha's birth, attempting to capture both my excitement and anxiety at impending motherhood, when Alexander walked into my boudoir cuddling our sleeping daughter in his arms.

"She will be a great beauty," he declared, with all the bluster you might expect of a new father. "None to match her in Moscow or St. Petersburg. She shall be the toast of all Europe and crown princes will fight for her hand in marriage."

I welcomed the distraction, for my words never had connected as brilliantly as Alexander's. It remained my fate in life to read rather than write. Besides, my husband's joy was infectious, though anyone with half a brain could see he would spoil Masha. Even as a baby, she had a sly look to her that made me worry. As a girl, her role in the world would be limited. I hoped she didn't find it too disappointing.

"Why stop at Europe?" I shut my leather-bound notebook softly, taking care not to startle Masha. With her head turned, and only her black curls in my view, she looked for all the world like a miniature doll Alexander had crafted in his own likeness. I set the notebook alongside my quill and inkwell on the night-stand, and picked up a vial of lavender-scented conditioning oil to run through my hair with a brush. "Our daughter could dazzle the gentlemen of the New World or claim her right to monarchy on the African continent."

"Ah! So you have been eavesdropping, madame!" He leaned into Masha to softly touch his nose to hers, but addressed me. "You've heard me speak of her illustrious ancestor, Abram Gannibal, and all the riches that will be hers once she is of age."

"I doubt she will wait until she is of age. I think she will run from us to explore the world as soon as her feet will carry her." Once I felt the first pains of labor, I had been prepared to suffer through the night, but Masha popped her head out like she couldn't wait to be a part of this world. Mother and Ekaterina both declared it a sign she would grow impudent and I'd need to keep a sharp eye on her. At the time, I was too exhausted to fight them, and only made a silent pledge to ensure my daughter avoided the influence of her grandmother and aunt.

"Either way, we want Masha to have all the advantages in this life," Alexander said. "Wouldn't you agree, my angel?"

His tone had flattened, as though he were hiding something from me and only now dabbled with the idea of finally sharing. I stopped brushing my hair and proceeded with caution. "I think you wish me to agree to something more specific."

"I shall come straight to the point then. We need a larger flat for this little princess-to-be and all of the princelings to come."

"A larger place . . . as we had in Tsarskoye Selo?" Alix's pretty little face flashed in my mind and I tried to banish the image to the furthest recesses of my memory.

"Not as such."

"We had agreed to remain in the city . . ." We had been through this already, but I endeavored to be a good wife and hide my frustration. Although I had not yet invited my sisters to live with us, they still needed husbands. If we moved away from the capital, and all of its dazzling bachelors, I would have failed my family. Ivan and little Sergey struggled to adjust to lives in the military, while Dmitry plodded through his dull government job in the Foreign Office and the unenviable tasks of heading our family's meager finances. I could not bear to think he might be burdened with my sisters as well.

"You know how much I've grown to loathe the shallowness of social life."

I bit my lip to stay silent. Alexander "loathed" society only because he had been able to partake in balls and dancing and concerts and theater and the attentions of the court when he was a bachelor. He married after thirty, whereas I married at the age of eighteen. And while I did not for one moment regret that decision, I thought it unfair my husband should tire of the lively city at the very time when I had only started to appreciate its excitement.

"I well understand the importance of our social station. We have not only your sisters to consider, but now this miniature angel." Alexander gave Masha a tender kiss on her forehead. "Not out of the city, but farther from the center."

It seemed to me such a momentous decision should be made between man and wife, but then he handed Masha over. I drew in the fresh scent of powder on her skin as she stirred and wiggled in my arms, reaching one of her chubby hands out to grab my hair. I thought she was hungry and had taken to nursing her myself, and so I was distracted as I held her in one arm and fiddled with the top buttons of my gown with the other hand, only managing to say: "I should like to hear more before we undertake a move, especially with a little one."

"I think you will like it. Besides . . ." Alexander moved to the window and drew the thin curtains aside. I could see the wrought-iron railing enclosing our private veranda and the little flowers in pots I had placed outside. He remained in the room and yet his voice sounded as though it came from very far away. "I need peace so I might write."

"I thought you had peace." I rocked Masha in my arms, but she still gazed at her father's back with adoring eyes. "Are you not content with our home? With your study? I leave you to your work during the day and try not to disturb you."

"Wifekin, please listen. It is not your fault. We have a family now. Perhaps we might have lived like wandering nomads once, but Masha needs stability. I know I should have consulted you before I chose the place, but the spirit moved me. This little one is a beauty to inspire any writer of prose or verse." Alexander turned to gaze at Masha once more, a besotted smile softening his features.

"You are writing again, then?" I said, glancing quickly at my own notebook.

"And what of you, angel?" He tilted his head at the soft brown notebook beside me on the nightstand. "Did I not hear your own quill scratching before the little one was born?"

"Don't peek," I told him, suddenly shy. "Not yet. It is only a first draft."

He said nothing, but managed a smile so winning I could not find it in my heart to ask why he had been reluctant to answer my question and diverted attention away from his own writing so quickly.

Alexander had said that since we were parents now, we shouldn't live as nomads, and yet I could not help but think that after moving not once but now three times over the course of our short marriage, we should be considered such. I wondered if we might save money by living in the same manner of those in the deserts of the Near East, and merely roll up our tent and pack our belongings on a camel when we tired of one place and wished to move to another.

At least Alexander had the sanctuary he desired, and a spacious study with giant picture windows and a balcony. I envied him such a marvelous space for his creative endeavors. After a few days of shifting his shelves and desk and swivel chair into different configurations—to the endless delight of Masha, who crawled about, tossing his bound journals to the floor and tearing expensive Goncharov paper from his notebooks—he eventually settled in. When I rose in the morning to have my hot cocoa and English buns, I heard the nib of his quill scratch on paper. Visiting his study, I saw he had set to work once more, but had deleted so many lines and rewritten them in such small and tight script that they would be nearly impossible to transcribe into a legible hand.

Happiness in our new flat was disrupted that September when we received word my grandfather, Afansy, had passed away. I spent an afternoon locked away in my room, sobbing, not for the man my grandfather had been at the end of his life, but for the one I knew as a child. He had held me on his shoulders while we toured the factories and shared the story of all the Goncharovs who had come before. He taught me to ride, letting me choose any horse from his stable, insisting I could manage any mount—at least until my father's accident. After that, everything changed. The Goncharovs changed.

Once I calmed myself, remembering Afansy had lived a long and, for the most part, content life, I made my way out of my room, calling for Masha to be brought to me from the nursery. When I reached the parlor, daughter in my arms, I discovered my grandfather had delivered a most unusual inheritance.

The life-size bronze statue of Empress Catherine that once graced Afansy's basement now stood watch between Alexander's bookshelves and the low mahogany divan Aunt Katya had given us as a housewarming present. I stood before the statue, Masha mewling softly. Catherine's gaze fixed straight ahead, right at me, with such steely determination that even Masha could not find it in her to howl at this strange new toy. I couldn't shake the same feeling I had when young, that the statue somehow held Catherine's spirit.

"Take a look at our own empress," I whispered in Masha's ear. "We may be born women, but we are not trapped by our bodies, nor by fate. We have no limitations."

I beamed at my daughter who gave the most delightful smile in return. She was already forming dimples that made her look a bit like her Aunt Katya.

"Where in the name of all that is damned and all that is holy are we supposed to put this old girl?" Alexander asked, disrupting my thoughts. He entered the room, tucking the evening papers under his arm.

"I consider it an honor to host the great Catherine."

Alexander greeted Masha with a kiss on the forehead before tenderly brushing his lips against mine. "You're feeling better?"

"Better." I managed a smile. "Just admiring our gift. It's a . . . surprise."

"And where shall we store this honored guest?"

"The nursery? Perhaps Grandfather meant her as a gift for Masha."

"It's no gift for Masha." He started pacing and rubbing his hands, a nervous habit from his childhood he had rediscovered in recent months. "Afansy asked me to dispose of this thing for a bit of cash. I failed and now we're stuck with her."

I did not feel "stuck" with Catherine. "We could keep her in the parlor to amuse visitors."

"We shall need to take care with what we say in her presence. For all we know, she is one of Tsar Nicholas's secret police force come to spy on me, convinced I am plotting the second coming of the Decembrists, no doubt. Or perhaps she is here to watch you. I have it on good authority the tsar has spoken of passing by your window when riding about town and complains when he finds the shade drawn."

I froze, trying to force the memory of the tsar's leering face from my mind. Alexander was rubbing his hands so furiously now that I feared he might scrape a layer of skin right off, and so I kept my tone measured for his sake, betraying none of my true panic. "You cannot be serious. That sounds like a tale designed by jealous rumormongers only to make you angry. Besides, if the tsar insists on a show at my window he shall remain forever disappointed."

Alexander forced his hands apart and gave an abrupt, mirthless laugh. "Perhaps it is all part of a grand plan to keep me in an agitated state." He held his shaking hands aloft. "My mother used to bind my hands behind my back to stop me from chafing them. Do you think I should reinstitute the practice? Would you help me with that, my love?"

I raised my eyebrows high, unconsciously imitating my Aunt Katya, but could not let the subject drop so easily. "I have a solution. Let's move Catherine to my bedroom. We shall lay a trap for Tsar Nicholas. We'll leave the curtains open, and if it's true he chooses to play the peeping pervert, he shall find his own grandmother staring sternly back at him."

This time, Alexander's laugh was genuine. "You have beaten the tsar at his own game. There must be some great reward in that."

"We shall make our own reward for the shades shall frequently be drawn." I adjusted Masha to hold her over my shoulder with one arm. "Perhaps my grandfather thought the empress would inspire us to create more strong Russian children."

"The great Catherine listening in on every private moment between us? I should have to blindfold the good woman before I could even consider such a thing." A mischievous smile played on Alexander's lips and he curled his hand into a loose fist and bopped it against his mouth. He had placed a blindfold over my own eyes at times during our lovemaking, insisting it heightened other sensations. He had been right.

Despite a pleasurable evening, both of us eager to play games with the blindfold once more, sleep did not come easily for me that night. How easily I envisioned the tsar keeping watch under my bedroom window. I tossed and turned while Alexander grumbled beside me. After an hour or so, he took the pillow from his side of the bed and retired to his study. Eventually, sleep overcame my senses.

When I opened my eyes again, an apparition had formed before me. I recognized her feminine figure: the elegant posture, beautiful simplicity of her face, and clear, purpose-driven eyes I had always so admired. Her bemused expression was half-cloaked by shadow in the pale moonlight. She said nothing to me but I heard an echo of my husband's voice, merrily declaring we needed to take care for the great Catherine could now listen in on all we said. With graceful little fingers, she beckoned me to lean forward until our noses nearly touched.

"Men are not worth the trouble. Their egos are never satisfied. Men bring naught but pain. Tend to yourself. That is the path to true happiness."

The words cut deep into my heart and surprised me. After all, Catherine had enjoyed intriguing men in her life. I had thought her a woman capable of power and romance at once. "How can you of all people say such a thing?"

She poked me gently in the chest. "You are a woman of passion and ambition, yet you consider yourself second to your husband. See the error of your ways. Put your desires before that of any man."

The walls of the room began to spin. Slowly, I realized I inhabited an alternate reality. As I came to my senses, my eyes opened once more, shaking. At first I thought somehow Catherine had commanded the earth itself to quake and then I realized Alexander was hovering above me, jostling my shoulder.

"You were screaming," he said, face pale. "I could hear it even from upstairs."

I sat upright and struggled to find my spectacles on the nightstand. When the world was again clear, Catherine no longer stood at my feet, and yet her words lingered in my mind.

"I believe I saw a ghost."

Alexander's features relaxed and his eyes widened in mock amazement, though I detected a hint of genuine worry in his expression as well. "Pray tell. Only I hope it was not your dear Afansy checking up on his beloved statue, still waiting for me to sell the poor old girl to some lonely country manor."

"No." I opened my mouth, feeling a fool for what I was about to say but also finding no way to keep the words in. "I know it was just a dream, but I saw Catherine. She spoke to me. It seemed real. I cannot explain it."

"Sounds like something worth committing to paper. What did she have to say?" Alexander reached under the blanket and tickled the inside my thigh. "Tell me she didn't spy on us in the bedroom. Tell me she didn't offer advice on that part of our lives."

"Stop it." I batted his hand away, giggling, and kissed his cheek.

"Then what did she say?"

Men bring naught but pain. Minding my words, I stilled my tongue before I could speak. I did not think Alexander would appreciate the great woman's advice for me. "I can't remember anymore. You know how it is with dreams. In your memory for a moment and then fleeting as the wind."

Alexander seemed to accept this, and eventually the apparition of Catherine dissolved into no more than a vague memory. But from then on, I took care when passing by her statue.

The following summer, I gave birth again, this time to a red-haired little boy. Though he resembled my husband's carrot-topped brother, I named him after Alexander and we called him Sasha. He was sweet enough, but unlike his sister, reluctant to leave the womb. He came during the humid days of July, right after the white nights of the northern summer, and his labor took two full agonizing days.

Afterward, as I cuddled the sweet bundle in my arms to nurse him, Masha held her father's hand and regarded her new brother with a mixture of wonder and disgust. I began to consider if there might be a way to prevent another baby, at least for a little while, so my body might recover, though that was but wishful thinking in those days.

Soon we fell into a routine. While Alexander wrote, I spent mornings with Masha and Sasha, took a respite midday as they napped, and then shared luncheon with my husband and later reviewed the household accounts. Despite a new infusion of capital from my late grandfather's estate, the numbers troubled me. I thought Alexander might insist on being paid in gold rubles rather than the creditor's slips that so often failed to be worth the designated amount. I resolved to confront him with this idea.

I looked all around our flat for Alexander and was surprised to find him at last crouched before the statue of Catherine, one of his notebooks splayed on his lap and a charcoal pencil in his hand. He was drawing furiously, as he liked to do when pondering ideas for a new work. I wondered if Catherine had inspired some idea or another and my heart soared. My grandfather's gift was not as useless as Alexander had previously supposed. I peered over his shoulder, expecting to see a likeness of Catherine rendered on the paper.

Instead, Alexander had sketched a rough outline of another statue, one Catherine had gifted to the city of St. Petersburg before either of us was born. It was the equestrian statue that stood near the banks of the Neva. The actual statue portrayed Peter the Great on a majestic mount, his long arm outstretched, indicating where his new city would stand.

When I looked closer, I saw the statue, at least in my husband's rendition, had come alive, for the horse was in motion, but there was no rider. "What is that? What are you doing?"

He lost his balance and fell to the floor with a thump. "Hurting my arse, apparently."

"I'm sorry." I started to laugh. I had not realized his concentration was so intense my soft words would startle him easily. "I was curious. I thought you were sketching the great lady."

"Not at present." Alexander rose to his feet, rubbing his backside with one hand while clutching the notebook in his other. "I have thought about her quite a bit as of late. After she appeared to you in your dreams. It wouldn't do to ignore such a sign." Alexander began to pace, curling his free hand into a fist and pounding the notebook with it as though keeping time with a tune in his head. "Your great Catherine wants me to speak of the statue she erected to celebrate her great predecessor Peter. It might be intriguing to write about the storm that nearly drowned our city in 1824 as well. You remember?"

I was but twelve at the time, and yet word of this disaster had reached even Moscow. "I do. They say the streets were flooded so high carriages were useless and boats used instead."

"I am not sure yet how it connects to this." He opened the notebook once more to the image of the horse and tapped it with a finger. "I endeavor to find out. I believe I shall soon have something new for you to transcribe."

"Then I expect you will need more time in your study." My lips trembled for it was good to see him excited about his work once more. "We'll stay out of your way."

"I am thinking rather that I shall spend the time traveling. I believe I should like to go research the history of Catherine's old enemy Pugachev and his insurrection and then go to the countryside and write in peace."

My lips stilled. I did not think my own husband would find it necessary to leave me in order to work, and I couldn't help but worry how the tsar would react to Alexander's newfound taste for the history of rebellion. "For how long?"

The question seemed to confuse him. "As long as it takes."

"We could come with you . . ."

He took me in his arms. "I take this to mean I will be missed?"

I tried to hug him back, but my heart was not in it. We had two small children now. He had responsibilities. If I wished to live without a man in my bed, I would not have married. Yet if he truly needed time away from us to write, I knew I should not try to stop him.

"The idea for the poem about Peter's statue and the flood *is* intriguing," I told him, mushed up against his shoulder.

"I hope so. What good am I to anyone as a husband, a subject, a man, if I am no poet?"

"You are that." The hint of sadness in his tone troubled me, and I hugged him back fully at last.

"Besides, it's not as though I expect you to spend every evening moping around this flat and pining after me," he said. "You are young and beautiful and meant to be admired. Surely you don't think I am so cruel as to deny you that? Bring the men of St. Petersburg to their knees. A little amorous torture will do those rascals some good in the long run, believe me."

The edge in his tone bothered me and I pulled back a bit. If Alexander were permitting me to coquette in his absence, I could only assume he intended to do the same while away. Romantic game playing was not only tolerated but expected, yet I could not help but think this separation would harm our marriage. "If you must go, come back to us as quickly as you can."

His smile would haunt me for the rest of my days, for it conveyed nothing but pure love and absolute trust. "I will write to you every day and kiss every letter you send to me."

It was one of the last times in my life I would put the needs of a man before my own.

Twelve

My lady's maid, Liza, put her hands over her mouth to stifle a smile. She was the same pink-cheeked girl who had been the first to address me as Madame Pushkina.

"What is it?" I said, making a turn before the full-length looking glass. "Don't you like it? I've spent hours . . . you've spent hours. I thought we agreed."

"It's beautiful! Only . . ." She lowered her hands and made a quick motion in the direction of my décolletage.

I looked down. "It is low cut."

Liza's giggle sputtered through her fingers.

"The actual women of the Minoan culture bared their breasts completely." I toyed with a bracelet, a gold bangle in the form of a snake that was meant to rest on my upper arm. "Do you think I should consider that instead?"

She gasped and then it was my turn to laugh until at last we collapsed into a heap together on the divan, fanning our faces and staring at the remnants of the afternoon's creativity scattered about the room I had designated for sewing: scraps of fabric, discarded paper patterns, gold braiding, and loose laurel leaves. I planned to debut this costume at the Anichkov Palace the last Sunday before Lent, the final and grandest costume ball of the season.

"The priestesses were certainly daring with their garb." Liza dabbed her damp eyes with a handkerchief she'd kept tucked in her apron pocket.

"They were powerful women. I intend to honor them as such."

"I've heard the tsar is an admirer of women, powerful and otherwise, but I don't know that he will let you go so far as to display your bosom."

"I suppose I could give him a lecture on historical accuracy." On Alexander's shelves, I had found a volume on the ancient civilization on the island of Crete and devised the gown based on illustrations of the matriarchal cults of the Minoan culture, particularly the high priestess in the Temple of the Bull. "Besides, I am an old married lady now, a matron with two children. Tsar Nicholas will hardly give me a second glance."

"He won't be able to concentrate, nor look you in the eye."

Though my shoulders tensed, we laughed a little more. Alexander had been gone for two months now, but the initial pain of missing him had dulled to a low ache. Fortunately, I found plenty to keep my mind occupied while he was away. I had set up a play school in the nursery where Masha could pretend to be governess every morning and lord over a small army of French dolls Alexander had bought for her. As Masha pretended expertise on mathematics, strutting about with my oval-shaped spectacles perched on her head, Sasha sat in my lap, wriggling his fingers in his mouth. Meanwhile I balanced a slate in one hand and did my best to keep pace with the mock lessons. In the afternoons, while the children napped, I conducted a perfunctory review of the household finances and then dismissed the steward, sure Alexander's new verse about the horseman would add a fresh infusion of income to our household.

Later in the evening, once the children were in bed with a nanny in the next room, and I read for an hour or so, the house grew too quiet for my taste. When I remained home alone, I stared wistfully at Alexander's side of our marriage bed until I broke down and re-read his most recent letter, bristling at every mention of an innkeeper's daughter or German actress he had met in passing. I kept our children happy while Alexander spent his time squiring hens to whatever traveling puppet show passed for entertainment in the country. If my husband could have fun without me, I could return the favor, and so I spent most nights at balls and public dances.

I confess that much as I longed for my husband, I found the attention of men a thrill. This was vanity, but Alexander had told me I might coquette while he was away, flirt with other men and even allow them to make small declarations of love, as per the conventions of the day. I chose to share the comments of my admirers with him in letters, hoping the playful tales of my small conquests of the heart might compel him to return home. He responded grumpily, complaining of men chasing after me like dogs, sniffing my arse, and cheekily asking for a list of men I had danced with in alphabetical order. Still, if he could mention other women in his letters, I saw no reason I could not mention other men in mine.

My efforts were soon rewarded.

In late November, while I danced a mazurka with a handsome member of the Calvary Guard, a footman tapped me on my shoulder. I turned, prepared to be upset. I hadn't been out in three nights because Masha was ill with a cold. The guardsman was a particularly skilled partner, lifting me as though I was made but of air, and gliding with me across the shining dance floor with such ease I felt as though we were flying.

The poor footman must have sensed my displeasure at the interruption for he was practically shaking in his fine blue livery and cowered before me. "I am so sorry, Madame Pushkina, but I was instructed to find you at once."

My stomach clenched. Masha had seemed well on her way to recovery this evening, propped up in her little bed in the nursery and ordering her nanny about like a field marshal, but now I wondered if I had left her too soon. "Is everything all right? Am I needed at home?"

The footman shifted from foot to foot, his youthful features reminding me of a masculine version of my own Liza. "It is . . . well, it is unusual . . . I was told to tell you the tsar . . . he would like to see you."

My initial relief reverted back to panic. "Is he in a receiving room?"

The footman looked at the floor. The music came to a halt and I thought the entire ballroom must have heard him say: "I have been asked to escort you to a carriage."

The handsome guardsman managed a quick "Madame Pushkina" before backing away. I swore every eye in the room had turned to me. I remembered Alexander's comments about his enemies at court. *Those who see fit to praise my writing while treating me like I'm beneath their contempt when I dare arrive at a ball.* Aunt

Katya had told me that as the poet's wife, I would attract more scrutiny. I tried to still my pounding heart, but no amount of concentration could accomplish this task. I couldn't be alone with the tsar in a carriage, but how could I diplomatically refuse his request? To say it was improper would impugn his reputation; to agree called mine into question.

"Let me just get my pelisse . . ." I walked slowly to the cloak room, the footman at my side. Perhaps I could feign illness. Or mention Masha! That might work. I felt a pang of guilt for using my daughter thusly, but she *had* been unwell after all, and it was not as though she shied away from intrigue, even at her young age.

Once I had my pelisse, the footman escorted me out into the cold November night. I hurried now, pulling the thin wrap over my gossamer ball gown, the perspiration on my brow freezing on my skin. I would just show my face in the window and greet the tsar. Then I would mention Masha at once and call for my own horses. As we approached the carriage, I located my spectacles in my reticule and pulled them on, thinking the tsar might be put off.

Once the world came into focus, I saw the coach before me bore no imperial insignia and the fine horses stomping their hooves in the cold were the ones I chose when we first moved to the city.

"You have tricked me!" I cried, as the footman set a stool down before me, not that I needed help. The curtains were drawn, but my heart skipped in my chest as I realized whom I would find inside.

"Have a good night." The footman closed the door behind me, a whisper of a smile playing on his lips.

And there was Alexander, now sporting a lush black beard.

I thought of all I might say to him about how badly I missed him and how much I had needed him at home.

"I missed you, angel." His features were contrite, at least so far as I could tell under the thick facial hair, but his eyes aflame. My limbs softened, my insides seeming to melt, just as they did when he pulled my body to his at night. An unseen force drew me to him and now I was the one who forgot all logic and decorum, and took his chin in my hand and pressed his lips to mine. Our kisses were always exquisite, slow and lingering, but this moment was so powerful I gave no thought that we were still in our coach parked before the palace. I knew only that my body was on fire and would have that which it desired. I guided his hands to the gown, helped him pull the thin material up over my hips, needing the intense rapture of his body united with mine. I was no longer human, but some primal creature of nature.

I had never felt more alive. Never closer to my true self.

Afterward, the pleasure seemed to float upward and then pop and dissipate, like bubbles in champagne. A delicious sleepiness overcame my senses as I cuddled against my husband's chest, but Alexander could not remain still and scrambled for the small valise he had stowed under the seat.

"It is finished!" he said. "I cannot wait for you to read it."

I had just dozed off and took a moment to comprehend what he meant. "Read what?"

"The tale of the horseman . . . the flood . . . Peter . . . here!"

I recognized his heavy notebook, the brown leather binding our elegant Goncharov paper and the lappet and old brass buckle protecting the contents. I knew he had written the verse quickly, for he had not had time yet to transcribe it in a legible hand and in some spots I could still detect the scent of the ink. Of course, I was well familiar with his writing and could decipher the words quickly enough, especially as it seemed he had revised this work little, writing cleanly from the start.

No doubt you're familiar with the great work that would come to be known as *The Bronze Horseman*, but permit me to describe what it felt like to read this verse for the first time. The impulse to sleep, so powerful mere moments before, waned. The carriage fell away; my husband fell away. Reality meant nothing. I was no longer Natalya Pushkina, but Alexander's lovelorn narrator, trapped in his insanity as the waters of the great Neva rose to flood, and the massive statue of Peter and his horse roared to life, chasing the tormented man through the once beautiful streets of our city. The same rhythm to his language that enchanted me when I read *Onegin* swept over me now, making me feel life was beautiful, and the possibilities endless.

By the time I finished, I was in tears. All of Alexander's time away had been worth it. I had already known he was the greatest poet our land had known. This only confirmed it.

"You enjoyed this trifle?" he said shyly.

I slapped his arm playfully, my fingers lingering on his bicep. "Do not pretend modesty."

He bobbed his head and tugged at the new beard, too excited to remain still. "It's good, then? I'm right?"

"I see so few corrections—"

"It came to me quickly in one of my stupid fits," he said, "as though inspired from above. I tell you, I feel a new man." He tilted his head. "But assure me this is not mere flattery. You're not simply hoping to get on my good side, are you? It is good, is it not?"

"Flattery is easy enough when you present me with such magnificent verse."

He grinned, but his fist tapped the inside of the coach. "From the tone of your letters, I know you've had much practice at flirtation while I was away."

So that's what this was all about. "Are you saying you're jealous, husband? Wish to have me all to yourself when you were the one who suggested I enjoy society? Surely you must realize you own my heart and my body. Did I not prove that a few moments ago? I only wish for you to remain close and not leave again."

He leaned back once more and I returned to snuggling against his chest, taking in the sweet scent of tobacco clinging to his neck. He stroked my hair as we rode home, but looked out the window the entire time. I would not say his mood had soured, but it certainly had turned more contemplative. I wished he would share the true thoughts racing through his mind, but I had not the courage to compel him to do so.

"Look at your pretty mamma." As I sat in the sewing room, continuing work on my Minoan priestess costume, Alexander popped in, rocking Sasha in his arms. He took in the headpiece and gown and jewelry while Sasha gurgled happily and scrunched some of Alexander's black curls in his blotchy little fists. "Look at what your pretty mamma made."

"Let him know he has a 'clever' mamma." I held up one of the gold bangles, meant to resemble a snake with imitation emeralds for eyes and a forked tongue.

"Look at your clever mamma." Alexander examined the costume once more and smiled at me slyly. "She is dressing as a priestess of the sun."

"Not a priestess of the sun, but a priestess of the bulls."

"I like the ring of 'sun' better. How many men do you suppose will fall in love?"

"No one will fall in love with me."

"You either underestimate your own charms or overestimate the ability of men to leave well enough alone. Even the tsar will follow the priestess into her sacred temple. Likely he will lead the way."

I stuck my tongue out and he chuckled and wandered off with Sasha. The thought of Tsar Nicholas still made my stomach tighten, but at least I was a matron now, not a fresh young wife.

Besides, my costume looked spectacular. I modeled it for Alexander later that night in the privacy of our bedroom, and he actually dropped to his knees. "I'm the first to fall," he told me, lifting the hem of the gown and kissing the inside of my thighs while I moaned with delight. "I am the first to worship the priestess of the sun."

His good mood was not destined to last.

By the night of the costume ball, I had confirmed I was two months pregnant with my next child. As we passed the enormous white Grecian columns and ascended the scarlet floor runner on the front staircase of Anichkov Palace, I was glad I had decided on the priestess costume, as its flowing shape was comfortable and easy to move in. Alexander had chosen not to wear a costume, but looked elegant in his evening frock coat with Dutch lace ruffles at his wrists and collar. We made a fine-looking pair.

"My Lady Pushkina!" Once we reached the top of the staircase, the tsar brushed past his courtiers and toward me without as much as a glance at my husband. "Welcome to my palace. How ravishing. What is this affair?"

His gaze seemed to drink me in, but I suppressed a shudder

and kept my tone light. "It was intended to represent a priestess in the cult of the bull in Ancient Crete, Your Majesty. But my husband . . ." I tugged on Alexander's arm to ensure he was included in this conversation. ". . . has renamed me the priestess of the sun."

"Clever fellow," he said, though his eyes had not left me. "Why don't you turn around then so we can appreciate the full effect?"

Hearing the tsar's request, several fawning courtiers joined our circle, drinking champagne as the orchestra struck up a merry waltz. I felt Alexander's temper seething—like a monster trapped beside me—and wished the tsar had shown more attention to him before throwing the weight of his flattery on me. Though wary, I twirled as requested. The ladies in gowns and costumes and the men in their fine uniforms swirled into a fuzzy but pleasant blur around me.

"It would be jolly if you assumed a pose the priestess might take," the tsar said. "I still remember how charming you were as Dido's sister. Would you be willing?"

In that moment, my fear of the tsar dissipated as this new opportunity presented itself. You might think me a foolish and vain woman in this moment, but you must understand I had found my true passion in masquerade. This was my art, my version of the poetry Alexander crafted, and I wanted nothing more than to transform into the priestess, powerful and feared, more so even than our tsar. Inspired, I slipped the bangles shaped like snakes from my arms and held one in each hand. Then I raised my arms like the woman in the picture, snakes aloft over each shoulder. I could not see my own face, but I was certain I had the same wild look in my eyes as the woman. I held the pose. I was no mere wife to a poet and subject to an all-powerful tsar. I *was* the priestess.

The courtiers clapped as though I had given a command performance of one of Mr. Shakespeare's plays on the London stage. The spell snapped. I smiled and curtsied.

"Smashing!" the tsar said. "I declare you queen of the ball."

"Most kind of you." I placed the bangles back on my wrists and up on my arms.

"It is only the truth, Lady Pushkina."

I heard a derisive snort beside me and realized it came from my husband. I am ashamed to say I had forgotten him. "You still address my wife in the English manner then?"

The tsar gave a careless shrug and smiled affably. Of course, Mother's tabby was playful with a mouse too before delivering the final bite that snapped its neck. "Seems appropriate for the beauty."

"And yet she is a good *Russian* woman," Alexander said. "My *Natasha* has many admirers here. I'm sure she will want to greet every one and honor them with her favor. It's not fair for one man to monopolize her, even if that man is her sovereign."

"Have you not monopolized the company of other men's wives?"

Alexander's hands bunched into fists while a cold prickling sensation ran down the length of my back. Alexander had deliberately contrasted the informal version of my name with the tsar's westernized affectation, and then insulted him on top of it. The tsar was lashing back and openly taunting him.

"But I see your point," the tsar added quickly. "Bad manners to monopolize the queen."

I wanted to say something to smooth things over, but Alexander pulled me away before I had the chance to gather my thoughts.

"You must mind your words," I whispered fiercely, once we were out of earshot.

"Is it not true?" Alexander's tone calmed as mine grew more heated, but his cheeks still flushed a dark, purplish color and his scent had grown heavy with the stress of the moment. "Have you not many admirers?"

"Every woman in this city has admirers. I have only one husband. You know this."

"A husband who looks a fool."

"You do not look a fool except when you snap at the tsar. Do you really wish to make this man an enemy? See our children raised in a prison camp?"

"It might do us good. I could write and you could learn modesty."

I shook free from his grip and turned, catching a flash of fear in his eyes.

"I'm sorry," he said, rubbing his hands now. "Please. Just listen."

Reluctantly, I allowed him to take my arm. Alexander steered me through the foyer, into a private alcove, under the watchful eyes of sculpted marble cherubim with pursed lips. He kept his voice low. "The tsar wishes to make a fool of me and not just in the way he drools over you. I should call him to the field of honor for his impudence."

The casual reference to a field of honor made me stiffen, but surely even Alexander wasn't so hot tempered as to challenge Tsar Nicholas to a duel. "I hear him flatter many men's wives because he can. There is nothing more to it than his desire to hold us all under thumb."

I gasped, realizing now what I had said, and glanced around to make sure no one heard. Alexander only chuckled and reached into an inner pocket of his evening coat to hand me a note. "Speaking of . . . I suppose I should share this. A summons from the tsar was delivered this very morning."

I held the thick paper in my hand, noting the imperial seal and extravagant handwriting. The tsar had presented Alexander with a loan for several thousand rubles and offered him the post of a junior gentleman of the chamber at court. I bit my lip, determined I would write again to Dmitry to ask for more money, and silently considered goods I might sell to a pawn shop: a pearl necklace and perhaps one of my better shawls. Anything to keep us from slipping deeper into the tsar's debt. For now, however, I chose to emphasize the second part of the missive. "This is an honor, not an insult."

Alexander snatched the letter from my hands and stuffed it back into his pocket. "If I were ten or twelve years younger perhaps, but for a man of my age it is an insult. I have no doubt the tsar is laughing at me behind my back. His silly coterie as well. I can hear them now: a junior posting for a junior-sized fellow."

"You're only being clever for the sake of being clever. It's a lower rank because you're new to court."

"I have an alternate theory," Alexander said. "And I doubt I'm the only one with suspicions as to the tsar's motivations in awarding me such a position."

I crossed my arms in front of my chest, the gold bangles jangling. "What might that be?"

"He wants *you* to attend official court functions and has contrived to assign me this lowered position as an excuse to see you more often. He has handed me the cuckold's horns and asked me to place them directly on my own head. After the display I saw a few moments ago, I suppose I can't blame the man. He likely feels he has been led to believe he can have what he wants from you."

I focused on the smirking cherubim along the thick crown moldings, trying to calm myself for the sake of the child growing inside me, but my anger demanded expression. "That's ridiculous."

Alexander rubbed his hands together again and then, realizing what he was doing, thrust them behind his back. "Do you find Nicholas attractive? It is said he is a handsome man . . ."

"You can't imagine my casual compliments anything other than flattery."

"You encourage his advances."

"I have done nothing wrong. If you wanted a drab wife you should have married one of the women you count among *your* admirers."

"I do not flaunt myself in front of my admirers."

"You do! You bask in attention and yet you would deny me the same pleasure." My voice was rising, but now I scarcely cared who heard us. "You dangled Alix Rosset before me. Even in your own proposal letter, you could not help but mention that foul Karolina."

Alexander looked as though he thought I might strike him. "I only wished to be honest with you and your family."

"At what cost? Do you not think that wounded me? Did you not think it would enflame my jealousy?" I began to feel dizzy and the floor seemed to slip out from underneath me, but I kept my footing and continued. "You were the one who encouraged me to be a part of the social life of this city and now that I take pleasure in it, you wish me to be holed up at home, as your prisoner. Then you should never be troubled with another man desiring what is yours."

Beads of perspiration began to glisten in his black side whiskers. "That is not the point. Tell me plainly. Has Nicholas asked you to be his mistress?"

"Alexander!" I cried. "Shame on you."

"I suppose you're a victim in all of this as well. If the tsar asks to take you to his bed, how could you refuse? You would never share the affair with me. So I will forever be doomed to uncertainty."

I could not control my words. "Our child . . . the one inside of me now. Do you wish to upset me to cause it harm? Would you have me miscarry?"

That was the moment the villain of St. Petersburg was born in her first incarnation: cruel and vainglorious wife. Alexander loved Masha and tiny Sasha beyond reason and I had accused him of trying to murder his next child. Yet my pulse raced so hard, my words had merit. He should never try to upset me, particularly not in my current state. The base of my temples throbbed and the back of my throat ached. "I don't feel well. Take me home."

His eyes hardened as though he had summoned the powers of Medusa to turn me to stone. "You are the queen of the ball. Surely you don't want to disappoint your admirers."

"I do not wish to remain in this place any longer."

"You will embarrass us." He inclined his head toward a group of women clustered near the dance floor, leaning in to one another and holding fans before their mouths so they could whisper to one another. "People will think we had a fight."

"We *did* have a fight."

"Even so, better to keep it to ourselves."

It seemed a wife was expected to stand proudly by her husband and ignore his female admirers, but a man might glower and pout whenever his wife was praised. I was proud of my costume, which I fancied a tribute to the powerful women of a great ancient culture. I had hoped my husband would take pride in it as well. Instead he had ruined the night. I stepped away, determined to find my own way home without his assistance.

The tsar could not destroy our marriage, but I feared Alexander's jealousy could.

After our fight, some of Alexander's usual circle gathered around him. Though the men looked me up and down, this crowd seemed far more interested in gaining proximity to the poet than flirting with me. Alexander was accepting pieces for his new journal and no shortage of struggling writers and artists sought paid assignments.

When I asked Alexander to take me home, I had exaggerated my symptoms, but now my mind and body conspired and my stomach turned so violently I feared I might vomit all over the glossy floor. I did not know what effects the grippe might have on the baby growing inside me and I endeavored to find a place where I might rest for a bit. I spotted a long sofa along the opposite wall, heavily carved with rosewood cornucopias but inlaid with an inviting, floral cushion and matching pillows where a woman feeling faint might rest her head.

Once I had settled myself on the soft cushions, and as I was staring at my husband's tense back, a man stepped before me. He was quite tall. At first I could see only his broad chest: full silver-plated armor and a staff with ribbons tied to the top. Tributes from fair maidens, I supposed.

"My lady." The Arthurian knight swept into a low bow that made the metal armor clank. He dressed from British mythology but spoke French with a lilting accent, like a native. "I've been admiring you from afar all night and finally have a chance to see you up close."

"I hope I did not disappoint, Sir Galahad." I knew this comment made me a coquette, but I was still furious with Alexander. I felt abandoned and hoped he might overhear.

The man drew himself upright once more: a fair-haired gentleman with a trim mustache and sparkling blue-green eyes. I confess I lingered on his face a little longer than I might have were it not so pretty, and temporarily forgot the pain low in my stomach.

"Sir Lancelot, actually," he said with a smile that animated his handsome features. "Though you're dressed as one of the ancients, I should like to think of you as fair Guinevere."

I looked about, fervently praying Alexander couldn't hear us after all. I had not meant to make him King Arthur—history's most famous cuckold—by proxy. "Priestess of the sun, actually. My husband dubbed the costume such."

The knight looked behind him, where my gaze had landed. "Your husband is the poet?" His tone couldn't have been less impressed.

"The finest in Russia."

"I suppose there is not much competition for that title."

My smile collapsed. "That's most unkind and nowhere near the truth."

The knight swept into another bow, the mischievous glint in his eyes mitigating the rudeness. "Forgive me, but you see it is only that in France poets are as common as the air we breathe. We are inspired by the beauty of life."

I suppressed a grimace as my stomach cramped. "If you feel Russians lack culture, you must find my company dull."

"You do not lack beauty." He looked at me intensely, even more so than the tsar dared. The last man who had looked at me that way on first meeting was Alexander.

I rose and extended my hand formally, hoping to break the tension. "Natalya Pushkina," I told him. "A simple girl from this simple land."

He kissed my hand softly. "Georges d'Anthès. Enchanted."

When he spoke, another cramp wrapped around my middle. I groaned and doubled over. My legs felt weak beneath me and the floor was unsteady. The knight's expression changed and before I could protest his strong arms broke my fall as my knees buckled.

"My lady . . ." His face, though hovering above me, had gone fuzzy and I felt another wave of sickness overtake me. Behind the knight, I could just make out Alexander's form, rushing toward me.

"My husband," I whispered, throat raw. It felt as though my insides were being turned out. "I need him. I need to go home. I need Alexander."

Thirteen

Our third child did not survive to see life outside of my womb. The pain gripped me until I screamed and then the blood came, dark and smelling of death. And just like that it was over. A court doctor was called and I spent the night in a delirium of fever. When the fever finally broke, the doctor chided me for nursing my first two babies. I had suffered from soreness and irritation in my breasts, which I had largely ignored. The doctor said my actions resulted in an infection. Though it was unclear whether or not this was true, he strongly advised a wet nurse for children to come, carrying on about the virtues of milk from a strong Russian peasant woman and the evils of following modern child-rearing notions from the west.

I nodded obediently, hoping the doctor would leave soon. Alexander paced on the opposite side of my boudoir, rubbing his hands together.

After another day, the children were allowed to visit. Masha and I played cat's cradle with yarn while Sasha gurgled happily at my side. Alexander watched us from the other side of the room, still seemingly unwilling to touch me, as though he feared he might hurt me.

"You almost died," he said despairingly. "I should have insisted on a wet nurse."

I sighed. Though the fever was scary, I thought the doctor had greatly exaggerated my condition. "I feel much better. I only need to rest and then I'll be fine."

"It's my fault," Alexander blurted.

Masha paused our game, the yarn caught in her pudgy little fingers, and turned to look at him. "Papa was bad?"

"He wasn't bad. He didn't do anything. Alexander, you mustn't say such things and especially not in front of . . ." I inclined my head toward Masha. "I will be fine."

"I was so angry with you . . ."

"You were upset. We were both angry at each other. It happens."

"But I was not even angry with you," he cried. "I was angry at *him* and I took it out on you. How can I live with myself?"

"Who?" Masha cocked her head, black curls dancing.

"Tsar Nicholas," Alexander spat. "The very ruler of this land. The man who can make all of us perform as puppets on a marionette string as he sees fit and if we question his authority—"

"Masha, why don't you take your brother? You can help feed him."

"Ooooh!" Masha cried while I rang the bell so that the nanny might meet them as quickly as possible. As soon as the woman entered I said, "Perhaps a snack for them both. Masha may help you feed the baby."

The nanny pressed her lips together in a judgmental manner, reminding me of Mother. Masha could be a handful and empowering her was likely a bad idea, but I thought it better than allowing her to hear her father rant about the tsar. Who knew what Masha might say outside our home and how easily word could travel to the ears of the tsar's secret police.

Once they left the room, I grabbed a brush and conditioning oil, for my hair was still tangled from the night in bed with fever. The motion helped calm me. "You can't say such things in front of her. You know how she is. She might repeat something."

"It's just . . . it is like he wants to toy with me for his own pleasure . . . and the way he looks at you . . ." Alexander rubbed his hands together so hard they were sure to chafe.

"Promise me," I said. "Promise you will stop saying such things to anyone but me."

He looked down at the floor as though kicking something that wasn't really there.

I stopped brushing my hair. "Promise me," I repeated.

"There is more to it than flirting with you and assigning nonsense positions to me, though that is horrible enough. I have received word the tsar's censor refused to allow publication of *The Bronze Horseman*."

"What?" The brush fell from my hands and to the floor with a clatter.

"It has been deemed seditious." Alexander still would not look at me. "They have agreed to allow publication of the prologue, but the rest of the work is to be revised if it is ever to see light of day in our fine country."

"But it is brilliant as is." I remembered the thrill of reading the words for the first time, how the carriage seemed to fall away and I stood in the middle of the flood and the madness of Evgeny's mind. "It would be a crime to revise it. Do not change a word."

"We think alike, my Natasha."

"The tsar must be mad. Madder than Evgeny in the poem."

Alexander turned to glance over his shoulder and then regarded me once more with a sly smile. "Now, who should watch their tongue? We wouldn't want that last comment out in the world. We might even have spies in our household. Despite his little love affair with you, I doubt Nicholas would care to be called mad."

I decided to let the comment about the love affair pass. Alexander's poem should have sold well enough to keep us in the clear for months if not years to come. To have it stopped on a whim . . . the injustice made my head spin. Yet Alexander was right. I needed to guard my tongue. Even at home.

"So you see I cannot make a promise I won't keep," he told me.

"Promise you'll try," I said, exasperated.

"Anything for my Madonna." Alexander kneeled at my feet and took my hands in his, caressing the inside of my palm. I shivered with pleasure, but knew he could not touch me more intimately, not in the way I liked, for weeks to come.

"I think time away would be good for your recovery," he said. "You mentioned you wish to see your family in Kaluga. You could spend time with your sisters. Perhaps it will be good for me as well. Being near you and unable to fulfill my husbandly duty? It is a torture no man on earth should be forced to bear."

I managed a faint smile. "How easily you turn everything to the dramatic."

"Perhaps you can take this opportunity to deliver the great Catherine back to her rightful spot in your family's basement."

"Never. She wouldn't have it."

"I shall spend some time away from the city as well," Alexander declared. "I can write."

"I like that idea. We are a growing family after all. It's only a matter of time until the next one."

"Down, but not out." The thought of writing once more seemed to chase Alexander's melancholy away. He tapped his mouth with a closed fist and I could almost see the wheels turning in his mind. "By the time you are back in the city, I shall have new work to sell and your charm shall help me get the highest price possible for my labors."

At the time, I had no doubt Alexander could write another piece as great as *The Bronze Horseman*. This time with no content to which the censors could possibly object. Once again he would be the adored poet of St. Petersburg and even the tsar could not touch us.

A month later, I was strolling around the lake on my late grandfather's property. The pathways were edged with fir trees and shrubbery formerly shaped into deer and rabbits, now neglected and grown wild. I drew in the fresh country air tinged with the scent of pine from the forest surrounding the estate, trying to ignore the rusting on the statues of the ancient gods that watched over the once-thriving English gardens.

I cannot adequately explain my feelings on returning to Afansy's estate. I found comfort in the space from whence I came. However, with my grandfather's passing, something was missing and I could not experience the wonder I had known when I spent time there as a small child. The looms that once ensured my

family's prosperity were too noisy and badly in need of mainte-
nance. And after the grandeur of St. Petersburg, everything our
family owned seemed insignificant. At least Dmitry had seen to it
that our stables still housed a few well-fed mares. I wished we
might have taken these fine Goncharov horses out to ride, but
Alexander had explicitly forbid me from riding "spirited" horses
during my convalescence.

Behind me, Ekaterina emitted a loud sigh. I turned. Masha
clutched Ekaterina's hand while Sasha bounced in Azya's arms.

"They are only doing what they think is right," Azya told
Ekaterina. "They want what is best for you."

"Who?" Masha asked, curiosity narrowing her eyes and making her look the spitting image of her father.

"Never mind," Azya said gently. "This is a conversation for
grown-ups."

I rolled my eyes. Azya could not have said anything to intrigue
Masha more.

"They want me to perish an old maid!" Ekaterina moaned, her
lower lip still jutting out in a pout. "They care more for their reputations than my happiness."

I waffled between a gentle lie and my honest opinion on the
matter. As a married woman and a mother now, I thought it my
duty to stick to the truth. "You're both right. They want what is
best for the family, but they also wish to protect our reputations.
You can't marry him."

Ekaterina had recently been bullied by Mother and Dmitry
into refusing the hand of a perfectly lovely gentleman in Moscow.
They cited the same reason that made me hesitate to marry my
Alexander—he was said to have been involved with the Decembrists. I felt sorry for my sister, but had to agree with my family's

decision. Particularly now that my husband's financial life had suffered at the hands of the censors, despite the tsar's promises to the contrary. Besides, if Ekaterina was so in love with this man, she could have fought for him, the way I fought for Alexander.

A white hare crossed our path, leaning back on its hind legs and twitching its dainty pink nose. Masha screamed with delight, breaking free of her aunt's grip and attempting to pet the little creature. It hopped away quickly at the sound of her scream, but this didn't stop her from racing after it. Alexander would have gone crazy at the sight of his daughter tempting fate chasing a bad omen.

Ekaterina continued to mope. "My life is over. I shall have no more prospects."

"Don't say that," Azya told her.

Baby Sasha squeezed his eyes together, face scrunched and red. I knew what was to come and extended my arms to take him from Azya before the full crying jag began, but my hands shook. I hadn't slept much the night before and my nerves were unsteady.

"If only I lived somewhere with more opportunities to meet gentlemen." Ekaterina raised her voice to be heard above Sasha's wailing, as though the two of them were meant to form some sort of tragic Greek chorus. "If only I might be presented at court."

Ekaterina was not exactly being subtle, and despite my rocking, Sasha would not calm down. I was supposed to be healing, and instead I found my heart racing as my mind worked itself into a fever of anxiety. While I was away, Alexander would get in trouble with the tsar, and my sisters would remain unattached their whole lives, growing dependent on us as our family's estate fell into greater disrepair. I could not stop the panicked thoughts from rushing through my head, and at the same time, my darling child would not fall silent. I heard a loud "Ow!" from off the pathway. Masha had tripped over a rock and now picked at her bleeding knee.

I needed it to stop. I needed peace, if only for a moment. In desperation, I blurted, "The two of you should come and live with me. You will meet more gentlemen in St. Petersburg."

"I should like nothing better!" Ekaterina declared. "Why, we could leave at once if you wished it. Don't you think so, Azya?"

"I think it would be most pleasant." Azya bowed her head so I could not see her expression. However, Ekaterina's mood instantly perked up. The two of them must have conspired, perhaps even with Mother or Aunt Katya's help, to compel me to utter those very words.

"Well . . . I shall write to Alexander and tell him the news." Irritated, I wished nothing more than to get Sasha into the hands of a nanny. "He shall be happy to hear it."

How easily the lie escaped from my lips as I abandoned my earlier pledge to tell them the truth of matters. I didn't think Alexander would be glad to see my sisters. But I didn't see how either of us could refuse them.

"It's rather out of the swing of things, isn't it?" Ekaterina sniffed as she made her way up the staircase of our flat in St. Petersburg a few weeks later.

"Good to see you as well." I bounced Sasha on one hip while Masha stood beside me, staring wide-eyed at her aunts.

"I think it's lovely." Azya wiggled Sasha's toe. Alexander's valet—a gray-haired gentleman named Nikita—had assisted my sisters with their luggage. Azya had taken one of the bags to help ease his load. "This is most kind. I would like to thank Alexander as well." Azya stumbled on Alexander's name, and her already large eyes grew wider as she searched the room. "I hoped he might greet us. I wanted to ask what he's working on now."

"Yes, where is he exactly?" Ekaterina twisted her lip. "Not out gambling with the boys or some such nonsense, is he?"

"Daddy isn't here," Masha piped up.

"Ah!" Ekaterina's lips spread into a smug smile. "I suppose many temptations keep a man busy enough in this city. Still, it's a shame. I should like to thank him for his hospitality."

"No, he is here," Masha clarified. "In his study. Papa didn't want to hear hens clucking."

Ekaterina's smile collapsed, but Azya and I giggled. "You may want to keep that to yourself next time, little one," I told her.

"Daddy likes to work," Masha continued proudly, swinging her perfect black curls over her shoulders. "He tells stories."

Ekaterina chucked Masha playfully on her chin. "You are a pretty thing, but you must know children are to be seen and not heard."

"Daddy said the same about you!" Masha exclaimed.

I knew I shouldn't laugh, but I couldn't help it. Why, it wouldn't have surprised me if Sasha removed his pacifier from his mouth and said something sharp to his aunt as well. Ekaterina was already exasperating, yet I confess I had missed sparring with her. "Those were not his exact words." I led my sisters into the parlor, where Azya plopped down on our mahogany divan and ran her finger along the smooth Karelian wood end table. "Rather it was more to the effect of 'Will this home now be filled with the sound of clucking hens?' I assured him we wouldn't cluck any more than his friends do when they come over and start fussing over their poetry and journals."

"So he does not wish us to stay here?" Ekaterina said primly, while Azya cut in with: "I hope we are not an imposition."

I released Masha who ran over to sit next to Azya while I shifted Sasha into my other arm and avoided the question. "I can do with the company. It will be such fun to take you to masquerade balls. We can make our costumes together!"

"That does sound fun!" Azya said.

"I have so many ideas! Now that there are three of us we might dress as the three sisters with glass hearts or the three sisters with wizards for husbands in the tale of Masha Morevna." Alexander's love of folklore had rubbed off on me and I knew many of the traditional tales now. "Perhaps we might even dress as the wizards. Dressing as the opposite gender was the rage in the court of Empress Elizabeth. Why not revive the custom?"

"And what will your husband say to that?" Ekaterina asked.

"He would warm to the idea quickly enough." After all, such a costume would require many layers of loose fabric and likely not attract attention from other men. A flash of memory hit me as it had with disturbing frequency over the past weeks. Sir Lancelot smiling down on me, appraising my costume as priestess of the sun. I found myself fussing with a bit of lint on my frock, thinking of the devilish glint in Lancelot's grin, knowing full well I should not return to that image as often as I did.

Sasha's squalling disrupted my thoughts and a wave of guilt hit me like cold water.

"May I try to soothe him?" Azya nodded at Sasha. I handed him over without hesitation, though I knew it would do no good.

As soon as he left my arms he started to wail even louder, despite his auntie's cooing.

"Your husband doesn't wish to see us at all then?" Ekaterina spoke loudly to be heard over Sasha's cries of despair. She nodded her large chin in the direction of Alexander's study.

"He works all day, same as any other man." I shook my arms, sore from lugging Sasha around the house. "He will come out of his study when he has come to a good stopping point and it makes sense to take a break." I had heard some of Alexander's writer friends say so much of the craft simply involves the will to place oneself in front of a blank sheet of paper. Perhaps confined, my husband would be forced to write.

"I adored *The Bronze Horseman*," Azya gushed. "It is a masterpiece."

I beamed at her praise, almost as though I had written the poem myself. Although Alexander's poem still languished in the office of the censor, we had shown it privately to a select group of trusted readers, including my sisters. Masha had begged to listen, and against my better judgment, I had allowed her to sit in while Alexander performed the poem for his friends; I had been afraid she would have nightmares the entire week. Instead, she simply clapped and begged her father to take her to see the statue one more time.

"What is he working on now?" Azya asked eagerly.

I tried to hold my smile, but it was difficult. I knew I wouldn't be able to fool my sisters for very long. "Many projects! His history of Pugachev as well as another fairy tale in verse. He also started a new project set during the time of Catherine the Great— a short story about gamblers. He continues his poetical works and the novel about Abram Gannibal he never finished . . ."

That all sounded convoluted and unfocused, even to my own ears. I stopped and looked down at my hands. Even Ekaterina didn't say anything tart, but merely busied herself locating a fan in one of her overstuffed valises. If Alexander failed to bring in income, it would affect her now as well and was nothing to joke about.

"You have your own work as well to keep you occupied." Azya gestured to my notebook, left open on a writing table.

"Mamma writes!" Masha exclaimed.

"So Mamma is a poet as well. I suppose this shouldn't surprise us." Ekaterina sounded as sincere as she could manage. "Have you shown the verse to your husband yet?"

"They are hardly worth his time. Only a few brief ditties." I didn't care to admit that after four years of marriage and two children, I had yet to show my poetry to my husband. I had yet to show it to any other soul. "Alexander is the poet in the family. I am a dilettante."

"Still, he might enjoy hearing your work," Ekaterina pressed.

"Yes! Let Daddy listen." Masha sprang off the divan and ran toward the study.

"No!" It came out louder than intended. I softened my voice. "I shall read them to Daddy in private. Sometimes that's better."

"I only hope we see the little fellow soon," Ekaterina said, back to her irritable self. "I hoped he might take us to a good restaurant this evening. Somewhere in town."

"We are in town," I said.

"Oh, you know. I meant the fashionable part."

I pressed my lips together. For a few moments, it had been pleasant to spar once more with my sister, but now I felt I could better deal with Ekaterina if I left my spectacles in their reticule atop my desk and her face remained fuzzy.

Alexander decided to take us to for supper at Andrieu's, one of the most popular restaurants in the city. We made our way into the bustling establishment, past finely dressed groups of handsome bachelors smoking cigars and elegant couples huddled over candlelit tables. The dining area already smelled of the men's tobacco mingled with the roasted meat and steamed vegetables being prepared in the kitchen. Ekaterina straightened her shoulders, and for once, looked almost satisfied with her situation in life. Azya stuck close to Alexander's side; my husband had already drunk half a bottle of iced champagne in the carriage—quite unlike him—but his mood was much improved from this morning. He patted Azya's hand and told her about Pugachev. I had not realized Azya took such an interest in Alexander's work.

When we received our menus, my sisters attempted to discern the names of the French dishes. The coq au vin was easy enough to decipher but they had a difficult time with *andouilletes de troyes*. I fretted, avoiding the champagne brought to our table, for I had missed my monthly cycle and my body felt uncomfortable in a way I hadn't noticed during my previous pregnancies. After Sasha's birth, my stomach retracted down to the small pouch I was accustomed to seeing. Alexander never minded the extra weight; he liked to squeeze the soft parts of me and lay his head on my stomach when our lovemaking was over. Still, I didn't care for the idea of growing overly stout. My breasts were still heavy and, looking down, I realized the gown I wore did not fit as well as it once had.

I was trying to adjust my top without anyone else noticing when a familiar masculine voice rang in my ear.

"Mademoiselles! You seem to be having some trouble interpreting the menu. Perhaps I can be of assistance."

The pretty face of Georges d'Anthès loomed above me, the white uniform of his cavalry regiment, the Chevalier Guards, immaculate down to the golden epaulettes on his shoulders, but his dark blond hair artfully tousled just so. Behind him stood an older man, pleasant looking enough, perhaps in his mid-forties, with a full brown beard and a receding hairline. He was dressed less formally than Georges, in a plain frock coat with two medallions shaped like stars on the right side of his chest.

A swell of panic rose, as I fancied that Georges knew I'd been thinking of him lately more than I ought, that somehow I had conjured him. With a flash like a firework in my mind, I remembered Alexander's fortune-teller warning him of a tall, fair man.

That was foolishness. I forced the anxiety to the back of my mind, giving a slight shake of my head, determined to behave like a normal human being. "Monsieur d'Anthès! The knight from Arthur's court." I extended my hand. He lowered his head to kiss it and I fervently wished I'd had more success adjusting my gown before he made it to the table.

Alexander stood, and when Georges rose back to his full height, he was a head taller than my husband—a fact clearly not lost on Alexander who straightened his back to make himself as high as he could manage.

"These are my sisters." I wished their first introductions in St. Petersburg society had been to someone different. "You must know of my husband, Alexander Pushkin," I added quickly, feeling ashamed to have not led with him.

"An honor." Georges nodded in Alexander's direction. "And enchanted." He kissed both Ekaterina's and Azya's hands. Azya looked flustered at the attention. Georges lingered a bit on Ekaterina's fingers. She simpered, whispering, "Call me Koko." The name was an old childhood affectation of hers and I felt a spark of jealousy in my chest followed rapidly by another dark cloud of guilt.

"May I introduce Baron Heeckeren, a diplomat of the Netherlands."

My sisters nodded politely in the baron's direction while keeping their enraptured gazes focused on Georges's handsome face. Ekaterina's foolishness didn't surprise me, but it seemed even Azya was smitten, though at least her gaze turned back to her menu soon enough. Ekaterina's heavy jaw might have dropped to the floor for all her lack of subtlety.

"How do you two know one other?" I asked.

Georges concentrated on me intently, like Alexander had early in our marriage, as though I had asked the most fascinating question in the world. I found myself struggling to maintain my neutral smile. "Baron Heeckeren and I met in court circles."

At that, the baron patted Georges's arm fondly. "We are more than friends, or will be soon at any rate."

I tilted my head, unsure what the baron meant to imply.

"Yes, it seems that now we are to be family as well. He plans to make me his heir. The baron will be my adopted father! Can you imagine the luck?"

"I cannot," Alexander said. "It seems fortune sometimes favors charming foreigners more than the bold."

The tips of my ears burned, but the baron merely dipped his head while Georges turned to Alexander and said: "I was most enchanted by your wife's costume at the last masquerade before Lent. I am so sorry the night was disturbed by her unfortunate illness."

Alexander leaned back in his chair, but his hands pressed into tight fists and then opened wide again. I imagined the flat of his palm smacking Georges across the cheeks. "That was months ago. How odd you should take note of it now."

"The image is still vivid in my mind. The priestess of the sun. Such a beauty."

"And who were you at this masquerade, Monsieur d'Anthès?" Ekaterina asked.

"Sir Lancelot. The fellow from the Englishmen's stories? He loved a woman who belonged to another."

"How scandalous!" Ekaterina declared, clearly pleased.

"I know the story. Poor Arthur," Azya added.

"Sir Lancelot was in love, in rapture," Georges said. "How could he be expected to behave in a proper manner? All is forgiven when love is involved. Don't you agree?"

Now I busied myself with the menu, wishing we had taken my sisters to one of the foreign restaurants far away from the more fashionable part of the city. Alexander said nothing further. However, his hands lay flat on the table to either side of his china plate and he focused on them as though at any moment they might spring to life of their own volition and box Georges between the ears. The silence grew awkward, and I could not let the final note of our conversation remain Georges's thoughts on forbidden love.

"I'm sure you had no shortage of admirers at the masquerade," I said, without considering the words too carefully. "Why would you ever stoop to chase another man's wife when you looked handsome as Apollo!"

Alexander's fingers curled into fists, and Ekaterina sneered. I vowed to say nothing more.

The baron placed his hand on Georges's upper arm. "We should find our table before Monsieur Andrieu releases it to another party." His tone was strangely irritable, even more so than Alexander's.

"Of course." Georges clicked his heels together and nodded at my sisters. "Charmed." He turned to me. "And I trust I will see you again, Madame Natalie."

I wished to sink under the folds of white linen draped over Monsieur Andrieu's table. I had not shared my husband's old western nickname for me with Georges; he had summoned this endearment on his own. Still, Alexander would assume I had shared this intimacy with Georges. I could not bear to look up again until I heard the thump of boots on the floor and knew Georges and the baron had retreated to their own table.

"Now *that* is why I came to the city," Ekaterina said. "What a handsome fellow."

"I trust that chap will find some way or another to see *Natalie*," Alexander muttered. "And then the rest of us will be forced to tolerate his company."

"Anyone else thinking of ordering truffles?" My gaze fixed on the lovely calligraphy on the evening's menu.

"I am thinking now of a different dish," Ekaterina said. I raised my head enough to watch her sip champagne while her gray eyes set on Georges's broad back as he and the baron took their seats near the window.

"You can do better." Alexander's voice changed. I didn't care for the switch from irritability to false joviality. "What did you think of him, Azya?"

I peeped at them. Azya's gaze flitted between Alexander and me. "Too tall."

"Too tall?" Ekaterina said. "What rubbish!"

"I found him excessively tall."

Alexander leaned back in his chair. "I think you are the diplomat tonight, my little sister, not our stuffy Dutch friend. Perhaps the tsar might hire you as an ambassador and send you to talk sense to the Poles or the Turks when they start causing trouble." Alexander may have been speaking to Azya, but he looked straight at me as though I had already shattered his heart. "I think you will do very well here in St. Petersburg."

"I have something I would like you to see." I tried to keep my voice as gentle as possible as Alexander removed his striped dressing gown and took a seat beside me in bed. His loose nightshirt was fully buttoned and he didn't reach for me as he usually did when we retired together for the evening.

"Is that so?" he asked, still as a statue.

I was trying to make amends, even as a faint voice inside insisted I had done nothing wrong. Except a stronger voice said it didn't matter. Alexander's shoulders drooped and he had spoken less than ten words to me since dinner. My heart beat anxiously underneath my nightgown. My husband was unhappy. And it was my fault. I needed to show him how much he meant to me. I looked down at the notebook propped on my lap.

"A poem!" I said. "Nothing but a lark. Still, I would value your opinion."

He stared at the notebook, making no move to take it in his own hand or read its contents. I pressed forward. "You were once kind enough to write poems in my honor. I thought it appropriate to return the favor."

I expected him to make a sarcastic comment then about Georges d'Anthès, the same way he would if the tsar had flirted with me over supper, but he remained quiet. I squeezed his hand. He didn't need to say anything. If only he would squeeze back.

"I did not mean to flirt with Georges," I said helplessly. The comment about Apollo had not been calculated and he was making me pay too dearly for it.

"Did I say you were flirting?"

"Your silence speaks plainly enough. Now I have something to offer and you refuse. You are angry and you won't talk to me."

At that, Alexander put his head in his hands. I saw tears in his eyes and I cast my notebook aside, taking him in my arms. "What is wrong? What can I do to make it better?"

"Do you know what people say about me?" Alexander asked hoarsely.

People said a great many things about my husband, but I chose to focus on the positive. "That you are a titan of Russian literature?"

He flashed a weak smile. "Good effort, but no. They say I am temperamental and hot-blooded, and it is due to my African heritage from Gannibal himself."

"What nonsense." I thought a moment and added: "Not that it is nonsense you have hot blood, but what shame is there in that? It is nonsense to think such moods are credited to your African ancestor. Who in St. Petersburg has even traveled to Africa? They speak like provincial girls who pretend to have seen the city."

At last, he squeezed my hand. "Thank you. My mother has more African blood than I and never even cracks a smile nor makes a joke, let alone loses her temper."

This was true enough. I didn't pretend to know Alexander's family well, but both his mother and father seemed cold fish. Besides, when it came to odd families, I considered myself something of an expert. "We shouldn't look to our heritage to explain our temperament, but the disposition God granted us."

"There is more to it than that. I fear I am going mad. As Evgeny did in my poem."

"Why would you think this?" I kept my tone calm, though I found the words chilling. But I saw no sign of mental illness in Alexander. And after growing up with my father, I thought myself well enough qualified to notice the warning signs.

"I feel my temper sometimes slip from my control. Why, the way that Frenchman looked at you . . . it is no more than any man would, considering your beauty. It is no more than *I* would have once upon a time, paying no mind as to whether or not a husband was involved. And yet now . . . I wished to smash the fellow's face in for a trifle."

"I have no need to see Georges again," I told Alexander. "Ekaterina seems taken with him. He can focus his attention on her. He need not flirt with me."

"Coquetry certainly does not line the path toward happiness, but neither does that." Alexander gestured at my notebook.

"Writing? Why not?"

"It causes naught but pain. I cannot even stand my own verse right now."

I had not thought writing an occupation that would bring sadness to either one of us; I only wanted to grow closer to Alexander by sharing my poetry with him. "Pursuing an artistic talent should be a joy."

"Writing is truth seeking and the truths of most lives are too terrible to bear. Better to live in happy ignorance. Then again, a happy ignorance is not possible for a writer either, for we always wish to tell our story, and when we can't, we feel nothing at all. I believe that too is responsible for my failing mental state."

I pulled him closer and kissed his cheeks. "You will write soon enough, I am sure of it."

"How wrong I was to think happiness could be mine. My mother always told me I was destined for misery. I should never have expected more."

My face burned at the thought of yet another cruelty inflicted on Alexander by his own mother, but I kept my own voice calm. "We must both exorcise the voice of our mothers from our heads. But, my darling, what is so terrible in our lives that you cannot bear it?"

He buried his head in the crevice between my shoulders and neck, his shoulders shaking, inhaling deeply while I stroked his black curls.

"That I do not deserve your love," he whispered quietly in my ear. "And that soon enough I will pay dearly for it."

Fourteen

Despite Alexander's troubling words, I tried to maintain a happy face in our domestic life over the coming months for the sake of our children and my sisters. My husband paced restlessly upstairs in his study, still unable to put pen to paper, while over supper, Azya tried every means of flattery to encourage him to write again. Meanwhile Ekaterina—*Koko*—asked about Georges so often I wanted to slap her. To avoid a scene that might upset Alexander, I smiled and assured her we would see him often enough at winter balls.

This turned out to be the truth, though it was difficult for Ekaterina to spend more than a few minutes at a stretch alone with Georges, for women were drawn to him like hummingbirds to a flower. Even so, Georges seemed willing enough to entertain my sister with his jolly stories. Yet even as Georges held Ekaterina's hand, his gaze followed me.

I kept my promise to Alexander, and steered clear of him. For a time.

In May of 1835, Grisha, our third child, was born. Alexander's mood improved at once, for he enjoyed having babies about the house almost as much as he enjoyed the process of creating them. I tried to share in his happiness, but felt unaccountably morose. It had nothing to do with Grisha, a darling baby with a mop of thick black hair. It was only that I didn't sleep well and took to crying for no reason, sometimes in the middle of the night, and did not want to bother Alexander with my problems. Were I granted a wish to return to those days, I would handle matters differently. At the time, I worried over Alexander's mental state. Not wishing to diminish the obvious joy of his second son's arrival, I kept my mounting sadness and frustrations to myself until they reached a tipping point.

One afternoon, after I had just put Grisha down for a nap and hoped to snatch a bit of sleep myself, Ekaterina returned from a shopping trip on Nevsky Prospect with gifts for the children: a soldier's drum for Masha and a pair of cymbals for Sasha, which he immediately began to clang together, waking Grisha, who began to wail. Bestowing these gifts and accepting kisses as reward, Ekaterina announced she had made plans with a new friend to tour the gardens at Tauride Palace and flitted away once more, leaving me to deal with the aftermath.

I already suffered from aches in my head, and the noise made the pain nearly unbearable. All I wanted was to lie abed for an hour. I threatened to withhold the gooseberry preserves that Masha loved almost as much as her father did. Still, she banged her drum and made her new baby brother cry even more.

"Take them outside!" The nanny was taking afternoon tea in town with a friend. So I shouted at my darling Liza, something I never did, shoving Grisha into her arms, grabbing Masha's blue down coat from the wardrobe in the nursery, and snatching Sasha's cymbals from his hands. "I can't stand it any longer."

Liza's mouth moved helplessly, but she had nothing to say at the sight of the wild children suddenly in her charge, while Sasha gave me a woeful look that made me feel like a monster. With an apologetic glance, I softened my tone as I kissed Sasha's head. "I will return them when you're back home. Mamma only needs some rest."

Once poor Liza had herded the children's army away, I flounced upstairs, thinking I should like to punch a hole in the wall and not even sure why. I only knew I needed a good night's sleep, and a brief nap would have to do.

As I walked to my room, I passed Alexander's study. A high feminine voice chatted gaily inside. I caught a light vanilla scent in the air. For a moment, I was convinced Alix Rosset—now Alexandra Smirnova—had found her way to our flat. The thought of Alix in the house with us made my head pound even worse than the cymbals and drums. The door had been left ajar and I shoved it open.

"Of course, our grandfather always spoke of the visit Catherine had planned to make to our family estate." Azya lounged on Alexander's leather couch. Her feet dipped off the ends and one slipper dangled from her toes so that her stockinged heel was exposed. The room smelled of vanilla-tinged oil. I quickly realized she'd dabbed her neck with cologne. "He hoped Catherine would rise from the grave and somehow her spirit would find her way to

Kaluga. I think he felt our family's fortunes were forever damaged after Catherine's snub."

"Is that a fact?" I said, too loudly. "I never heard Grandfather say such a thing."

"Oh! Natalya! Natasha! Natalie!" My sister jumped to her feet. I wish she had remained seated. It would have made her seem less guilty. "I didn't hear you come in. Alexander was just sharing new verse. He has asked me to transcribe his drafts."

I surveyed the notes on Alexander's desk and the sheepish look on his face. I thought then of our cozy house at Tsarskoye Selo, when I spent my mornings happily copying Alexander's rough drafts into more legible work. Why had we ever left that happy place? Why had I ever agreed to share my home with my sisters?

"When do you intend to do this?" My calmness must have scared Azya, for she stepped back, nearly falling over the sofa behind her.

"Why in the mornings . . . I suppose . . . perhaps after breakfast . . . should it matter?"

I faced Alexander. "Are you not happy with my work, sir? I thought I did a fine job with your transcriptions."

"Of course you did, Natasha . . . my Tasha . . ." Alexander had adopted this informal endearment permanently now that both the tsar and Georges referred to me as Natalie. "Yet we have a third child now. I thought you needed rest."

"I'm fine. Azya should be too busy for such matters."

"It is only a trifle . . ." my sister began.

"You need to make new friends of your own, as Ekaterina is doing. You cannot remain trapped in this house all day waiting to die an old maid."

Azya's wide eyes, which had looked on me with love so often, brimmed with hurt. I had put those tears there, a monster once more, and yet I had said no more than the truth. But she was not the only culprit. All of the frustration of the past weeks had been churning inside, waiting to reach a head, alongside my physical discomfort and lack of sleep. "You shouldn't encourage her," I told Alexander. "It isn't fair."

My husband still attempted to make light of the situation. "Your sister merely takes an interest in the arts, as you once did."

"As I once did?" I had not helped Alexander with any further poems only because he had not asked me to do so. Besides, he didn't think to ask again about my writing. Rather, he wanted to keep me like a prized bird in a cage. It seemed to me in that moment life was always about him: his feelings, his work, his ownership of me.

Even then a small voice inside my head said Azya likely had nothing more than a harmless schoolgirl's crush on my husband, and Alexander had not asked about my poems because he suffered from the same melancholy that now had me in its clutches. Still, I could not bear that my favorite sister should swoop in with her unseemly affections.

"You were the one who didn't even want my sisters here in the first place," I told Alexander. "You thought they needed husbands and lives of their own rather than to leech off ours. Why would you ask my sister to behave now as your personal secretary? If you are in need of someone to transcribe your work, I'm sure we could sell more possessions to a moneylender and you could hire a fellow. Or do you wish to keep my sister at your beck and call?"

I would not look at Azya but heard the heartbreak in her voice as she addressed my husband. "You do not want us here?"

I spoke before Alexander had a chance to answer. "You need to find a husband of your own. You wouldn't want to live on our charity forever. You're here only because I allow it. Never forget that."

After behaving so terribly to my sister, I found my own company intolerable. More and more, I sought escape from our little family dramas in masquerades. When I was not working on costumes, I thought about them or made lists of materials, addicted to the thrill of fashioning a new identity. I riffled through the books in Alexander's voluminous library, searching for ideas. When I wore my costumes, I was no longer a wife and mother with debts and a distracted husband, but a character from a fairy tale, a figure from history—a goddess. Once a group approached me at a ball to tell me how fine I looked, I longed for more people to do so. I was no longer the decorative poet's wife. For once in my life, I felt valued for myself, not for how well my presence reflected someone else's glory.

I was working through the first steps for a costume of Queen Esther, and instructing Liza to tighten my corsets accordingly, when someone rapped on my boudoir door. Irritated and assuming one of the children was playing a joke, I called: "Come in only if someone is afire."

Alexander stuck his head through the door. "In your presence, I am always afire."

"Alexander!" I motioned for him to enter. "I have an idea for a costume from the Bible . . . Esther from the book of that name. Do you know her?"

"Of course I know her." He seemed in a good mood, yet he

was rubbing his hands together. "Intent on saving your people, are you?"

I bowed low, in mock subservience. "Ever at the command of my people."

"Perhaps you might start with your own husband."

I smiled coyly, thinking he meant to take me to his bed that afternoon. "Liza, why don't we get back to this later . . . perhaps you could check on the children for me."

Liza gave a quick curtsy, and left the room, giggling.

"Alexander, you know it is not a matter of me not wishing it, but the doctor said to wait. Still, I think there are other ways we might express our love for each other . . ."

"Don't put ideas in my head!" He sat at the foot of my bed and I took a seat on his lap. "You see, I have a gentleman coming this afternoon to pick up a new manuscript."

"That's wonderful!"

He made a dismissive motion. "Only a few verses, but I have given thought to our finances and wonder if it might make sense to start asking for more money for my work."

"I have said as much."

"Yes . . . but you see I already agreed to a sum with this fellow, in gold rubles of course. It would not seem gentlemanly to ask for more when we already came to terms. I had not the foresight to think of the expenses we might incur after Grisha's birth."

"You will ask for more next time," I assured him.

"Or . . ." He hesitated. "I can't ask for more money, but you know when a fellow's wife asks something of him? Most gentlemen understand there is little that man can do."

I pulled back, searching Alexander's seemingly innocent expression. "You wish to tell him I am making you back down from the original agreement and ask for more money."

Alexander grinned. "Or better yet—you might ask him."

I dropped my hands and made my way to my feet as best I could, my body still sore from carrying Grisha. "What?"

"Think of the boon to our accounts. How can he resist the plea of a ravishing woman?"

I sighed and moved back to my chair in front of the vanity looking glass. I looked a fright, but knew Alexander was correct in saying a gentleman would be unwilling to refuse a lady. Considering how my stomach twisted into knots when I considered our accounts, and how I had already offered several items of jewelry to pawnshops, I can't say the thought of a financial windfall didn't appeal to me. "How much were you thinking?"

"We had originally settled on fifty."

I flinched, for the amount was far too low. I wish Alexander had thought to ask for more when selling his work in the first place, instead of having me come to clean up the mess later.

"Now I am thinking one hundred."

"Twice the original price!" Still, I thought how far an additional fifty gold rubles would go to paying our expenses.

"He will not complain should the request come from you."

So that's what all this was about. I sighed, too exhausted even to protest the outlandish plan. "Fine. When am I to meet with this gentleman?"

Alexander consulted the pocket watch he kept chained to his trousers. "In ten minutes."

"I'm not even dressed."

"Not to worry. You need only pull on an appropriate day gown. He is coming here."

"Alexander!" I said, exasperated.

"It will be fine."

The doorbell rang. "He's early. Let me just go to talk to the fellow. It will all be over soon." Alexander squeezed my shoulders. "Remember, you are a woman of business."

I looked back in the mirror. I had played with arranging my hair in black curls framing my face to assume the role of Esther. I supposed a woman of business was yet another role to play, so I practiced a pleading but formidable expression. I only wished I might lose the feeling I had been reduced to beggary. Our family's precarious financial situation made me think I had lost grip of the very world beneath my feet, and that my own husband could neither save me, nor even see the indignity of our situation.

I longed for escape.

With such disloyal thoughts running through my head, I didn't dare tell Alexander about the notes.

They came infrequently at first, slipped into my hand discreetly by Liza, and smelling strongly of a woodland-scented French cologne I had come to know well. The romantic words of Georges d'Anthès seemed harmless at first, praising my beauty in simple but earnest language, the effect my presence had on him, and how the world seemed a better place for me being in it. Nothing more than he might have copied word for word from a French journal for gentlemen. And certainly nothing more than one might expect from the courtly flirtations that were common enough occurrences in those days.

And yet . . . I found my heart beating faster than it should have when I saw the devilish look in Liza's eyes as she approached me with these little romantic letters. Either she relished her role as the rogue agent of this courtly affair or she had a crush on Georges herself.

Georges appeared frequently at balls and other public events, surrounded by his usual coterie of giggling women, and nearly always accompanied by his good friend and mentor, the baron, who had taken to reminding everyone that he had formally adopted Georges. Every so often, I caught him looking wistfully at Georges, the mixture of pain and joy in his eyes far from paternal, instead more akin to the looks Alexander had given me when he began his courtship.

Or the looks Georges now directed at me.

Georges and I danced often enough, I admit. Women must not wound a man's ego by refusing. Besides, he made me feel as though I flew across the floor. In addition to his florid notes, Georges was quick with compliments, taking note of some detail of my costume or gown lost on my own husband. Though it pains me to admit, there were times when I drifted to sleep at night, Alexander lightly snoring beside me, thinking of Georges. Please don't think too ill of me, for I didn't fantasize about him in the way most people envision a wicked wife would. Rather, my mind wandered to memories of Georges's amicable and unchallenging chatter. He had not the genius of my husband, yet I wondered if life might be more comfortable with someone like him: a man whose finances were in order, who didn't need his wife to ask a publisher for more money, who wasn't prone to melancholy or fears of insanity. Perhaps once or twice, I did wonder what would happen if I allowed him to kiss me. The thought of it leaves me burning with shame now, and yet who among us has not dreamed of some alternate life.

One evening, while attending a costume ball with Ekaterina and

Alexander, and finally dressed as Queen Esther, my old acquaintance Ida approached me. When we first met, she had dressed as a Muse, but now she wore a simple milkmaid's gown. "How darling your costumes have become! I must have you help me with mine."

I gave a quick nod, my dangling gold earrings swaying.

"You must show this newest creation to Georges d'Anthès!"

Georges stood on the opposite side of the dance floor, wearing a scarlet robe over a Roman tunic with sandals. I believe he had patterned his outfit after *The Last Day of Pompeii;* a painting that so entranced Alexander, he'd composed a poem on the doomed Roman town. I tried not to stare, nor think about how well-muscled his shapely bare legs looked. "He is more than welcome to come and chat with me, as always."

"Is he really?" Ida said slyly.

I turned to her, vexed but trying to hide it. "What do you mean?"

Ida shifted her gaze about the room, her large blond curls bouncing on her shoulders. She leaned in close to my ear. "People say you choose not to play the coquette with Georges because you are afraid of your husband."

"What?" I tried to keep my temper in check.

Ida shrugged. "I hate to be the one to tell you and of course it's nothing *I* believe. It is only that your Alexander is so proud of his African blood and known to have a temper."

"What rubbish!" I was stunned, but remembered the hurt in Alexander's eyes when his great-grandfather Abram Gannibal was subject to insult. At that moment, I caught Georges's eye by accident and he moved toward us, but then hesitated. Ekaterina stood to the other side of Ida. I saw his gaze flick between my sister and me.

"Georges!" I called. "How fine you look this evening! Are you perhaps one of the doomed patriarchs of Pompeii? It is as though you stepped off the canvas!"

At that, Georges beamed and headed in my direction. Ida gave a quick giggle and slapped my arm. "I knew it! You are a true coquette after all."

The orchestra played the first lively notes of a quadrille. I thought even Alexander couldn't object to such an innocent dance with Georges. After all, we would do naught but bow at one another for the most part. When Georges offered his hand, I accepted. His hand might rest lightly on my back for a moment, but what was the harm in that?

"And how ravishing you look, Queen Esther," Georges said, the gentle French accent making the words even sweeter. "I am not sure I should say you have stepped off the pages of our Holy Bible, though. It makes me feel a blasphemer."

"Sin can be a most enjoyable occupation," I said, without thinking.

If he had been beaming before, Georges was now positively aglow with pleasure. "I could not have put it any better myself. What a delightful evening this has turned out to be."

I would say no more on the subject of sin, nor would I refuse a harmless flirtation and have wicked tongues flapping over Alexander's supposed temper. I nodded and gave him a small smile as we took our places on the dance floor. I glanced over my shoulder just long enough to see Ekaterina's lips pressed firmly together and Ida regarding Georges with a look of utter satisfaction.

"People are talking about Georges d'Anthès and our family," Alexander told me later as we waited for our carriage to be summoned.

I straightened my skirt before sitting next to him on a chaise longue in the annex of the palace, knowing I needed to take great care with my words. "I can hardly refuse a dance."

He gave me a half-smile. "I have no criticism of you. Is that surprising?"

"Of course not," I said quickly.

"I meant they talk about your sister and the scoundrel d'Anthès."

I lowered my gaze, a few seconds too late. Alexander had caught my expression.

"This bothers you?" I could feel his mood souring.

"I shall be delighted if Ekaterina makes a good match."

"But you wish for d'Anthès to remain your special toy and moon after you alone."

"Certainly not." I shook my head, a little too dramatically. Georges had asked Ekaterina to dance several times throughout the night, and I had watched him take her hand, whispering something in her ear that made her face flush with pleasure. I chose to ignore my own petty resentment at the thought of it. "He does not moon after me. He is just a nice boy."

Alexander's tone grew affable, which somehow made it worse than if his temper got the best of him. "Remember Ekaterina needs to find a husband. Not you."

I felt a burning at the back of my eyes, tears threatening to fall. Deep down I knew he had reason to chide me and this flirtation was not as innocent as I liked to think. Still, I protested. "How can you say this to me? I love you."

Alexander's eyes grew tender and gently he moved back a tendril of hair that had fallen into my face. "I didn't mean it like that. I only meant words are malicious. I wouldn't want you caught in any of the stories people float around to embarrass me."

Alexander had confided his suspicion he was going mad; I couldn't imply he was imagining things. I didn't want him to feel worse than he already did, so I didn't deny anything, nor did I try to assure him that his worries were unfounded. Instead, I said something meant to flatter him, but which I would soon come to regret: words with which I will have to live for the rest of my days.

"I trust you will defend my honor, husband," I told him. "You have always been my protector and I know you always will be."

Fifteen

When he heard the bell from the front of our flat, Alexander grumbled and threw a pillow over his face. "What time is it? What scoundrel arrives so early in the morning?"

I rubbed the sleep from my eyes, grabbing a chiffon dressing gown from a hook near our door. "My aunt," I whispered, massaging my swollen stomach. "She said she would call this morning, only I had not realized she would come so early."

He groaned. "She knows this is not court? We're not on a schedule here."

"She wouldn't come so early were it not important."

Alexander leaned forward and planted a kiss on my belly. "Fine. Only make excuses for me, if you will."

I doubt my aunt had come here to see Alexander; likely she wished to check on my sisters and scold them for failing to attract worthy suitors yet. She had resumed her former practice of bringing used dresses from court for Ekaterina and Azya and seemed particularly adept at finding gowns that made Ekaterina's face seem less tiresome. Perhaps Aunt Katya thought Ekaterina had a chance with Georges, and despite my rather unfortunately confused feelings on this matter, I was as eager for my sisters to be married as anyone.

I greeted my aunt with a hug and kiss for each cheek, before reaching for the bell pull so my sisters might be summoned to the parlor.

"Not yet." Aunt Katya raised her hand as my fingers wrapped around the rope.

A harsh note in her words brought my hands down to my lap, where I folded them like a naughty schoolgirl caught stealing cookies from a jar. I felt somehow in trouble but did not yet know why—though I had my suspicions.

"You are a great success in St. Petersburg." Aunt Katya opened her fan, fluttering the gauze panels before her eyes for effect. My shoulders shivered. I wished I had thought to bring a blanket with me downstairs. "How far you've come. Why, you hardly have time to visit me anymore."

"I'm sorry for that," I said, meaning it. "I will make more time to call on you."

"Still, I hear so many things."

Not all of them good, I supposed. Otherwise she would not ask to speak to me alone. I thought of Ida's whispers about Alexander's temper. "What have you heard? I can assure you my husband is a good man and I don't fear him in the slightest."

"I hear rumors you are a minx who dishonors her husband."

"What nonsense!" I had no need for a looking glass to confirm my cheeks had reddened, for the parlor no longer felt cold. Aunt Katya never had been one to mince her words.

"They say you dance all night. You whisper with handsome men . . ."

"That is no more than other married women do. Why should I be singled out for humiliation? I have held myself to the highest standards."

"Would your mother agree with that assessment?"

Thankfully, what Mother might think had long since ceased to be a concern of mine. "Mother is welcome to visit and attend any function."

"Have you invited her?"

I had not. I had taken her grandchildren to visit her, of course, but could never find it in me to actually extend an invitation here. "My conscience is clear." My private thoughts were my own affair.

"Perhaps you feel that way, but it does not stop the rumormongers of this city. You are married to our great poet. Surely you understand the pressures of that position. We have spoken of them often enough. You are held to a higher standard than ladies married to common dolts for their fortune. I would be remiss in my duties if I didn't speak with you."

"In that case, you have done your duty," I said primly. "Consider any further matters to be entirely my responsibility."

"And the consequences entirely your fault."

My fingers clenched. "I anticipate no consequences."

"What about your sisters? They still need husbands and rumors about you reflect poorly on the entire family."

I thought of Georges bending down to kiss my hand, the light in his eyes when his gaze caught mine. "I have done nothing wrong."

Aunt Katya lay her fan down alongside one of Alexander's stray journals, which had made its way from his study onto the end table in our parlor. She picked it up and began leafing through the pages. "It isn't selling as well as he'd hoped, is it? I worry for you and your children. It can't be easy living on the edge of financial ruin."

"I wouldn't go that far," I told her, even though my heart raced. I knew in my heart her words were only the truth. Despite a run of intriguing true-life tales, the journal hadn't attracted as many subscribers as Alexander had thought it would and was contributing to his general sense of disquiet.

Aunt Katya gave me a tight smile, more melancholic than a smile had a right to be. "You say you have done nothing wrong? What does it matter? Neither did your mother."

A dry, cottony sensation prickled my tongue. "Whatever do you mean?"

"Do you know why your mother is no longer a lady at court?"

"She is married . . ."

"Yes, but how do you suppose that came about?"

Though my aunt's voice was kinder now, I didn't care for the direction of this conversation. I knew Mother had once served at court and at one point was a favorite of the previous tsar's wife. I imagined my mother as a young woman and confidante, lovely with her high cheekbones, but with a haughty air and a tension in her pursed lips that made her impossible to befriend. "I assume she said something ill-timed."

"Your mother turned heads once," Aunt Katya said, "but sometimes a woman turns the wrong head and the wrong man falls in love with her."

My mouth dropped, but I contained my emotions. "Who did she love?"

"Oh, she didn't love him. It was one-sided. She had an admirer, not an affair. But the attention made her glow and so she acted a fool around the gentleman in question. Unfortunately, that admirer happened to be the empress's lover."

I flinched, understanding now why Mother had warned me about a life at court, near the tsar and the empress.

"Your mother thought an innocent flirtation could cause no harm, that her reputation was beyond reproach, but tongues will wag regardless and eventually the empress learned of it."

Though afraid of the answer, I asked the next logical question. "What happened to Mother then?"

"Her admirer satisfied himself with another woman and sparked a crisis all on his own. As I'm sure you well know by now, in such cases the woman is always blamed. It was thought better for your mother if she took leave of the court. That's when she married your poor father."

I stared out the window, at a bit of dew clinging to a birch tree. The muted sound of horses' hooves clomping past and a group of couples singing from atop an open coach reached me. Once, Alexander and I had been part of such merry rides. Hadn't we? Or had Alix and Karolina and the tsar and others always been there, always interfered? The early years of our union seemed a haze now. And yet I realized with a jolt that no matter how my attention diverted when Georges drew near, my passion for Alexander remained. My love remained. Despite our troubles and quirks, I wouldn't trade my life with him for anything. How low had I sunk that Aunt Katya felt the need to scold me?

"Surely you know your parents were not a love match," Aunt Katya was saying. "Although I suppose they got on well enough before your father's accident . . ."

That might have been true, but I had spent so much of my

time with my grandfather at his estate and factory in Kaluga as a little girl, I hardly knew of that time in their lives.

". . . even in the best times, your mother never forgot the excitement she had once known at the court. After your father's accident, she grew bitter. Your mother wouldn't want you to repeat her mistakes. Don't ruin your life over a man who has lost his head over you."

"It's not mutual. It's not my fault if he lost his head. I did no more than flirt. I have given no encouragement. For God's sake, I am expecting again . . ."

Aunt Katya maintained her cool expression.

"Alexander's child." My behavior had been so disparaged my own aunt needed the clarification. I wished to sink into the floor and disappear.

"I know." Aunt Katya drew her dainty little hands to her chest. "Yet there will be cruel whispers and jests. There always are."

"So what do you suggest I do?" I asked, still defensive.

She leaned forward. I caught a whisper of jasmine fragrance in her facial cream. "Georges already courts your sister at balls. Encourage that."

"Gladly. But what am I supposed to do when he approaches me?"

"Treat him with coldness. A man's ego cannot abide it."

"I can't be rude to this man."

"Why not?"

I would miss the attention. I cringed as the thought ran through my head. "Wouldn't that look even worse than a flirtation? It would look like I had something to hide."

"Bring up your sister before he has a chance to say anything more to you. It won't be a shock. This would be a prudent match for our family, and Georges d'Anthès should settle down. He can't continue to have the run of the court's maids like a wild stallion."

I blushed and dipped my head.

"You are a married woman now, with children. Don't pretend to be embarrassed or offended. I hope your reaction is not due to jealousy."

"Of course not!" I blurted. "I love Alexander."

Aunt Katya tilted her chin. For a moment, I saw a slight resemblance to Ekaterina and imagined my sister's elation should Georges ask for her hand.

"We both have a temper, I suppose," I told her. "Alexander and I."

"An artistic temper," my aunt mused. "That's the price of marrying a poet. It's not surprising. But now, the eyes of the court are on you and you must watch yourself."

Our next child, my namesake, Natalya, was born that May. We spent most of the summer at a peaceful dacha on one of the so-called Stone Islands on the delta of the Neva River. Our country house remained cozy and quiet, even as the island grew crowded. My sisters joined the evening picnics on the shore, near sphinxes that kept watch over the Neva, and the public balls held in newly constructed mansions. I instructed them to make excuses, so I might avoid society: I was still recovering from childbirth, or a summer cold, or a lightly sprained ankle. I stayed inside with baby Natalya in my arms and Alexander at my side, cross-legged on the bed we shared, working on a set of poems inspired by his long walks around the island. It reminded me of the early days of our marriage, and though I felt content, a part of me sensed this was merely the calm before the storm.

When we returned to St. Petersburg, we moved for the last time, to a flat on the banks of the Moyka River.

I had taken Aunt Katya's words to heart. I could no longer excuse a flirtation with Georges, no matter how innocent, and would steer him toward Ekaterina. While we were away on the island, she chattered on and on about Georges: the perfection of his dance steps, the humor of his stories, the way his legs looked in tight breeches. Azya confided to me that rumor had it they stole private moments alone together. With Dmitry far away, splitting his time between Moscow and Kaluga, I decided I must speak for our family and ensure Georges's intentions were honorable.

I next saw him at a ball honoring the victory over Napoleon in 1812, hosted by the tsar at the Winter Palace. As we dressed that afternoon, I talked Ekaterina into wearing a sea-green hand-me-down gown that flowed bewitchingly. I gave the fabric a longing look as Liza whistled a tune about an American dandy with a feather in his hat and worked on last minute restitching to ensure the dress flattered my sister's figure. I let my imagination play, fancying that with a flowered wreath made to look like seaweed and glimmering jewelry like fish scales, I could have kept the gown for myself and made a fetching mermaid. Reluctantly, I chose a simple black dress instead, with a modest neckline and a matching lace shawl. I wanted all attention focused on my sisters this evening.

As we entered the Winter Palace, Alexander and I walked hand in hand and my sisters flanked us on either side, not unlike the tsar's two guards who stood on either side of the front staircase, I noted with some amusement. The guards wore the uniform of that fateful year of 1812: stiff collars, high-plumed helmets, and bayonets.

Ekaterina had taken special care to make her cheeks rosy with rouge, and even Azya, normally shy at balls, perked up as we made our way through the room. I squeezed Alexander's hand before I released it and gave each of my sisters a glance. As we ascended the marble stairs, we withdrew fans from our reticules and fluttered them before our faces in unison. When we acted as though we commanded the room, people treated us with greater deference.

The tsar stood directly in our path, arms crossed, before a life-size portrait of his late brother, Tsar Alexander. In the painting, his brother looked stiff and grim, back erect, ready to face down the impudent little French dictator who dared to invade Russia. Tsar Nicholas didn't smile as he usually did when he saw us, but rather looked as glum as his late brother, brow lined. Without thinking, I clutched my shawl tighter around my chest.

Yet the tsar didn't have his eye on me, nor my sisters, but my husband. Alexander had worn his official court uniform, even down to the feather in his old-fashioned cocked hat, which he said reminded him of the Yankee Doodle in Liza's song I knew he loathed. Although his outfit was complete, he'd thrown it together in a hasty fashion, cravat tossed over the short uniform coat. Alexander preferred a careless look for bounding about town during the day, but in the evening he usually took more pride in his appearance. I wondered if he wished to purposely vex the tsar. I had been too preoccupied with making Ekaterina presentable to worry over it before we left.

Now the tsar approached us straightaway, his guards struggling to keep pace. "Pushkin! My lady!" I curtsied low, but he

seemed impatient and beckoned for me to rise. He kissed my
hand and nodded approvingly at my sisters. Ekaterina nearly tipped over with excitement, as she always felt particularly full of
herself in the presence of the tsar, but he turned his attention at
once to Alexander. "I know you are a creative type, bound by
whims and such, but this confuses me." He indicated Alexander's
uniform. "Did these lovely ladies kidnap you off the street, man?"

To my horror, Alexander looked bored with the tsar's reproach.
"Oh? Were we not to appear in uniform this evening? Your guards
are done up to the nines. It seems I never can keep the dress codes
for these affairs straight in my mind."

The tsar's lip twitched. Clearly, he had anticipated an apology.
"The invitation specified evening dress for guests, and after loan-
ing you a goodly sum, I don't imagine money is an issue. I only
think it proper that our great poet look presentable when appearing in public."

I drew in a deep breath, unaware the tsar had loaned us more
money. Purplish blotches appeared on Alexander's cheeks, and
his hands closed in and out of fists. The tsar spied on his wife,
blocked his work from being published, and left no doubt of his
power over him. It was only a matter of time until Alexander's
temper got the better of him. I thought of the young Decembrist
officers, lurching and swinging from ropes, forever silent.

"It is only that my husband adores his new uniform so! I think
he cannot bear to part with it . . ." The tsar frowned. No sweet
words would relieve us of his judgment. Alexander turned to me
as though to add something cutting to my comment and I gave a
quick shake of my head. I leaned in close. "Perhaps you might
consider a change of clothes. We'll be all right."

"Yes! They'll be fine." The tsar easily changed his tone to sound merry. "I'll keep my eye on them for you. No mischief, I promise."

Hearing that, I wondered if Tsar Nicholas was one of the rumormongers Aunt Katya had warned me about, laughing at my husband behind his back. I was afraid now to look anywhere but the floor and Ekaterina's tapping foot in a pretty green slipper. I feared Alexander might say something sharp to the tsar and I had made the situation worse.

Tonight, however, Alexander kept his anger in check. "Take this one." Gently, he guided Azya to the tsar. "She deserves to enjoy the best company in St. Petersburg."

I think the tsar would have preferred myself or even Ekaterina, who could babble about gossipy nonsense with the best of them, but he was nothing if not gallant and offered Azya his hand. "It would be my honor."

"I will see you later, lovely wife." Alexander leaned in to peck my cheek, his side whiskers brushing against my face. Given this convenient excuse for escape, I realized why he had remained calm and knew I wouldn't see him the rest of the night; he preferred a card table to the stuffiness of the ballroom any night.

Azya and the tsar strolled off in one direction, toward the crystal punch bowl, and Alexander veered to the opposite door. I watched his back, hoping beyond hope he might turn to look at me one last time. He once had asked me a question no one else ever thought to consider: *What do you want from your life?* Had I ever answered? Did I even know? I wanted time to read and love my children and perhaps even return to my own writing, but the allure of the balls had been so powerful . . . I wanted that to be a part of my life as well.

I felt a sharp jolt in the rib cage as Ekaterina jabbed me with her elbow. "There is Georges. Are you going to dance with him?"

"Why would I dance with Georges?" Already this evening was shaping up as a disaster, but at least my sister had the decency to wait until my husband was out of earshot. I turned once more to look at Alexander, but he was gone.

"It is how you have started your time at our previous affairs." Ekaterina waved her fan before her pink cheeks and took stock of the room. "Why should this one be any different?"

I bit my lip, assessing Ekaterina's face and wondering what she knew, what rumors she had heard or even started to spread. Could she be that petty?

Ekaterina squeezed my hand, her voice now strangely sincere. "Might you get us started? You seem to have an easy rapport with him."

Before I could answer, I spotted Georges on the opposite side of the dance floor, the details of his face too far away to be clear without my spectacles. Still, I recognized the gleaming red sash he wore under his evening coat and the sparkle of the golden medallion with the tsar's face on it that he wore near his heart. His entire form drew to attention when he spotted us. I averted my gaze, suddenly finding a great need to adjust the thin lace shawl over my shoulders.

"He's coming our way." Ekaterina glanced anxiously this way and that, like a coy country milkmaid in a melodrama.

"Give me a few minutes and then he's all yours."

This comment seemed to cheer Ekaterina. She headed toward a long table draped with patriotic imperial banners, where preserved rose leaves were served on a platter alongside figs and honey.

I toyed with my fan as Georges approached. I could smell his French cologne before he reached me, the scent earthier than the citrus and sandalwood Alexander favored, somehow tantalizing and off-putting at once.

"My lady." Georges swept into a grand bow and kissed my hand, as he always did, but with an extra firm press of his lips against my skin. Now that he was near, I noticed his bright blond hair, golden as the sun, flopping on his forehead as he bent down and the smile that made him appear as Apollo himself. I closed my eyes and then, fearing I would appear a coquette, opened them wide again.

It may seem strange that such a thing could happen at this particular moment, when I was trying not to think of Georges as anything but a potential brother-in-law, but I swear it was then that I realized exactly what I wanted from this life. Freedom. I wanted space to speak and think and know the path I chose was mine alone, and not limited by what others might think of me. And I wanted to share this exhilarating freedom with Alexander. He was the one who had made it all possible. My heart sank to my stomach as I realized how dangerously close I'd come to losing it all.

Tonight, I was a woman of business, as I had been when I spoke to Alexander's publisher, and I arranged my features into an appropriately solemn expression.

"I must speak with you," I told him.

Georges seemed ecstatic at the notion. "Anything, my lady." He took my elbow and tried to steer me behind a wrought-iron trellis garlanded with climbing wisteria and bougainvillea. I stopped cold before we could get any farther than a footman carrying a tray of crystal goblets.

"We shall speak here."

His brows pinched as he leaned over to fetch a goblet of punch for me. "I thought some measure of privacy—"

"We do not need privacy. It is unseemly for us to spend further time together alone."

He took it as a joke. "Unseemly? Why we are simply enjoying one another's company." He waved at the other pairs of dancers. "We take no more pleasure than anyone else."

"My flirtation has caused injured feelings. I wish no appearance of impropriety. I wish no further attention drawn to my family."

Georges clicked his tongue between his teeth. The sound was most irritating and he suddenly seemed far less handsome. "Your husband has no problems with his own flirtations. Does he not fear a loss of honor? Here, drink this. You'll feel more at ease and more yourself."

I shook my head and refused the punch. "I cannot deal with further distractions."

Georges's sunlit features now paled and his voice grew hoarse. "My lady, I was under the impression you considered me more than a distraction. I thought we had come to an understanding and could take what pleasure we might in one another."

A sudden chill passed over my shoulders, but then I grew so warm perspiration beaded my brow. We had done nothing more than share a few sweet compliments. I hadn't spoken to him a moment too soon. "We are friends. I wish you happiness. That is all."

Georges dropped the crystal goblet and it fell to the ballroom floor with a crash, splintering into a thousand pieces. Everyone in the room turned to look. I was glad Alexander had left before he could witness this humiliating scene. Had he heard this poor man declare his love for me, he might have taken Georges down in a brawl in the center of the palace.

"I am mad for you. I love you. If you wish me to be happy, then tell me you feel the same."

He might as well have struck me in the face, for though I knew Georges desired me, he could have any woman and I had not considered our flirtations more than amusement on his part. I certainly had not thought him bold enough to make such a declaration in a public space. I hoped to spare his feelings so my words were ill chosen. "I wish I might tell you the same."

"Then why won't you do so? I have seen it in your eyes often enough."

I shook my head. "You have not." I stumbled over my next words, knowing I needed to speak plainly. "I'm sorry if you're hurt, but you have misread my intentions. Your love was not the outcome I sought, nor that which my heart demands."

"Surely you share my feelings."

"I do not love you. I cannot love you. I have a husband."

His expression gentled. "So if you were free—"

"I do not wish to be free, not in that way," I said. "I wish to be with my husband. I love him."

"You are saying only what society expects you to say. You are a good soul who cannot abide hurting your family, but they would recover, darling. We could run away together if you only say the word. People do it all the time."

He kept twisting my words. How could he have possibly thought I would even entertain the notion of abandoning my family? "You don't understand . . . my sister Ekaterina . . ."

Georges sputtered, but when he saw that I was serious, he

frowned and released my hand. "I see. You wish me to believe your attention was on behalf of your unmarried sister."

This was not exactly the truth, but it seemed like a useful version of our history. "Nothing would give me greater pleasure than to see the two of you together."

"Nothing, Natalie?"

"I'm sorry," I told him. "I'm sorry you developed feelings for me. That was not my intention. Now that matters are clear between us, however, I'm sure you will do the right thing. If you give Ekaterina a chance, you will find her company most pleasurable and see the wisdom of what I say."

His gaze landed on my sister, still hiding behind her fan. She had caught up with the tsar and now whispered something to Azya.

"You are a beautiful family," Georges said softly.

It was a start. I smiled at him. "Ask her to dance. She will jump at the opportunity."

"No doubt." After the glass shattered, Georges had made an extra effort to look congenial. I was sure the other guests passing by suspected he was apologizing for making a scene, but his tone remained morose.

"You spend a great deal of time with my sister Ekaterina. I do nothing to dissuade the bond between the two of you . . ." I wasn't sure where I was going with the sentence, for it didn't feel quite true, but I needed to say something to fill the silence as servants swept the shattered glass into dustbins.

He grabbed hold of my wrist and twisted so hard I cried out. I looked at him, astonished. His eyes were burning, though the rest of his body stayed rigid. No one near us would suspect anything amiss. I knew differently. My wrist throbbed.

"Clearly you wanted no more than to toy with me for your own amusement. Now I am besotted and you discard me like a frivolous plaything. I love you. Why do you not see it?"

When Alexander told me he loved me for the first time, he looked at me with anticipation, not expectation. Later, he told me he didn't know if I would say I loved him back. He merely found it necessary to express the words, to live free of regret. Georges looked like a wild little boy who, experiencing desire but denied the pleasure of possession, has his first tantrum. His gaze came to rest on an empire-style chair in the corner. I wondered if he might take the chair and hurl it at some innocent soul just to make himself feel better.

I searched desperately for the baron, the only person in the world who I thought could bring Georges to his senses, but his "father" was nowhere to be found. It seemed the baron was as anxious as my Alexander to be free of a formal court ball.

I needed to defend myself.

"Release me or I shall make sure that everyone in this ballroom sees you're hurting me." It was an empty threat. All eyes had been on us since the moment Georges dropped the glass, but I could think of nothing else to say.

"They shall see truth and beauty," Georges declared. "In France we worship these ideals. No one will blame me for acting foolishly for they know I am in love."

"In Russia, we are ruled by an iron tsar who metes out justice as he sees fit, answering only to himself."

At that, Georges let go of my arm. It seemed he feared exile in Siberia, the same as any of us. The threat of the tsar's temper and a random sentence carried out on a whim was enough to dissuade Georges from his abominable pursuit. When he let go, I shook my arm and took stock of the room. I longed for my spectacles, but then they would only confirm what I knew to be true. Backs turned to us, whispers behind fans. They had all overheard our conversation and would report the scene back to Alexander, as snidely and dramatically as possible. Among those who had heard the whole dreadful encounter were men who envied Alexander's literary successes and women who envied me for having the great poet as a husband.

"It's late, Monsieur d'Anthès," I told him, as loudly as I could manage without shouting. "My husband has taken ill. I am going home to see him."

As I flounced past Georges, I saw the tsar. He had been watching us the entire time. Though his features were but a pleasant mask, I could not shake the feeling he knew exactly what had transpired, knew I had invoked his protection, and that this was exactly what he had wanted all along.

Sixteen

That evening, I covered my bruised flesh with white powder and arranged my nightgown carefully so Alexander would not see the injury. I worried he would go after Georges with his pistol if he knew. How could I have let myself befriend a man who would lay hands on a woman? I felt a fool, and yet anyone present at the ball would assume I had led him to such a scene, that I must have encouraged him in some way. It was just as Aunt Katya said: women are always to blame.

Alexander was taken with the great Englishman Shakespeare, collecting all of his works and attempting to read them in their original language. I stuck with French translations and had read the tragedy about two adolescents in love. People spoke of it as a grand romance, but hadn't Romeo been madly in love with Rosaline before falling for Juliet? It confirmed my suspicions. Men are fickle creatures and easily distracted. With any luck, I was a mere distraction to Georges, as Rosaline had been for Romeo, and soon enough he would forget me.

When Georges did not attempt to visit, nor slip a note in Liza's hand, I gradually came to believe that either my admonitions had the desired effect or the tsar had spoken with Georges and he now understood the foolishness of the situation.

I avoided social occasions for a few weeks, but by the time the weather cooled, I grew restless and rummaged once more through the costumes I kept in an enormous closet in our hall, all lovingly catalogued and hung on hooks. I stroked the velveteen lining of a half-finished medieval cloak. I hoped to dress as Maid Marian and convince Alexander to appear as Robin Hood at a celebration to honor the tsar's name day in early December. My old friend and enemy, Ida, had hinted she might hire me to assist with her gowns as well. I liked the idea of doing something productive to earn a bit of extra income, and with four small children in the house, I needed a respite. Yet Ida lived near the barracks of the horse guards, where Georges was stationed, and I had not forgotten her encouragement to flirt with him. I consistently found excuses not to visit.

I shut the closet door, resolved to work on Maid Marian's costume after I put baby Natalya down for her afternoon nap. As I crossed the hall to the children's nursery, I spotted Ekaterina in the parlor, legs tucked under her bottom, the way a little girl might sit. She held a letter in her hand and a look of sheer victory on her square face made me pause. "What's that?"

"Oh!" Ekaterina tried to cultivate an air of mystery and failed entirely. "Wouldn't you like to know?"

I actually didn't want to know that badly. How easily Ekaterina set my nerves on edge. "If you want to keep secrets, do so. Your correspondence is none of my concern."

Ekaterina's lips twisted and she waved the thin vellum paper in the air triumphantly. I caught a whiff of gentlemen's cologne, knew in an instant who had sent the letter, and instinctively clutched the cross hanging around my neck, thanking God Alexander was out of the house. He would have recognized the musky scent as well as I.

"Georges d'Anthès was your special friend." Ekaterina pressed the letter to her chest. "Yet it seems your reign as master of his heart has come to an end."

My heart engaged in a quick war with itself. I had Alexander. I had the world. I would do nothing further to damage that which I had earned. Marrying Ekaterina off to Georges might lay this tawdry business to rest once and for all. Even so, I worried for her. I remembered Georges twisting my wrist. For all Ekaterina and I fought like two dogs trapped in a cage, her blood was my blood. I felt compelled to say something. "Watch yourself around him. He has a temper."

"He seems like a dream to me. Gentle as a lamb. Perhaps he only behaves abominably to women he has no intention of marrying."

"I'm not convinced he would make a good husband."

Ekaterina let out a loud, sputtering laugh. "You would say no less to keep him near to you. Who knows what witchcraft you cast?"

Of course Ekaterina would insist I had cast some crone's spell on Georges. "I have no desire to keep him for myself."

"You mean you have no desire to play fair. You only want to dangle him on a little string along with any other men who strike your fancy. To the humiliation of your own husband."

"Take that back." I fought the urge to hit my sister. "I would never hurt Alexander."

She snorted. "Really? You convinced many people otherwise. Carrying on like a strumpet. And then when one of your male harem decides to focus his attentions elsewhere—well! You can't have that. Particularly not if his attention turns to your own sister. How that would damage your ridiculous legend as the Venus of St. Petersburg."

I was keenly aware of a shadow lurking in the doorway to the nursery and felt sure Ekaterina's loud voice had summoned Masha's curiosity. I took care to keep my own voice to a minimum level. "All of this sounds like some fantasy you have conjured. My concern is that Georges put his hand on me sharply and in anger."

Ekaterina thrust her chin at me. "What did you say to make him angry?"

The woman is to blame. Always to blame. "Why do you think *I* said something? That is neither here nor there. His behavior was hardly chivalrous."

"So this lecture is for my benefit? You only think of me?"

"I do not believe you should entertain this man's attention."

"Is that so?" To Ekaterina's credit, she had inclined her head toward the nursery and made an effort to keep her voice down now. "You wish me to be underfoot forever so that you might feel you are queen of the palace with all your little minions in place."

"I won't hear another word. We've been nothing but generous to you."

I heard the front door open and then the click of heels on tile in our foyer. Liza appeared in the open entranceway to the parlor, rubbing her hands briskly in her apron, her cheeks red and teeth chattering from the November chill outside. "I'm sorry to interrupt, Madame Pushkina. May I see you?"

"If you must."

"How convenient. Walk away then." Ekaterina returned to her seat on the divan. Our mahogany divan. All Ekaterina had in the world was due to my generosity. My sister's pale hands trembled and she clutched her stomach. Whether she was madly in love with Georges or not, something troubled her. She was old enough now that wicked people might begin to call her a spinster behind her back. She needed a husband to have any chance at a place in the world and she knew it. My anger began to dissipate. "I don't wish to leave when we're still mad at one another."

"I'm not mad. I only wanted you to know I am in love with Georges, and it is the thrill of my heart to think he might be in love with me as well."

I doubted Georges spoke of love in his letter to my sister, but she was hopeless. I shrugged, determined to speak to her again only after her temper had calmed. I followed Liza into the foyer, out of my earshot. "What is it?" I asked, still testy.

Liza's hands had not left the apron. As I looked closer at her face, I realized her reddened cheeks were more than a flush of cold. "A gentleman arrived earlier with two letters. One was for your sister, but the other . . . he asked that I wait until I saw you alone to deliver it."

My heart fell. "Georges d'Anthès."

Liza nodded and looked at the floor.

"I'll take it," I said quietly and Liza slipped the note into my hands.

I reviewed the contents quickly, feeling every second I held the paper in my hands was a betrayal of my husband. Georges insisted he must speak with me. He vowed to be cordial and wrote that Ida had agreed to remain with us the entire time at her house. The gall of this man—*the impudence of the scoundrel*, as Alexander would have put it—thinking I would be fooled by his sugared words, after all that had happened.

And then I read the last sentence. Georges said this matter concerned my family, someone close to me, and he had to speak to me at once, for he knew my mother and eldest brother were far away and my father indisposed.

I glanced over my shoulder, toward the parlor, where my sister still sat. Perhaps Ekaterina was not as delusional as I thought. If Georges had turned his romantic attentions to her, I needed to know. I couldn't bear the thought of Ekaterina seduced by a man who would lay a violent hand on her. I folded the note in half. My mother and brothers were in Moscow, my father was useless, and my grandfather was dead. I was the only one left to protect the Goncharov honor, even if it meant facing Georges once more.

"Please go to Ida's house," I told Liza. "Let her know I'll be there in an hour."

"The lady of the house sends her apologies," Ida's footman assured me as I followed him inside. "She was detained unexpectedly. One of the children is ill and she is upstairs in the nursery. She asked that you take a seat and make yourself comfortable. Would you care for tea?"

"Oh, I'm sorry to hear that." I kept my voice steady, but shot an anxious glance about Ida's tidy and practical little house before taking a seat on one of the armchairs in the parlor, feeling as though ants pranced over my shoulders and upper back. "Tea sounds lovely."

After the footman left, several minutes passed, each loudly ticked off on a Bavarian cuckoo clock with agonizing precision. I tried to make myself comfortable. I twiddled my thumbs and took in the clean scent of the dried mulberries hanging across the mantel of the hearth. I tried not to think about my fight with Ekaterina, and what promises might already have passed between my sister and Georges.

The door creaked open and I sprang up from the chair, startled. "Ida? Is everything all right? One of your children took ill?"

The tread of the footsteps was heavier than I'd anticipated. A moment later, the handsome face of Georges d'Anthès appeared before me, figure pristine in his formal white uniform. "I knew you would see me. My dream has come true."

He spoke as though nothing had happened, as though he had not grabbed me so hard he left a bruise. As though I had not told him plainly that I took no interest in his romantic affections. My heart beat so wildly I thought I might faint. "Georges?"

"I had to see you." Normally every one of his blond hairs was perfectly tousled just so, but today his hair was wild. Even the simple words he spoke were slurred. He must have been drinking. "I love you."

"You said Ida would be here. You said you wished to talk about my family."

"Didn't you hear what I said? I love you."

Georges's features remained passive even as my head spun and my cheeks burned with humiliation. This had all been a ruse. I should have known. My gaze darted around the tasteful little parlor. Ida may have been a part of this all along, arranging a meeting as some sort of cruel prank. But even so, I prayed Ida or her footman would arrive and put a swift end to it. "Did I not make myself clear? I love my husband."

He must have heard me, but you would never have known it from his expression. "I think you're scared." His tone was gentle, but condescending. "It is understandable. I should not have been so abrupt with my confession. You see, my feelings have rendered me senseless. I tried to forget you. Truly, I did. You must understand." He began to bang his hands against his head, harder and harder, until I worried he would hurt himself. Yet I remained too frightened to stop him. "My words are truth and the truth must always be spoken, no matter the cost. Still, I should have known your gentle soul would find it difficult to comprehend."

He reached for my hand, but I snapped it behind my back and out of his reach. "I am not simple. I understood perfectly and your words offended me. You wish me to become your lover and I made it clear that would never happen."

"No, no, no." Georges pressed his lips tightly together, but small bubbles of spittle still formed at the corners of his mouth. I backed away from him. "You misunderstand. Forgive me. I ask only for your assurance. And love. I expect nothing more." He waved desperately at the cross around my neck. "You're a virtuous woman. I only ask for one word to assure me I might hope someday to be with you. I only ask you to respond with the word 'yes.' A simple word. A simple favor."

No man would be content with a mere whisper of love from a woman he desired. And even if by some stretch of the imagination Georges only wanted a word assuring him of my love, I could never say something so far from the truth. Even if his senses had taken leave of him, as though he suffered from the same mental ailment that plagued my father. Even if it might quiet him for a while, long enough for me to leave this room at least, I could not say anything so horrible.

"If truth is paramount, as you insist, how can I lie?" My shoulders heaved, as though some malevolent spirit had taken control of me. "How dare you say these things when you have sent a letter to my sister encouraging her feelings? How cruel you are."

The muscles in his face tightened as his jaw clenched. "Your sister has been clear about her feelings and I have no wish to embarrass her. I have engaged only in a harmless flirtation."

"Not so harmless." I couldn't believe I was about to defend Ekaterina. "You have played with her heart."

"She must know the truth now. That is why I insisted you see me, for the sake of your family. Koko is a pleasant enough thing, but I belong only to you."

"That is your cross to bear," I told him. "It is not a mutual passion."

"You don't know what you want. Women are fickle. You must trust me."

"I know exactly what I want! I want you to stay away from me."

"You don't mean that."

"Don't tell me what I mean." How could I have wasted even one careless thought on this man? "Don't tell me what I want. I can think for myself and have no desire to trouble you any longer."

"You are no trouble," he said helplessly. "You are my love."

"Consider your heart free to pursue another."

"How could I even think of another woman when you exist?"

"You hope someday I might love you? I don't love you now. I

have never loved you in the past. And I foresee no circumstance in which I would love you in the future. Ever."

"But my Natalie . . ." For all that Georges treated me as a decorative plaything, the crushed expression on his face still wounded me. From the look of panic in his eyes, you would have thought I had taken a pillow to his face and pressed it down to drive the last breath from his body. It made me almost feel badly about what I needed to say next, but it was his own abominable persistence, his refusal to take me at my word, which had led us to this place. He needed to hear the truth in no uncertain terms.

"I cannot stand the sight of you," I said in a low, fierce voice I scarcely recognized as my own. "You disgust me. Stay away from me. Stay away from my family."

"You can't mean it. You ask the impossible."

I did not wish to invoke the tsar's protection once more, further indebting myself to him, but saw no choice. "If you fail to do so I will take the matter up with Tsar Nicholas."

Without a word, Georges reached into a pocket of his uniform coat and retrieved a pistol, similar to the one Alexander kept locked in his study. The roof of my mouth parched and I made a strangled gasp. I was about to die. Georges would say something demented. If he could not have me, no man would. I prayed fervently, begging God to spare me if not for my own sake then for my children. Alexander's intense gaze the first time he saw me flashed through my head, the feeling that anything in the world was possible. I'd held the world in my hand and let it go over a silly flirtation. I'd been a fool. And now I would die for my stupidity.

I screwed my eyes shut. If I had to die, I wouldn't give Georges the satisfaction of knowing the fear in my heart.

Nothing happened.

My heart still raced, but I managed to crack my eyes open. Georges looked at me, the pistol turned to his own head. "If this is how it must be," he said softly.

A wave of dizziness threatened to knock me off my feet, and yet, through some divine intervention, I stood my ground and kept my voice measured. "Georges, don't do this."

"What choice do I have?" His deadened eyes looked through me.

"You're not thinking straight."

"My thoughts have never been clearer."

"You have family," I said desperately. "The baron loves you. I don't think he could bear this world were you not in it."

Georges hesitated. From the sadness in his eyes, I knew he returned at least some degree of affection for the man. Misery keened his voice. "He has never understood me. He thinks we should be attached at the hip at all times. Perhaps some men are happy this way, but my passions are not so easily bound. No one understands."

"God understands! God has created you for his own divine purpose!" I raised my voice, hoping someone in the household might hear. "It is a mortal sin to end your life!"

His shoulders sagged, but he did not lower the pistol. "God abandoned me long ago."

"God abandons no man."

"You are but a child. You cannot know your own mind, let alone the ways of God. What a cruel fate to be bound by passion to a mere infant. No wonder I have been driven to such desperate acts."

He closed his eyes and I was sure he would squeeze the trigger. "No! No!" I made my way to try to free the pistol from his hands, but Georges stepped back and I tumbled over the side table. I regained my footing, but now the table stood between Georges and me. I could not hope to wrestle the pistol from him.

"You wish me to drop this weapon?"

"You're not thinking straight. You're not right in your own head. You need help."

"I need only one word," he said. "As I requested before. I need you only to admit I stand a chance of gaining your love yet. I need only to hear the word 'yes.'"

Around me, the room seemed to take on a crimson tinge. I felt the tears swell and forced them back as best I could. This man had granted me power over his own life and still I hesitated. Surely they would all understand if I said the word now. I would run from this place and tell Alexander everything. I would warn Ekaterina not to accept any more letters from Georges. I would approach the baron and explain that this man he loved needed the care of a sanitarium. The baron would understand. They would all understand. They would know I said the word yes under extreme duress.

Except, no matter what happened, no matter the circumstances, the woman was always to blame. Aunt Katya had taught me as much and I had seen it myself many times over. Creeping doubts filled my mind. People might not believe me, not even my own family. Ida would casually mention Georges had planned a secret rendezvous with me and that I had agreed to meet him privately at her house. Georges would tell everyone I loved him, convinced in his own heart this was the truth despite everything I said to the contrary. I would have only my own reputation with which to defend myself. And how easily that had already been damaged. I was the villain once more, the vindictive Venus who could not be bothered with the care of poor little Vulcan. I thought of Alexander and his pistols, the lure of these monstrous things for men.

I said nothing.

Georges continued to hold the pistol to his temple, but his lip started to quiver. "You cannot say it! Even to save my life you will not speak the truth of your heart."

My silence might condemn this man to his death. I wondered what tortures might await me in hell, but I would not risk hurting Alexander.

The door clicked open once more and tiny footsteps pattered. The footfall was too light to be Ida. A little girl, nearly the same age as my Masha, popped her head around the doorway, her blond hair twisted into braids tied with pink bows on either side of her head. "Are you Natalya?" she cried merrily. "Mamma said we might have visitors, but she made me stay upstairs."

The little one ran forward, not even noticing Georges or the pistol, and hugged my legs. "I have new dolls from France. Would you like to see them?"

I squeezed her back, never so grateful to see another human being in my life. "Dolls! How lovely." I glanced across the room. Georges had withdrawn the pistol and was now opening and shutting his mouth as though unsure what to do next. It seemed he had enough sense left to stay his hand rather than blow his brains to the floor in front of a child. I muttered a silent prayer of thanks. For so long I had resented Mother's piety and the limitations it placed on us, forever trudging behind her on the way to church. Now, I was grateful for the faith she had instilled in me. It would grant me strength.

Georges had lowered the pistol, but not put it away. I made a quick gamble. "Speaking of France, do you know your mamma's friend, Georges? He is from that land."

Intrigued, the little girl turned to Georges who quickly placed the pistol back in the pocket of his uniform coat.

"You are?" She said, with reverence. "Have you seen Paris?"

Georges still looked confused but kept his voice charming. "I have, little friend."

"Perhaps Georges could talk to your dollies," I suggested. "I'm sure they might want to meet one of their fellow countrymen."

"Oh!" She clasped her hands together. "I'm sure they would enjoy that."

"Are you up for such a discussion, Monsieur d'Anthès?"

Georges was not about to disappoint this child. "I could manage," he stammered.

"Very well then." I pressed her hand. "Georges will keep you and your mamma company."

Ida's daughter nodded and released my hand. I brushed past her without so much as looking at Georges and made my way out of that house as quickly as I could manage.

Seventeen

I managed to steady my hands during the bumpy ride home, but once I was safely back at our flat, and approaching Alexander's study, my fingers trembled once more. Ekaterina and Azya had taken it upon themselves to accompany the children on a walk, leaving Alexander to his own devices. The furious scribble of his quill against vellum gave my battered heart some reason for hope. If he had conjured inspiration to revise his poems from the Stone Islands, and abandon his card tables at the club for the comfort of his own study, perhaps he might return to the Alexander I once knew: the Pushkin who marched across St. Petersburg and Moscow, pounding his silver-tipped walking stick on the cobblestone and tossing his hat in the air solely for the pleasure of catching it once more in his hands.

I felt a sudden pang in my heart. How terribly I had missed that person and how badly I wanted him back. My hand hovered near the doorknob, and I considered keeping the entire sordid incident with Georges to myself, so as not to disturb him. To create, his mind must remain free of worry. And yet word of the drama would reach him; Ida would never keep such a secret. Besides,

Georges had put enough distance between Alexander and me already. I would not allow him to create further havoc in our marriage.

I gathered my courage and rapped my knuckles against the door.

"Who is it?" Already he sounded irritable. "I asked not to be disturbed. Come in only if it's important."

"Is your wife important?" I whispered.

The door creaked open and Alexander stood before me, eyes wide. "Natasha! I thought you were busy with your costumes, determining how best to break all men's hearts . . ."

When he saw my expression, his brow creased. "What happened? Are you hurt?"

"No, but . . ." I clasped his hand. "Please let me in. Please let me hold you."

He drew me first into his arms and then we moved to the large sofa he kept in his study for relaxing and *pondering*, as he put it. For the next quarter hour, as he stroked my hair, I told him of what transpired at Ida's house. Hot tears began to flow and when I related the appearance of the pistol, my shoulders convulsed and Alexander's body went rigid beside mine.

"Tasha," he whispered, devastated. "I am so sorry."

"I shall never go there again. I was tricked into the meeting, but I should have known not to trust either of them." Alexander handed me his monogrammed handkerchief and I blew my nose before sinking my head onto a worn velvet pillow. He had the sofa placed before one of the shelves in his library, as though the sight of so many words bound in old leather might inspire him. I stared blankly at the shelves upon shelves of books and elaborate folio volumes that took up nearly half the room. Why had I started thinking of costume balls again? Why hadn't I been content to stay here with him, curled up in a corner of the study on the deep burgundy leather cushion of his armchair? I could have read quietly and withdrawn from the world. At one time, hadn't that been all I desired? "I will never see this man again."

"I have no objections, only our holy tsar awarded me his little post at court as a token. We can hardly avoid society, which means we can't avoid this scoundrel."

Alexander was right. We had numerous obligations to appear at court functions and we still owed the tsar money, but I shuddered at the idea of facing Georges. "The man is mad!"

"Mad with love."

I slapped Alexander on the arm. "Do not take it lightly. He held a gun to his head."

Alexander leaned back on the sofa. "I did not mean to make it so. I wish to protect your honor at all costs. I simply do not know what to say."

"An illness of the mind must be no different than an illness of the body," I said.

"Surely there are doctors who could help. Treatments that might be administered."

"It is difficult for a man to admit to such shortcomings."

"An illness is no shortcoming." I thought of my father roaming my grandfather's estate. Dmitry had taken charge of my father's care, but a sanitarium had never been discussed, for we all feared such places. I wondered now if that fear was misplaced. Babette did her best when Father visited. She made sure he was fed and at least somewhat clean, but I wondered how much differently my father's life might have unfolded had he been under the care of professionals.

"Perhaps," Alexander said, "but diseases of the mind are rarely admitted. When a man is committed to a sanitarium or some other course of treatment, it is often at the behest of the person who loves him most."

It might have been too late for my father, but perhaps there was still hope for Georges. I remembered the baron's tender eyes as he looked at Georges. He would want what was best for him, no matter the personal cost. "I know just the person."

"Let me guess." Alexander tapped his mouth with a closed fist. "Our friend, the baron? I could confront the man, I suppose, in the interest of your honor. I don't care how old this Georges d'Anthès is, his father needs to give him a proper thrashing."

"That was *not* my thought." I felt his arms and shoulders tremble beneath me. I squeezed his hand to steady him, already imagining Alexander and the baron screaming at one another in a crowded ballroom, while ladies whispered and giggled behind their fans, no doubt blaming me for the entire tawdry scene. "I have caused the damage. I shall solve this problem and speak to the baron myself."

First thing the next morning, I called on Aunt Katya and impressed upon her my need to speak with the baron. She proved quite useful, for she had chatted with Georges's adopted father at a recent supper party and learned he was to escort the ambassador from Bavaria to a performance of *La Sylphide* the following night. I wished to keep the business between Georges and myself private, at least for the moment. So, I made vague references to Alexander's struggling new journal and the possibility the baron had useful connections in Europe. With a suspicious tilt of her head, my aunt finally agreed to ensure two tickets for the ballet awaited me at the box office that evening.

For the occasion, I chose a pale pink chiffon gown with a modest neckline. Alexander found himself conveniently ill and unable to attend, while in a twist on the usual state of affairs, Ekaterina declared herself content to stay home and care for the children so that Alexander might rest. Though she did sneak in a rude comment that she must fill this role since no one else seemed to take interest in them of late.

I wanted to slap my sister, but liked the idea of avoiding her company for the evening and didn't want her to change her mind. Azya, usually the one to stay at home, seemed glad enough to go, but she gave Alexander a sad look as we left our flat.

Even in my agitated state, the ballet entranced me. I held a lorgnette to my eyes so I might see every detail. The dancers wore loose skirts that hit just below their knees to better showcase their impressive work *en pointe,* a feat I thought I would never grow tired of watching. I felt sure Alexander would get tickets for himself after he heard how ravishing the ballerinas looked, although I didn't think he would like the character of the fortune-telling witch.

When the red-and-gold velvet curtain dropped after the first act, we left our seats and entered the crowded lobby for intermission. Despite the crush of people, I immediately spotted the baron near a crystal bowl filled with punch and sliced oranges, and a lavish cake ornamented with graceful miniature sylphs. He was speaking with a bearded man I assumed was the ambassador. Assuring my sister I wouldn't take long, and giving her coin to purchase an iced sherbet if she so desired, I worked my way through the people gathered in the crowded lobby to the spot where the baron stood and gently tapped him on the shoulder.

The baron spun around, startled. When he saw me, his expression remained neutral, but his shoulders hunched underneath the thick fabric of his uniform coat. The Bavarian diplomat stopped talking and took a pinch of snuff from a silk pouch.

"Madame Pushkina," the baron said, between gritted teeth.

"Madame Pushkina?" the diplomat exclaimed, huffing through the words as he stifled a sneeze. "Of course! I heard you were the most beautiful woman in this city or any other and now I see you do not disappoint. A pleasure!"

"The pleasure is mine. I'm sorry to interrupt, but might I steal the baron for a moment?"

"Your wish is my command." He bowed gallantly and kissed my hand. Though I was in no mood to flirt, I appreciated the Bavarian's good manners and he left of his own accord, stuffing his pouch of snuff back in his pocket and helping himself to a glass of the fruited punch before crossing the room to examine a collection of posters advertising the season's ballets.

"What do you want?" The baron asked coldly. I took a step back. He had always regarded me with subtle contempt, but this was the first time he actually seemed angry to see me.

I steeled myself and pressed forward. "I must speak to you about Georges."

"The man I last saw at home weeping with a broken heart?" he said. "You see, he grew infatuated with a beautiful woman, and when he was led to believe she felt the same, this infatuation turned to love. Yet it seems he was but a toy to amuse this same woman's ego and now that she has no further use of him, she left him devastated and alone."

In my heels, I was as tall as the baron so I looked him straight in the eye. Hopefully, he still held his adored ward's best interests at heart. "Is that the story he has told you?"

"It is the tale I have seen unfold before my own eyes."

"He received no encouragement from me. We did nothing but flirt, trifling coquetry at that. He lives in a fantasy of his own making and now cannot leave it." I glanced nervously about the lobby and lowered my voice. "When I saw him last it was a surprise to me. He pulled a pistol. He threated to shoot himself. Georges is not well. He needs help."

"This is not the version he related to me."

"It is the truth," I insisted. "You are his father, in legal right if not in blood. Surely you could intervene so that his mind might settle and be well once more."

"All Georges needs is a person who loves him for who he is and not for his pretty face or flattery."

I didn't know whether it was diplomatic, or even wise, to say what I truly felt in my heart. I only knew that when he spoke of a person who loved Georges for who he was, the baron spoke of himself. I had seen his longing gaze fixed on Georges enough times and heard whispers the baron preferred the company of men. "Surely he already has that. He has that in you. He will see your intervention for the true affection it is. You love him."

The baron looked struck, even as his eyes grew tender and his voice softened. "It is not as simple as that. I wish it were."

"Perhaps it could be," I said. "You have heard rumors about the Goncharov family, have you not? You must know of my father's troubles. We lived in denial for so long, but it has gotten so bad that my mother cannot tolerate his presence. Now he is shuffled back and forth between my late grandfather's estate and the home of my brother Dmitry. It is a sad state of affairs. I wish we had done something sooner . . . sent him somewhere."

The baron raised his defenses once more, shaking his head and looking at me as though I were a demon in female form. "Now we see the true nature of the matter. I will not send Georges away. To a sanitarium or whatever other ghastly place you suggest. *That* would be madness."

"It is not a permanent situation. It's what is best for him . . ."

"It's what is best for you." The baron's words were like frost in the air. "Wouldn't that work to your advantage? Instead of taking responsibility for your own actions, you would be absolved. Georges d'Anthès the madman. Poor Natalya Pushkina." He waved his hand in disgust. "You are even more selfish than I imagined."

My heart quaked from the shock of his words, wondering if there was not some truth to them and I truly did care more for my own reputation than Georges's well-being. Perhaps that was why I had asked to speak to the baron alone, without Alexander present. Could I be so horrible? "That is not my motivation. I hope you will reconsider."

"I will do no such thing," the baron snapped. "You have reduced a splendid man to feminine hysterics. You think he might end his life over you? I cannot tell you differently. If you wish to help, abandon your husband and run away with Georges. Go to Europe, to the French countryside. Such affairs happen all the time."

Cramps twisted my middle. I regretted the day I ever laid eyes on Georges, but still had one weapon at my disposal. The baron could not mean what he said. He couldn't bear to lose the man he adored. "You would have me take Georges away from you? You love him."

"You don't know the meaning of love. When you love someone you want that which will make them happiest. You are willing to sacrifice your own happiness to make this so." At that, the baron turned his back to me and I knew I had been dismissed.

I barely felt sensible and couldn't see past the blurry veil of my own tears. Making my way across the lobby, I had no idea where Azya had wandered off to. I only hoped she would spot me and guide me outside to the courtyard, serving as my eyes as she had before I married. Once she saw my state, surely she would call for our horses and we would go home. I wanted nothing more than to be in my own bed with my children and Alexander for comfort.

Instead, I felt a strong hand grip my arm and found myself spun around and staring up at the tsar. He held me with one hand and a chilled glass of champagne in the other.

"My Lady Pushkina," he said in his deep, booming voice. "Darling! You look a fright. Are those tears? What has happened to upset you so? A lovers' quarrel?" His expression was subdued, yet I knew our tsar well enough now to detect the subtle smirk on his lips. No doubt he was laughing inside, laughing at me. Laughing at Alexander and Georges and the baron and our silly feelings, all of us merely entertaining players on a stage to him.

I could not summon words, only a tepid curtsy.

The tsar motioned for me to rise. "Georges d'Anthès is not here this evening. Such a shame. It seems the two of you are good friends."

I gathered myself together. "We are acquaintances, nothing more."

The tsar looked casually around the room, as though his next words would not destroy me: "Yet it seems you have set tongues wagging. Why even my wife has heard rumors from her ladies you took a secret meeting with this fellow. Rubbish, I'm sure." He drew a step nearer, so the sheer mass of his body seemed to block any escape, as though he wanted to leave no doubt he could overpower me if he wished. He leaned in close. I could smell the mint sprigs he used to freshen his breath. "Still, if you're in need of another 'acquaintance,' I can fill that role."

No matter what anyone might say, or what Georges thought, I was not simpleminded. It was clear enough to me what the tsar meant when he said "acquaintance," and the ghastly implication made me feel I was not a true being, but merely a physical body, good for one thing only. He knew I had been alone with Georges in Ida's house, believed us once lovers. Now that this fictional affair had been torn asunder, he wanted to take me as his mistress. Anything I might say in my own defense would only make matters worse. And now the tsar hovered over me and I was trapped in every possible sense.

My first instinct was to duck to avoid being so near his face. Instead I swept into another curtsy, the lowest I could manage, trying to stretch the moment so I might calm my trembling hands and determine what to do next. Our holy tsar had chosen to wield his infinite power. If his suggestion evolved into an explicit proposition, I was in no position to refuse. "Forgive me, Your Majesty. I have not felt myself all evening and believe I will be ill."

The tsar's forehead wrinkled in annoyance, but his words remained smooth as honey. "What troubles you, dear lady?"

I cast my eyes down in mock embarrassment. "Pains in my stomach. I must make my way home before it gets the better of me."

Though such matters were meant to be private, everyone knew I had suffered a miscarriage two years ago: the first night I had met Georges. On reflection, I should have seen this as an omen and known better than to pursue any relationship with him, no matter how seemingly innocent. I did not think even the tsar would risk a woman's health under such circumstances.

Sure enough, the tsar paled. "As you wish. By all means, take good care of yourself and fetch a physician if need be. Why our little Pushkin need merely say the word and I shall send the court doctor to your flat. We shall renew our friendship at a later date."

He took my hand, turning it over so my palm faced upward, and let his tongue slip between his lips. I repressed a shiver, feeling as though a reptile had slithered onto my wrist and caressed me.

"I look forward to seeing you again, my little vixen." The tsar drew me forward, pressing himself to me in a hug. I tried to pretend this was nothing more than a platonic affection while simultaneously working my body away from his. "Remember to take care with the way you behave in public. People are talking and word might reach your husband. You would not want to arouse a great man's jealousy."

The tsar would not refer to Alexander as a great man. He was the "great" one whose jealousy had been inflamed. I had reached my darkest moment with the worst possible decision before me: betray my husband's heart or risk my family's safety by angering the tsar.

I didn't know how much more I could bear. I only wanted Alexander.

When I arrived home, Alexander was locked away in his study once more. As I stared at the flicker and glow of candlelight in the crack underneath the door, I was torn between craving my husband's arms around me after another terrible night and not wishing to disturb him at all so that he might work.

As I wavered at the door, a figure approached me, tall and thin in her nightdress, holding a candle aloft in a holder.

"Finally!" Ekaterina said. "I thought you would never get home."

"I'm home earlier than usual." I had no patience for my sister's nagging, not tonight.

"You need to go in and see your husband."

I intended to do just that, but wasn't a field soldier at her command. "He's working. I thought I would wait so as not to disturb him."

"He has been in there all evening and will not let anyone inside. He will not eat. He even refused dessert." Ekaterina tossed one long braid over her shoulder. "It's hardly like him."

I was in no mood to cede this truth to my sister. "You understand his profession? He is a writer. Writers need privacy."

"If he is writing, why have there been no sounds of scratching nibs and the like?"

"Have you stood outside his door all night?" I said, exasperated.

"Listen to me." Ekaterina used her free hand to take me by the shoulder, still holding the candle aloft. The light shone on her face. I saw the creases lining her brow. This was not some drama of her own invention; she was truly scared. "A letter arrived earlier. He would not let me see it. But he looked a fright after reading and has since locked himself away. Believe me, he isn't working. Who knows what he's doing?"

I thought of the pistols in Alexander's desk and my body froze. I heard the light steps of Azya coming up behind Ekaterina, and sensed her terror, nearly as great as my own.

"You haven't seen him all evening?" her voiced wavered.

"No one has. Not even the children." Ekaterina leaned forward, right past me, and knocked on the thick wooden door. "Your wife is home," she called. "Will you leave her out here to worry herself to death?"

After a moment, the chair scraped against floor, and I heard the heavy plod of Alexander's footsteps, so different than the light steps he took when happy. The lock unlatched and Alexander stood before us, his black curls a mess and his eyes dazed. Behind him, atop his desk, the flame of his candle wavered, wax dripping slowly down the edges and into its copper holder. I spied a letter on his desk and an envelope with a broken red beeswax seal tossed to the floor. Though I could not make out the particulars, a few words stood out from the rest, as though they had been written in blood.

The Most Serene Order of Cuckolds.

My chest turned to ice.

"You had a good time with the tsar?" Alexander's words were a monotone.

"Will you leave us?" I turned to Ekaterina, trying to control the tremor in my voice. "I need to speak to my husband alone." I glanced over her shoulder at Azya. "Both of you."

Alexander seemed to suddenly realize Azya was there and came alive with anger, storming toward her. "And you accompanied her? Did you have a good time? Did you watch the men drool all over her poor little hands and the women laugh behind their damnable fans?"

No matter the true nature of my sister's feelings for Alexander, she was intimidated by his temper and stammered: "Well . . . I had a time . . ."

"How many men did you meet? Or were they all so captivated by my wife they made no time for you?"

"Alexander!" I cried as Azya turned stone white.

He stopped himself, hands bunching into fists. "Listen to my wife and leave us." And then to Ekaterina, "You too."

Ekaterina gave me one last irritated look before taking Azya by the arm and stomping away.

"What is this?" I pointed to the letter. "Who brought it to you?"

"The messenger is not the salient question, but rather the author: your tormented pursuer, Georges d'Anthès."

I wished to believe Georges incapable of such foolishness, but his erratic behavior had proved otherwise. I could not forget the dead look in his eyes when he held the pistol to his head. "May I read it?"

My husband gave a hollow laugh and beckoned for me to enter the study. He pushed the letter toward me. Quickly, I read. The words were as terrible as I had supposed. I had betrayed him with another man. I had made a fool of him. Word of my time with Georges at Ida's house must have spread across the city, just as the tsar had said. Nausea weakened me, but I refused to collapse. I needed to stay strong and read through the terrible missive. Just as I got to the last sentence, he snatched the letter from me.

"I changed my mind. This isn't your problem." He locked it away into the same desk drawer where he kept his pistol. "I should not have shown it to you."

"We are husband and wife. We will deal with this together, only you cannot believe I have ever betrayed you." My voice started to break. "I carried on a modest flirtation. That is all. I have already told you of my last meeting with Georges. He is not well. Now he's trying to rile you. However . . ." I glanced at the drawer where Alexander had stashed the letter away and hesitated. "The writer may have meant to reference Georges, but this isn't from Georges."

Alexander didn't miss a beat. "How do you know?"

"He wrote little notes . . . trivialities, no more. I ordered Liza to avoid them, but I did see a few . . . and then the invitation to Ida's house. That isn't his handwriting."

Alexander slumped in his chair, head in his hands, looking defeated. Why was this happening? Why did I continue to hurt my husband? I felt like a beast. Worse than a beast. A devil. "I acted a fool. I'm sorry."

"If this wasn't written directly by Georges's hand, I wager it is from the good Dutch baron, on behalf of his adored *son*." Alexander sprang to life once more, startling me, opening the drawer and waving the letter in my direction. "Look at this paper. Have you seen anything of the like? Expensive stationery from a man of society, from a foreign shore."

As Alexander worked himself into a greater fit, I found it easier to maintain my composure. One of us needed to keep their wits about them. "That is pure conjecture. I don't believe the baron would ever facilitate something so rash. You have no evidence that the baron is involved at all."

"Then I shall have the paper examined! I am sure enough of its provenance. Georges d'Anthès must get his way with that fellow even more than Masha gets her way with us."

Alexander threw the letter on his desk and collapsed onto the large sofa he kept in his study. Clasping his fingers, he covered his face. I could not stand that he had been brought so low. I moved to his lap and wrapped my arms around him, needing to shield my husband from the cruelty of the world. Resting my head on his shoulder, I started to cry again. He stroked my hair and I cried harder, grateful for his gentleness.

"I must face him," Alexander said.

"No." I shook my head, dreading what was to come next.

"I must face him on the field of honor."

"Alexander, please," I said. "This is what they want you to do."

"What who wants?"

"Whoever is responsible for this cruel letter. You once told me you are like Mozart and the court is filled with jealous Salieris. Could it not be that one of them wishes to plant foul suspicions in your head?"

"Or Georges d'Anthès wishes to make you a widow and the baron is willing to do his foul work for him."

"Then why does Georges keep writing to Ekaterina?" I asked desperately. Even as the answer popped into my head, Alexander gave voice to it:

"He wants to be near you in a way that puts him beyond reproach. It makes me sick."

"Georges will not marry my sister, and I will see to it that he doesn't come anywhere near me. Please do not escalate this foolishness. It's beneath you. Promise me."

Alexander's gaze fell past my shoulder, as though he didn't

hear me. "You have no idea the power you possess, the power of a beautiful woman over a man." He pulled away, clasping my shoulders now. I was grateful for the weight of him holding me. "Don't you see the lengths this swine will go to, to make you his? I must protect you. You are not safe around him."

"You do not need to protect me. We must let this conjured controversy pass."

Slowly, he shook his head. "I have already sent a response to the man who has declared his love for my wife and made a fool of us both. I only await his response to know the day and time he wishes to face me on the field."

I saw the deep pain in his eyes and hated myself. That sensation has never left me, but lingers as a ghost to a tormented soul. Alexander was being pushed into a duel over my reputation. No matter what happened, I was to blame.

I recalled what the baron had spoken of before: sacrifice made for true love. Alexander had always said it would be cheaper to live in the country. I wanted nothing more than to leave St. Petersburg altogether. But first I needed to find a way to stop this duel, another pointless affair of honor among men, from ever occurring.

Eighteen

Have you ever see a man so trampled by life he loses his appetite, his swagger, his very reason for being? I pray you never do, for this is what happened to my Alexander. When I look back, I see my husband in two frames: the time before the letter and the time following. The man who came before—mercurial, jealous, passionate—and the broken man forever after.

At first, I did not realize this damnable letter had also been delivered to Alexander's friends, twelve copies in all. One of those same friends, having seen Alexander's name on the envelope, and not understanding it to be a cruel jest, had forwarded the letter to him without reading the content; so not only had my husband read the devastating words, but knew he had been made the laughingstock of St. Petersburg.

Those first few nights I knew nothing of this and still hoped we might contain the problem to our own household. The baron himself arrived at our flat the morning after Alexander issued his challenge to Georges. His normally impeccable clothes were in disarray and his features sallow, as though Alexander had already shot Georges straight through the heart on a ghastly field of honor. I was not privy to the conversation, but stood near the door of Alexander's study, gently rocking my little namesake in my arms. I heard the gist well enough. The baron had lost all sense of pride. He was crying, a muffled wail, as he begged Alexander to grant an extension and give Georges a week to determine how to avert the duel. After the baron left, Alexander calmly told me he had given him two additional weeks.

"You still believe the baron is responsible for the letter?" I asked Alexander. "After seeing him this way?"

"I don't know what to think anymore." He rubbed his hands together, but even this nervous affect was slow, as though his body went through the motions of living, his mind elsewhere. Drawing two fingers to his mouth, he kissed them, and then bestowed that kiss on our baby's sweet forehead. "I only know I could not be so cruel as to deny a broken man's request. Two weeks makes no difference."

Alexander was wrong. Two weeks could make all the difference. I had time now to determine how to end this sordid mess.

One portion of the letter still puzzled me. The unknown author had mentioned by name the grand master of this obscene order of cuckolds: Naryshkin. I did not see how this man was connected to the business, but doubted his name had been dropped by chance. Not wishing for Alexander to fall deeper into melancholy, I decided to call once again on Aunt Katya.

As my aunt sat sipping hot tea in her posh flat, I related the contents of the letter. When I mentioned Naryshkin, her face instinctively wrinkled, and she set her saucer down hard on her fine French table, causing her little pot of elderberry jam to quiver.

"You know why the author would mention this man?" I asked.

Aunt Katya smoothed her hair over her ear and straightened her shoulders. "His wife was the mistress of Nicholas's late brother." She hastily crossed herself. "It is said the last tsar paid him handsomely for the privilege of bedding his wife."

My thoughts clicked into place like jigsaw puzzle pieces. "Then this affair may not be over Georges at all. Whoever wrote this letter wants Alexander to believe I am the tsar's mistress?"

Aunt Katya's lovely features clouded with worry. At first, I thought she was being sympathetic. As the minutes ticked by on her grandfather clock, I realized she might be waiting for a confession. I should not have to do this. I should not have to plead innocence to my own mother's sister. She was family and should know me better.

Yet what choice did I have? She still held sway at court. I needed her on my side.

"It is not true," I said flatly. "It is the worst kind of lie."

"I needed to hear you say it. Even if everything in the letter is a lie, sometimes such matters have a kernel of truth exposed as a result of the gossip. I know it's difficult, but if I am to help, I must know the extent of the matter."

"I flirted with Georges, as you know," I spat, hating every word. "It was foolish. I have put a stop to it. He is the one who keeps pressing the matter."

"And you have flirted with Tsar Nicholas?"

"No more than any other woman at court. What else can we do? Ignore him?" I felt pressed into a corner and spoke plainly. "I believe the tsar wants to make me his mistress."

She didn't even blink. "How do you think he might go about making this so?"

"It is only an implication at this point. I intend to avoid him."

"Forever? How?"

I dropped my head into my hands, wishing I might disappear. I was so tired. "Someone is ruining my reputation and driving my husband mad. They hate Alexander so much they wish him to duel."

"Does Alexander believe you have been unfaithful?"

"No, but he still believes he must defend my honor. He has already issued a challenge to Georges. Should I now worry he will challenge the tsar himself?"

Aunt Katya tucked a stray lock of hair under her ear. "I doubt even your husband is so rash and challenges can be withdrawn with no loss of honor. We now have two weeks to convince Alexander to do so. We can divert Georges easily enough. After all, your husband is known to be a keen shot."

"Georges is mad!" I said. "I told you, he threatened to shoot himself. He doesn't care about his own life."

"Monsieur d'Anthès may not care about his young life, but the baron cares for him deeply. Don't you agree?"

"He adores Georges, no doubt."

Aunt Katya's pretty features remained placid, but I fancied I could see gears turning in her clever brain. "Our family must be as transparent as possible. We must declare any rumors about you and Georges to be rubbish as quickly and loudly as possible. The baron wishes for Georges to avoid this duel at any cost, so he will help. Plus, we have an additional ally."

I bit my lip. "Who?"

"Your own sister."

"Azya?" I thought of my sister's feet dangling over the edge of Alexander's sofa and the tips of my ears burned.

"My namesake, Ekaterina. I believe she would be thrilled to receive a proposal of marriage from Georges."

"Wait . . . what?"

"He must be encouraged to propose to Ekaterina. As quickly as possible."

A brass samovar hissed and my stomach lurched as I processed what my aunt had said. "Why would he do that? He doesn't love her. He's only playing with her affections the way he accused me of playing with his."

"I believe he will do it."

"Even if Georges agrees to such nonsense, Alexander will assume it's a ruse and fear seeming the fool once more."

"Your husband may fear seeming the fool, but he is no fool. Ultimately, he'll see the sense of it and be glad enough to let your sister live elsewhere."

Guilt gnawed at my chest. I could not stop thinking about Georges's handsome features distorted as he held a dueling pistol to his head. If he were willing to turn on himself in such a violent manner, he could turn on my trying sister as easily. "It wouldn't be fair to Ekaterina."

"Ekaterina will be over the moon. She is sick with love for that boy, anyone can see it."

"But Georges has shown he is . . . unstable."

"I am confident your sister can handle herself." My aunt leaned forward. Her voice lowered to a whisper, as though we were in a crowded ballroom, rather than alone in her parlor. "You don't know everything that happens underneath your roof."

"What?" I shook my head vigorously and found myself unable

to control the trembling of my own hands. "What is happening? What do you know?"

"I know this arrangement is best for everyone involved."

Aunt Katya's features were set and I realized she had already decided the matter in her own head. I could not stop her from setting this plan in motion. The baron would do anything to save Georges, and Ekaterina had already proven she was too far gone in her infatuation to heed any warning about Georges's temperament. Alexander had backed himself into a corner by issuing the challenge, but I did not think him so melancholic he would risk his own life in a duel when he had an opportunity to withdraw and still maintain his honor.

I had only one person left in this world I thought might help save my sister.

"Your husband doesn't look well," Mother told me, nodding toward Alexander's study. "He should be under the care of a physician."

The betrothal happened quickly. Though Alexander grumbled, the baron met with him personally to swear this was a love match Georges had made of his own free will, and that he had declared his love for Ekaterina long before this foolish note had been circulated about town. My husband remained unconvinced, but eventually—after several private meetings with my aunt and the baron—withdrew his challenge. Even as I spent the Christmas and New Year holidays helping Ekaterina sew petticoats and delicate lingerie for her trousseau, shame haunted my every thought. My husband was no longer in danger, but my sister was about to make the biggest mistake of her life and no one seemed willing to stop her.

In early January, our mother came to town for the wedding. She was my last hope.

Mother looked stern and stoic as ever, dressed in black from head to foot, a large silver crucifix dangling from her neck. One could easily have mistaken her for a nun. She towered over my children, who were so intimidated by their grandmother that once obligatory kisses had been bestowed, they quickly scampered off to hide out with their aunts in their back bedroom. After a perfunctory greeting, apparently a fresh wave of inspiration struck Alexander and he moved to his study, closing the door with a thud.

Now I wondered if he'd heard what my mother said. Even though the challenge had been withdrawn, Alexander looked gaunt and haggard from lack of sleep. The letter still wounded him, no matter what he might say. And though he was but three years from forty, he stooped at the shoulders and groused like a much older man.

"He's under tremendous pressure," I told Mother. "As you may have heard, he has started an almanac in the English style—the first of its kind in Russia."

"Then why doesn't he seem happy?"

"Well . . . he is limited in what can be written on political topics since everything is subject to censure. So he has not attracted as many subscribers as he hoped . . ."

"I think his pressures extend beyond the financial. I think he experiences the pain of a beautiful wife who is careless with his feelings."

So many years had passed since she could intimidate me, since she could pressure me to live the same bitter, cold life she had endured. And yet the tender little girl inside of me felt hurt and

ashamed because I had displeased my mother, the most important person in the world.

"Surely you know I exchange frequent letters with your aunt,"
she continued, "or are you such a part of the high Petersburg society now that you believe you are out of my reach?"

I tapped my fingers on a piece of glasswork hanging over our
mantel, steeling against her, forcing my heart to turn to stone.
"I am only surprised my mother would believe such blatant and
evil lies."

Mother pressed her lips together. I had never spoken sharply
nor contradicted her before, at least not to her face.

"You were not carrying on with your own sister's fiancé?"
Mother asked at last. "You wish to deny this? And if you are innocent, why is your husband so upset?"

I recalled what Aunt Katya had told me about Mother's own
experiences at court, how she had been driven from her position through no fault of her own, but by the unrequited love of
a man and the whim of an empress. "You well know how easily a
woman's reputation can be damaged."

Mother took a seat at the kitchen table and for a moment
looked her old self, emotions impenetrable, like the Turkish fortress of Kars, just as Alexander had once told his friend Tolstoy. In
another minute, however, her head was in her hands. She released
a sigh that threatened sobbing, but managed to hold back her
tears.

"Of course I do," she said softly. "That is why I am so worried."

"Then why harass me with accusations?"

"I had to be sure. I had to see your reaction. You wouldn't be
the first woman caught in an ill-advised affair of the heart."

I joined my mother at the table, the sight of her so upset inclining me to forgiveness. Though my true feelings still made me sick to my stomach with shame, I decided to risk sharing with her. "I admit . . . I found Georges attractive. I thought about him. I was disloyal to my husband in that respect, but I love Alexander. I have always loved him."

"Then you must protect him," Mother said. "You know this."

"By sacrificing my own sister to a man who does not love her?"

"Your sister is attractive enough, even if you cannot see it. She has had suitors in the past. This man must have some feelings for her or he would not have asked her to marry him."

I looked at my hands. My normally impeccable cuticles were ragged. "He's only trying to avoid a scandal."

"He could have left the country. He's a foreigner, is he not? If he wished to avoid a fuss then he could have returned to France or wherever his father might want him to go."

"I think there is more to it than that." *I think he wants to ensure he remains near me.*

"I hope your sister is not right in thinking you wish to block her path to happiness."

"Georges is unstable," I blurted. "I think he needs help." At last, I shared with my mother the tawdry tale of what had happened when I saw Georges at Ida's house in the barracks: his declarations of undying love, the pistol to his head, and the appearance of Ida's daughter. By the end of the tale, Mother's face had paled considerably.

"I cannot let Ekaterina marry such a man," I said, "but she will not hear reason. And what would Alexander say if the wedding was canceled? Would he stand with me? Would he still believe me when I assure him I do not return Georges's affections?" I thought of the tsar's proposition as well. This I did not share with

Mother; she had heard enough for one night. "I feel like a fly ensnared in a spider's web. I fear there is no right answer."

Mother rubbed her cheeks. My children's feet thumped the floorboards at the back of the flat, punctuated by the merry sound of Ekaterina laughing. I hadn't heard my sister laugh in such a genuine way since we were girls, yet her engagement to Georges had made it so.

"Koko is old enough to know her heart and determine the direction of her own life," she said at last.

I blinked hard, unused to hearing this endearment for Ekaterina from Mother.

"Besides, you couldn't stop the wedding if you tried."

"You could."

"Have you noticed anything . . . odd about Koko as of late?"

"She is always odd."

"She does not look herself. She is pale, tired, complains of nausea . . ."

Slowly, the meaning of my mother's words became clear to me. Aunt Katya's words rang in my head: *You don't know everything that happens underneath your roof.* "You think she . . . ?" I could not bring myself to ask if my sister was with child, tried not to imagine Georges capable of such a crass seduction. But I didn't know what to think about anything anymore. Besides, it made sense. If it were true, or at least if we were made to believe it was true, Alexander would have no choice but to relent in order to save Ekaterina's reputation. Aunt Katya must have shared her suspicions with him. That is why he had finally called off the duel.

"For once in her life, your sister is happy," my mother said. "She wouldn't be the first woman with an unstable husband. Leave her be."

"She doesn't understand what she's doing," I cried.

"She is a clever enough girl. She will find a way to manage the situation." Mother pressed her lips together and I knew there would be no further discussion of the matter. "Your aunt is right. This marriage is in everyone's best interest."

I claim no powers to foresee the future. Still, I have come to believe human beings capable of intuiting how events might unfold not with the rational reasoning so beloved of philosophers, but only a queer feeling in one's stomach. The heart feels what the mind might not yet know or accept. Alexander had withdrawn his challenge, Georges and Ekaterina were wed on the tenth of January, and yet still I dreaded what was to come.

Alexander hoped to avoid any contact with Georges and Ekaterina. Once my sister had moved out, he declared they were no longer welcome in our house. Yet, St. Petersburg society was a complex thing, and we both knew we could not avoid them entirely. A mere week after the wedding, we were all invited to a lavish supper party at Count Shuvalov's mansion, where the tsar was to be counted among the honored guests. My mind ran in circles. Despite everything, the vile order of cuckolds was still the talk of both St. Petersburg and Moscow; that the letter to my husband had been filled with lies and libel was irrelevant. After the wedding, Aunt Katya had confided to me that the empress herself asked one of her maids whether she thought Georges married for love or to save the honor of the woman he truly loved. Even if Georges was my brother-in-law now, I wished to avoid him. Yet I could well imagine the vicious rumors were Alexander and I to avoid social functions with Georges and Ekaterina: that he was gambling and I was home crying, pining over a lover I gave up to my own sister.

Unable to sleep, I placed a tender kiss on Alexander's still cheek, and tossed the covers aside. With no fires yet lit in the hearths, I laced my flannel robe tight around my neck to fight off the chill in the air, and then lit a candle in a wide holder so I might wander our flat.

As I walked, the shadow of dancing flames cast about me, landing on the statue of Catherine. She was tucked into an alcove in the corner of our main hallway, beside potted ferns Azya had bought from a passing vendor. Catherine's stout bronze figure called to me and I held the candle higher to better see the subtle hint of a smile tempering her stern expression. I thought of what Catherine might do in my place, what my grandfather Afansy would have done when he was a younger man: hold their heads high.

I determined to do the same.

The evening of the supper party, the four of us stood at the foot of the palace's ironwork staircase, waiting with the other guests for the announcement to enter the dining room. I hadn't seen Georges since the wedding, and though he held my sister's hand, he would not tear his gaze from me. Alexander could witness this plainly enough, as could everyone else in the foyer. I took care to keep my features amicable and conversation light, commenting on the beauty of a marble nude, a woman reclined seductively with her arms outstretched, at the entranceway, and the portraits of Count Shuvalov's esteemed ancestors hanging on the wall above the hearth. I tried not to stare openly at Ekaterina's belly, nor wonder whether it had grown larger. Meanwhile, Ekaterina thrust her left hand forward to show off her ring at every opportunity. She babbled about wedding gifts, still sailing on a cloud over her good fortune.

"The most generous gift came from Tsar Nicholas himself," she declared to an elderly countess, who wore an emerald-studded tiara over her gray hair and held a lorgnette to her weak eyes. "One thousand rubles! Can you imagine?"

When Alexander heard that, he smirked and rolled his eyes, but held his tongue. A slow burning irritation churned in my stomach. Ekaterina had not the wits about her to realize the countess would see this gift for what it was: the tsar viewed our family as a charity case. In fact, the thousand rubles had been delivered to me with instructions to purchase a suitable wedding gift for my sister, but I did not view myself as the tsar's private servant and had just given her the money instead.

"I always fancied the mahogany divan in my sister's parlor," Ekaterina prattled on. "Why, with this generous gift I can decorate our entire flat with such finery."

Couples in elegant evening coats and gowns stared blatantly, quickly looking away once I caught their eye. I would not let them view Alexander, nor even Ekaterina as figures of pity, even if I came across as empty-headed in the process. I would not give them the satisfaction of watching our family fall into disgrace. My sister's unchecked words made matters worse, but somehow I would salvage the situation.

I bit my lip, trying to recall the countess's name. When it came to me, I cut into their conversation: "Countess Burlova! How marvelous to see you." I kept my tone modest, but my voice grew louder than intended. The countess turned her lorgnette to me, nose wrinkling. "I am so sorry to interrupt, but I only now remember that I wished to ask my good sister about a podiatrist she once recommended."

Ekaterina looked as though she wanted to tear off her new

jeweled brooch and throw it at me. "Whatever are you talking about?"

"It is only that my feet are not as fine as they once were . . ." This sounded like the smallest of small talk, even to my own ear. Alexander crooked his head and gave me an incredulous look. Hopefully, he found this nonsense amusing at least. ". . . and yet I cannot recall the gentleman's name."

"And you must have his name right now?"

"Yes," I insisted. If my grandfather, Afansy, could have seen me, I think he would have been proud of the effort I made for the sake of our family's reputation. Perhaps after my mother's disgrace, my father's descent into madness, and this newest scandal, there was still time to redeem the Goncharov name after all.

Georges turned to me, seemingly intimate but in a voice that let anyone who cared to make an effort overhear our exchange. "Yes, what is this doctor's name? Perhaps he can confirm something that has been troubling me." He whispered the next words in French, but I was certain everyone could hear. His voice seemed to roar in my ears. "I know your feet are more beautiful than my wife's."

A bead of perspiration trickled down my forehead. He had spoken in French to play on the similar sound of *cor* for feet and *corp*, the word for body. Georges was a newlywed and still he could not contain himself. Not even when my husband stood at my side, his anger seething like a living presence among us.

When Georges tried to catch my eye, I cast my gaze elsewhere: the silver tinsel draped around the banister of the staircase, an exceptionally large emerald on the countess's tiara, the head of a deer mounted above the family portraits and the poor creature's vacant gaze.

Georges raised his voice to tell Ekaterina: "I see I am not well received. Perhaps my conversation is more welcome elsewhere. Come, my *légitime*."

My stomach turned so violently I thought I would be sick. Georges had used a derogatory expression for my sister's status. From the corner of my eye, I spotted a young man, stifling a laugh, then making the cuckold's horns, two fingers held over his head like antlers, to the delight of his friends.

I pulled Alexander closer. He felt stiff as a statue. Everything else happened quickly and yet I saw every movement drawn out slowly before me: Ekaterina's scowl, Georges's intense glare, and the sagging of Alexander's shoulders right before he straightened himself up again. Alexander dropped my hand, crossed the room, and then stopped abruptly before the mounted stag. He reached up to tap the horns with one finger.

"This is the right place for husbands, is it not? Next to the cuckold's horns? Some in this room would see it as a perfect position for married men such as me."

Some of the couples giggled, while others looked at their feet. For all of their finery, I imagined them a mob in rags, gathered around a guillotine as crowds once had on the streets of Paris. Yet as my pulse calmed, I realized this was only my imagination. Given the drama playing out before them, the reaction of the other guests seemed fairly subdued.

Several people turned their gaze from Alexander to the top of the staircase. I looked up and froze. Before the entrance to the dining room, stood the tsar in a formal white uniform coat ablaze with medals that glittered in the candlelight of a high chandelier. He did not look at the red-faced Ekaterina, nor the oblivious Georges, nor even me. He glared at Alexander.

"Might we speak?" Tsar Nicholas requested, his tone a command. "You and your wife."

We glanced at one another and then turned to the staircase. Without a word, Alexander and I reached for one another's hand, clasping them together tightly as we ascended. The buzz of ordinary conversations resumed and this mitigated the humiliation somewhat, but my face felt afire.

"I don't know what strange affairs take place within the confines of your own home," the tsar admonished, before we had even taken the final step to the top, "but when you are engaged in a public space I expect your behavior to reflect that of a seemly Russian family."

I found it unbearably hypocritical that this tsar should trumpet family, and calling Catherine and Afansy to mind, I tried to draw on their strength. "I don't know what you—"

The tsar raised his hand, still staring at Alexander. "Silence your woman."

My heart dropped to my stomach. For all of his affability in polite company, all of his compliments, all his desire, the tsar spoke of me as though I were property rather than an individual being. I had thought myself somehow elevated beyond that. Now my true standing was made clear.

"It is bad enough she carried on with this foreign fop before . . ." Though he had specifically asked for me, the tsar spoke again as though I were not present. I could only conclude he wished to publicly humiliate me; he might have flogged me were it possible to do so without shattering the illusion of a civil and modern society. ". . . now she continues to flirt while he is married to her own sister. Can you not control your own wife? Do you need instruction?"

Alexander was not nearly as tall as the tsar, but at that moment he appeared every bit as formidable. "The fault lies entirely with the other party. He has insulted my wife's honor."

"Then another man has violated your wife's reputation? The remedy for that is clear."

Alexander released my hand, and shaking, balled his own into fists. Everything we had endured had been for naught, all because Georges could not control his emotions and Alexander would not bear the humiliation.

I heard murmuring from downstairs. Alexander had not bothered to keep his voice low. He had as good as publicly challenged Georges once more.

The night after this disaster, I sat rocking the baby on my knee. The other children gathered around me in the drawing room in what I thought made a nice domestic tableau. Azya joined us as well, perusing a hymnal and clutching the prayer beads she had taken to carrying about. I wondered why I had ever desired more, why the excitement of the balls and masquerades held appeal when we had such contentment right here. But I knew the answer already. Quiet evenings at home were well and good when balanced with a rich life on the outside. I was already considering a new masquerade costume, an ode to Alexander's greatest heroine, Tatiana from *Evgeny Onegin*. I had also determined to wear it only for the pleasure of my husband, sister, and children. It was a small price to pay for our family's peace of mind.

My ears perked up at the click of Alexander's key unlatching the front door and his footsteps in the vestibule. I was afraid he might head straight to his study and so I called his name as merrily as I could manage. He popped his head in, looking haggard.

He had not slept the night before and his olive skin had taken on an alarming ashen undertone. I assumed he had been gambling at his club, and prayed he hadn't been drinking as well. My husband seldom had more than two glasses of champagne at a time, but the smell of liquor on my father's breath remained a powerful memory from my childhood. I could never overcome the suspicion that under trying circumstances, all men succumbed to the temptations of rough wine or vodka.

"You're home!" Masha ran to hug her father's knees. *Good girl.* I gave silent thanks for the tenderness I saw in Alexander's eyes when he looked down at her.

"A quiet night in?" He sank into an armchair, his features gaunt, as though he already floated between this world and the next. "How unusual."

His tone held only sad resignation. "I hope to enjoy many more of these, husband, now that . . ." I was going to say *now that Ekaterina is married off* but dared not allow any hint of Georges to enter this room. ". . . now that I have had a taste of St. Petersburg society. I find I appreciate time at home all the more."

"This is a refuge from the world." Alexander leaned back and closed his eyes.

"A refuge is exactly what you need." I reached for a manuscript I had found in our bedroom and moved to the parlor. "I hope you don't mind, but I took the liberty of reviewing the latest revisions on the history of your noble ancestor, Abram Gannibal."

That brought him to attention. "You have been in my study?"

"You left it in our bedroom. I thought you meant for me to see it, that perhaps there were scenes of passion you wished me to read."

Alexander relaxed and managed a small smile. "Nothing but

random thoughts as they came to me. And what is your opinion of my new ideas?"

It seemed to me he had placed too much emphasis on his ancestor's jealous nature, but at the moment I only wanted to encourage him to write. "I never thought you should have abandoned it in the first place." I gestured to my sister. "Azya agrees."

"I do!" Azya's eyes were positively glowing.

"At times I miss our little house in Tsarskoye Selo," I told him. "Do you remember? The peaceful walks. The days you spent in your study."

"Until Tsar Nicholas took up residence."

"He isn't there now. I think we would enjoy it even more the second time around. Do you miss those days as well?"

"The happiest times of my life. My school days. The first months of our marriage."

"I think it might be worth looking into at the least." I turned to Azya, whom I had already enlisted for help. She had paled, perhaps at his reference to love. "What do you think?"

"It is a wonderful idea," my sister enthused, trembling slightly.

"Don't you wish to stay here?" Alexander's voice turned bitter. "To have your go at the marriage market?"

"It is more important that you are somewhere conducive to writing," Azya said. "I will be all right. We could leave at once if you so approved."

Alexander rose from his chair and kissed the top of Sasha's red head. He saw through our ploy, but was too gallant to call us out on it. "Thank you, Azya. Say a prayer for our children, sweet wife. Before they get to bed tonight. Say blessings for all of our children. You know I have always admired your soul even more than I desire your beautiful self."

"You could join us, husband," I said, attempting to control my quavering speech. "You could say the blessing over us all."

"It would mean little coming from me and so much coming from you. I want to give our children every possible chance to find favor with the Lord."

"They have the favor of our Lord, as you do, even if you don't know it yet."

I saw a hint of the old twinkle return to his eyes, but his next words stunned me. "I suppose we shall find out soon enough."

"I pray we do not," I said firmly. "I ask you as your own dear wife. Do not take any actions that would hasten your death. We could not bear it."

Alexander glanced at Masha, but the light in his eyes had gone out and the creases on his face deepened. It seemed even his children could not draw him out of his depression. "I'm not capable of defending myself should matters come to a head?"

Alexander was more than capable, but affairs of honor were messy and Georges a trained shot. I attempted to clarify, for the last thing I wanted was to fight over his skills with a pistol. He might take his out and fire bullets into the wall and my nerves couldn't handle it. "I do not wish you to take unnecessary risks over foolish words."

"Words are never foolish, Tasha." He stared straight ahead, his gaze fixed on some demon only he could see, and then shook his head as sorrow roughened his voice. "Words are the most important things on earth. I thought you of all people would understand that."

Nineteen

It seemed an ordinary day.

That afternoon, I sipped the hot cocoa and coffee concoction I'd had the cook prepare after luncheon and wandered our flat, mentally composing a letter I planned to write not to Dmitry, but Sergey—since I trusted him most—asking him to make discreet inquiries into rental properties in Tsarskoye Selo. I did not want it known I was looking to leave the city. I feared it might provoke Georges and force a duel I still hoped to avoid.

Alexander had been up early, huddled in his study all morning. He left right after lunch, bundled in his thickest overcoat, giving me a peck on the cheek and cheerfully declaring he would likely stop for pastries and perhaps he could bring some home.

I came to a halt before the enormous bureau in our bedroom, drawn as usual to the costumes I stored inside. I pulled the knob and looked over the outfits I had assembled for masquerade balls, prominent among them the gown I had worn as "priestess of the sun." I remembered the tsar's praise, which I had once been foolish enough to consider a high compliment. I shuddered, remembering how low his hand had rested on my back when we first danced, the lascivious inflection when he asked me if I wanted another *acquaintance,* the humiliation of being scolded at the top of the staircase of the Shuvalov mansion like a serf.

My eyes narrowed. I no longer desired to play at being someone else, no longer wished to summon my power from others. Rather, I wanted to wipe the slate clean and find peace with myself. I glanced toward the nursery. The children were supposed to sleep another hour at least. Azya was still huddled over a book in her room, but she usually played with them for some time after they woke. I wouldn't wait a moment longer.

Inspired, I set my coffee down on the nearest end table and rushed to the back of our apartments, locating a large cedar trunk in the storeroom. Gathering all of my strength, I dragged the trunk to our bedroom and began to stuff costume gowns, robes, bangles, headpieces, and other trinkets that had once accessorized them into the trunk. I didn't know whether such items would hold value, but I knew I felt better doing something other than pacing and worrying over money. Even a small sum would help toward the ultimate goal of taking my family away from St. Petersburg to start anew.

I called for Liza so that I might quickly dress, and asked her to make sure the horses were ready as well. I was determined to arrive at Nevsky Prospect before the pawnbrokers closed. Alexander's valet and a footman assisted with lifting my trunk into the waiting carriage. If my wares were of no interest at the first shop, I would continue from venue to venue until I found someone willing to take these items off my hands.

A sharp gust battered the windowpanes, kicking snow about like dust in the dazzling winter sunshine. Drawing my velvet cloak tightly around my shoulders and chest, I gave instructions for the cook to prepare supper at home. When I stepped outside, the freezing wind penetrated the cloak, seeming to reach through my skin to chill my bones. I merely pulled it tighter. I had much to accomplish and didn't care to delay even one more day.

As we moved through the city, a sense of peace settled over me and I put on my spectacles so I might see more than a bright blue blur from the window of my coach. I raised my hand, shielding my eyes. Though it was bitter cold, the churches and palaces and frozen Neva River sparkled in the winter sun and the snow was so deep it reached the knees of grown men. The streets were crowded with families taking advantage of the clear weather to go tobogganing on the hills outside the city. Even to my weak eyes the city seemed made for fairy tales, as if the beautiful snow maiden herself might appear out of nowhere to wander the streets. I would miss this magical city, but Alexander and I could only find our happiness elsewhere.

My driver swore at a carriage that rushed by too close, and our horses hit a buckling cobblestone in the road. I was jostled in my seat, my spectacles dislodged. Perhaps it was for the best. If I could not see the graceful lines of our imperial city, I would not be tempted by its beauty. I could concentrate on my marriage, my family, my intellect, and my spirituality—all I truly valued in my life.

With my spectacles off, I barely made out the form of the sleigh crossing the other side of the embankment. The clomping of hooves and the slight neigh of my own horses in recognition met my ears, but in the haziness of my compromised vision, I could not place the carriage nor the team. Besides, I was intent on the mission at hand.

And so I did not see the bulky fur-lined coat, nor the *chapeau Bolívar,* nor the silver-tipped cane, nor the box holding the dueling pistols. I did not have the opportunity to beg Alexander to turn around and avoid his ultimate destiny.

As it turned out, the pawnshops accepted only a few random baubles and a ring that had been a gift from my grandfather long ago. I couldn't count the trip a success. Exhausted and admitting defeat, I instructed my driver to return home. I hoped Alexander was done with his errands for the day and we could spend a quiet night at home with the children. Perhaps I would even work up the courage to tell him what I had been doing, emphasizing my commitment to our relationship. I felt sure he would see the sense of my plan to leave the city and think of a way to gather the money quickly.

When we returned to our apartments on the banks of the Moyka, Alexander's sleigh and horses remained haltered and out in the cold, the animals huffing and prancing in the freezing air. The queer feeling that so often upset my stomach assailed me now, a new premonition I had no wish to acknowledge. I alighted from my carriage, shouting at the driver to see to Alexander's horses as well as mine, and flew up the eight steps that led to our front door. I burst into our flat calling out my husband's name.

It was quiet inside, the table set in the dining room with our everyday china and flatware for supper, but no aromas of roasting meat or simmering soup drifted in from the kitchen. Usually, I came home to find the children running about and knocking things over, begging for a treat while servants chased them away telling them they shouldn't spoil their appetites. But now I was greeted only by a tomblike silence and a strange metallic scent clinging to the air. The door of Alexander's study was shut tight. Farther back in the flat, from Azya's bedroom, I heard quiet sobbing.

The door of Alexander's study flung open and three men rushed out. Alexander's friend, Danzas, followed by Alexander's stooped valet, and a stranger clutching a black bag in his large hands. A doctor. The pain in my stomach worsened and my heart pounded so loudly I felt sure it would explode.

Danzas approached me, eyes wet with tears. I have never seen men cry before and have no desire to see it again. His soft features tightened and when he opened his mouth, no words issued forth. He raised his hands as though he might try to place them on my shoulders.

"Alexander?" My voice was a strangled echo in our vestibule.

The doctor turned to Alexander's valet. "This is the wife?"

"I am." Though on the edge of hysteria, I tried to maintain some measure of dignity.

Out of the corner of my eye, I caught Liza peeking out from the kitchen, pale as the moon, rubbing her hands in her apron. The doctor eyed the men again, his expression glum.

"He was shot in the abdomen. I can't dislodge the bullet. All we can do now is try to make him comfortable."

Danzas and the valet began to speak at once, competing with the doctor, their voices seeming at first loud and then barely audible. The devastating images taking shape in my mind were made more vivid by the phrases swirling around me as they tried to explain what had happened on the field of honor.

His opponent took the first shot.

At first he hesitated and we thought he would not take aim, but Pushkin insisted.

Even crumpled on the ground he managed to get his own shot off and fired at d'Anthès, the scoundrel. Pushkin played it like a gentleman to the end.

There is still a chance he may regain his strength.

I think d'Anthès might have fired early, the foreign swine.

No, it was a fair fight. Pushkin charged and d'Anthès had to take his shot. And then he stood his ground after Pushkin fell, when it was his turn to fire.

I still say the swine chose his outfit with care. Why the buttons on the foreigner's coat were like shields. Pushkin's aim was perfect, but the bullet deflected off the brass.

Their voices grew more agitated. The room spun around me and my legs failed. They took me by the shoulders and hoisted me upright. I refused to believe it. Matters could not have progressed this far. Alexander wouldn't risk leaving me a widow and his children orphans. He loved us too much. These men were lying. They had to be. "I must see him."

"He asked us to keep you in another room," Danzas murmured in my ear, his gentle hand finally resting on my shoulder. "Perhaps you might stay with the children. We've seen to it they remain in the nursery. Alexander has no wish to upset you."

"Do I not seem upset already?"

"He will recover," Alexander's valet said in a shaky voice. "There is no need to worry."

"Did he ask you to tell me that?"

The poor old man fell silent.

"If Alexander will be fine, then surely I can see him. Let me see him!"

Danzas still had his hand on my shoulder, but when he hesitated, I broke free from his grip and ran to Alexander's study.

The next part of my tale might sound familiar. It has been told already a thousand times in our land and beyond: the great poet, fatally wounded and yet lingering in this life. The guilt-ridden wife vacillating between denial and grief and wild proclamations, begging for forgiveness, promising God and anyone else who would listen that she would do anything if only her brilliant husband might survive this ordeal.

Now I will tell you the whole truth of the matter and what my family endured.

When I first saw Alexander, I wanted to thrust a knife in my chest and be done with the world. I had never seen him look so ghastly yellow in pallor, as though the blood had already drained from his body. He sprawled on the sofa in his study holding a cloth towel filled with ice cubes to his abdomen. Wet with perspiration, his black mass of curls stuck to the sides of his face. Though I saw the shallow rise and fall of his chest, the smell in the air made it seem death himself was already a presence in the room.

I screamed and ran to his side.

My children were still hidden away in the nursery, and for their sake, I gathered my senses. I stifled my wails and tried to remember happier times we had spent on this sofa, my legs curled around Alexander's waist, his lips on mine, my face nuzzled in his chest. Why had I not counted those seconds as precious? Why had I not done everything in my power to make the world stand still, so that I might remember and savor every one of those moments? The tears returned, with a small scream. I couldn't do it. I couldn't think about the better times, not now. I could not think of anything except letting him know how much I loved him.

Despite his agony and instructions to keep me away, Alexander smiled and moved the towel and the ice, carefully tucking his shirt back over his chest so I couldn't see his injury. He opened his arms to me, as he had in better times, when he wanted no more than a caress and the pleasure of my body. Now, he was in grave pain, past such base desires, and longed only for comfort. When he lifted his arms to me, his movements were weak and his skin felt cold and sticky. His waistcoat, stained with blood, had already been removed and was slung over the back of his desk chair.

"Who is this doctor anyway?" I drew Alexander close, taking care not to disturb the wound. "Has he the credentials to pronounce life and death so quickly? We could talk to Aunt Katya. She'll know physicians of greater talents who have thoughts beyond abandoning all hope."

"Danzas said more doctors are coming," Alexander rasped. He wore no cravat, his throat and upper chest free, yet he still struggled for each breath. "I have asked for leeches."

I could not imagine draining more precious blood from his body, but I had made so many poor judgments over the past few years that I was not about to risk questioning the established medical wisdom of our time. "May I see the wound?"

Alexander recoiled. "I cannot bear it."

"Please." Some deep painful instinct inside me needed to know the extent of the damage.

Reluctantly, he raised his shirt just enough for me to see. Bile rose in my throat. The bullet wound was clear enough, a puncture in his abdomen that had blackened to an alarming degree, surrounded by jagged red lines, dark as the clotted blood speckling his chest and his upper legs. Farther out, the skin had turned yellow and green with bruising. But the wound itself had already taken on the appearance of infection. If the damage inside did not drain life from him, he would risk succumbing to an even more dreadful death as his body poisoned.

I screwed my eyes shut, hoping against hope that I would open them to discover this had all been but a nightmare. Alexander's face would appear above mine, healthy and vital once more, his hands shaking my shoulders to waken me. Somehow I would be granted the miracle to do everything over again—never to dance with Georges nor accept his notes, never to insist my sisters should come to St. Petersburg, never to find myself in the presence of the tsar. Never to make a fool of my husband, driving him to such lengths.

"You've seen enough." When Alexander spoke, his voice rattled in his chest, the sound of air fighting to travel through his lungs, moist and terrible as the roar of the steam engine pumps my grandfather once used in his factories.

"I needed to know," I said quietly, opening my eyes, heart despairing. "I needed to see what I have done."

"This isn't your fault." He covered the wound once more and I wrapped my arms around him. The duel flashed before my eyes as though I had been there myself, Alexander and Georges struggling toward one another, plowing through the deep snow in their boots, breaths misting in the cold. Alexander falling, his blood stark red against the white, and then struggling to get his shot and firing at Georges. What fools men were with their guns, how like terrible and thoughtless little boys.

"How could you do this to me?" I cried, even as I knew I had done it to myself.

"I'm sorry, Natasha, my Natalie, but nothing could have stopped it. This duel was my fate. The fortune-teller told me as much all those years ago. Death at the hands of a tall, fair man. I should have known from the moment I first saw the scoundrel."

I rocked him. Nothing justified what had happened, not even destiny. Even if Alexander had survived the duel, Georges could have died. Though I hated the man, I had no wish to cause his family such suffering; I would spare even the baron such pain.

"Forgive me." I could hold the tears no longer. They spilled freely, the two of us bundled together in a cold wet mess. "I should have publicly ordered Georges out of my presence whenever I saw him. I should have slapped him right across his smug face and shouted at him to leave me be."

Despite the terrifying sounds emitting from his chest, Alexander managed a quiet laugh. "And how would you have accomplished this? We would have been the laughingstock of St. Petersburg. He was playing the role of the courtly romantic and you played along, as a thousand women before you have done."

Alexander still refused to understand. He refused to allow me to take any blame, instead he shouldered the entire burden and this I could not abide. There was no worse hell than allowing my husband to go to his grave bearing such a weight. "I should have known his feelings were deeper. I was a fool."

"He is his own man. He should have mastered his emotions."

"I murdered you. I might as well have held the gun myself."

Danzas had peeked his head around the corner. I believe he heard every word we said, blanching at my last declaration of guilt. Later, such eavesdroppers would return to haunt me, but in that moment, I only cared about getting my point across and allowing my husband to travel onto the next world without worry.

Alexander clasped my hands feebly in his and kissed the tips of my fingers. His light touch still sent a thrill of excitement through my body, tempered now with the weight of knowing such moments would never come again. "You have only known the sorrows of a beautiful and clever woman. You did nothing wrong."

I started to shake. "I could have done something. I could have taken you away."

"Weren't you trying to do just that? Isn't that why you spoke of our happy times in Tsarskoye Selo so frequently these past weeks?"

I hesitated. "You knew."

"You are clever, but hardly subtle."

"I should have gotten you away from here sooner."

Alexander stroked my face, each exquisite brush of his fingers wonderful and terrible at once, for his skin was deathly cold. "Perhaps in some future world women will hold power to make such decisions, but you must live in this world with only the power of your charm."

I buried my head in the crook of his shoulder. I wanted to die in his place. I said a silent prayer, begging God to take me instead of Alexander. Let Georges storm in here with a pistol and fire it at my head as long as Alexander might return to life. I listened to the ticking of the clock on the mantel and knew this was impossible. So I changed my prayer. Instead I asked God that I might die with Alexander, even if it meant leaving my children behind, in the care of Azya and my brothers. Later, I would experience a guilty dread when I looked at them, wondering if they had guessed I was capable of such abandonment despite my love. I just couldn't bear to think this was the end. "You will not pass on without recognizing my complicity."

"I don't see it as such. We have but mere hours together and I have no wish to dwell on what makes us both sad. Would you give me peace? Is that your heart's desire?" He cupped my chin and lifted my face to meet his gaze. The simple movement gave him difficulty. "Let me see you no longer blame yourself. Let me move on to the next world with that knowledge in my heart. I cannot bear to think you might suffer on my account. I had no choice. This was our fate. Let us accept it with grace. We shouldn't spend these last moments together fretting over what cannot be changed. Let us simply enjoy one another's company. I love you."

"I love you," I said, though I was still crying.

"I only need a little rest . . ."

"No!" I shook his shoulder. "You must not close your eyes."

"My love, the body must rest so it can continue to fight."

The doctor had made his way into the study and I felt the press of his hands on my shoulder. "Let him rest."

"No!" I cried, insensible. "No!"

More of Alexander's friends had rushed to our flat. I would learn later that word of the duel spread quickly throughout the city and those closest to him knew it would be their last chance to see him. Hearing my hysterics, three men entered the study and pulled me away. Alexander was so still I began to cry anew, but they barred me from his study so that he might sleep. I collapsed in our hallway, weeping.

My husband's agony continued. Still, I tried to make him as comfortable as possible. I had not words to explain to the children what had happened, but only referred vaguely to an accident. He asked for them, wanting to fuss over their tiny heads for the last time. They remained solemn, even baby Natalya who lay quietly in her father's arms. Only Masha broke ranks. She would not accept this as an act of providence, instead remaining sullen and angry at her father, a four-year-old child already acting fourteen. When I suggested she bring Alexander his favorite dessert, gooseberry preserves, she broke down in helpless sobs. It was the middle of the night, but time no longer held meaning. I allowed her to feed Alexander a bit of the confection and then asked the children to leave the room so that I might spend some time with him alone.

Alexander managed to taste the treat, but the rest of the dessert remained in the crystal bowl, barely touched. "I didn't make much of a go at that."

"Don't worry about such nonsense now." I rolled up the sleeves of my dress with shaking hands. It was the same one I had been wearing since his friends brought him home. Trying not to think of the dried blood that still clung to my garments, I dipped a soft cotton towel into the basin of water by the sofa. I wiped his face and his chest, still hoping somehow this small comfort would return the beautiful dark golden tone to his skin. "Concentrate on regaining your strength."

"You're saying prayers for the children?" Alexander grasped my wrist, his grip so light it was as though he had already transcended this life and become a ghost.

"I always say prayers for the children, and for you as well."

"I need every one." He leaned back on the many pillows we had brought for him, and shivering, pulled the goose down comforter tighter about his shoulders. "Please hold me."

The playfulness had drained from his soul, only fear and resignation remained. I cuddled next to him and held him in my arms.

"I wish to pass with you into the next world. I could take a knife from the kitchen. The pain would be intense but brief, then we might slip away together . . ."

He squeezed my hands, his body trembling and cold. "Do not even think such an abomination. You will remain here and care for the children and live a long and wonderful life. It is all that gives me peace now. Thinking of your future happiness."

"I shall not be happy. I should die, not you."

"Please do not say such things." He turned to face me. I could hardly meet his pale eyes. "I ask only that you grieve for me as long as a proper widow should: two years."

Despite the darkness in my soul, I allowed a smile. I knew he wanted to see me smile. "Everything according to protocol? A poet should be more subversive."

His face briefly lit with joy, the banter and playfulness in my voice reminding him how things used to be. I allowed myself the faintest hope he would recover yet. "You look fetching in black."

"I shall be the most fetching pretender to widowhood and wear black for you every day."

"If there is a heaven, then I think I shall be allowed a glimpse."

"Live to see it yourself."

Alexander kissed my hand. "After those first two years, I promise I will look away and you will have no further obligation to my memory. Find a second husband, find joy once more."

I touched his cheek with the palm of my hand. "I shall wear black for the rest of my days and never even consider another man. I won't abide such foolishness, you scoundrel."

He arched an eyebrow, but then started to cough with another alarming rattle in his lungs. "I've spoiled you for all others, then?"

"You have spoiled me completely. I am worse than Masha."

"Impossible."

I laughed again. "I have no desire but to honor our life to-gether. I shall never remarry."

"You say that now." Alexander closed his eyes. "Know that I would never hold you to such absurdity."

I squeezed him tighter. "I love you. I have loved no other. You have made me whole and you have changed my life. I shall love you forever."

"You have sent me to heaven a happy man," he whispered.

He closed his eyes.

I felt it deep in my chest, a puncture in my heart. He was gone.

My thoughts grew insensible. I fell to the floor. A sharp pain shot up my back, but I was aware of it only in the dimmest sense, as though watching someone else. Once more, harsh hands squeezed my arms and shoulders, lifting me to my feet. As they dragged me upright, I caught a glimpse of Alexander's body in the dim candle-light. Using the last reserves of my strength, I bolted free and rushed back to my husband, throwing myself on him and weep-ing, the primal sounds emanating from my body more animal than human. A bitter masculine voice hissed in my ear, telling me to pull my wits together for the sake of my children. They were scared and cowering in the nursery, only half-understanding what had happened. I would have to explain. I needed to be strong.

But the very substance of my being had shattered. All I wanted was Alexander.

His friends pulled me from his body and dragged me to the kitchen, where a kind-looking boy with rosy cheeks and a round face attempted to serve me hot water from our samovar with slices of lemon. When he handed me the cup, I flailed and knocked it from his hand. He yelped as the china crashed to our floor. "Leave her alone," I heard someone murmur. "I'll stand guard by the door."

The world turned gray around me and I sank to the floor again, wishing nothing more than to disappear forever.

Twenty

A tender spot radiated pain across the small of my back. Squinting, the speckled ceiling and pots and pans our cook had affixed to hooks high on the kitchen wall came into focus above me. My dress smelled rank. I had not eaten in over two days and my empty stomach rumbled. Low voices murmured in the other room; Alexander's friends were still here. I did not wish to face them, but I had to see my children.

The kitchen door creaked when I opened it into the dining room and then the parlor. The voices hushed and all heads turned to me. I braced for meaningless words and ill-advised hugs.

They said nothing.

The sickly scent that permeated Alexander's study had made its way into the rest of the house, the silence a crypt. The men stared at me. None offered words of comfort, not even the boy with the kind face who had tried to offer tea. I worked my way through the room to find the reticule with my spectacles. I wanted to see if Azya had come down, for I thought I could bear her touch. I wondered if Liza were near, but I believe she had been enlisted to help with the children in the nursery.

I was alone.

Alexander's friends kept their eyes fixed on my back, shoulders, feet, face, and the disarray of my hair. I was accustomed to men staring at me, but not in this fashion, not with such hatred. They were all part of St. Petersburg society. They attended balls and masquerades. They knew Georges and might even have witnessed me flirting or dancing with him. Guilt weakened my knees, but I clung to Alexander's words. He wished to move on to the next world in peace, knowing I did not blame myself for his death. He had framed it as a last wish and it was my duty to honor his memory. A small voice inside my head insisted I should wish to honor myself as well, that I did not deserve the loathsome looks of these men. Alexander would have wanted me to stand up to them. I now wanted the same for myself.

I heard shouting, and as I moved to a window in the drawing room, I put on my spectacles and drew the curtains to one side. People had gathered on the street below, their coats and mittens bright spots of color in the otherwise gray world, waiting to pay their last respects to Alexander. Some waved. I saw the publications in their hands and fancied I could see the adoration in their eyes. I knew Alexander's work was popular, but this was beyond what I imagined, the queue to see him stretching down the street and around the corner.

A spark ignited in my heart, pushing the cruel, dull pain aside. As Alexander's widow, I had a responsibility to everyone who had been touched by his work, a responsibility to preserve his memory. Alexander's body still lay where he had died. It would make his readers weep to see him, but they needed to do so.

"Look." I gestured outside. "We can't make these people wait. They can come to see Alexander while he lies in state."

Danzas made his way to the window. "I'd no idea he had so many admirers."

"Of course he did," another one muttered. "Genius, in general, is good."

I recognized the words from Alexander's tale of Mozart and Salieri. They strengthened my resolve. Alexander's admirers needed to pay their respects. "We should prepare him."

Alexander's valet addressed me. "Do you have his uniform coat in the closet? We might change his clothes and make him look presentable."

I thought of Alexander itching and clutching at the uniform he had so hated. "I would rather you fetch his old frock coat, the one he wore about town, and his walking stick and hat. His favorite cravat. Let them see him as he truly was."

The valet nodded and went to gather the items I requested from our hall closet.

"Bring him out to the vestibule," I said. "Perhaps one day people will see his study, but for now I want to respect his privacy."

The men did as asked and moved Alexander's body to a high table in the hallway.

I smoothed my skirt down. "All right. Let them in."

"Will you say a few words in his honor?" Danzas asked.

Nothing I could say would come close to paying Alexander justice. They were here to see their beloved poet, the man who spoke to their hearts. My presence seemed superfluous. "I haven't had a chance to tell the children their father is gone." I looked down at my hands again, forcing the tears back. "That must come first. But you can start letting people inside. There's no reason to wait."

The men nodded and started moving, seemingly grateful for something to do. I looked down the hallway, toward the nursery, dreading the look I would see in Masha's eyes when I told her Papa was in heaven now.

I wandered around Alexander's study, trailing my finger over the rows of books on his shelves, the bric-a-brac and yellowing papers and sketches on his desk, sniffing the air for any remnants of his citrus and sandalwood cologne or sweet tobacco. Two weeks had passed since we had laid him to rest, yet I still yearned for him to materialize so I might wake from this nightmare. Danzas and the valet kept asking me if I wanted the sofa moved, if I wanted anything moved, and when I told them to leave everything alone, they exchanged worried looks. A small part of me accepted the horrific reality of my loss, and already considered how best to memorialize Alexander. So many mourners had gathered to view his body; surely there would be readers in the future who would wish to see the rooms where he created the verse they so loved. It was my duty to preserve everything as it had been while he still walked this earth.

Truth be told, I wasn't ready to let go, not while a part of me could still fool myself into believing he was still here, somewhere, that I would come home one day to find him hunched over his desk, finally finishing that novel of Abram Gannibal.

The last two weeks were a blur. I kept my spectacles tucked away, for I had no desire to see the world clearly, only wished to be alone with my memories of Alexander. I struggled to keep myself together and hugged my children close. Mother insisted we should return to Moscow, but that city held too many memories: the first time Alexander and I had met at the dance master's ball, walking behind Mother to church, our first kiss. Meanwhile, though Azya was wonderful with my children, I often caught her staring at the study, a wounded look on her pale face, stroking a crucifix that one of Alexander's friends had found buried underneath a cushion of the sofa. Since then, I had taken to either snapping at her over the merest trifle or ignoring her altogether. Azya had done nothing more than gaze worshipfully at my husband, but that alone was enough to vex me.

As for Ekaterina, she had made all the proper expressions of sorrow, but refused to acknowledge her own husband's culpability in the matter. Meanwhile, I was told Georges said nothing of me or Alexander, as though we had never known one other at all. He walked away from the duel with nothing more than a graze to his arm, walking the streets freely, still regarded as a man of honor.

How easily some people can live in denial.

My aunt was the only adult member of my family who provided me with any real comfort in those first days after Alexander's death. When she saw me, she offered neither hugs, nor hollow words of pity, which too often felt like a muzzle shoved on my face. Instead, she took action so that my seemingly endless list of tasks and chores might lighten. She procured clothes appropriate for a grieving widow, arranged for the servants to stay longer than usual, and paid long-overdue bills without pawning any more of my jewelry or Alexander's treasures.

So when the footman let me know my aunt was waiting for me in the front hall, I put on my spectacles, ready to face the world once more.

Liza stood in the hallway, hands shaking and legs locked into half a curtsy. Aunt Katya had not come alone. A tall man in a drab overcoat stood next to her. I sensed he meant to travel incognito, but he could not fool me.

She had brought Tsar Nicholas into my home.

As I stared up at his smug face, memories raced through my mind: the pain in Alexander's face when *The Bronze Horseman* was locked in the brutal censors, how tightly the tsar held me when we danced, and worst of all, his last words to Alexander: *Another man has violated your wife's reputation? The remedy for that is clear.*

He had as good as murdered him. He was as culpable as I. More culpable.

I wanted to slap our holy tsar right across his arrogant face and order him out of my house. If that meant torture and death I would bear it gladly.

And then I thought of Masha's expression when I told her Alexander was gone. She had hit my legs and tried to punch my face, calling me a liar at the top of her little voice, until at last she collapsed weeping into my arms. She couldn't bear the loss of another parent. None of my children could.

I curtsied low, looked down at the floor, and said: "I am unwell and fear I can only visit for a few moments. I am so sorry Your Majesty was troubled to come today."

"The tsar wishes to speak to you alone." Aunt Katya's tone left no room for argument. "I will give you those few moments and then perhaps you'll feel better."

I had no choice in the matter, never had any choice in the matter when it came to the tsar. Or at least that is what we all have been led to believe. Liza still waited in a corner of the foyer, locked in that damnable curtsy. Aunt Katya took the girl by the ear and steered her out.

"Please take a seat if you wish," Tsar Nicholas told me, once they had left. "I know how terrible the past few days have been. We all miss him."

I tried to listen, but my ears were ringing and all I could think about was the impudence of this man, entering my home uninvited, scaring my Liza.

"Natalya Nikolaevna," he added formally. "You and your children will be provided for under my rule. It's the least I can do to express my respect for the greatest poet of this land."

I should have thanked him. I should have kissed his hand. Instead, my hands bunched in and out of fists, the way Alexander's once had, anger rising in my chest until my face turned hot. I could not control my next words. "You knew about the duel. You could have stopped it. You could have saved him. Instead, you encouraged him. For all I know you encouraged Georges to pursue me as well, for your own amusement. Maybe you were the one who composed the first dreadful letter to Alexander."

I looked back down at my hands, the nails digging into my skin. I had ruined my husband and now my children as well. I only hoped the tsar's wrath rained down on me alone.

"I didn't send any letter." I peeked up and saw the tsar had gone pale, that in his plain overcoat he looked like nothing more than a paunchy middle-aged shopkeeper, just as I'd always thought. "These matters go beyond the reach of a head of state . . ."

"You knew the specifics of the duel then?"

"I heard of it only through rumor. Dueling is illegal."

"Then these matters *are* within the reach of the state. You will try Georges d'Anthès?"

For a few days after my husband's murder, it was thought Georges might be arrested. To calm the people's anger, someone needed to be held accountable for their great poet's death. At first, the tsar vacillated on the matter, but ultimately he relented to the opinion of his courtiers—many of whom had been caught at one time or another in their own affairs of honor—and ordered Georges out of the country instead. Georges and Ekaterina were to live in France, free to start their lives anew, while my husband remained deep in the frozen earth.

The tsar's voice was steel. "I know you're upset. I will forgive your impudence if you will at least have the decency to look at me."

My chest felt as though it were caving in on itself. I gathered what little remained of my strength and looked at him. The tsar stared back, gaze hard but eyes rimmed in pink. He had been crying. That seemed impossible, yet the evidence was there before me. The tears did not make me hate him any less, but they helped me summon courage.

"I'm sorry, and yet I still pose the question. Why didn't you punish Georges?"

"It is not as simple as that," the tsar said. "Dueling is illegal, yes. Technically, he committed a murder, yes. On the other hand, your husband willingly participated in this affair of honor. Everyone knows Georges had no choice."

"Alexander felt he had no choice either."

"And had matters gone a different way, I would not pursue a legal case against him. Georges d'Anthès is exiled. He cannot return to Russia. I'm sorry but I suppose this means you will not see your sister Ekaterina again."

I almost smiled. I had no desire to see my sister ever again. I wished I could have shared this turn of events with Alexander before he passed to hear his laugh one last time.

"As for you and your children," the tsar continued. "You may live wherever you wish, and in whatever manner you wish. Your husband's debts are forgiven. I will see to them myself. It's the least I can do for our great poet. You need never worry about money again."

Finally, the right words came out of my mouth. "Thank you, Your Majesty. I am humbled by your generosity and wish I had the words to express my gratitude."

He took my hands limply in his. I felt something cold on my finger and saw that he had slipped a ring onto it. The ring I had sold to a pawnshop on Nevsky Prospect the afternoon Alexander had been shot.

I stared at the ring. The tsar couldn't have been coarse enough to suggest I become his mistress, not now, and yet I couldn't help but feel some sort of proposal had just been proffered. I couldn't reject his money, for that wouldn't have been fair to my children. I did, however, remove the ring from my finger. "It never fit right, but thank you for returning it."

"My pleasure." The tsar's lip twitched, as though implying something more with the word "pleasure." "I am your servant. I am the one to help you through this. After all, who knows what wicked rumors might spread regarding your own culpability in this disgusting affair? Under my protection, you need never worry about the damage these gossips might cause. I will never allow them to hurt you or your children, nor your place in society."

"Such an honor!" I said, simultaneously impressed and repulsed at my ability to suppress my true feelings, instead replacing them with pandering nonsense.

"And I hope you will do me the honor of remaining nearby." He kissed my hand, which had turned so cold I could scarcely feel the press of his lips. "You know a secret? I used to pass by your window at night in the hope of seeing you. How seldom I was granted that gratification, but perhaps now I might hope for something more from you."

Have you ever had a moment where it seems as though you

just woke from a dream? As if the world's true nature is suddenly known, and all that was hazy is now crystal clear? As I stared at the tsar, I realized I had not accepted the facts of *my* life; I was in as much denial as Ekaterina and Georges. Alexander was gone forever and I had no life in St. Petersburg without him, nothing beyond my dubious worth as an object to be pursued and caught, and this I could not bear. I needed to establish a space for myself away from the tsar and his malicious court.

"I have already spoken to my eldest brother about relocating," I said. "I feel the place for myself and my children is at my late grandfather's estate in the country. My eldest brother is in charge of it now."

The tsar pressed my hand and I recoiled instantly in fear, remembering how Georges had twisted my wrist. The tsar's touch was lighter, but far more cunning.

This was the moment when I took the greatest risk, for though the outpouring of grief and despair at Alexander's death had shocked the tsar—so much in fact that Alexander's state funeral was moved for fear of the unruly crowds—he was, after all, still tsar. Would he be so callous as to take the widow of his people's beloved poet as a mistress? Or did he realize the people did have power in numbers and could, someday, present a threat to his power?

"It has already been decided," I said, trying to keep my voice matter-of-fact. "I wish to focus on my children and the preservation of my husband's great works. What could be more appropriate than that? A simple Russian home in the heartland for a simple Russian woman. What could better honor my husband's memory and help his readers find peace with his untimely death?"

The tsar hesitated, then straightened his shoulders and made the pragmatic choice, as I'd hoped he would. "Of course. Only don't forget your friends here in the city while you're gone playing the peasant girl."

I managed a smile. "I will never forget St. Petersburg. I will never forget everything that happened to me here."

Even in Kaluga, the slightest sound made my head cock up like a rooster waking at dawn. On those rare occasions when the footman announced a visitor, my heart raced, for always I was afraid the next caller would be the tsar and I would have no way out of his clutches. For the present, I was financially dependent on his good graces.

He never came; our holy tsar wouldn't lower himself to travel this far to pursue a mere woman. Gradually, the tension in my shoulders dissipated and my stomach settled. I began to feel like myself again: the true self who had once been a small and carefree child exploring Afansy's estate.

The provincial pace of life was slow and our entertainments modest in scope. Still, as I breathed in the clean country air and strolled the old Goncharov factory, I felt at peace. When I stopped to run my hand along a broken waterwheel, I wondered what the grand ladies of St. Petersburg in their luxurious palaces would think. *Naught but a sad mess: a broken operation and a silly woman, a vainglorious coquette who drove her brilliant husband to his death.* But their imagined opinions meant nothing. I had successfully chased Mother's judgments from my mind, and I did the same to theirs now. I had no one to answer to but myself.

My children began to relax and play again. Their little faces grew less pallid and they greeted the morning with the excitement they once had. They still asked about their father, but I had rein-stituted Mother's practice of evening prayers at home every Sat-urday. Azya joined us in Kaluga, and together we made sure each of my children said a special prayer for Alexander. Unlike my mother, however, I did not follow prayers with stern admonitions to get straight to bed. Instead, Azya and I popped corn on the stove, poured fresh apple cider into tin mugs, and shared stories of Alexander.

I still worried about Masha. She had been closest to her father and resembled him most. Her black curls ran wild over her shoul-ders and though sometimes she allowed me to tame them into ringlets, she preferred to wear her abundant hair loose and free. When we went for a walk, she ran farther than the other children and never wanted to turn back. If we had chicken for dinner, she cried over the loss of an animal she fancied a pet, demanding we live on bread and cheese instead. She alone missed St. Petersburg and frequently asked when we would return. I simply told her I didn't know, shaking my head until she stomped her foot and flounced off in a temper as I rested my face in my hands, knowing my firstborn could not be kept from the world.

Just as my family was growing accustomed to this routine, a message was delivered from our old friend Tolstoy the American. I saw the scribble of his handwriting on the note first: *Thought this might be of interest should you ever wish to return to the city. It is a copy of a verse addressed to St. Petersburg society by a young writer named Mikhail Lermontov, who is sometimes spoken of as the next Pushkin. It is officially banned now, but copies are in circulation. I enclose one for you. T*

Alexander had mentioned this young fellow Lermontov once or twice, praising his talents. No doubt, the boy had been shaken to the core by my husband's death. I stared at the letter. Had my peace in this place been so fragile that a mere mention of the past could disturb it? Tolstoy had been a friend to our family, but infrequently in recent years, finding time to see my brothers or Alexander only when he happened to be on his way somewhere else. I wasn't sure I trusted him, and I dreaded learning Lermontov blamed me for Alexander's death.

I could not stay in the dark forever, though. I slit the envelope open with my fingernail and read Lermontov's first words, the title.

Death of the Poet

In his neat and even hand, Lermontov blamed the society of St. Petersburg, the aristocrats of court, for Alexander's death, claiming they didn't appreciate Alexander's talents and hounded him to his grave. In this version of events, the court indeed played a similar role to Salieri in Alexander's tale of Mozart, while my role was almost nonexistent. I was not the villainess of St. Petersburg, but merely another pawn. I was grateful to this talented fellow Lermontov, who understood the truth of our story. He reinforced my decision to stay in the country. I had no desire to return to the viper's nest.

Yet life sometimes takes us in directions we do not expect.

SIX YEARS LATER

I tried to convince myself I had returned to St. Petersburg for Masha, and to further the schooling and future careers of my two sons, but deep down I knew the same desire for a life in this world burned inside of me, if perhaps not as brightly as before. I no longer wished to play the hermit in my late grandfather's shadow.

As our fine team of Goncharov horses trotted through the city, effortlessly traversing the damp streets, my spirits began to rise. Through the window of our coach, the Neva glistened in the spring sun, and the sleek carriages of the elite sped across the city's bridges while more humble residents waddled by foot to market and church. I sensed Alexander's presence, calm at my side whereas his spirit had seemed restless in the provinces. I saw it embodied in Masha. If she remained in the countryside, she would find a way to run away, as her father might have done in her place. So we returned to live in St. Petersburg. But while I enjoyed the public gardens, shops, and the art, I did not plan to make a formal return to society.

Until Sergey came to visit.

My brother had finally found his happiness in the army, much to my surprise. And though his face had lost its plumpness and he treated life with a seriousness he once lacked, he still made jokes and teased me and tickled my children. On leave from his regiment, he invited us to a Springtide masquerade at Kikin Hall, a mansion built during the reign of Peter the Great. Over and over, he assured me Masha would be safe: the ball was held early in the evening to suit the schedule of the cavalry units and their families stationed nearby. She was sure to find people her own age milling about. This was precisely what I feared—she would find a pretty boy of her age and who knew what trouble—but at least this way I could keep an eye on her. And truth be told, I wanted to assemble a new costume.

Using pieces I had once worn to dress as Queen Esther, I fashioned an ensemble after an old painting of the biblical Rebecca by Benjamin West: loose silvery gown, blue scarf tied around my waist, orange cloak, and my hair done full up front and then down one side of my shoulders in a long braid. I lost hours and then days to sewing and fittings and giggling with Liza over the low-cut bodice, always the fashion of court, it seemed. Not that I would be the center of attention. Masha dressed as Little Bo Peep from the English story in white pantaloons, short blue dress, and matching poke bonnet, with a shepherd's staff to accessorize. She looked adorable.

The horses came to a halt now before a three-sided, gabled entrance to the hall. After we made our way inside, I let Masha roam as she wished as long as she checked in with me every hour. She agreed, patted my arm, and bolted out of my sight.

I hesitated. The way she touched my arm and tapped her shepherd's staff to the floor. Even the lively mazurka melody, the chatter of conversation, the scent of savory pastries heaped on side tables, mingling with men's cologne and candlewax. Everything reminded me of Alexander. I spotted a large fern in a pot and half-fancied I would see my husband step out from behind it, a sherbet or some other iced treat in hand, calling my name and steering me to a secluded spot so that he might steal a kiss or share a ribald joke.

So many years had passed and still his image remained fresh and alive in my mind, though I clung to no delusions. I was here and Alexander was gone. Only his spirit, the sense of him about, remained with me and I had learned to be satisfied with that, even at my loneliest.

I found Sergey and greeted him with a warm hug. My brother stood next to a tall, slender, clean-shaven gentleman. From the gray at his temples and the wrinkles at the corners of his eyes, I guessed the man was past forty. Even so, he had an impish, almost boyish look I found appealing, and his laugh was so jolly I had heard it even from across the room.

When Sergey formally introduced me to his friend, Peter Lanskoy's good-natured eyes lit with interest. I did not sense the world shift beneath my feet, as I had when I first met Alexander. Still, I *had* noticed him and even smiled when I saw the glint of admiration in his eyes. I had not received such attention in a long time, and I confess, it gave me great pleasure.

We found a divan to the side of the dance floor and talked for an hour. Nothing complicated, nor earth shattering. I learned Peter was forty-five and a career soldier; from the reflective nature of his conversation, I intuited he had reached a stage in life where he wished to focus his attention on one woman and the comforts of a domestic life. I was in need of such focus. The more we talked, the more I realized this amicable tête-à-tête—with a fellow neither rattled, nor offended with ease—was exactly what I needed. I even asked him to fetch one of the hearty potato and mushroom–filled *piroshki* I had spied on the side tables. When Masha came by to check in, I waved her away with a pleasant nod and nibbled on the stuffed bun, trying not to burn my tongue.

Peter watched Masha's black curls, held loosely back from her face by the poke bonnet, as she returned to a group of giggling girls. "Your daughter is a beauty."

Thankfully, I detected no hint of entitlement in his voice. It had been an innocent observation. Everything about Peter seemed innocent, despite his age. I paused midbite. "She looks a pretty little mirror of her father. If he shaves his whiskers and attends a masquerade ball as a woman, they might pass for twins."

Peter grew quiet and looked uncomfortably at the slanted tiles beneath us on the floor. I set the *piroshki* down on its china plate, appetite suddenly gone. I had spoken of Alexander as though he yet lived, a mistake I hadn't made in years.

"I hope you won't think this rude, but I wanted to ask about your late husband."

I stared at the half-eaten pastry, bracing myself for questions. Our entire meeting could have been a ruse to convince me to relate scandals of years past. Aunt Katya had warned me of unscrupulous writers who wished to tell stories of the end of Alexander's life in the most shameful manner, and Peter could have been dispatched to cajole me to utter a careless revelation, some tidbit that might make for a fine addition to a tawdry novel to be sold abroad.

"I didn't intend to raise the subject," I told Peter primly, making a subtle move away from him on the divan. "I don't care to speak of Alexander at length."

Peter's cheeks colored, and he looked even more like a younger man, despite the gray. "I did not intend to offend you, Madame Pushkina. It is only . . . you see . . ."

He was stammering now and I waved my hand to encourage him, the way I did with Grisha or Sasha when they stole cookies and were oh-so close to confession. "I see what?"

"It is only that I am an admirer of his work," Peter blurted at last. "I followed *Onegin*, of course, but my favorite is *The Captain's Daughter*."

I smiled, but the contentment I had felt a moment ago had vanished. Once again, I was valued only for my relation to another human being, not for myself. Still, this Peter Lanskoy had good taste. *The Captain's Daughter* was one of Alexander's last works, set at the time of Pugachev's Rebellion, with a love affair between a man also named Peter and a woman named Masha. Perhaps he had his eyes on my daughter, despite her youth, after all. "Did you wish to speak with me only to hear tales of my late husband?"

Peter was still blushing. He set his china plate on the floor so that he could take my hand in his and squeeze it. "I wished to speak to you because you are the most beautiful woman in this room. I suspect you are the most beautiful woman in every room. That doesn't mean I love Pushkin's work more or any less. But it seemed . . . inappropriate to mention it from the start."

I allowed his hand to linger on mine. "You didn't want me to catch you reading Alexander's tales behind my back? Under the covers at night when you should be asleep?"

He laughed a little, but did not respond. Alexander would have thought of something sly to say in response, and we would have enjoyed our banter for another quarter of an hour at least. Peter was a different sort. That was all right. Now that I understood his intent, I was glad he had brought up Alexander. I could not dwell forever in the past, but neither could I embark on this new phase of life without speaking of him at all.

As I left the ball, I felt Alexander's presence once more. He had asked me to mourn for two years and I had now been alone for nearly seven. Peter Lanskoy was a pleasant distraction, but no threat to his memory. Beyond that, he was a reader, and my late husband deemed no quality more important than that. If Peter and I were meant to be together, I knew Alexander approved.

My wedding to Peter Lanskoy was a small affair, consisting only of my children, Azya, Sergey, Aunt Katya, and Mother, who if she had any negative opinions on this match at least had the decency to keep them to herself. Peter invited a few family members and soldiers as well, but seemed grateful enough to keep it a small affair. We agreed on such matters. We fit well together, both in our day-to-day life and when we sought comfort and pleasure from one another in the privacy of a bedroom.

The second night after we had returned from our honeymoon, I flipped through a stack of letters while standing next to the hearth's crackling fire, and paused at an envelope addressed to me in French. One of Ekaterina's letters, delayed by a year from the looks of it, but as far as I was concerned ready to be stacked with the rest. I had never opened any of them.

I tried not to follow news of Georges, but Aunt Katya hinted he was viewed with some disdain in European social circles. I think she was only trying to make me feel better. While Alexander remained well-loved in Russia, I hadn't been asked for permission for his works to be translated into other tongues, and so had no reason to believe readers in Europe or the New World appreciated him as we did here in Russia, nor that Georges suffered for his role in Alexander's death. I only felt sorry for the baron, who had gifted property and a title to a man he loved, only to lose him forever, sacrificed to a hasty marriage to my sister, which ultimately did nothing to avert the duel anyway.

A letter had arrived from the tsar as well, telling me how much he liked Peter, and how glad he thought my first husband, the great poet, would be if he knew I had found happiness once more. I smirked, past fear. As I made my way around St. Petersburg, I saw Tsar Nicholas on occasion. He walked the streets without guards, as he had walked the public gardens of Tsarskoye Selo so many years ago, still oblivious to the idea that his subjects might feel anything but love for their mighty tsar and he could be in danger. I encountered him once while shopping at an English store on Nevsky Prospect. Up close, he looked much older than he appeared on our currency and in official portraits.

By now, I was numb to it all. Seeking justice on this earth seemed a futile endeavor. All we can do is seek momentary pleasure and leave the determination of right and wrong to whatever might await us in the hereafter.

I crumpled the envelope with Ekaterina's letter and then the tsar's note into small balls and threw them both into the fire, watching them glow, bright orange and red, before dissolving to naught but ash.

The following week, I visited our old flat on the Moyka with a bouquet of red roses. The wind blew softly in my hair as I riffled through the reticule slung at my side to find my spectacles. It pleased me to find a slew of other flowers at the site, but I had a powerful need to be closer to him, to have a moment alone with one another, and so I knelt on the cold ground outside the flat where I had told him good-bye for the last time.

"So I am married," I whispered. "I'm happy, but it's a different type of happiness than I shared with you. Peter Lanskoy is a good man and I love him, but not in the same way."

I bit my lip, for I was about to say something disloyal to the man I had vowed to devote myself to for the rest of my life. But once out, I would never say a word against him again.

"He is kind and good, but he has not your wit nor your unique way of seeing the world. I will miss you until the day I die. You changed my life. You helped make me who I am today. I will keep you in my heart even as I stay loyal to Peter. I know you understand, but I needed to share with you."

"Madame Lanskoya!" the coachman called. "Pardon the interruption, but we need to leave now if we are to make your next appointment."

I touched the cold wall. "I will come back. I'll bring our children."

Our next stop was the archivist's library. I delivered the bundle of papers, tied with ribbon, to the grateful man: all of the letters Alexander had ever written to me. For years, I kept them on the little table at my bedside and read them at night, especially when I had trouble sleeping. Tolstoy and Danzas and other friends of Alexander had encouraged me to release them to the public, but the thought made me nervous, for some of Alexander's most tender, most erotic words to me were in these letters, as well as some of our old quarrels. I was beyond caring what the world thought, but not quite to the point of inviting any further scrutiny of my personal affairs. Besides, I didn't want to part with the private world Alexander and I shared.

Except now I was a married woman again. The timing seemed right.

"I know these will interest future biographers." The archivist smiled as he set the letters on a table, reverent as a priest before an altar, and placed thin cotton gloves on his hands so that he could look at them carefully without damaging the material. His hair was thinning and he adjusted his own spectacles as he spoke. He seemed gentle and his reverence touched me. "I understand you have spoken to several people about releasing new editions of Pushkin's collected works."

"My husband and I have spoken to publishers, yes." Peter remained an avid and loyal admirer of Alexander. I wanted to make sure he remained in this conversation.

"Did your first husband by any chance preserve your letters,

Madame Lanskoya?" the archivist asked. "I am sorry to pry, but such correspondence would also be of interest."

I had been expecting this request and returned his smile. Alexander had saved all of my letters to him, even proudly showed me the little wooden chest where he kept them, but I could only furnish the world with so much of my heart. To tide the man over, I said: "Oh, I fear those may have been lost, but I did find one that he kept. I included it at the end."

The archivist nodded. "Thank you." He hesitated. "And might you have any other writings of your own you wish to include with your husband's work?"

I thought of my verses and short history of Russian poetry. Those were mine alone.

"Thank you for asking, but no."

I left the archivist to Alexander's beautiful words. The past was settled and I felt confident that I had helped secure my husband's place in the future.

I was ready to begin the next stage of my life.

AUTHOR'S NOTE

Empty-headed. Frivolous. Selfish. Slut. How often are words like these used to describe women? How many times do they accurately describe the truth of a woman's life?

History has proven particularly unkind to women who fall outside of the traditional norms of dutiful daughter, faithful wife, and saintly mother. Historical accounts, written largely by men, sometimes fall into the habit of ostracizing women, particularly if there is any hint of romantic or sexual "misbehavior." And yet nothing is more fascinating than a beautiful woman with a bad reputation.

I've long been intrigued with Russia's greatest poet, Alexander Pushkin, and the circumstances behind the duel that led to the tragic end of his tumultuous life. At the center of those events? His young wife, Natalya.

In several older portrayals of the Pushkins' marriage, Natalya is depicted as a vacuous flirt, focused on balls and gowns and liaisons with other men, carelessly spending Alexander's money, oblivious to his emotional pain and his genius. Natalya's role in Alexander's duel was a fruitful source for shaming, as allegations of her inappropriate flirtations and even a possible affair with the handsome Georges d'Anthès lingered long after Alexander's death.

Though Alexander himself absolved his wife of any wrongdoing, Natalya was sometimes viewed as complicit and even responsible for the duel between the great poet and his perceived rival. In an age where a man's honor meant more than his life, some sources continued to blame Natalya for her husband's death. By this line of thinking, a scandalous woman robbed us of whatever future works Alexander might have created, had his life not been cut prematurely short. To my mind, the tragic end of Alexander's life and the Pushkins' marriage is connected to a culture that presented women as delicate objects to be fought for and defended, and the pressure Alexander felt to preserve his own sense of masculinity and purpose in life.

Fortunately, more sympathetic interpretations of Natalya's personal story have emerged, honoring her emotional complexity and status as an intriguing historical personality. This newer interpretation of Natalya's life, which I first found presented in a Newsweek write-up by Anna Nemtsova citing the research of Larisa Cherkashina, inspired the fictionalized version of Natalya presented in my novel.

One issue in Natalya's personal history which seemed keenly relevant to readers today was the question of whether or not she slept with the tsar, Nicholas I. He certainly seemed smitten with Natalya. I can't imagine the tsar's interest put her in anything but an incredibly uncomfortable position she would then have been forced to negotiate as best she could. Natalya did not have the benefit of the vocabulary we use to understand sexual harassment today. Still, her story might resonate with anyone who has ever been at the mercy of the romantic whims of an individual with power over their lives. In some respects, Natalya's experiences may seem strange or even sad to us, but in other ways, the challenges she faced may seem all too familiar.

Although this is a work of fiction, I relied heavily on the research of historians to re-imagine Natalya and Alexander's world. In the interest of narrative flow, I made minor adjustments in the timeline, while trying to stay faithful for the most part to the Pushkins' lives. For English language readers interested in learning more about Natalya and Alexander, I strongly recommend T.J. Binyon's *Pushkin* and Elaine Feinstein's *Pushkin*. A more extensive bibliography is available on my website.

ACKNOWLEDGMENTS

I can think of no better way to spend a scorching hot Central Valley afternoon than wandering the stacks of a university library. During the research and early writing stages of this novel, I spent several happy months at the UC Davis Shields Library, among shelves and shelves of Alexander Pushkin's writing and books devoted to his life and times, his charming sketches, and many gorgeously rendered visual and written portraits of nineteenth-century Russia. Midway through drafting the manuscript, personal circumstances brought me back to my hometown of Stockton, where I continued to research and write in the elegant University of the Pacific William Knox Holt Memorial Library.

I have been fortunate to enjoy the talents and expertise of early readers and editors who helped me navigate Natalya and Alexander's complex world. As always, Melissa Jackson provided invaluable insights after reading an early draft. My agent, the ever marvelous and perceptive Erin Harris of Folio Literary Management, and reader Maya Chung helped me polish and add further depth. Editor extraordinaire Vicki Lame at St. Martin's Griffin brought me through the final stretch of revisions with her graceful and keen observations. Copy editor Naná V. Stoelzle helped put the finishing touches on the manuscript. I am immensely grateful to Lisa Marie Pompilio, who has provided beautiful, evocative cover art for all three of my books.

Writing can feel like offering your heart to the world. I appreciate the endless support and good humor of the Sacramento Area branch of the Historical Novel Society, including Erika Mailman, Erin Lindsay McCabe, Mark Wiederanders, Erika MacDonald, Anna-Marie McLemore, Gini Grossenbacher, Kathy Boyd Fellure, Marcia Calvin, and Ed Moore. I would also like to thank my family—Jon, Karen, Brett, and Liz—who are always there to pick me up, brush me off, and get me back in the game.

ABOUT THE AUTHOR

Channa Vance

JENNIFER LAAM is the author of *The Secret Daughter of the Tsar* and *The Tsarina's Legacy*. She earned her master's degree in history from Oakland University in Michigan and her bachelor's degree from the University of the Pacific in Stockton, California. She has lived in Los Angeles and the suburbs of Detroit, traveled in Russia and Europe, and worked in education and nonprofit development. She currently resides in Northern California.